D0424884

# BLOOD
# MAKES
# NOISE

DISCARDED

# BLOOD MAKES NOISE

Gregory Widen

**THOMAS & MERCER**

The characters and events portrayed in this book are fictitious. Any similarity to real persons, living or dead, is coincidental and not intended by the author.

Text copyright © 2013 Gregory Widen

All rights reserved.
Printed in the United States of America.
No part of this book may be reproduced, or stored in a retrieval system, or transmitted in any form or by any means, electronic, mechanical, photocopying, recording, or otherwise, without express written permission of the publisher.

Published by Thomas & Mercer
P.O. Box 400818
Las Vegas, NV 89140

ISBN-13: 9781611098990
ISBN-10: 1611098998
Library of Congress Control Number: 2012918814

*For my parents*

**Based on True Events**

# PROLOGUE

**April 21, 1947**

It was late, nearly midnight, and everyone else had left the bank hours ago. Home to wives, girlfriends, warm social dinners made more perfect in his mind because he had neither friends nor dinner invitations—just his last name on the front of the building and a hatred for this minor errand-boy assignment he'd been left with.

His desk was large, prominently placed, and if you didn't know better, you'd think this was a young man of responsibility. But everyone did know better—even, seemingly, the ancestral portraits glaring at him now.

The bank was an old, family one. Never a fertile dynasty, theirs produced a single son each generation to carry on the family crime. But every gene pool has its shallow end, and this son was trusted with little but the time to concentrate on the growing shame that was becoming his inheritance.

And so Otto Spoerri sat there, waiting, and threw crumpled paper balls at a wastebasket he never hit.

The note, hand delivered that afternoon, was predictable enough. A wealthy foreign individual—unnamed of course, this being a Swiss bank—would send a representative at midnight—it was always midnight, wasn't it?—to arrange a large, VIP safety deposit box. The representative undoubtedly would be some colorless suit straining under the weight of some monster or other's fleeing, bloodstained fortune.

At twenty past midnight he was dozing when there was an insistent rap at the rear glass doors. Otto got up and opened them on a broad-shouldered man in livery costume. "Herr Spoerri?"

"Of course." Who the hell else would be stuck here at this hour? The livery costume nodded, walked back to the idling limousine, and opened the rear door.

From it emerged a beautiful woman in her late twenties. She wore mink, her blonde hair up in a fierce chignon. Otto Spoerri recognized the face immediately, and his surprise was sufficient enough to leave him momentarily without manners.

"Are you the banker?" she asked in Spanish. Finally coming to attention, he took her hand and bent with a snap. "Senora. I am surprised. Please, welcome to Kredit Spoerri."

She nodded. He led her inside, offered a chair, muddled his university Spanish. "You needn't have come in person, Senora. We accept transactions through intermediaries."

"Had I wanted intermediaries, Herr Spoerri, I would have sent them."

"Of course."

He laid out the relevant papers for her to complete. Eva Duarte Perón. Evita. First Lady of Argentina—a dictator's wife but widely considered the real power—she was here on her grand European tour. In the utter dreariness and hunger of postwar Europe, the more dreary and starving the country, the more fabulous—if often clenched—the reception this cattle-rich nation's First Lady had been given.

But things had gone sour in Switzerland. The world's recent insanity hadn't lapped over this side of the mountains, and its people were neither hungry for Argentine beef nor amused by its demanding maiden. Otto could glimpse tomato stains clinging to the limousine's finish, souvenirs from the Zurich crowds protesting her visit.

"I apologize for the hour and whatever appointments I've kept you from. Are you married, Herr Spoerri?"

"No, Senora."

"You do not love women?"

"Perhaps too much, Senora."

"If you cannot love one woman, then you can love nothing."

"Wise advice, Senora."

"The marriage between my husband and I is the light of my nation."

Her bosom swelled under cashmere, and he wondered if it was *my husband* or *my nation* that did it.

She sat back, crossed her legs, and took a cigarette from her purse. Otto struck his lighter and held it across the desk. She placed the cigarette in her mouth, bent forward, and, as the flame licked the end, turned the shaft between red lips and allowed her eyes to rest an instant on his.

"Our standard procedure, Senora, is to issue you a completely private account number. With this—"

"I would like a key."

"Senora?"

"One key. Nothing more."

"It is usual to have an authorization list of who may have access to the box. It provides security against—"

"No list. Just a single key. The key, only the key, is my authorization. It will, however, be a very *special* key."

"All our keys at Kredit Spoerri are special, Senora."

"I am quite sure. But this key is already made. It is manufactured to such a temperance that if a false one is placed in the lock it will disintegrate instantly."

"I'm not sure I am aware of such a lock."

"It too has already been made and will be installed in the box."

"An outside lock? No security list? I'm afraid such an arrangement is unprecedented."

She took a breath from her cigarette and rested her elbow on the chair's armrest, cocking the smoldering end off the side of her cheek. "Of course."

What a woman, with her harlot lips and shopgirl swagger, the heat of an absolute confidence that dried his eyes. A woman who'd come to a country that despised her, waded through seething crowds and splashing fruit, all to sit in the city's oldest bank at midnight and calmly wait for what she wanted, turning the cigarette between moist lips, and the contest was over before she ever walked in—over the day she was born.

"Such an arrangement is probably against Swiss banking law."

"I'm sure."

"I'd be putting myself personally at risk."

He watched as his words were dismembered and eaten by smoke.

"Yes."

And he thought of her in bed. Imagined that focus pounding itself down on him. As if divining his thoughts, she leaned forward. "I will deal only with you, Herr Spoerri. There will be no statements sent to me—if I need information I will contact you alone. My name will be on no records. There will be only our friendship, our understanding, and the key, for which I will pay handsomely, also to you."

"Why should I do this?"

"Because you are a young man in an old man's bank. A young man with dreams of a different future. I would like to be a part of that future."

Smiling from a place unmapped, she handed back the sheaf of government deposit forms—blank.

"If I may view my deposit box now, Herr Spoerri."

And he lingered, jealous of the moment, listening to the rustling of her stockings, then stood with proper Spoerri formality. "This way, Senora Perón, please."

Her limo driver brought in the leather cases, nearly a dozen, and in private Evita and he transferred the contents to their new home and sealed it all with the custom locking mechanism, carried in a shiny aluminum attaché.

Otto knew he would never tell his father, or the bank, that the box was Eva Perón's. He printed up the single sheet with the number and laid it in her warm palm. She left then, and he had waited for her return. There followed hand-delivered notes, short, fragrant sentences. But Eva Perón herself never appeared again. In five years she was dead and the box remained, untouched, and he grew older, coming to the vault sometimes, sitting there, thinking of it and her.

Her legacy had plenty of company. This was a room full of midnights: tax evaders, gangsters, Nazis—many dead, like her, their reeking fortunes marooned under the devil's quilt of secrecy that was his family's crime. His nation's.

**April 9, 1953**

Juan Duarte never liked the river, and now it lay outside his window, scaly with moonlight, taunting him. It was his first memory of this cursed city and would likely be his last. A bitter wind off its surface rattled his reflection—the same wind that had taken his sister, coming for him. Juan drew in a tired breath and dreamed of floating away. To his village, its hopeless roads. They had danced circles in the dust as children there, his sister and he. They had needed only each other...

"Where is it?"

Juan recognized the voice without turning. Bluff and baritone, with the crack of jackboots. Juan's eyes stayed on the window. "I don't know."

He wished he sounded tougher, for once confident in the presence of the peacock. Instead his voice was only sad.

"Come, Juan, be reasonable"—spoken with a reasonable voice. This would be the peacock's shadow, announced—always—with the tap of his dog-headed cane; everyone's favorite demon uncle. "You're among family. How can you keep secrets from your own blood?"

"I tell you, I don't know." A gust of wind jarred his reflection: pencil mustache and hair pressed flat with brilliantine. A dandy.

"Liar! She..." The baritone peacock again, his voice breaking on that word as it broke every time he uttered it since...

"She was your sister. She told you everything."

And nothing. He had known her better than any, and he had known her hardly at all.

His eyes dropped to the dresser, where they'd placed his suicide note, the handwriting and syntax better than his own, and he appreciated that.

"Answer me, goddamn you!"

He didn't care anymore. Had stopped caring since she died eight months ago. He felt himself drifting. Away from this place. Toward a thought that made him smile. "Did it ever occur to either of you that my sister, of all women, could have taken it with her?"

Sighs. A cock of gunmetal. His favorite demon uncle: "I always had affection for you, Juanito, even if I never liked you very much."

The last thing Juan Duarte thought, as oblivion tapped the back of his skull, was how much he hated that goddamn river.

**June 6, 1955**

The terrorist bomb that exploded outside a Recoleta café during that long year of bombs was unremarkable but for the fact that it misfired. Black powder packed so loosely it went off more like a firework than an instrument of political pressure. Still, when the police picked through the shattered glass and broken bamboo chairs, they found it had, despite its ineptitude, managed to claim one victim.

His name was Tomasso Villa, but everyone knew him as Tomi, a genial drunk who earned his gin money making deliveries for a Spanish doctor on Juncal. He'd stopped that afternoon for his single nonalcoholic drink of the day, an espresso, and was blown into bloody hieroglyphics for his trouble.

The satchel he had been carrying was ripped open and its contents cast haphazardly across the park fronting the café. When the Buenos Aires cops collected them, they found only lab reports, some correspondence…

…And six X-rays.

X-rays of a young, dead woman.

*In Argentina a call at midnight is always a lover,*
*but a call at four a.m. is always destiny.*

**November 23, 1955**

# 1.

It was a sound Michael Suslov never got used to.

After four years back in the capital, still it was a sound of childhood. Shrill, angry, coming to take your life away.

"Yes?" His voice croaked with sleep. The old-fashioned receiver was heavy in his hand—hard Bakelite thick enough to kill someone. Everything was old-fashioned here. It was a national obsession.

"Michael?"

Only two people in the world called him Michael: his wife, Karen, and Hector Cabanillas.

"Hector."

"I apologize for the hour, Michael." It was a bad sign when Hector started apologizing. "I must see you."

He looked at the bedside clock—4:13 a.m.—and thought of telling Hector it was late, to go back to bed.

"Give me half an hour."

Michael dressed, put some coffee on, sat in humid silence as it perked. The walls around him rang with the evening's fight. It had been over a bridge invitation. A barbecue. Something.

He poured his coffee and stood at the window. It was open, and he could feel a muddy breeze blow through him. The back garden, laid out in tidy European rows by the house's former, tidy European owners, glowed gunmetal under a sliver of moon. A dog barked somewhere.

Karen and he had always fought, even used to be proud of it—flash fires clearing the deadwood. But the fires were coming more often, and they lingered now, scorching the stalks beneath.

She was sleeping when he crouched beside the bed and whispered he had to leave. She mumbled something in her sleep. Michael smiled. When they still lived in Arlington, Karen had slept through a snow-heavy cedar branch crashing through their bedroom window.

At the first roadblock on Avenida del Libertador, Michael slowed the car, showed the peach-fuzzed militia soldier his diplomatic ID, and drove on. Sweat rose under his shirt. It was only a day before Thanksgiving back home, but in the backward seasons here at the bottom of the world, the capital already groaned under the hammer blows of summer. There were fewer roadblocks now than the last time he came this way. The generals were starting to relax, starting to believe that *this* coup might stick.

He could glimpse the Rio Plata now. Too big for a river, too small for an ocean, in winter it threatened grayly; in summer it lay fetid brown and coffin still. He followed it south to the Federal District and its buildings of state. Drowsy sycamores appeared on the streets, some pocked with age, others gunfire.

Behind the sycamores lay Government House—Casa Rosada—until recently the home of the president, its century-old pink walls, originally colored with beef blood and lime, now stained with the gray shudder of five-hundred-pound bombs. The work of good Catholic boys in good Catholic airplanes taking it to heart when the pope excommunicated El Presidente. The pilots missed their man but killed four hundred civilians. Good Catholic bodies broken and strewn over the Plaza de Mayo.

He slowed for another roadblock near the burned-out basilica, one of the dozen churches torched by unionist mobs in revenge for the pope-inspired bombing of Casa Rosada. Squatters drifted in the gloom, their candles lonely, bobbing sparks.

Hector had asked Michael to meet him at the Confederación General del Trabajo workers' union center on Azopardo. Michael parked his car one street over and walked to the CGT's art deco front door, tonight dark and silent. Not surprising. Once the powerful lightning rod that juiced, then mouthpieced, a working-class *descamisado* revolution, since the coup half its leaders were in hiding or across the river in Uruguay. The CGT of the moment was a distinctly low-key institution.

There were usually two of the generals' armed hard bodies at the door, and their absence surprised Michael. What didn't were the piles of wilting flowers stacked against the wall. Every morning the military took them away and by the next they were always back—roses, tulips, small handmade crucifixes—delivered by a legion of ancient women armed with feet so light, dedication so complete, the guards never saw them. A cycle played for three months now that ended every morning with still more laid against the wall. Their devotion not for this arrogant hunk of concrete, not for the CGT...

For Her.

Michael's head snapped suddenly at the sound of boots. Two uniformed soldiers, rifles slung over shoulders, came into the light. Between them bobbed the short, gray head of Hector Cabanillas, deputy commander of Argentine military intelligence. Palace guardian. The new residents of the palace had taken a shine to quiet, measured Hector. But then, they always did.

"Michael." The handshake was reliable, the smile playful under a wilderness of wrinkles. Hector had on the dark-blue suit that was his trademark, winter or summer. "I'm so glad you came."

"It's four in the morning, Hector."

"I apologize, Michael." He was apologizing again. Hector patted Michael's arm affectionately. "Let's get off the street, no?" He nodded to one of the soldiers, who produced a key for the door. Michael meditated on the soldier's face: brighter, sharper than those of the typical grunts here, most of whom were illiterates culled from the ferociously poor *Barrio Miserias.* Despite the olive uniforms, these were clearly Hector's private reserve.

The entryway smelled of must. Michael knew people still worked here—army-installed yes-men caretaking the CGT workers' union in name only. Still, it seemed crowded with stale ghosts.

Ghosts…

They took the stairs to the third floor, snapping gloomy lights as they went. Hector lagged cheerfully behind, favoring a crippled leg with his silver dog-headed cane. Before the war, Hector had been tortured by a previous regime until the cartilage in his knee disintegrated. Years and several governments later, that same torturer rose again to authority, had the cane handmade in London, and with a boyish lack of irony only Latins can truly manage, threw a lavish banquet and presented it to Hector. That regime was, of course, also long gone now, but Hector endured. Still the quiet, patient voice in dark alleys.

The third floor felt even more musty than the two below. This time it wasn't an illusion; all the offices in the north end of the building had been cleared out three years ago. The thought chilled something in Michael.

At the end of the hall stood a sealed wooden door, its edges plugged with wax, yellowish and crumbly. Room 63. Hector, his soldiers, and Michael stopped before it. "We are waiting for one more," Hector smiled.

He was short in coming, his bald pate clearing the landing, and the chill in Michael's gut rolled into a snowball.

Dr. Pedro Ara, cultural attaché to the Spanish embassy, approached them on soundless loafers. His eyes went straight to the door and lingered, as if waiting for it to speak. Only after a long beat did they reluctantly shift and pass without enthusiasm over Hector, Michael, the soldiers.

"Is there no one here of rank?" Ara's Madrilenian Spanish hummed with imperiousness.

Hector stepped forward. "I am Hector Cabanillas, representative of the government."

"There is no government." The accent was leased from dead aristocracy, composed to humiliate those like Hector, their New World dialects marked by the cadences of immigrants. Hector let it go, his face the mask of the ever-patient host.

"I have complete authority to speak for Casa Rosada."

"So Casa Rosada finally speaks."

"This is Michael Suslov, of the American embassy."

Michael had been introduced to Ara before, by other people in other places, but the good doctor's eyes showed no recognition. Michael was low rung, a twenty-eight-year-old diplomatic nobody. Ara was more than a senior rep; he was the social track's magician, its dwarfish undertaker. It was Ara's career that landed him in the capital, but it was his hobby—his obsession—that gave him access to the most rarefied circles of the oligarchy. That obsession now brought him to the third floor of the CGT.

He didn't shake Michael's hand.

Hector nodded to the soldiers, who removed bayonets from their belts and began prying the wax from the doorjamb. It peeled and fell in crumbly strips that skittered on the tile floor. Hector brought forward a key, but the lock had frozen. As the boys in olive went to work on the door, Michael stared at Ara.

What a strange-looking bastard, he thought. With his puckered chin, his elfin ears, his ubiquitousness—like a bad dream, perched on the edge of every night here. The station had vetted him a dozen times, and the conviction held that he wasn't a spook. He was just...Ara.

The soldiers tore out the hinges and the door came down, drawbridge-like, onto their forearms.

And Michael knew.

Knew the moment the smell, a wakened dragon, snicked through them. Mold, carbonized incense, lilacs.

Ara shouldered past Michael to the room's threshold of darkness and breathed deeply the scent of things dead, things changed—and his face took on a kind of beatific satisfaction. A soldier snapped his flashlight. Ara pushed it gently aside. "No. Candles."

Hector nodded, and the soldier produced one. Michael wondered if candles were standard combat equipment or if Hector had anticipated this, understood the moment. A match struck the wick, and with candle held high, they crossed into the room.

A few feet inside stood a pair of tall votives. Ara took the candle from the soldier and touched the two others with an air of private ceremony. The room rose and sharpened. It was large and windowless, with a high ceiling of pressed tin. The walls were empty but for a pair of curtains framing a portrait of the Virgin. At the room's center was a raised pedestal draped in the blue and white of the Argentine flag. They stood around it now: Michael and Ara, Hector and the two soldiers with intelligent eyes.

"Remove the flag, please," Hector said. Voices had fallen to whispers. The soldiers reached for either end.

"—With care."

A soft tug, and silk slid silently away, revealing beneath it…

Her.

Dust shivered in amber glare.

Michael had been prepared for nearly anything: a corpse, a wasted shell, a shrunken effigy. But not what lay before him. Blonde hair glistening in dancing light. Smooth porcelain skin. This was Her. Eva Duarte Perón.

Evita.

In life she'd shattered the pointless cycles of Argentine politics, flung open the gates of history to the great ignored, and ruled them as their pampa Cinderella. This bastard of a cow baron's toady, the kept daughter of a kept mother of a kept town, rocketed into history on the shoulders of a dream-crazy mob that sang of her, named stars after her, and on her death, at a still-beautiful thirty-three, choked and paralyzed a country with grief.

This was Her.

A hundred and sixty thousand people signed petitions urging the pope to declare her a saint. Santa Evita, who fed the mob and exploited it ruthlessly. Even in death, her corpse carried within it such imagined power her husband had it sealed away here, in a $30,000 bronze casket with an inch-thick clear-crystal cover, at the bosom of the building that had once been the heart of her obsession.

She seemed so small now.

Michael conjured their only conversation. The strange words passed between them. It tugged unexpectedly, and he wondered if it showed. Michael tried to place those words now in the tiny mouth before him. They wouldn't fit.

Everything around him—the air, even the light—creaked with rot. Everything but Her. Here time had been shackled to an ageless instant. Ara hovered over her protectively, beaming with pride at his creation. "She's beautiful," Ara murmured, as if to a stuck butterfly.

"Yes. She is." Hector's voice was soft. For the first time Michael thought he caught a glint of fear in the soldiers' eyes. Hector's boys perhaps, but boys of the pampa nonetheless.

Hector cleared his throat. "You will bear witness, Doctor, that no damage or disrespect has been done to Her." The dampness seemed to close around his words, crush them in midair.

"...Doctor?" Hector prodded.

"Yes, yes, of course," he answered impatiently. He was lost to them now. Cooing to her. "You're so lovely..."

In life she wrapped herself in nothing less than the most exclusive Christian Dior, but here lay only a humble, pious servant of God clad in a robe of simple white muslin. She wore none of the half-million dollars in jewelry that had flashed and dazzled paparazzi on two continents, just a rosary from the pope knitted between unpainted fingers.

Hector ordered the crystal lid removed. Ara knelt down beside her head, examining rouged, waxy lips. "Look at them," he mumbled—to whom Michael wasn't sure—"the downfall of nearly every artist. Two weeks I spent on these alone. Perfect."

The first time Michael had seen Ara was at an embassy reception where the doctor had brought with him a stitched leather hatbox. Sometime between dinner and cigarettes, he removed from it the embalmed head of a Spanish peasant. The work was so remarkable, the reconstruction so flawless, it inspired not horror but wonder among the guests, most of whom were used to this nightly unveiling and treated it as a rare objet d'art taken from a host's safe for viewings among friends. No longer belonging to its original owner, yet not the grave, it had emerged as something more: a piece of expressive art, with Ara its proud sculptor.

Michael didn't remember what condition the lips were in.

Evita didn't look dead, but she didn't look alive either. She looked…Ara's. One hundred thousand dollars he'd been paid by Juan Perón to preserve his wife, returning to him nearly a year later an incorruptible effigy he declared would last a thousand years. It was his masterpiece to eternity—a monument that would never fade.

And that was exactly the problem.

Michael hadn't noticed the soldiers leaving, but they returned now, carrying between them a long, simple pine box. Not a casket. A box. They set it down beside the raised bier.

"What are you doing with Her?" Ara demanded. He had placed himself between Hector and his masterpiece.

Hector's chestnut eye, the good one, seemed to soften with sympathy. "No one here doubts your devotion to the Senora, Doctor." Hector spoke quietly, without hurry. "Your work and loyalty are beyond reproach. But outside"—Hector's eyes gestured to a world beyond blank walls—"are dangerous times…"

Beyond those walls it was now a crime to read of her, to own her photograph, to utter her name. Yet every night that name rode the breezes above the city, screamed in a thousand flowers stacked at the foot of a shuttered building, in a million gallons of spray paint that everywhere demanded over and over WHERE IS SHE?, in the kitchen pipe-bombs that crackled through the barrios.

Hector took in a breath and released the words that would forever change their lives: "It is time Evita Perón was removed from politics."

Together they lifted her—chilly and weighing all of a twelve-year-old girl—from the half-ton casket and set her into the box with the maximum dignity possible while still putting someone into a box. The eyes remained closed and serene, the hands still clenched their rosary, the pleated gown found its old rhythms.

They screwed a wood top over her.

The box was taken down back stairs to the rear alley, where an army truck waited. The soldiers loaded it onto the bed and secured a tarp. Suddenly everyone was left standing with nothing to do but avoid one another's eyes and listen to the bleats of tugboats on the Plata. It was Ara who finally spoke. "Where will She be taken?"

"She will be given a Christian burial," Hector answered, anticipating the next question by adding quickly, "in private."

Ara seemed ready to fight the idea, but the moment receded. His eyes drifted to the tarp. "She is a symbol to so many, Senor Cabanillas, but please remember that she is also a woman."

"Thank you for coming, Doctor."

They didn't shake hands. Ara looked Hector up and down, as if to memorize his features, then turned and walked through the alley, his dwarfish figure slipping into a fragment of night.

"An unmarked grave?" It was Michael's turn to speak. They were alone now, the soldiers busy with the truck.

"A sanctuary."

"From whom?"

"History."

There was purple in the sky now, deep and low over Uruguay. Hector removed his wire-rimmed glasses and cleaned them with a cloth. A job-completion ritual.

"Thank you for coming, Michael." His myopic eyes were aimed at the wall but focused beyond it, to the docks and river that lay on the other side.

"Why did you call me?"

"I needed you."

"For what?"

The glasses were returned to the bridge of his nose. He faced Michael now. "To be a witness."

Hector squeezed Michael's arm, turned, and climbed into the truck's cab. There was a dry cough of pistons, a lurch of gears, and the prewar Mack whined away down the alley with its cargo. The sound lasted three blocks, fading behind the hum of the city's waking, cranky infrastructure.

And Michael was alone.

The sides of the CGT were bluish now, the light from street lamps retreating in tiny halos. He walked back down the alley to his car, paused to put the key in the door, and smelled it again for the first time.

Wafting up the alley on gusts of memory: slaughterhouse blood atop dead canals. The warm stench of half-sunk fishing boats. The rot of night-old tango sweat. It was a smell of childhood, of La Boca, which for Michael were one and the same.

He hadn't realized how close he was to the old neighborhood, just a few blocks south and a million miles away, with its crumbling piers and crazy immigrant homes. La Boca. The dockworkers would be up now, setting off for work, swinging lunch bags thick with *fugazza*. The children would wake soon. Hammering feet on slick cobblestones, school-bound voices catcalling in an Italian-accented Spanish that was true of all Spanish here but no more so than in La Boca.

After four years back in Buenos Aires, he had yet to visit the old docks. It seemed another world now, too far away to touch, close enough to burn if you stared too long. His innocence lay there. So did his mother and sister. He thought of them, let the dull spasm reach stiffly over years…

…Then started his car and drove away.

## 2.

A first memory:

His mother, young, raven hair brushing his cheek as she kneels beside him, smelling of spoiled milk. Something weak and small twitches in her arms and he's only two but he knows it's trouble. "Michael," she says to him in Italian, "this is your sister."

His father, an old man even then, towering sinew with a shock of arrogant white hair. He picks Michael up roughly, bellows at him in Ukrainian: "Not king of the hill anymore, eh?"

They lived in Chicago. West Taylor. His father had played clarinet with the Kiev symphony, had survived the Reds in '18 but not his brother's reputation in the White Army. The Cheka sniffed his house, sniffed his friends, sniffed his back as he picked through a pile of frozen, massacred corpses on Christmas morning for the body of his brother. The symphony was disbanded the next day on Stalin's orders, and on New Year's afternoon Nikolai Suslov read the writing in the snow and walked out of Russia.

Through Poland, where he slept in church doorways with his clarinet. Into Germany, where he hunted rabbits in the Black Forest to stay alive. Across northern Italy, where he stole grapes in the shadow of the monastery at Monteriggioni and was discovered by the vintner's daughter, Constantina D'Oro, a moody, restless woman, who brought him pecorino and Sienese prosciutto. He was thin, broke, and had only his clarinet. She was bored, sharp, and had only her swollen, veiled chest. She was eighteen. He was fifty-seven.

They came to America, to Chicago, where he looked for an orchestra, then a band, and ended up with one-nighters in gangster speakeasies. He grew frustrated. She grew pregnant: first with Michael, then Maria.

Not long after, Michael's parents gave up on the Depression, on America, and emigrated to Buenos Aires, where Constantina had relatives.

*"Love her, Michael. Love your little sister..."*

Michael and Maria grew and came to understand, then love, their La Boca neighborhood. He palled with the other immigrant kids, and they ran in gangs through the narrow rainbow streets; drew chalk dragons on apartment walls painted red, yellow, and green; sailed waste-wood battleships in the putrid canal; pestered dockworkers, who'd make them sing sweetly before surrendering candies from Bolivia or Scotland. And always there was Maria, following, just wanting to be near him.

*"Watch out for your sister, Michael."*

His father now, and Michael vowed he would. Though she was weaker and sickly, Michael allowed her to tag along and bloodied the nose of any of the gang who complained. And Maria steeled herself, built forts with them, slayed demons, helped spook the ice man's old cart mare with Chilean firecrackers, only occasionally lying down to gulp, to search for her breath and medicine. Never telling their mother, always climbing to her feet and running with Michael home when she called for supper.

There would be evenings she caught up to Michael and he'd be standing on the sidewalk, looking up at the riotous hulk of their apartment building—purple corrugated walls, green shutters, orange cupolas trimmed with blue-and-red doors. The lights would be coming up in each window, and with them the tumbling smells of *bifes*, pasta, and burbling tomato that mingled with canal garbage into something unreally sweet that shot to the back of their mouths. Struggling through it all, as the sky fell and the gas street lamps ticked and fussed, would be the thin, drifting sound of their father's clarinet, and for a moment Michael knew his universe worked. As the certainty swept out from his heart, he turned to Maria and she was looking at the same building, feeling the same confidence, and he put his arm around her and promised his sister he would always look after her.

Inside, supper was hot and clanging. His father would uncork the Chianti, bought cheap off the docks, and alternate with straight shots of Finnish vodka as his family waited nervously to see which side of the mountain the sled of his emotions would tip to. Sometimes it would be the gentle slope of his better nature, and with a stamp of his boot and an open gesture with bony fingers, he would tell stories of his days in Kiev, of the orchestra and legions of doe-eyed Ukrainian flowers that had wept for his attention. Sometimes he would skip a part on purpose, and his children would catch him and demand the full version, for they'd heard these stories a thousand times and loved them for the certainty of their cadence.

But sometimes the sled would tumble the other way, his father's face darkening with frustration. He had twice the work here in the music halls of Avenida Corrientes than in Chicago—at half the pay. His nights were busy but the days were spent watching the Suslovs sink further and further into Constantina's relatives' debt. He hated the half-breed orchestras here and their bombastic, mercurial conductors. As his rants broadened and soured, he would sweep his eyes over each of them, looking for a blink, a rise that would stoke a flash of temper. Sometimes it was Michael; a wrong look, a half sentence, and his father would be on him, boxing his ears till the tears stung and his head rang.

More often it was his mother, unable to contain another slur against her family, who would take the bait, their voices leapfrogging over each other, and Michael and Maria would dive for cover, knowing one would eventually brush its mate and release a furious, scrapping brawl. In the face of Constantina's flailing rage, Nikolai's temper would collapse into belly laughter as she'd struggle and shriek and finally collapse into tears. There'd be kisses, and a pause, and the scoot of a chair as he'd carry her to the bedroom. Foreplay in Michael's home usually involved broken furniture.

And once a broken body.

Up past the docks. To the tanneries, where the canal fermented with cattle guts and bone. Where they were never allowed and where they stood now—his gang, and he and little Maria— on a rise over the tannery's waste pipe, shouting over the roar of chemical entrails blasting—too heavy, too slow—in their tumble to the canal. There, even though it was forbidden, to see an older girl living in one of the tar paper shacks clinging to the rear of the tannery—a girl who, for a fistful of dock candy, would lift her dress and let them touch her thing.

A boy's moment, and Maria can't come. She's to wait by the belching pipe. Because she's a girl and most of all because she's his sister. So he lines up with the others, passes down his toll of Belgian taffy, reaches, and feels something to his eleven-year-old mind mind horrifying, thrilling, impossibly important. When it's over he stands with the gang, wired and anxious and a little sick, making it better with bravado. Making it go away. Finally he remembers Maria, goes to the churning wastepipe, and she's not there. Annoyed at first, he calls her name harshly, looks briefly around the mushy rise, and decides, even as a shiver rattles his guts, that she got bored and left.

He starts home, slowly, then faster, then finally in a blind, stumbling panic. Her room is empty and Michael stands on its threshold, feeling the stare of her only doll.

His parents were in the kitchen, and hadn't heard him come in. He waited, shivering, till they saw him, blurted out that Maria was gone in a single, tangled breath. Watched his mother's face grow and distort into reaches unfathomable. His father leapt from the table, demanded to be taken to the spot. Neighbors followed—the D'Annunzios and Spitalieris, Calabresis and Mottos. They searched the banks, the shrubs, pulled the ears of each boy till they were satisfied none knew. Except Michael. No one pulled Michael's ears. He was left on the muddy embankment, alone.

They searched till nightfall, then beyond with lanterns, calling her name, roving like fireflies over the tannery grounds. Michael sat in the dirt and watched as his father—crouched in the wan glow of a neighbor's lamp, tears streaming his cheeks—plunged both arms to the shoulder in to the roiling entrails of the canal, raising them empty and stiff and bleached with acid.

And Michael lay down, pulled the earth over his head, and willed himself to die.

There was never a funeral, just a day they gave up looking. His mother never cried, his father never cried again, and both seemed to lose track of Michael. He lay in his room, missed school, left at first light each day to sit above the pipe, where he coaxed clouds of lye and blood to scald him clean. He tried to imagine Maria in the blurry rush below, tried to imagine her tiny bones rolling and mingling with those of steers and sheep. His mind would reach from there to death and forever empty night, would just touch its truth before disappearing under a smothering curtain of survival.

They may have tried to carry on as a family, but the rhythm was gone. Meals grew silent, his father came home later and later, and Michael's mother retreated to a place Michael could not follow.

She burned herself sometimes now at the wood stove, sometimes forgot to make dinner, sometimes never got out of bed. When one day she didn't come home at nightfall, her husband and neighbors took to the streets, calling her name. It was Michael who found her, above the tannery pipe, staring into the rust-colored water below. He didn't know if she'd heard him approach, but she turned in his direction, looked at him with eyes long moved on to other things, and whispered, "I have nothing. Nothing in this world is mine."

And Michael fell howling at her feet. Gurgled in a finished voice that he was sorry—for Maria, for being born—that he would do anything, anything, if she would only come back to him.

And his mother stroked his hair absently, like he were a vaguely familiar dog, and listened to the rush of tannery waste speak soft, soothing words.

Eight months later her body burned with cancer. She embraced it, shoveled it her flesh. At the end her husband was there, her relatives, the neighborhood priest. Everyone but Michael. They'd forgotten to fetch him, and on the curb he waited in his Sunday best, drawing pointless circles of chalk, till someone remembered to tell him she was dead.

The next day his father packed their bags, closed the apartment, and, without a word between them, booked a ticket back to Chicago.

He died on Michael's first day of college. No brother to sort through a pile of frozen bodies, no wife to throw herself at his casket, no daughter to weep softly. Only quiet Michael, not tossing in a handful of dirt like they do in Italy, or lighting a candle like they do in the Ukraine; just standing there stupidly and apart, waiting for it to be over, like they do in America.

**May 12, 1956**

# 3.

The sun threw lances into a cloudless sky as Michael parked at the American embassy on Roque Sáenz Peña—actually three rented floors in the turn-of-the-century First Boston Bank tower. In London and Paris, US government representatives worked out of palatial structures blocks long. Even in the new, instant capital of Bonn they had broad lawns, brick patios, and colorful gardens. But South America was still an afterthought in the Eisenhower State Department, its diplomats to the Republic of Argentina tenants between accounts receivable and domestic loans.

Michael got off on the middle floor of the embassy, where the CIA station was located. The theory was that by sandwiching the station between the upper and lower floors, they could cut down on electronic eavesdropping. It was a joke of course, what with all the pipes and elevator shafts running between here and the bank offices above and below. The consolation was that this particular station rarely did anything worth bugging it over.

It wasn't even seven and the floor was deserted but for Wintergreen, the marine who sat at a desk guarding a single door labled MILITARY LOGISTICS—embassy-speak for a CIA station.

"Morning, Jarhead."

"Morning, Spook."

"You could save my life with some coffee."

"Why would I do that?"

"I'm bigger than you are."

"I'm armed."

"I sign your time card."

Wintergreen poured him a cup. "Yours is the mug with 'Asshole' on it, right?"

Wintergreen and Michael were the only ones on the floor under thirty. Barely old enough to drink back home, the marine guard was a good-looking Wyoming kid for whom *semper fi* had been a plank off the sinking ship of his Basque parents' sheep ranch.

Michael glanced over the marine's shoulder to the comic book he was reading. "*Superman*?"

"In his greatest struggle with the arch fiend." The Wyoming kid's accent still had, despite his constant effort, tiny tracks of Basque over it.

"How is Lex Luther?"

"He has a new titanium-blade snapping arm. I'm concerned."

Michael signed for the overnight dispatch pouch from Washington, left the guard to his early morning Eternal Struggle for World Domination, and headed for his own pathetic little corner of it.

Just beyond the "ML" door were the station support offices where an administration assistant, record clerk, and three secretaries worked, most drawn from the wives of ex-pat vice presidents of locally based American internationals like Dun & Bradstreet. The room was empty.

Through a second metal door was the inner station itself where five of them worked. Norris, the station chief, had the large corner office. Esther, the code clerk, worked in the windowless communications center. There were a few storage rooms, a darkroom at the end of the hall, and, across from it, the cluttered corner the three remaining case officers—Lofton, Miller, and Michael—shared.

Michael dropped into a chair and slid himself on squealing casters. His desk faced an ornate, curved window typical of the building's design, which he liked to think of as Early Robber Baron. Parquet floors, scooped lintels, even roof-line figurines—of whom, Michael had no idea. His view was the corner of Roque Sáenz Peña and Calle Florida, the fancy pedestrian shopping street. There was a cable car stop directly below, and his mornings here usually began with the strangle of metal brakes. Casa Rosada and the Plaza de Mayo were just a few blocks away at the other end of Roque Sáenz Peña. When the anti-Perón pilots bombed it in June, every window was blasted out of the embassy, and Michael had spent weeks picking fragments of glass from his typewriter. Someone on the State Department side claimed to have found a hand blown onto the roof. Just another weekend at the First Boston.

Michael unlocked the dispatch pouch and spilled out the usual: requested files from Records Integration Division, cipher updates, budget forms, name checks, and a red-striped envelope marked TOP SECRET SELF-RESTRICTED HANDLING EYES ONLY addressed to Michael—in a manner of speaking. Upon induction into operational intelligence, each wet-nosed neophyte is issued an official pseudonym to use in all CIA correspondence. At first the idea appealed to Michael—a sort of nom de spook. He imagined such dashing possibilities as L. L. Shadow or Maximilian Devereaux. When the name finally arrived, dreamed up by some chinless functionary in a Potomac basement, it didn't have quite the ring Michael had hoped for: FRANK SNIFF.

**FRANK SNIFF BUENOS AIRES STATION**

**TOP SECRET SELF-RESTRICTED HANDLING EYES ONLY**

Michael debated opening it now or after lunch and decided to get it over with.

**FROM: PETER NORTH AC/WH/5/**
**TO: FRANK SNIFF BUENOS AIRES STATION**
**SUBJECT: RYBAT BI LETTER**
**MESSAGE:**
**I HAVE, AFTER CAREFUL CONSIDERATION, COME TO THE**
**CONCLUSION THAT YOU CAN JUDGE THE DEVELOPMENT**
**OF A CIVILIZATION BY HOW LATE YOU CAN GET A PIZZA**
**ON A TUESDAY NIGHT.**

**END MESSAGE**

Michael sighed. "Peter North" was the working pseudonym of Billy Patterson, a grinning, murderous carrottop he went through CIA boot camp with at the agency's newly acquired Camp Peary. They were partners on field exercises, including a mock border-crossing, where Patterson managed to nearly kill an instructor in a watchtower explosion. After graduation, both ended up in the Directorate of Plans Western Hemisphere Division—Patterson in Branch 5 communications—and it was then the TOP SECRET SELF-RESTRICTED HANDLING EYES ONLY messages from Washington started haunting Michael's desk, their contents always a different, meaningless whimsy that had crossed Patterson's deranged mind over coffee. Michael had tried begging him to stop, telling him that so much EYES ONLY traffic directed to him personally from division HQ was further alienating his already alienated coworkers, but Patterson had responded by gleefully doubling his output and upping the security clearance.

Michael had considered showing them to Norris and the others, but that would only get Billy into trouble, and the fact was Michael owed him. Billy might have almost gotten them killed at Camp Peary, but he also happily, almost perversely, stood up and taken the fall later for a team failure that was entirely Michael's fault. This resulted in Billy being punished after graduation with a desk rotation in Washington while Michael was assigned immediately on an FI rotation abroad. He owed Billy, so he kept his mouth shut and took his lumps in cold stares from his boss.

Michael fed Billy's dispatch to the shredder, put his feet up, stared at the plaster ceiling—at cracks running through it like veins—and thought of Evita.

Of her funeral and the thousands who stood in the rain for hours to glimpse her ravaged body. Of a city that came to a shuddering stop as if it would never start again. Of a gloating oligarchy and shattered peasants. Of a note left fluttering on his front door.

Of her frightened husband.

With Dr. Ara's work finished, Evita was brought to the third floor of the CGT to lie in wait while her husband and president, Juan Perón, began work on a monumental tomb. It was to be based on Napoleon's, a towering marble facade topped with a 450-foot shirtless laborer—a *descamisado*—standing taller than the Statue of Liberty.

But Evita was Perón, and Perón was Evita, and only together were they that improbable political fantasy of Peronism. And during those first nights, when Perón would climb the CGT stairs alone to sit outside her door, he came to realize that not only did his wife lay dead in there, but also half his power. In public he began to bang his fist harder, drive his motorcycle faster, sleep with women younger—a howl of exorcism against a wife that had gone from his greatest love to his greatest yoke.

In three years he was gone. A pathetic creature in a seedy smoking jacket, escaping to a Uruguayan gunboat that would lead him away from the hounds, from memories, into exile.

He left plenty behind: a nation in economic chaos, a thirteen-year-old lover, a dead wife sealed behind wax. The first thing the new government—a government of generals—did was dynamite her monument. And they banned her. Banned even the notion of her.

Yet they never gathered the courage to touch Evita herself. She lay where her husband left her, stowed in silence. But not forgotten by voices that grew louder each passing night, spoken with flowers, and now more often, violence. She wouldn't go away, so they had finally come for her. To take her out of politics.

In Michael's desk was a letter from Evita, written near the end of her life in a shaky, chemotherapy hand. Of the lines she wrote, the one that stuck with Michael these three years since her death was always the last: *You Will Never Forget Me.* At the bottom of the envelope was a single lock of blonde hair...

"Mike."

Michael jerked awake. It was Ed Lofton, one of the case officers he shared the room with and the only one who came close to liking him, which wasn't much.

"Spend the night again?"

It was an old station joke. Michael had a habit of falling asleep in his chair. Once, during a particularly insufferable lecture from Ambassador Nufer, he'd curled up into a fetal ball and begun snoring. This time he had at least an excuse: Karen was four months now into a pregnancy that seemed to be a scientific experiment in continuous vomiting. Neither of them had slept the night before.

Lofton had a copy of the local rag, headlines screaming about the latest Peronist bombing. "Cocksuckers are getting on my nerves," he sighed. Lofton was in his midforties and lanky, with a soft belly, seersucker suit, and Gallic nose that was a web of exploded capillaries. Michael had stumbled on some of Lofton's more debauched moments during stakeouts, and the fact that he had never brought them up had earned him, if not the affection of his fellow case officer, a certain respect.

Lofton tossed the newspaper on the desk. "Bud wants to see you."

"How's his mood?"

"Usual."

Robert "Bud" Norris's office was across the hall. The door to the station chief's domain was always closed, and Michael dutifully knocked.

"Come."

He entered. Norris was behind his desk, going through the day's cable traffic. "Did you get an 'Eyes-Only' this morning?" he asked without looking up. Norris had the cable inventory list in his hand, and for the millionth time Michael cursed Billy's name to all the sprites in redheaded hell.

"Yeah."

It hardly mattered anymore. What few fantasies Michael might have entertained of fitting in here had been choked in their crib years ago.

At sixty, Norris's face was still remarkably handsome but for the beginnings of a jowl that was edging inexorably forward with each year. Norris would be a turkey-neck by sixty-five. He stretched his chin and ran a finger along it as he studied Michael, a habit picked up from his wife, a strained, brittle *Porteño* beauty named Flavia.

"Anything I should know about?" he asked. The routine. Michael, keeping up his end of their kabuki dance, answered exactly the same way he had for four years.

"Nah. Nothin' special."

In the entire time Michael had been assigned here, no one else had received an EYES-ONLY. Norris stroked his turkey-neck-in-training. "Have a seat."

Michael obeyed. The wall behind Norris's head was blank but for a framed photo, not of CIA Director Allen Dulles but FBI chief J. Edgar Hoover. The significance of this was made abundantly clear on Michael's first day here, when, after leaving Michael's extended hand hanging stupidly in midair, Norris had eyed him up and down and growled, "So why the fuck are *you* here?"

Norris had the bullshit file open on his desk. The bullshit file was green and thick and dictated most of Michael's waking moments in the Republic of Argentina. "So how's Schmidt coming?"

Rudolph Schmidt. Volkswagen dealer. Ex-son of Deutschland who may or may not have once been an SS officer and may or may not be ranked about nine billionth on the attorney general's list of escaped war criminals.

"No ID yet. State doesn't have any prints, and I still haven't gotten a wire photo from Army CID."

"You've snuggled his neighbors? Opened his overseas mail?"

"I'm working on it."

"I've been on you a month about this."

"I've still got the GRU SPR file updates to finish. They're due next week."

"Schmidt's an ODENVY liason request. Give it priority."

Michael sighed. ODENVY was CIA-speak for the FBI. Which meant the FBI legal attaché at the embassy, Cosgrove, had made a call to Norris on behalf of Hoover or the US attorney general's office for help, which was now, once again, being dumped in Michael's overflowing lap. It was utter bullshit, but it was the way life worked down here.

"We understand each other?"

"I'll talk to Gulliano this afternoon."

"And Mike…" Norris leaned back in his chair, took the time to light a cigarette and stroke his advancing chin. "Last few months…some of my ears…have been hearing rumblings…"

"Rumblings?"

"Buzz in the corridors. Lights left on in Casa Rosada. Whispers…"

"Saying?"

"I thought you might have picked up something."

In four years Norris had never outwardly admitted that Michael might have a source better than his. Michael wasn't completely sure he was now.

"I'll ask around."

He turned to leave.

"Mike."

He hesitated.

"Is something going on?"

In a normal universe, in a normal field intelligence office of the United States of America, to any other brother station chief, Michael would have sat down and told him of dust and Ara and women who wouldn't fade being laid in pine boxes. But this was Norris and Buenos Aires, and Michael had learned a long time ago that though they occupied the same floor of the First Boston Bank building, that didn't mean they worked for the same company.

"Not that I know of, Bud."

# 4.

In the beginning there was nothing.

Then there was World War II, and with reluctance was born the Office of Strategic Services, a nervous America's first spy agency, a birth not marked with joy by either of its older siblings: the War Department and, more important, J. Edgar Hoover's FBI. For the FBI had always been the nation's answer to interstate robbery, be it banks or state secrets. And with the war there was plenty of the latter. But Hoover's flatfoots were by temperament cops and never really developed a love of the cloak or a feel for the dagger. But it was still a big, bad world only getting worse, and a frightened Uncle Sam finally decided he needed people that could find that peculiar love and feel, so the OSS came into being.

Hoover's FBI fought the idea, watching in horror as Roosevelt handed the OSS and its smug Ivy League sociopaths the cloak for Europe and the dagger for Asia, till he finally drew a line in the sand. And that line was South America. In a wartime compromise, Roosevelt left South American espionage, its bananas and generals and odd Nazi cruising dockside bars, to the FBI.

But soon World War II ended and another, chillier war began, and Uncle Sam decided to unite his frat boys and equatorial flatfoots under one roof, and so the OSS and the FBI's Latin American SIS branch were given a shotgun wedding in '47 and renamed "CIA."

But South America had always been FBI, and though their stationery now had "CIA" in its letterhead, the boys down there were still, in their hearts, Hoover's boys. And Hoover's boys just looked at the world differently.

In the internal struggle that followed the wedding, it was the frat boys, the old OSS, that ended up running the new CIA store. But the old World War II FBI hands didn't give up easily. They dug in behind the walls of the Western Hemisphere Division, where their boss, J. C. King, kept them physically separate from the rest of the CIA by running WH operations out of Barton Hall, an old wartime dormitory in Potomac Park, far away from the other CIA division headquarter staffs grouped together in the former OSS buildings along E Street.

During those first years, the frat boys on E Street would send memos south, and the ex-FBI flatfoots would ignore them. And they grew older, married into the local oligarchy, and carried on as they always had, targeting Hitler's ex-doormen, Mafia dons, and the odd unionizer screwing with General Motors.

By 1950, in the frat boys' minds, Buenos Aires was a basket case. There was zero penetration of East Bloc missions, the station was completely frozen out of the Perón administration, and its reports, when Norris bothered to come to work and file them, were legendary in the halls of the DOP for their inaccuracy. Norris was even credited—after leaking to the press a boneheaded report connecting Juan Perón to Nazis—with helping get the peacock, whom Truman hated, elected president of Argentina in the first place as a vote against "US meddling."

But despite all this, J. C. King, who had bonded with Norris and the others running deception ops against the Japanese in Buenos Aires during the war, continued to be a firewall between the WH Division and the rest of the CIA, and as long as King was WH chief, Norris, Lofton, Miller...all of them were protected. And J. C. King—who everyone assumed must have pictures of Dulles either with a dead hooker or a live boy—wasn't going anywhere.

It was '51 before the DDP Wisner, could finally muscle one of their own into Buenos Aires station: an expansion of the case officer staff by one to create a designated Russian-speaking Soviet Bloc desk.

Since none of Norris's team spoke Russian, in August, 1951, Michael Suslov, twenty-four years old and fresh from spook camp and the frat-boy world view, was sent south, the first new blood in these parts since the consolidation in '47. The first of the new CIA.

And they hated him on sight. Ignored him, fucked with him, and every moment of every day for four years reminded Michael that he worked not for Buenos Aires station but for *them*.

From Norris's office Michael went back to his desk and picked up the Ramirez 201 file. A gift from Hector, Ramirez was a Chilean military attaché anxious to fund a mistress habit by acting as an access agent to a female Czech code clerk, whom he claimed to also be sleeping with. There was so much going on in the world. Moscow station was riding the whirlwind of a nation shaken to its foundations by Khrushchev's ascension and execution of Lavrentiy Beria. Stations in Iran and Guatemala were changing whole governments, while in Indochina the SE Division was in the middle of a shooting war, trying to keep the French from giving an entire subcontinent away. All that history being made, all those *careers*, and here he sat, chasing senile Krauts for Norris. The station chief of course forbade Michael from tasking Lofton or any of the others with his Soviet Bloc work, which meant Michael was essentially alone in trying to keep tabs on the USSR missions here and the half-dozen spooks and support staff operating out of them.

The absurdity of all this reached a peak the previous spring when Michael discovered that the station actually owned an empty property that shared a wall with the Soviet commercial office lying along the back of the Russian embassy compound. Though it was a God-given opportunity for audio surveillance, Norris had inexplicably refused to authorize the budget for a listening post, so the possibility languished to the point where Norris was now openly talking about *selling* the building to conserve station resources. Norris's strategy was obvious. If a bugging operation, if *anything* Michael was doing down here, turned up something interesting, DDP Wisner would insist on expanding the Soviet Bloc desk in the station with more Michael clones, which would weaken Norris's grip on the place and the lifestyle he and his crew had comfortably built for themselves. So rule one here was simple: keep Michael from finding anything interesting.

Michael had tried appealing directly to WH HQ in Barton Hall, but he was still recovering from an operational fiasco with the Polish ambassador during his first year here and was, for the moment, radioactive with the SB branch. That and the unshakable J. C. King/Norris bond meant the building continued to sit empty while Michael spent another in a series of late nights here alone, processing Rameriz's 201, finishing the KGB/GRU SPRs, managing his Argentine contract agents in the police department, and basically running half a station by himself.

Michael was reaching the end of his emotional tether here, but if he could hang on a little longer, get some traction on any of this, he just might finally impress his bosses, his *real* bosses—not in Barton Hall but across Potomac Park on E Street. That would eventually mean a promotion. Which would mean a transfer. Which meant getting the fuck out of Buenos Aires.

Michael left early for lunch and strolled Calle Florida, ducking into three different tobacco shops on the bustling pedestrian way before finding what he wanted: a carton of imported Sobranie Black Russians. He'd come far enough down Calle Florida that, despite the humidity, he decided to loosen his tie and walk the rest of the way to the Central Post Office.

Michael had never requested Argentina. With his Russian and Romance languages he'd hoped for the East Bloc, and would have settled for Italy, even Spain. But with the perverse accuracy of a silver bullet, they'd shipped him back to the one black hole in his life: Argentina.

The fit, physically at least, was not a bad one. Unlike his station mates—all of whom seemed recruited from the same Minnesota football team—Michael, with his medium height and dark hair, blended easily into the lunch crowds around him. His Slavic blood left him with blue eyes and it was that, if anything, that marked him.

As a child he'd liked the Central Post Office, a gaudy monument of stone and iron. He remembered calling off echoes in the massive marble lobby, the tellers smiling patiently at him from their art deco cages. Entering now, he couldn't resist striking his heels hard on the floor to hear the echo come back to him off the muraled ceiling.

Assistant Postmaster Alphonse Gulliano's office, a large room with a small window through which no air moved, lay on the second floor. Gulliano, a slight, meticulously dressed man Michael's age, stood nearby signing time cards and smoking a Sobranie Black Russian.

"Senior Suslov."

"Senior Gulliano."

"Please. Come sit in my office. It's cooler."

It wasn't.

"Cigarette?" Gulliano offered the pack, careful as always to make sure Michael saw the crested label on the box.

"No, thank you."

"My only vice." It was, in fact, what first attracted Michael to him. One afternoon three and a half years ago, feigning some problem with his overseas mail, Michael had wandered in. There were over a dozen employees and several managers, but it was the acrid, heavy smell of the Sobranies that caught his attention. Imported, they were several times more expensive than local or even American brands. Bitter, Sobranies were at best an acquired taste, like caviar—a status symbol, and that was all Michael needed to know about Gulliano.

"You are here about one of your international renegades, no? One of the *alemanes malos*?"

That first afternoon Michael had segued their conversation from his alleged postal difficulties to international correspondence in general, and how, back home, his own father was a mailman. Gulliano had eagerly given Michael a tour, explained their procedures, and as he spoke, Michael took inventory of the young man's slightly above-market slacks, the occasionally dropped Spanish theta, the stench of the Sobranie Black Russians. A poorly paid civil servant heroically struggling to maintain airs above his station.

Michael shifted in his chair. "Rudolph Schmidt."

"On Juncal?"

"Yes."

That first afternoon quickly turned into lunch, and lunch again, where Gulliano would alternately pontificate on the failures of Peronism and devour Michael's stories of his college year in France, demanding the most mundane details—how strong the coffee was, the fashionable length of men's ties—and furrow his brow as if memorizing them. Michael spoke little of his work—embassy paper shuffling—except to hint at his difficulty in gathering evidence on certain notorious criminals wanted by the US attorney general. For his part, Gulliano spoke rarely of his wife and family and never invited Michael to his flat for dinner— ashamed, Michael assumed, of the lie it would give his cultivated exterior.

"This could cost me my career, Senor Suslov."

"I understand the difficulty of your position."

Michael pulled out the carton of Sobranies he'd bought on Calle Florida. "Here. These are for you."

"I couldn't possibly. They're very expensive."

"We get them free at the embassy. I don't smoke. They might as well not go to waste."

"Well, if you insist. Thank you."

It was always thus. Gulliano wasn't a bad guy when you got past the posing, and Michael began to see more of him. Lunches became dinners, coffee became wine, and talk of politics and airmail slid away into deeper regions of dreams, women, and fathers. Gulliano was surprised, then impressed, when Michael told him he was raised as a boy in working-class La Boca. Only then did he dare to bring Michael home to his sad flat in a sadder building in an old and tired outer barrio. There, surrounded by children and a harried, tiny wife coached not to speak, Gulliano would talk of his crippled mother, his fallen sister, and his eyes would mist with emotion. Sometimes in these moments, Michael would confide in Gulliano stories of his own family. Some of which were even true…

It was during a walk through Recoleta Park that it finally happened. They'd been talking about something trivial. The afternoon breeze was off the pampas, full of March and the snap of camaraderie. Gulliano's voice had suddenly changed, and with it Michael's heart leaped and his palms dampened, because he knew, after months of work, that he *had him*. In a tone struggling to remain casual, to brush it off as inconsequential, Gulliano let drop that Michael could, if he was discreet, perhaps glance at the mail of certain individuals of concern to his embassy. Through the blood slamming excitedly in his skull, Michael managed to protest that it was too great a risk to ask of a friend, but Gulliano had waved it away. "In the interest of justice…"

Schmidt's mail was in the side drawer of Gulliano's desk, a half a dozen or so letters, all postmarked Germany but for one from Chile. That would be Schmidt's brother, who owned a small farm in the Lake District. Michael would steam them open, have an old German couple the station kept on retainer transcribe the contents, seal them again, and have the packet returned the next day. He already knew what the letters would say—pathetic drivel from aunts and uncles back home complaining of shortages and demanding money. There'd be no secret Fourth Reich codes or reminiscences about gas chambers and firing squads.

"You must stay for coffee. I have some West African roast, just the way you like it." Meaning the way Michael drank it when he was going to school in France.

"If it's not any trouble, thank you."

After the third time Gulliano had slipped him somebody's mail, Michael had suggested that perhaps his friend, who was clearly running a risk, might be incurring certain costs. Surely it was only fair that he be reimbursed by the embassy, say, a hundred dollars a month? Michael knew that was at least double the struggling civil servant's salary, but he knew also, as he did that first day, that Sobranies didn't come cheap…

With his bullshit FBI Nazi hunt out of the way, Michael felt free to at least make a stab with Gulliano at some of his real CIA work—the GRU Soviet Personality Reports. He was, of course—despite a direct policy command from Washington—the only spook in the station trying to finish the damn thing. But then he was the only spook there that actually bothered to work for the CIA.

Gulliano handed him a stack of incoming East Bloc mail. Michael didn't expect any state secrets—those were shipped by pouch—but sometimes the staffs wrote private letters to friends and lovers within Argentina, letters they didn't want passed through the diplomatic system. It was these letters that could give a small hint about the personalities of his potential targets: who hated his wife, who was broke, who might be looking for a way out. The staff at those embassies weren't stupid enough not to at least suspect some of this sort of mail was being read, so there were no outright confessions. Still, if you read between the lines... Michael would do it himself, being the only Russian speaker and damn near the only *Spanish* speaker there. More homework, more nights away from Karen...

On the way out, Michael lingered and looked back at Gulliano, returned now to his work, and treated himself to that first memory. How the thrill had been not unlike the day Kimberly Mann let him clasp her hand when he was twelve. Something pure, almost childlike. A singular instant Michael had never before experienced with another male. The jolt of tasting for the first time the knowledge that someone will betray their government, their work, possibly their life, not for patriotism or money, but for friendship. You never forget your first...

Michael didn't see as much of Gulliano as he used to. The money changed it. Without anything being said, their relationship had become...business. Still, Michael wouldn't let Miller or any of the other flatfoots near Gulliano. Like with an old girl-friend, he couldn't stand the idea of someone else manhandling the slightly built postal clerk who was not only Michael's first, but the CIA's first agent-in-place in Buenos Aires.

# 5.

It was dark when he finally got home, and he felt foul with it. Loosening his tie in the foyer, he could see Karen grilling a steak in the kitchen for dinner, her growing belly keeping her nearly a hand's length from the range. Five months. Five months and their lives would be changed forever.

"Barefoot and pregnant in the kitchen. I finally feel like a real Argentine husband."

She smiled, eyes still on dinner, and he came up and reached around her from behind. She leaned into him and the damp smell of her neck wiped away his day.

"I didn't hear you come in."

"I'm sneaky that way."

His strokes moved south and took on another character. "Your *asada* is going to be *negra*," she breathed, "again."

By the end they were lying in a blanket, half in, half out of the garden's french doors. The night was peaceful, he was peaceful; even the alien constellations seemed on their side.

"How was work?"

"Stupidness. Another day of stupidness."

"I hate it here. Hate what this place is doing to us. To you. We never talk anymore. Not really. You're never here, and when you are you're still not here. You're still at work...or La Boca..."

He stroked her head absently. "It's okay. You'll feel better. It's just the baby. I'll be here more..."

She stiffened suddenly and stared fiercely at him. "Don't work me, Michael. Don't *ever* work me like one of your johns."

"I'd never do that." But he wasn't sure if he just hadn't. *Christ. I'm not at work. This is my wife. This is my real life.* He caressed her arm. "I'll get us out of here, Karen. I promise. I'll get us out of here..."

And he still wasn't entirely sure what part of him was speaking.

She went to bed early, and he read till he couldn't stand the heat or the stare of his living room and went out.

There was a small café on Juramento that served sidewalk cappuccinos. The owner, a transplanted West African who did little but nod, dispensed drinks from a bar behind which a record player spun solely '30s French cabaret tunes. Michael sat there, the only patron, and listened to the flare of bugs against an electrified lamp, the singing of damp power lines, a bruised recording of Jean Sablon.

Christ, the alienation didn't help their marriage any. Karen and he had rented a house in the wealthy Belgrano district, a city's-width away from La Boca. But still his childhood kept creeping in around the edges of his vision, cutting him off from her. To make matters worse, nobody at the American mission would talk to them. To the legit embassy wives, Karen was a spook's spouse, to be tolerated for cover's sake but not drawn close. The station support wives and flatfoot spouses had their own inner circle, forged over years here, that effortlessly froze her out. That left the BA oligarchy, the serrated generals' wives whom Karen loathed. Michael had his work, such as it was, and Karen had nothing. Long, wet days with no one to talk to but a distracted husband slowly turning to smoke...

"Michael."

That voice. The one that always seemed to come from the hollowed end of dark alleys. He hadn't heard him come up. But then you never did with Hector.

The crippled deputy head of Argentine military intelligence took a chair beside him. It had been nearly six months since Michael had seen Hector, candlelit beside the embalmed remains of his former employer's wife. It seemed a thousand.

"Such heat so late in the year." Hector dabbed his forehead with a handkerchief. "You're out late, Michael."

"I could say the same about you."

"It is my natural condition."

Hector smiled his Hector smile, but there was something wrong with it.

"How is Karen?"

"Confused. Pregnant. A little pissed off at me tonight."

"Our life is hard on the ones we love."

"You're not married."

"It is an academic observation."

Michael toyed with his coffee. "I lie to her every day. About my work, my thoughts, my life, really. It's become easier than telling the truth."

"The fear of being truly known. Perhaps it is that, more than anything, that unites people like us."

"I think I was known only once, and then just for a moment."

"Where?"

"Italy. A thousand years ago. Her name was Gina. I didn't know her long, but she's still the only person who ever stared straight through the chaos in me."

"What became of her?"

"No idea…"

"You've never called her?"

"It was complicated…" His thoughts drifted a beat on the memory before returning reluctantly. "Everything feels so out of control lately…"

"You're young, Michael. Soon you'll understand that the basic condition of life is chaos. Given enough time, you'll even grow to prefer it that way. And with your abilities, Buenos Aires isn't forever."

"It's sucking the life out of me."

"Talk to Carmelina, Michael. You must tell these things to your wife, not your coffee."

Carmelina was Hector's pet name for Karen, from that night four and a half years ago when the CIA's first real man in BA stood with his wife, alone on the edge of their third embassy reception, where no one would speak to them. The other foreign missions, the local power elite—none of them had yet figured if Suslov-and-spouse were worth talking to. So they were left standing next to the shrimp bowl, bored, ignored.

Then Hector appeared. Smiling and arms wide with charm, he asked their names, brought them drinks, pointed out who was who and told funny stories about each. They liked him instantly, were flattered by his attention, his smile, his uncliquishness. It wouldn't be long before Michael learned that a foreign intelligence officer is always the first to bring you a drink.

But that night Hector was just a free radical, a friendly uncle who suggested they three become their own clique. Declaring himself clique president, Hector moved that the first order of business be to adjourn somewhere else. The motion was seconded and passed unanimously.

The night was freezing, and Michael's tux kept grabbing at his crotch. The cabbie Hector stopped spoke English and turned out to have played two years of AA ball in the Carolina league. When the cabbie asked "Where to?" Hector deferred to the vice president and secretary of the new clique, and the secretary declared, "Music!" Hector mumbled an address to the former third baseman, and soon they were down along the nervous side of the river, past shadowy docks, and finally at a blank door that opened with a hot red gust onto a working-class tango bar.

They took a bug-gut-stained table right up front, their tuxes ludicrous, the lights and noise and arrogant thrusts of the dancers prickly on their skins. They drank, got drunk, laughed, and slurred stories they wouldn't remember to people they'd never see again. He remembered Hector's ease with everyone there. That unique confidence with kings and prostitutes, possible only by vice cops and spooks. And somehow Karen ended up on the dance floor, whirled and spun and locked hip to hip with a lustful ship mechanic who kept insisting she was a woman named Carmelina. And Michael remembered Hector's laugh and his promise that from now on Karen would always be Carmelina to him. He remembered the heat and the music and the bites of his tux. But most of all Michael remembered looking at his wife, sweaty and naughty in the hands of her tango partner, and thinking that he loved her and that their lives here were, after all, going to be good.

The taxi ride home had been a blurry hiss of tires and damp hair. Impossibly, they hailed their AA ballplayer again, and joining in their sloppy harmony he missed the turnoff, plunging through a strange, shuttered neighborhood that with a hollow thump Michael realized was that of his childhood: La Boca. As if a part of his thoughts, Hector had leaned close to his ear and whispered, for the first time in Spanish, *"Welcome home, Michael..."*

"How is the Senora?" It'd been several moments of silence before Michael said it. He couldn't keep his eyes off Hector's dog-headed cane, the way the light spun off the silver from the café's single lamp. Its master spoke carefully.

"History is sometimes...difficult."

"Argentina loves a corpse."

This nation had an unreal fixation with the remains of their famous. School children here were taught to dutifully recite the last words of national heroes, like San Martin, and celebrated not their birthdays but the day of their deaths. General Manuel de Rosas, a nineteenth-century strongman who died in England, had been buried there more than a hundred years, yet the government was today using all its wheat power to blackmail a hungry Europe into shipping his moldy bones home. The dead have power everywhere, but nowhere, it seemed, did their bodies themselves speak more forcefully than in Argentina.

"I've heard the rumors," Michael said. Everyone had. That since that night at the CGT five and a half months ago, each time they moved her, no matter how secret the new location, how remote, flowers would follow. Always.

"A woman loves her flowers." It was perhaps Hector's first joke, and Michael knew something was wrong. "We have never spoken of that night." Hector calmed the dog head with soft strokes.

"Then we're the only two people in BA that haven't."

"Do they press you? At work?"

Michael shrugged. "They've got their rumors too. Ninth-generation cocktail drivel."

"These are very strange times. You can feel it everywhere." On clear nights you could hear it too. The muffled thwack of kitchen bombs. The hiss of spray paint, someone's thirty seconds of four a.m. courage bled across a wall: WHERE IS SHE? The first snips in the fabric of a society deciding if it should unravel completely.

Hector stared down the dark throat of road fronting the café. "Michael, within the confines of our relationship, would you say you trust me?"

He couldn't place the emotion behind it. "Within the confines of our relationship, I suppose so."

"I trust you, Michael."

That silence again. The buzz of damp transformers.

"Michael, I may someday—possibly someday soon—ask you to do something. It will not be a favor but a request. Of someone I trust."

"What?"

The familiar smile but now weirdly dysfunctional. A fun-house mannequin out of sync. "With any luck, and in all probability, we will never have that discussion." One of Hector's friendly squeezes on the arm that suddenly wasn't Hector's at all. "Ah, but the time. I'm not as young as you, Michael, I belong in bed." He stood. "Please give my love to Carmelina."

Not long after that first night in the tango bar, Michael had screwed up an attempt to bug the Polish ambassador's new residence with a direct-current listening system. In the middle of wiring it up, a maid Michael hadn't accounted for appeared suddenly, forcing the pair of Technical Support Division guys down from Panama City to bail in such haste they left gaping holes in the home's plaster walls.

For a day and a half Michael had waited for the phone call that would say the maid had fingered him, that he was officially burned operationally in DO and would be sent home, to the utter delight of Norris, to spend the rest of his career disgraced on a desk in Barton Hall.

But when the call finally came, it wasn't from Washington but Hector. Apparently the Argentine spook had already bugged the residence a week before Michael's attempt, and in the interest of protecting his own operation had, under some official pretext, delayed the Polish ambassador that night, paid off the maid, and had an emergency crew repair the mess Michael's TSD team had left, all of which probably saved Michael's career.

But what Hector did next put it on a whole different trajectory. The deputy head of military intelligence then offered to share his recordings of the ambassador's residence with the CIA, but with a catch: Hector would only deal with Michael. Not Norris, not anyone sent down from SB Division to replace him, only Michael. And from that moment onward, Michael became Hector's personal conduit to Washington. Any messages to be sent, any insights that suited Casa Rosada, and some that suited merely Hector, went through the junior CIA officer. It saved Michael from being yanked home, but it also made him a prisoner here. Hector had became his only real friend in BA outside his marriage, and that made him another kind of prisoner. Hector had never asked anything in return, but Michael had always known, someday, that the request would come. Favors were, in the end, the grease that ran their worlds.

"Walk home careful, Hector."

Hector turned and his eye—the damaged, wandering one—caught the light, and for an instant it took on the dead glisten of a reptile.

"The night holds few surprises for me, Michael."

A tap of his cane, two at most, and he was gone.

Michael walked home, through a night full of the flinty whisper of clouds and the lonely warp of sirens drawing pointless circles in the asphalt...

Over the last six months he'd dreamed four times of Her. The dried husks of flies, the spark of candles, the weight of a twelve-year-old girl. In the dreams, always, as they were about to close the lid of her box, the eyes would open, the lips smile, and three of the times she said what she had written to him in life: *You Will Never Forget Me.* In the fourth dream, the last dream, the smile grew larger and the words changed.

*I Will Always Be a Part of You.*

**June 9, 1956**

# 6.

Michael was at the window, stripped to his undershirt, sitting beside the camera tripod. Attached to it was a 400-mm lens aimed across the street at another window in another apartment, known to be quietly leased by the Soviet embassy as a safe house. Lately it seemed to be used more for sex than debriefings, though sex certainly had its place in Michael's SPR files.

"Anybody moving? Fucking?" The gravel voice belonged to Ed Lofton, who was sitting across the room, reading the paper.

"Not yet." The routine window-watching was done by a retired American couple on retainer with the station. After logging a Monday evening assignation between two members of the Sov embassy, it was decided to send down a pair of case officers the following Monday to check it out for themselves.

"Bombs, bombs, and bombs…all for that stupid, arrogant cunt." Lofton was having his usual go-around with the morning paper. Seemingly oblivious to the heat, he still wore a jacket and tie, his bloodless, veined face sporting a moist, toxic sheen. "South America's biggest secret. 'Where's Evita?' Just give the bitch back to them, I say."

Lofton grinded on Michael, but he was the only case officer that would even consider helping him out with this work, though Michael suspected the attraction was more likely the opportunity to spend an afternoon sipping bourbon, there in his seersucker suit like a Tennessee Williams character, than anything to do with policy directives from E Street in Washington.

"Ever read her file? There's something to keep you warm on a winter night. Lady spread her legs faster than day-old butter in her youth. But always for a price. Good ol' Evita always knew the price of everything. Use to be a betting pool in the station on how many millions she'd stolen from her beloved citizens. Or where she put it. How that thieving whore ended up a national saint should be proof by itself of the existence of miracles. But then you knew her, right?"

A dig, and Michael ignored it. His strange and brief friendship with the former First Lady was something he never spoke of.

"She ever talk about it?"

"What?"

"The money."

Michael snorted and shook his head. "Argentina's favorite ghost story."

"Well, can't blame a boy for wondering."

Lofton flipped through a few more pages and then abandoned the paper, bored.

"How'd you get into this business, Mike?"

"Like everybody else. Wrong word in the right ear in college."

"Never went to college. Bud neither. Johnny Miller for that matter. None of us down here did. Just old-fashioned cops. Not as *educated* in the ways of world domination as you boys."

There were stirrings in the apartment. Two couples, midthirties. "Company." Michael stepped up to the 400-mm lens. Lofton turned the page of his newspaper. "Looks like Federov and Guylina. The blonde's Alexis's wife. Don't recognize the other woman."

"Tell me when the clothes come off."

Michael clicked off a few shots. The four took seats on a couple of sofas, produced a bottle, and started pouring. Michael took his eye from the camera and paged through his notes. "All four are married, though not to one another."

"Way of the world with Sovs, isn't it?"

It was. Moscow kept its kids on such short leashes, about the only peccadilloes possible were with fellow staff from the embassy. Russian culture seemed remarkably elastic on the matter, and such activities rarely caused ripples through the Soviet station. Still, it never hurt to know who was doing whom. At least in Michael's training.

Lofton lit a cigarette, bent forward, and held his temples between two fingers. "Amazing, really, the trouble they've gone to trying to keeping her hidden."

"Who?"

"Evita."

Michael was back up at the camera. The foursome was laughing it up now, getting touchy-feely.

"Maybe they just want to protect her." Michael tried to keep his eye on the lens, but his sweat kept fogging the view finder.

"From what?"

"Themselves."

And just like that the clothes came off. No preamble. One minute chat, next buttons working their way down, exposing pale flesh. "The clothes are coming off."

Lofton groaned as he stood and leaned against the window frame. "Lovely."

"Don't let them see you."

"Don't think their attention's on me, butch."

Their skin looked pocked through the lens's ground glass. Mouths on breasts, buttocks dimpled with carpet indentations.

"Did you know even President Aramburu doesn't know where she is? Nobody at Casa Rosada does. It's Argentina's only secret."

*Except for whoever brings those flowers. Every night.* "I'm sure someone there knows."

"You mean Hector?"

Hands groped into pants. You could see sweat on the women's backs. "Whoever."

"We all know that means Hector. Anything that happens after midnight in this country has Hector's name on it. Coups rise and fall, but Hector always endures. Casa Rosada's resident demon. Just comes with the furniture." Federov was climbing atop the blonde now. Lofton let out a sigh. "I was hoping for something a little more exotic from our communist friends."

"Four on four isn't enough for you?"

"You haven't lived in Argentina long enough."

Yes he had. Strangers' sweat in unventilated Buenos Aires rooms brought up foul memories of his own, not involving his wife. It was an ugly association.

"How'd you like it, someone photographing you?" Lofton said it right against Michael's ear, and the alcohol rot of the man's body pushed him to the edge. He took his eye from the lens. Rubbed it. "It's just for the SPR files."

"Millions of pictures of humping Russians. That'll change the world." Lofton straightened up, looked out on the clumsy orgy. "Your bosses must be proud."

They'd all been switched from FBI to CIA down here since '47. Eight years and still they were *Michael's* bosses. *Them.*

Michael clicked off a few more shots without even looking through the lens, then sat down on the carpet with his back against the window.

"You're missing the big finish."

"I got enough."

Michael would have to wait, though, for the obligatory sidewalk shots. He wanted to go home, get away from sweating Russians and Lofton. Yet he craved Lofton's approval, craved one—just one—accepting face among his spook partners.

"Why do you think Hector picked you out, Mike?"

"Who says he did?"

"C'mon. I read the cables. The guy likes you. Ever since your belly flop at the Polack ambassador's house, he's been giving you stuff."

"Maybe I'm the only one that's interested."

"Oooh. FBI bashing. Wondered how long it was going to take before your right hook came up." Lofton winked and took a long, leisurely drag on his pocket flask. "No, I don't think that's it. Want to hear my theory? Isn't that you used to live here. It's because you're the only one of us that wants *out*—your Sovs are on the sidewalk, butch."

Michael rose to a crouch and squeezed off a few more. Federov had a stain on his pants that no one was going to mistake for coffee. The others weaved and faded into the sidewalk crowds. A last shutter frame of the back of someone's head and he was done.

Michael started breaking down the camera. "Hector likes you, Mike. He tells you things. Things he doesn't tell his own government." Michael slipped the 400-mm lens into its cut-foam suitcase. "Think he'd tell you where she is?" Michael loaded the camera body into the case. He just wanted to go home. "Do you know, Mike? Do you know where she is?"

Michael stopped and the two stared at each other as Wintergreen, the station guard, came barreling suddenly through the door in his civvies. Lofton smiled, "Master Wintergreen, everyone's favorite marine. Favor us with some Basque, dear boy."

"*Zoaz infernu.* It means 'Go to hell.'"

"Warms the heart to see a boy speaking the native language of his parents."

"Only when I'm pissed off."

Michael looked in disbelief from Wintergreen to Lofton. "You always tell the marines where our safe houses are?"

"Well, young Wintergreen here is hardly just *any* marine. He's *our* marine."

Michael thought, *Scratch one fucking safe house.* He shook his head, buckled the case, and stood.

"Ed and I were just getting some dinner," shrugged the marine.

"Raising a little *infernu* tonight," Lofton said, walking back to retrieve his newspaper. "We'd invite you, Mike, but most of your hell seems to be pretty much self-contained."

**June 22, 1956**

# 7.

They were in the land of frightening skies.

Here, the earth was an afterthought, a pathetic strip of taupe running away without character or form. It was the sky that consumed everything: color, movement, texture. It was the sky that was real and the earth insubstantial. So hungry, so big, you lost trust in your feet, as if you could tumble upward into the maw. Vast, empty blue that was an arrogant, mean piece of forever.

Karen liked the pampas. She had spent summers as a child in eastern Colorado, and it spoke to her. To Michael it was a vaguely evil place in which he never felt at ease.

Michael studied his wife's profile, fuller now with pregnancy. That same profile first glimpsed against a foggy morning in the Reynolds coffeehouse at the University of Chicago. Her hair was full of midnight, like his mother's, with just a few silvery strands she'd had since sixteen, like her mother. It cupped a face the color of no color, with eyes so startlingly gray Michael had never seen them on anything but wolves. When he'd finally glanced over her shoulder, she had the worst handwriting he'd ever seen…

They shot past a pampa town, its grim coupling of expressionless buildings low and fearful of rising from the earth's safety into the swallowing sky. A poverty fragment sucked away in a dusty second.

Karen was in a good mood. These flat, expressionless miles west of BA always lifted her morale, and they were playful with each other—careful play, cautious of the hidden hair triggers that had grown into the fabric of their lives here. But nobody misstepped. Karen was in too high a spirit, happy just to be freed from a city they'd begun to see as the enemy.

The estancia's gate was white between two gnarled ombu trees. It was swung open, a shotgun gaucho checking names. The ranch house lay three miles farther along a sycamore-shaded road, where two dozen cars already crowded the circular drive. The house was like most out here: a sprawling, Mediterranean one-story. The floor was cool tile, the furniture covered in treated hide. Everything had a tricked-up, kitschy feel: the Lore of the Gaucho. Like most pampa estates it didn't feel lived in, and it wasn't. The wealth of Argentina came from these pampas, but it didn't stay. Like the owners of the estancias, it slipped quickly away to the city and rarely returned. The lords of these nation-sized plots lived most of their lives as urban *Porteños*, putting on their grandfather's gaucho knife only on the weekends when they'd return to the muddy source of their cars, furs, and perfume. The only people that truly lived out on these horizon tracts were the impoverished peasants who worked them. Half-breeds whose flat noses were all that remained of an Indian culture Spanish colonialists wiped out in just six bloody years. There were no Indian reservations in Argentina.

Across the entry hall, a pair of latticed glass doors stood open, the sound of laughter riding thin breezes. Off the back of the house sprawled a brick patio with a raised fire pit, flaring now with the juices of an entire steer turning above coals. It could feed fifty, and fifty milled about waiting, biding their time with gossip and gin and tonics. They were the usual mix: half BA upper crust, a few foreign diplomats, a blend of American ex-patriots—businessmen, technocrats, CIA station Buenos Aires.

Their host was still out on his horse—tradition at these gatherings—the lord leading a group of husbands on a manly gallop across the estancia. Heavy drinks appeared in their hands—also a tradition—and hoisting them, Michael and Karen took their place on the rim of the party, waiting for a point to enter the fray.

The point today was Norris, Michael's boss. Two tall ones' worth of mellow, he smiled at Michael, something he did only in public. Standing with a knot of British utilities magnates who owned most of BA's power grid, he had his arm warmly around Michael's shoulder now, one happy family. It was what Michael disliked most about these weekends. But Michael was good at his job, and a CIA officer is nothing if not the most outgoing person at a party.

The rules were looser away from the city, and a group had taken Karen in. His wife was attractive and intelligent if you gave her a chance, and it warmed something hopeless in Michael to see her fawned over by listing men hanging on her anecdotes. When she was angry, when she was depressed, it gave Michael's life a kind of certainty. But when she was happy, grasping the reins of her life, it confused him.

He'd downed his first two drinks fast, just to swallow the road dust, and they were slithering up on him now, warm numbness across the top of his skull. The house stood on what in these parts passed for a rise, and thousands of acres drew away from it to where land and sky smacked in silence. A hard line of clouds had taken station there, hitching the thermal up from Patagonia.

The pampas.

No one was sure how deep the topsoil was. Eight feet or eighteen, black richness that sprung wheat like weeds and grass a hundred million cattle couldn't finish. So effortless the wealth of this place that its ability to absorb the abuses of its owners was legendary: *"Dios arregla de noche la macana que los argentinos hacen de día."* God puts right at night the mess Argentines make by day. So effortless, this wealth, it stunk with the stale tragedy of how a nation so endowed had added up to so little. For Argentina should have been great. But the easy land didn't require talent, and its people produced none, becoming instead a place obsessed with its dead and alive with the thrill of its own self-destruction.

Evita had seen her country as great, and for a shining instant the country believed it. But she was just an echo now across a nation sliding out of control, ruled by nonruling generals stalling and clucking and driving the whole show into the ground.

There were plenty of them here. Norris's polo teammates, bemedaled and snug behind their new authority. The queen was dead, the king stateless, and maybe if you did call her a thief, maybe if you ran her underpants up a flagpole to show her commonness, maybe if you ordered her memory disappeared, she would disappear.

Maybe if you moved her body.

They'd tried to show she was just a whore mimicking the rich she supposedly despised. They displayed her diamonds, proved she stole magnificently from the treasury. But they missed the point. She had started poor and so, in becoming wealthy, fulfilled the Cinderella dream so many fantasized about. And if she stole from the rich for herself, she also stole for the poor, and no one had ever done that before. No one had shaken down international corporations to build hospitals and dedicate schools. And if it was all vanity and greed, who cared? No one had ever spoken to the great unwashed as an equal, held them to their breast, cooed to them like lovers, whispered hatred for those they hated: the rich; the privileged; the whole pointless, pathetic history of their nation.

She was dead, and she lived on in the stares of servants. And all the generals' medals, all the posturing Michael knew only underlined a fear so deep none had the courage to destroy her. Because maybe her corpse really was protected by God, or the devil, or the stares of servants.

He was drunk.

Nothing can sneak up on you in the pampas, and *El Amo's* riding party was already a mute plume of dust at vision's edge. Valets prepared cool towels and *mate* for the returning adventurers, flushed with the ride, sun, and booze. A gaucho bringing up the rear carried in one hand half a dozen strung pheasants, the day's shotgun catch. Each horseman half dismounted, half spilled out of his saddle as the chef rang the bell announcing the meal.

The beef, sliced from the side of the mammoth rotating carcass, was sweet and so juicily raw Michael's mouth sang as his gut sagged. He'd held Karen's hand under the table at dinner, felt her brush his arm in suggestion, but he'd lost her now somewhere among the greasy laughter on the patio, the piles of bones going red in the retreating day.

He was cornered now, pinned against an adobe planter by his host, his office mate Lofton, and a nonspecific *Porteño* whose name he couldn't keep straight over the growing gin rush in his ears.

"Tell him the story, Mike." It was Lofton, living up to his reputation as the drunkest man in Argentina. The veins in his nose had taken on a life of their own and were rivaled only by the pulsating red in his eyes. "Come on, Mike, tell him." The conversation was in English, despite the two Argentines; Lofton in fifteen years here never bothering to pick up the language.

"Please, Mr. Suslov," his host, Senor Carenza, said, swaying. Carenza was spectacularly fat in gaucho *bombachas* and a cotton riding shirt. His face was easy and drunk and listing dangerously to one side. Lofton had heard the story a dozen times and had never shown any particular interest in it. But Lofton liked to be around people without having to deal with them, liked being at the center of a good story he didn't have to tell.

"Once, when I was a kid..." His tongue felt bloated and alien in his mouth, the words unwieldy blocks to scale. Michael knew the story by heart—how his father, stuck with him for the evening, had dressed Michael up as an adult dwarf so he could take him drinking in the local tavern. It was a funny story, but Michael knew if you looked closely enough it was a sad one too.

"Where did you grow up?" Carenza asked. *I grew up in La Boca*, Michael thought, *tasting the malevolence of your class.*

"Chicago."

Days died fast out here, twilight lasting just long enough to find the light switch. The gnats had risen and with them bats, blurry shapes dashing through the glow of strung party lamps. The drinks had stopped slithering and were now outright tackling his body. His face was numb, and it was getting hard to concentrate on what anyone was saying. So he stopped trying. The gaggle of husbands had grown tight enough around Karen he could barely glimpse her brunette head. It was always the same out here: endless drunken weekends on endless pampas, heat and booze and husbands flirting with his wife.

"So. Mike."

He slurred his head to look. "Barbara."

"You're drunk."

"Old news I'm afraid."

Barbara DeVries was a full inch taller than he. From his slouch it seemed ten. She had a frosty glass in one hand, surveying the party. "Saturday night in Argentina."

She was his age, with short, severe brown hair and a face so mannishly angular it could cut paper. Her British education left her talking Oxford, but she was Dutch, here as a secretary for the Dutch mission.

"Where's Short Eyes?" He was hammered and probably said it too loud. Barbara smiled.

"Oh, he's around. Probably on his knees in the stable boy's quarters by now."

Short Eyes was her boss, the Dutch mission's economic atta-ché. Notorious for his fixation with dark-haired boys, Barbara was his beard, someone over fourteen to have on his arm at social functions.

Barbara drank from her glass. A rivulet of melted frost rolled over the back of her hand.

"I've been checking the BA obits for a month now to see if you were killed in a car accident or something."

"What?" His face was stupid, and it annoyed her.

"It's a joke, Mike. You haven't called."

"Oh. Yeah. It's been, y'know, sorta crazy lately with—"

"It's a *joke*, Mike."

Last year, with work sinking to new lows and Karen's morale beginning its ruined turn, Barbara had asked him to lunch. She didn't eat meat—a weird, lonely practice in cow-crazy Argentina—and they ended up at probably South America's only beat café. There, surrounded by Latin hepcats, she had ignored him, taunted him, then taken him home.

She was thin, and it amazed him how breasts so large belonged to shoulders so narrow. When they got to her place nobody spoke, and before it was over he was already gone, reading the little paper notes around her phone as she gulped breaths in his ear. He thought how weird it was; how you spend most of your life thinking about sex, except during it, when your mind wanders.

It was a rotten time for him, before the resignation set in. He hated his work and he hated going home, so he concentrated on the empty peripheries of his days: the wiretaps, the late-night interviews, Barbara. They met all that summer in her small flat, lay sweaty on a mattress, listened to the squeak of a fan shoveling leaden air from one side of the room to the other. Just like Russians…

Sometimes he told her stories. But Barbara liked to talk, so they talked mostly of her: old lovers, home, life in the Dutch embassy. It was during a story about an argument between her boss and the ambassador that she stopped suddenly and drew away from him.

"You're working me, aren't you?"

They'd been making love that afternoon on her floor. She'd scooted against the wall.

"What?"

It was a kind of admiration worn on her clenched, half smile. "Sitting there listening about the ambassador and Short Eyes. You're working me."

Michael understood finally and collapsed on his back in frustration. "Aw, c'mon, Barb. You know I'm not."

Her face changed. The weak smile disappeared as she studied him. "No, you're not, I suppose." A sigh, then as she pushed a damp strand of hair from her eye, "When I first met you, I used to think you were a spy by accident. You were too open, too boyish to be a real spook. But I was wrong. All those silly stories you tell, the innocence, you know it makes people feel intimate with you. But it's all a lie, isn't it?"

"They're real stories, Barb."

"But they're nothing to do with the real you. They *feel* intimate, but they're just a screen. By the time people figure that out, they've spilled their life to you. The sickest part is that you don't even do it consciously. It's just who you are." She laughed then, hollow. "Dulles got a bargain when he hired you. The boyish cherub who's really a cunning, ambitious little fuck and doesn't even know it."

They didn't talk much after that, and somewhere along the line he just stopped coming. Since then Barbara was ironic when she saw him. Not because he had worked her, but because he had worked her without noticing it.

Her look fell from the party back to him. "So I was just a summer's distraction."

"Jesus Christ, Barb, do we have to talk about it now?"

"We *never* talked about it."

There was something dangerous about her today Michael didn't want to provoke. So he did what he always did. Smile. It provoked her.

"You're a chickenshit, Mike—is that the right word?"

"Close enough."

"You're not happy with your life. When are you going to wake up and do something about it?"

"You don't know me, Barbara."

"Sure I do. You really think this new fatherhood thing fools anyone? You're a rotten son of a bitch, Mikey. You think if you ignore something long enough it'll just go away. Well it's not going to. Not this time. Not unless you do something about it."

Old, ugly truths. Barbara shifted her gaze to something neutral. The edge of the planet maybe.

"Do you ever think about those nights?"

"Sure."

"Bullshit."

"I do. Honest." It sounded stupid and high-pitched to himself. Barbara smiled and shook her head.

"You never were a fun drunk…"

The temperature didn't drop much but the sky darkened and darkened till it seemed to glow with darkness. Stars raked powerfully over them, and the dusty breeze stilled and bedded for the night.

Fluted glass lanterns appeared as small cliques formed around wrought-iron tables. Most of the party had stumbled off to home or bed in the guesthouses, leaving remaining knots of laughter, toasts, and ghost stories tossed into the insect cry.

Michael was with Karen now, alone in their own warm circle. Her eyes caught the night and it hurt Michael to think that her eyes probably sparkled all the time, but he didn't notice like he once had. She touched his hand, let her hair fall into her face as she studied the fingers. And Michael felt the world sharpen for just a second. He leaned over, reached up under her cotton blouse, and touched their child.

They made love in the guest room. Careful. Mindful of the life pressed between them. And it was better, fuller for the care. Afterward they stood naked at the window and watched heat lightning flash somewhere over Montevideo. There had been lightning that first time in Michael's college dorm, a slashing storm that shook the walls with fury. They had stood at that window too, and below them blue stutters of light had lit up green, copper roofs. They'd counted softly together the space between each flash and its following thunder. "One, one thousand…two, one thousand…three, one thousand…" All night, a chant: "One, one thousand…two, one thousand…three, one thousand…" Till the storm passed with dawn.

From the guesthouse now they could see sputtering arcs low in the sky. But neither of them counted, for on the pampas no thunder followed the lightning. Like everything else in Argentina, it was different.

On the way home they blew a tire and limped into the pampa town. It was Sunday morning, everyone in church but a few suspicious dogs circling the only gas pump. Michael got out, walked to the storefront, and pressed his face to the dusty glass. A kitchen was on the other side, quiet, the beginnings of a noontime meal on the counter. As he pulled his face away he saw the kid on a stool in the corner, planted absolutely still in profile, his gaze—as best Michael could see—fixed on the blank wall across from him.

Michael rapped on the pane, and the kid's head pivoted, not startled, slowly toward him. He was maybe ten, good looking but for a brutal scar that ran ear to ear across his throat. His hair was lighter than most here, reddish.

"Tire. We need our tire fixed," Michael said in Spanish. Something seemed off about the kid, who only after a beat rose from his stool and opened the door.

He put the tire in a barrel of water, felt for the leak's bubbles. Karen had wandered down the dirt main street to the town's tiny plaza. Michael stayed with the car, watched the kid watching the tire. When he looked up, Michael saw what was off. The eyes. The kid had the eyes of a tight, ruined adult. Michael smiled. The kid looked back down at the tire.

Michael pushed off the car and walked across the street to a weedy lot between two low adobe buildings. A small pile of stones stood there.

A shrine.

You saw them out here, rocks stacked together into an altar, and atop the altar a cardboard box containing sometimes Evita's picture but this time a small, blonde-haired doll. On either side were heaped runny remains of a hundred candles. Fresh flowers carpeted the top.

They always seemed more pagan than Christian, these shrines, part of the obsessive spiritualism that was the glue of these empty places. A way to ward off Indian ghosts blowing over the land, to invoke the protection of Her.

She had come from a town like this, and in towns like this they would never forget Her. Always theirs to stroke and polish and call up against the frightening shapes that drifted through their lives.

A crow called. His eyes jerked into the great bowl above him and for an instant he felt his feet slip. It was just sky. Buckets of sky and a little land...

A stone had tumbled from the shrine. Michael bent down and replaced it. When he looked up, the kid was watching him.

# 8.

A memory:

His nose had filled with the smell of crushed June bugs. Sickly sweet, made sweeter still by the sweat of half a million people cheering shoulder to shoulder on the Avenida 9 de Julio—widest thoroughfare in the world and still they filled it for blocks, on stoops, atop cars, hanging from lampposts. It had been August 1951. Michael had been back in Argentina, now as a CIA officer, only two weeks and never had he seen crowds like this. In a moment it would be the first time he'd see Her.

They'd come down on a lark, Karen and he, and been swept into the center of the throng. They shouted to each other over the pounding *bombas*, the loose cannon blats of tubas, the echoing bursts of "*Perón! Perón!*" Around them the crowd jostled in a rage of tones: red ponchos from the northern mountain country; black bowlers from the Patagonian farmers; the loose, white cotton blouses of the urban working class. All bused in for free, the biggest street party ever, thrown by Papa Perón. Even the revered *Cabildo Abierto* of 1810, the open town meeting on this spot where the country had decided on separation from Spain, had drawn fewer people than this.

The day failed like the cue of a house manager, and spotlights brightened two five-story-tall posters of the president and his wife, Evita. They could feel the temperature in the crowd rise. A heavy tree branch, bowed with spectators, snapped like a rifle shot, spilling them into the sea of bobbing heads. Loudspeakers, a hundred of them mounted along the avenue, began to blare the CGT union stomper "We Are the Peronista Boys." The crowd picked up the tune, sang it robustly, and congratulated itself with whistles and howls. A piercing trumpet sounded, like a bullfight announcement, and Juan Perón, El Presidente, appeared on a mammoth stage decorated with the blue and white of the Argentine flag. The crowds erupted in "*Perón! Viva Perón!*"

Perón basked in the warmth of his audience. This was to be his greatest moment: nomination to the presidency for another term by acclamation. Raising his arms, he stood there alone on the dais. It wasn't long before the cry began to rise, "*Where is Evita?*" Perón feigned surprise and announced that, of his wife's many virtues, modesty was her greatest. However, she would be sent for.

Michael and Karen had rolled their eyes. Latin theatrics. The whole thing was an orchestrated CGT circus: people bused in, given time off and beer, just to cheer the president's ego for renomination to a job no one else was allowed to contest anyway. What a peacock. Sending for his wife with such surprise. Michael looked at the faces around him. They might as well have been at a soccer match.

Then, as Michael began to gloat at his insight, to congratulate the crowd for being in on the joke, She appeared.

And everything changed.

A weird noise grew around them. It started as a gasp but fed on the surprise of its own sound, building into a guttural howl of excitement that rocked the avenue and blew into the night. Michael felt a chill shoot down his back and with it the realization that every flatfoot status report he'd read before coming down from Washington was wrong. This was no brain-dead peasantry led from the nose by beer and free bus tickets. That was an oligarch fantasy. There was juice in these people's eyes, and for Her, he saw clearly now, there was *devotion*.

She stood at the microphone, five foot five but looking taller in heels and bearing, dark-brown eyes flashing. Her honey-colored hair piled fiercely atop her head as it always was in public. In private it was said she could sit on it. Her features were sharp and so was her voice as she began to speak: "Friends, *descamisados*, I stand before you, a humble, lowly servant." There was a quarter-million worth of jewelry around that humble neck. She spoke in a kind of edgy trill. As if the searing commitment to Perón could rupture the body that held it. She played her part well, applauded the people's nomination of her husband, made veiled threats against the entrenched oligarch, pledged again, hand over breast, to lay her life down a thousand times for Perón, Peronism, and Argentina.

Perón had yet to announce his vice-presidential running mate, and the crowd seized the moment, chanting "*Con Evita!*" and "*Evita con Perón!*" Evita beamed and drifted from the prepared speech for her finishing remarks: "I have always said I would rather be Evita than the wife of the president if this Evita could do anything for the pain of my country, and so now I say I would rather be Evita."

A beat rolled through the street. Had she accepted their call for the vice presidency? Murmurs. Evita off the dais now. Perón at the microphone. No, she hadn't. Voices now rising. Shouting. Interrupting Papa Perón. "*Evita! Evita!*"

And all at once the evening went off the script.

The crowd had taken on its own dynamic and knew it, making it impossible for Perón to continue with his acceptance speech, and the annoyance was clear now on his face. Espejo, the CGT's chairman, tried to save the moment and, taking the microphone, asked Evita to accept.

And even down there on the street you could see it: a look between husband and wife. Perón had not nominated his wife for the vice presidency because it could simply never be. The army hated him but nothing like they hated his steamrolling wife. Evita as second-in-command they would never allow. But there was something in her eyes. The way you could see Perón's uncertainty reflected in them. She turned to the microphone, to the chants, not with defiance but inevitability.

"My beloved *descamisados*..." Her voice quavered, jacked on emotion. "I ask the comrades of the CGT, the women, children, and the workers gathered here, by the love which unites us, that for so important a decision in the life of this poor woman, you give me at least four days for consideration."

The crowd refused, threatened strikes. Evita pleaded for a day, an evening, to decide.

"No! No! *Now!*"

The dais became full of arguing people—Espejo, Perón, other CGT functionaries—shouting at one another with confusion. And standing apart from them, in her own pool of light, the focus of the crowd's love: Evita. In the back rooms they'd always known she was the real spirit of the movement. Now it was in the open for all to see, and her husband and his lackeys were reeling from the heat.

The crowd bellowed that it would not leave until she accepted. Newspapers were rolled and lit into torches, their sparks burning snowflakes on the avenue. Perón looked hopelessly adrift, mute and astonished by the power of his wife's bond with her *descamisados*. Without any discussion between them, without even looking at him, she stepped up to the microphone.

"Comrades, I will do what the people say."

They would have given their lives for her at that moment, would have marched into the fire of any enemy. They held her with their cheers, and Evita, lit by a thousand torches, with June bugs rocketing through spotlights, stood before them, threw back her head...

And laughed.

It couldn't be of course. Perón knew the military would destroy itself destroying him before they'd allow it. So, nine days later, in a voice hoarse and broken, Evita announced over the radio her renouncement of the nomination. She wouldn't have served anyway. Soon after that night—her greatest night—Evita began to die.

**August 23, 1956**

# 9.

July came, drifted. Russians threatened Hungary, and the backward winter finally announced itself in August. Days were short, their unborn child grew, the embassy radiators began ticking on, squeaky with disuse.

After most of a morning at his cover job in the commercial attaché office, half-listening to corporate flacks looking for import licenses, Michael made his way upstairs to the station and tried to catch up on field reports. The SPR survey he'd finally completed turned up a couple of possibilities, only one of which had bitten after a planned accidental meeting. Yuri Kraganov, forty-four, married, bored, a cultural liaison with the Sovs, and 100 percent spook. They'd had a few meals, Yuri and Michael, attended an opera at the Teatro Colon one night—wives along—and spent an afternoon at El Tigre sailing a borrowed boat. Some laughs, no dark-alley talk. The SB desk was encouraging, but Michael was starting to wonder who was working whom.

A paper airplane thumped his scalp.

Michael opened it: *Hector the Gimp buzzed. Phone him pronto—your loyal servant, Wintergreen.*

The embassy guard was at his station, feet up, nose down in a *National Geographic*. "Run out of comics?" Michael asked, approaching.

"Improving my mind."

"I didn't know you subscribed."

"Stole it from Miller. When they start putting naked *white* girls in here, then I'll subscribe."

"Hector called the security desk?"

"Well, he didn't use his real name, but I recognized the voice."

"How would you know his voice?"

"I know everything around here, Spook."

"When did he call?"

"I don't know. Hour or so."

"Why didn't you tell me?"

"Jeez, you were upstairs or somethin'."

"Why didn't you come *find* me?"

"Oh, I'm sorry, did I accidentally leave my apartment this morning with *secretary* stamped on my forehead?"

As Michael sighed and started back, Wintergreen's voice lowered, his eyes still fixed on topless Nubians. "If I'd called downstairs to the commercial attaché office, I would've had to use the intercom." Wintergreen's gaze lifted briefly in the direction of the station secretarial support staff and, implicitly, Norris.

Michael got it. "Okay, I owe you."

"Yeah, yeah, you and everybody else."

Hector had never called Michael at work before, and the feeling was strange.

It was one o'clock, Buenos Aires slow out the window. The streets would be lousy now with *olor Porteño*, the smell of grilling steaks. Every citizen, from Recoleta aristocrats to sewer workers crouched over sidewalk barbecues, would devour their two-pound *bife* and afterward stumble, bloated, for a piece of shade and a siesta till four o'clock. Michael looked at his watch. If he called Casa Rosada now there'd be no one there to pick up. He'd go out, get some lunch himself, and try Hector later in the afternoon.

Hector was waiting for him on the sidewalk.

At the streetcar stop. Quiet against the wall, just a voice first at his back.

"Michael."

Hector liked the privacy of being public and did most of his dry work in cafés and nightclubs. But today he wanted to go for a ride in Michael's car. To Palermo Park. A quiet spot, near the pond.

"What's on your mind?" Michael asked. It was a clear day, broken patches of light falling through twitchy leaves. Hector tried a smile, gave up on it.

"Shall we have a walk?"

It was cool here. Michael rolled down his shirtsleeves. Hector set off along the pond's edge, favoring his cane. A horse came down the bridle path, passed, and they were alone.

"I wanted you to know first, Michael. This morning General Olivar died."

Not a junta member but a boy with brains on the fast track up. He was young, maybe forty.

"How?"

"Olivar was many things, but discreet was not among them. A jealous husband found the general with his wife and…well…"

That helpless Latin gesture. *Y'know, men…*

"Shot him?" Michael asked.

"Cut his throat."

"Jesus."

Argentines loved cutting throats. The Lore of the Gaucho.

"You won't read about this. I doubt even Norris knows."

Michael studied Hector. More fissures in the mask. "That isn't why you called. It's about Her, isn't it?"

Hector smiled. "The smartest CIA man in Argentina."

"The *only* CIA man in Argentina."

Hector probed the dirt with his cane. "You already know how every time we moved the Senora, flowers followed. So I moved her again and told only ten. The flowers returned. So again I moved her and told only three."

"Olivar was one."

"Yes."

"And the flowers?"

"Like a shadow." Beat. "I once said I trusted you, Michael."

"I remember."

Hector bent down, picked up a twig and folded it over. It was too green to snap. "Eva Perón must leave Argentina."

"I don't get it."

"It has become clear that as long as Evita remains on Argentine soil, she will continue to be found by those fanatically devoted to her. And if eventually found by its more violent elements—"

"Peronist terrorists fighting for the return of her husband Juan Perón from Spanish exile."

"Disorganized, fractional. But if stupid old women bearing flowers can find her, sooner or later one of them will too. She cannot be allowed, even in death, to become their symbol."

"Put a guard on her. Put a hundred on."

Hector smiled. "You think like an American, Michael. To Americans, the power of myth rests in ideas and people. Here the power of myth rests in objects. They need not actually possess her body to stand before it and invoke her name as their name. It is not her works that electrify the crowds but *Her.* Reveal where she lies with such large-scale protection and there would be thousands of *campesinos* at the gate in an hour, and our enemies would have succeeded the same as if they had run her up a flagpole. She would become their flag, something to rally opposition around the way ideas never can in this nation."

"Burn her, then. Dump her in the river."

Hector took his arm as they strolled. "That's an American solution, Michael. You see history as linear. Cause and effect. The evolution of events. But Argentina is a land where nothing happens. History here is an endless cycle, and one day the Senora will become the friend of the state, *its* flag. So we must keep her safe, away from politics."

"On deposit."

"In Argentina everyone is on deposit, Michael. Even the dead. You look cold."

"I should have brought a coat."

"We'll go back to the car."

They sat there. Watched the horse pass again through the windshield.

"Evita Perón is a secret Casa Rosada cannot seem to keep and so will never be safe on Argentine soil. For the same reason, if she is removed through Argentine hands, she will never be safe abroad either."

"Why are you telling me this?" Michael hated the way it sounded. Worried.

"I would like you to use the resources of your embassy to move her out of Argentina."

"You want *me* to get her out of the country?"

"You and the engines of the US State Department. It is imperative no Argentines be involved."

"You're insane."

"Perhaps. But I have something to trade. Files. Years of secret material gathered on governments all over South America."

"If I asked Norris it would take weeks to get an answer, and even then it would probably be no, however much WH Division might want those files."

"Then don't ask."

"You expect me to do this *alone*?"

"The protection of the Senora cannot wait."

"This is it, right? The big withdrawal from the favor bank?"

"I'm asking you as a friend. But also as someone who knows you. Knows what you want. You'll be thirty years old next year, Michael. With a new child and a life you hate here. You want out of Buenos Aires. You *need* to get out of Buenos Aires. Do this quietly and you'll finally have that ticket. There are so few chances in life to grab the future, Michael. This is one."

Michael could hear the dash clock counting.

"Let me think about it."

It was stupid, it was dangerous—and it was probably doable if he put his mind to it.

Michael sat in the living room of their house, listened to the first rain in a month, and stared out at wet darkness beyond the patio door. Karen was on the sofa, writing a letter to her mother.

If he did it and Norris found out, he'd be canned. Hector's intel sharing had given him some credits with the SB branch, but to be collared shipping boxed first ladies without authority—well, that was a little beyond the pale, even with Hector's promised files. He'd grown to hate this job, but he wasn't ready to give up on it yet; there'd be retirements, other postings. It could get better. He was a foreign relations college major in an antiforeign recession economy back home. What the hell else would he do?

Karen looked up from her letter and saw the faraway look.

"What are you thinking?"

The snap answer was already halfway up his throat. This time he choked it down.

"Hector wants me to…to deliver something for him through our channels, without telling Bud. It's a pink slip if I get caught, but it's also probably our way out of here if I don't."

"Are you going to do it?"

Michael stood suddenly, kissed his wife, and softly told her he loved her. She took his hand and held it to her belly.

"We're going to be okay, Michael."

That night was Michael's turn on Ara watch. He tucked his wife in bed, turned off the lights, and reluctantly drove down to the apartment building on Avenida Cabello. Dr. Ara was so connected in the diplomatic community, had found himself at the center of so many goings-on, that WH refused to believe that he wasn't somehow on someone's spook payroll. Norris just laughed at their naïveté about how things worked down here. As usual, he wouldn't make Lofton or his other buddies pull shifts, so it fell on Michael to do one all-nighter a month in the safe house across the street and report the same thing to Washington in the morning: nothing.

Michael couldn't care less if Wintergreen or Yuri Kraganov himself knew about *this* safe house. It was only for Ara, and Ara was a waste of time. Michael had wondered why Norris didn't take a stronger stand on the obvious waste of station resources but had come to suspect, by the odd empty bottle of wine left behind, that his station chief was doing some private entertaining up here. Probably Lofton and Miller too. Hell, maybe even Esther. Maybe the whole fucking embassy Marine Corps detachment.

Like with the Russian OP, the apartment was a small studio with one window, a mattress, and a single armchair aimed out to Ara's apartment across the street. The lights were off, and Michael kept his off too, spending the first two hours staring at his reflection or the odd pedestrian haunting the avenue. He had a thermos of coffee, Roquefort pizza picked up on the way, some station homework, and his thoughts.

*What I am doing here? Why doesn't the station at least buy a comfortable chair? Because the only thing in here anybody else uses is the bed. My wife is in bed. So is my unborn child. My mother and sister are in graves, one kind or another, not far away. And I'm here, waiting on the Spanish dwarf.*

With a penlight clipped to his shirt pocket, he browsed the station files he'd brought to keep himself awake. Most of them had the opposite effect: endless stakeout reports from his contract agents in the Buenos Aires police, wiretap transcripts, expense accounts.

One of the folders Michael didn't recognize. Apparently filed among his by mistake, it was a source interview, dated February 1953. The source's code name was WOLLSY, the transcript a dialogue between him and his interviewer:

*INTERVIEWER: She never told you?*
*WOLLSY: No.*
*INTERVIEWER: Have the others looked?*
*WOLLSY: What do you think?*
*INTERVIEWER: Have you?*
*WOLLSY: I wouldn't know where to begin.*
*INTERVIEWER: Well, if not you, who?*
*WOLLSY: You presume too much.*

The transcript continued in that vein—elliptical questions and vague answers—for two pages. One part caught Michael's attention:

*INTERVIEWER: That's all she said?*
*WOLLSY: At the end, yes.*
*INTERVIEWER: That one word.*
*WOLLSY: She was at God's gate.*
*INTERVIEWER: Only that one word.*
*WOLLSY: Yes.*

During his years in Argentina, Michael knew of only one person that used the old-fashioned Spanish expression "God's gate"—Juan Duarte, Evita's brother. Michael knew Duarte had had contacts with the embassy before Michael's time and during his sister's heyday. A gambling playboy forever in debt, he'd have sold them his grandfather's watch if they'd wanted it. He had little else of interest, though; most of the Perón administration rightfully kept him at arm's length. Michael assumed the station had lost interest in him years ago, but this transcript was dated just a few months before his suicide. Evita had been dead since 1952, and the world had turned several times since by the time of this interview in '53. Who would have still cared about Juan Duarte?

Michael flipped back through the file, looking for the word Juan Duarte was referring to. It wasn't there. On the bottom of the last page was an endorsement of the case officer doing the interview. His name was Ray Tynnes, the working pseudonym for Ed Lofton.

Michael looked up. A taxi was dropping off Ara and a woman he didn't recognize. A moment later Ara could be seen in his living room, lighting a few candles and settling the woman on a couch. Michael knew next would come the dusty bottle of wine, the one Ara specifically told his maid *not* to wipe off. He was not disappointed. It was followed, as always, by Stravinsky on the hi-fi, Italian *cantuccis* from the kitchen...

And the hatbox.

The one with the embalmed peasant's head. And it must work with the ladies, because he does it every time.

Ara opens the hatbox and Michael's blood freezes because it's not the peasant's head inside.

It's Evita's.

Only it can't be, because Hector has her. Yet it's an exact copy, grafted onto someone else's skull. It's too real. It's *Her*.

And as Ara lets the woman hold it, as the candles catch Evita's features and bathe them in amber, Michael feels the room around him shift and speak to him of a future, and that future is only chaos and destruction.

**September 10, 1956**

# 10.

It was a pretty night and Karen and Michael strolled Recoleta Plaza, hand in hand, past minstrels and the colonial church lit up with floodlights. It was breezy and the coral trees squeaked with birds. They walked along the old cemetery wall, resting place of presidents and magnates. *It's easier to get into heaven than Recoleta Cemetery*, the saying went. The city's fanciest restaurants lay in a row across the grass. Michael and Karen lingered on a park bench, watched lovers and children pass, and waited for the restaurants to open, which in Buenos Aires never happened before ten.

Recoleta Plaza. A hundred years ago they dumped the heads of slaughtered cattle here. Then came the cholera scare in the southern barrios, and the money fled north to safety among the rot of their fortunes. Michael thought of the millions of bones beneath his feet, couldn't help thinking of his sister Maria…

"It's a beautiful night," Karen said.

"Yes."

"There are times when I almost like this city."

"Almost."

She smiled, rested her head on his shoulder, and held up their intertwined hands for inspection. And for a moment it was like it once was. Easy and right, and he prayed for it not to end.

They sat there past opening time, just being with each other, and when they rose Michael picked a restaurant off the row at random, for they were all excellent. Karen and he took a quiet table in the back and only after ordering a glass of wine noticed that the other corner was filled with former FBI South: Norris,

Miller, Lofton, a handful of generals, and the usual assortment of strained wives.

Michael and Karen, slumped with disappointment, smiled politely. Tried to leave it at that. The flatfoot contingent was already happily adrift on Chilean red. Lofton started waving for the Suslovs to come over. Michael waved back, tried to laugh it off, but they were all gesturing now, even the generals.

"It's not that big a deal," Karen said.

"We'll just say hi."

They walked over. The generals stood up for Karen. Norris scrounged for chairs. "C'mon, have a seat. Pedro here was just telling us about the parties during his academy days."

"Well, not *too* much," Pedro guffawed.

Brittle smiles from brittle wives, drunk husbands insisting on pawing Michael's child.

"We've got a table over there. We just thought we'd have a quiet—"

"Don't be crazy, Mike, c'mon, sit down. Karen, don't let your husband be a drip *every* night."

"Really, we…"

Then a look behind Norris's grin: *Don't fucking embarrass me here.*

"We'll take a rain check, okay?"

A catch in Norris's voice. "Sure, Mike. Stop by for dessert." Another death look, and back to Pedro's hilarious story. Suslovs dismissed.

The meal was okay, but the night was on the wrong foot. They tried to enjoy it, stuck their forks in each other's meals, looked out at the plaza, breezy and lit up prettily with strung lights.

The flatfoot table was in full swing. Lofton slumped in his chair, head rolling against the wall, Norris on his feet, telling in a voice just under a shout about a club girl in Tijuana and the skill she showed with just a groin and Ping-Pong ball. Pedro the general up now, to better the story—a girl in Lima—his English slipping under several vodkas.

"Let's get out of here."

She touched his hand. "It's okay, Michael."

"We'll do better down the street."

"Promise?"

"On a stack of flatfoots."

She laughed, and it cooled Michael off. He waved the waiter over, asked for the check. The waiter shrugged in the direction of the other table. "The gentlemen there took care of it." A curdled wave from Norris.

He could just walk out—he wanted to—but then all of BA would be hot with the buzz by morning.

They walked over. "Thanks, Bud."

"*Ajo* good?"

"Yeah, Bud. Great."

"Karen? Yours?"

"Really good, Bud."

Norris was hammered, maybe the most hammered Michael had ever seen him. Something dangerous smoldered in his eyes.

"You've met Generals Hoyos and Perez." Michael shook their hands. The table fell into an awkward pause.

"Well, we'll see ya, Bud, huh? Thanks again." Michael turned for the door, waiting for it.

"Say hi to Hector, Mike." Aimed between his shoulders. A look from Karen: *Let it go.*

"Doesn't stink, does it, Mike? Your shit?" Michael turned to the table. Latin faces trying to smile neutrally and just looking imbecilic.

"You got something to say, Bud?"

Lofton and Miller looked nervous, eyes alive between him and Norris, the station chief clearly not caring now: "I mean, your shit stinks to *me,* but goddamn they lap it up with breakfast on E Street, huh?"

"Big talk from Hoover's gin bottle. You need that with Flavia?"

"Fuck you, Suslov."

Miller was all over Norris now. "Why don't you just shut the fuck up, Bud, huh?"

"OSS's own little pussy spy. Casa Rosada's butt buddy. Everybody loves Mikey, don't they?"

Michael felt the air ready to burn. Norris hissed at him, "Say something, you little shit."

It could happen. He could smear the turkey-neck's face against the wall and it'd feel good. Somehow he held his voice steady instead.

"Y'know, Bud, after all these years, I think you were right after all. We don't work for the same company."

*Fuck them.*
*Fuck it all.*

He'd do it.

# 11.

How?

Regular, legit postal service or straight air courier was out of the question. Somebody, somewhere, was going to want to peek inside a six-foot box. For sensitive transfers, the station used a trusted in-house courier company—Hapag-Lloyd—which would crate, seal, and label the item in question as a US diplomatic shipment, which made it immune to customs or foreign government inspection. This was the obvious choice but for a rather significant problem: getting something into this pipeline required a notification filed with WH Support under a station chief's signature.

Bud Norris.

Michael had some juice with the SB Branch, but not over-Norris's-head juice. How then?

Billy Patterson.

His spook camp playmate and EYES-ONLY tormentor. Billy worked on the comm desk that was the link between Norris and the WH staff offices in Barton Hall. He was flaky, unpredictable...

And maybe just weird enough to do it.

An ocean of white noise, drifting clicks, a faraway ring.

"Yes?"

"Peter North." Billy Patterson's working pseudonym.

"Who's calling?"

"Frank Sniff."

"One moment."

Adrift in hiss. Finally, "Well, if it isn't that cheap half-breed who never calls, never writes…"

"That's because I don't *like* you."

A kissing smack from the DC end. Patterson: "So what do I owe the pleasure of…Where the hell are you, anyway? Sounds like a goddamn whorehouse."

"I'm on a pay phone."

"Norris getting cheap in his senility?"

"I want *you* to get on one."

"Oooh…What's it called again?…Damn, I used to know…"

"Peter—"

"Wait, it's on the tip of my tongue—oh yeah, *TRADE-CRAFT*."

"Just do it, huh?"

"Okay, okay. Give me the number…"

Michael hung up and waited by the phone as busboys bashed back and forth into the kitchen. He wished he'd gone further out of town, convinced someone from the station was going to walk in, as five, then ten minutes, clicked by.

Ring.

"CIA calling Senor Misterioso." Patterson.

"Where are you?"

"Ptomaine Tavern."

"Pizza gotten any better?"

"Two hundred stomach pumps can't be wrong." Michael could hear Billy shift the phone from one hand to the other. "I assume this isn't a social ring, since we aren't social."

"I need a favor."

"Animal, vegetable, or mineral?"

Michael reflexively glanced over his shoulder. "I want to ship something secure courier under diplomatic protection."

"Wrong department."

"I want to do it without Norris's signature."

"Cute. Hang on a sec"—quarters dropping—"How big is this item in question?"

"Six feet."

"What is it?"

"It's just six feet, okay?"

There was a hanging moment on the line as Patterson's voice changed. "Haven't gone Sov on me, Frankie, have you?"

"What? Shit, no. Just something I don't want the station to have a piece of."

"What do you want from *moi*?"

"I can't send it without a station chief cable through WH."

"'Tis true."

"I want you to fake an incoming cable from Norris authorizing."

Silence.

"You in?"

More silence.

"You miserable little poison dwarf. Four years of 'Eyes-Only' bullshit. Don't you play button-down now."

Chuckles from the cheerful sociopath. "Okay. What the hell. I kinda like tweaking flatfoots—hang on." More quarters. "You're costing me a fucking fortune, Sniff."

"Then you'll do it?"

"Whoa. Down boy. Not that simple. Big brother has a lotta machines up here, and one of them counts incoming cables. I fake one that wasn't sent, it's gonna pop up orphan. Can't you just send a phony yourself?"

"I don't know Norris's sign-on, and let's just say our cable clerk is on the wrong side of this discussion."

"Jeez. Paranoia in Patagonia. Okay, here's what you do. Give her some cable traffic over your file name—only mangle it—use the wrong interfaces or something, so it transmits garbage. Then tell me when it's coming, I'll catch it, chuck it, and replace it with your authorization. That'll keep the incoming count straight. *Comprende?*"

"Got it."

Again Patterson's voice shifting: "You okay?"

"Yeah. Honest. Like I said. Just a favor. A gag on these guys."

"Don't do anything I would."

"I'm not that crazy."

"Ha—oh, what are you going to label this mystery package you're shipping?"

"I don't know. Something outlandishly boring."

"Boring's bad, son. Red flag. Tell ya what works. Label it 'Decomposed Human Remains,' toss in a couple a fish heads to give it a little stink, no State Department goon's gonna want to mess with that shit. Promise. You there? I know it sounds goof but trust the Pete on this: 'Decomposed Human Remains.' That's the ticket."

Michael was still laughing at the irony when he hung up.

◎ ◎ ◎

He told Hector he'd do it. The deputy head of Argentine military intelligence finished his sip of *mate*, pushed the straw aside, and took in the junior CIA officer's face. "Thank you, Michael."

There was still a complication: even if Billy Patterson faked an authorizing "approval" cable from Norris, any courier pickup would be logged at the main embassy security desk—courier in, courier out. The only realistic way to do this anonymously would be to piggyback Evita onto a courier shipment that was already scheduled and hope nobody looked too closely. The problem with *this* was the reality that Buenos Aires station wasn't exactly the Grand Central Station of spydom these days; legit station courier requests were relatively few and far between. There was, however, one scheduled for a week from Tuesday that might work.

Panama City station handled all of Branch 5's Technical Support Division needs: communication hardware, secret writing kits, disguises, bugging equipment, etc. A year ago WH Division decided to experiment with basing an area TSD officer at Buenos Aires station. An insanely eager-beaver fresh from training, the kid they sent was all over everything, trying to turn the simplest op into a TSD issue and generally driving Norris insane. He ordered crate after crate of audio, photo, and other technical equipment, including, bizarrely, five hundred pounds of car keys—one for every vehicle made anywhere in the last twenty years. The station had been quickly running out of space to store all this crap—and Norris close to strangling the kid—when the young TSD officer did the favor himself by breaking his hip in a boat accident at Los Olivos. So the TSD went home to Panama City but all the boxes stayed, as Norris sent out cable after cable asking, *begging*, if someone, *anyone*, wanted this stuff.

This month he finally got as nibble: five crates of photographic equipment to be shipped via Genoa to the CIA Milan substation in Italy aboard the SS *Conte Biancamano*. So if Hector wanted Evita out by secure diplomatic courier before Christmas, it would have to be to Milan and it would have to be a week from Tuesday—nine days away.

Michael had already decided he would squeeze Norris for a few emergency personal days, meet the casket in Milan, sign for it, and pass it off to Hector. End of story.

Except why he was doing it.

"You're going to do it, aren't you?"

He was staring at the ceiling in bed, Karen beside him. She was right, and it was coming off him like radium.

"It'll get us out of here."

"Is that really why?"

"I don't know."

"You should know why, Michael."

They fell asleep, and he dreamed hard. Someone in the house, coming for him, stuffing a rolled newspaper down his throat, splitting his larynx…

He shot awake gulping for his life. The bed was soaked, and in the dark it felt like blood. He rolled over—Karen not there—and it panicked him. He coughed her name blind with fear. "Karen!"

She was in the doorway with a glass of water, and he was back in his skin in his home in his bed. "Michael? What? What is it?"

He coughed, unclenched his muscles. "Sorry. I…a dream. Sorry…"

She always got a drink of water at night from the kitchen, and never had he dreamt like that. Acid death in his mouth.

"This doesn't feel good, Michael."

"I know."

"But you're going through with it."

"Yes…I think so, yes."

**September 13, 1956**

# 12.

First stop a pay phone. Nine thirty a.m. Washington time. Other end: "Yeah?"

"This the poison dwarf?"

"Speak, you Latin fuck."

"Cable coming through in twenty under my name."

"Here we go."

Up to the fourth floor of the First Boston Bank building, a.k.a. Embassy of the United States of America.

"Morning, Mike." Lofton—Michael's only hello on the floor. A wave from Wintergreen, something like a nod from Miller. Michael sat at his desk, tried to look his usual bored self as he slipped a colored pencil from his coat and wrote a cable.

Knock on Norris's door. "Come in." Today was the third morning since their restaurant confrontation and their first words.

"Got a cable."

"For?"

"OTS."

If Norris looked closely he'd notice the cable was unnecessary bureaucratic double-talk. Without looking closely at all he'd notice it was written not in blue ink but blue pencil. He didn't. His eyes never left Michael's as he initialed the sheet and handed it back.

Ducking into the toilet, Michael erased the blue pencil code interface numbers, wrote in expired ones, and handed it to the cable secretary, Esther. If *she* didn't look too closely and catch the expired numbers, the transmission would lock out of phase en route and dump on Patterson's end as a bowl of ink gumbo.

If Norris's eyes had never left Michael's, Esther's never even found his end of the room. Hunched chain-smoking over the encoding machine, an arm reaching out behind was her greeting. "Cable?"

"Yeah." He dropped it in her palm and walked out.

"Message received." Patterson on the pay phone.

"A mess?"

"You could finger-paint with the stuff."

"Thanks, man."

"You're committed now, wonder boy."

Next night. Tuesday. Hapag-Lloyd courier pickup set for a week later. Hector weird on the phone—a call to Michael's house, his voice broken glass.

"I have to see you, Michael."

No footsie this time. "Where?"

An address in Belgrano—not far from Michael's—dead this hour, the well-heeled in well-tucked beds. The house was faux French colonial, iron balconies and painted granite. It sat at the end of a cul-de-sac. Michael parked at the lane's mouth.

The gate was open and the front door ajar. Michael knocked, and Hector himself answered. He stood there strangely a moment, as if Michael had called on him unexpectedly, then blinked hard, and with difficulty opened the door wide. "Please. Come in." As Michael did he saw the door had been forced half off its hinges.

The furnishings were mismatched and unkempt. If there were servants—and a house this size had to employ servants—they'd taken the month off.

"Who lives here?"

"Come. Please."

Hector grasped his arm and led him across the hall to a sitting room darkly paneled and overstuffed. A pile of empty gin bottles, crusted dinner plates, and rancid *mate* gourds littered the floor. At its center reclined a middle-aged man who had neither shaved nor washed, nor done much recently but drink. His eyes were filmy, ruptured pools.

"Well." Phlegmatic and authoritarian. The man had a cocked Luger in his lap. It was then Michael noticed six or seven bullet holes around the door frame.

"Michael, this is Colonel Moori Koenig." Head of military intelligence, Hector's latest on-paper boss.

Michael knew Koenig, had met him a few times since the coup, but hadn't recognized him. The stubble. The rice dried on his chin. The whole four a.m. craziness of this.

Koenig sat straight up and squinted down Michael with eyes adrift in private hysteria. "Do you have proper papers?"

"Michael is a friend of ours, Moori."

Koenig grasped his Luger. "I've watched Her well, Hector. Never have I left my post."

"I know, Moori." Michael couldn't take his eyes off the gun. Hector led Michael out into the hall.

"A good man, Moori."

"He's out of his fucking mind."

"Moori is the third person who knew." One dead. One insane. The third watching Michael now out of his good eye.

"You gotta think about expanding your circle of friends, Hector."

"And so here you are."

"Where is she?"

Hector withdrew a key and opened the hall closet on their right. It was larger than Michael expected, a walk-in. Instead of clothes, the glow from the hall revealed a long pine box. "Moori, Olivar, and I moved her here eighteen days ago. Moori was to stay with her until transport could be arranged. The servants were dismissed, food brought in. During that time…something happened to him."

"He went quietly nuts."

"Not so quietly. After a week he began calling me, Olivar, and finally this evening, the president himself, to say he was on the job. There had been screams but tonight there were shots. When I came the door was barred…" The box had dings, souvenirs of its restlessness. "It must be moved, Michael."

"The courier pickup is next Tuesday." A week away.

"It cannot wait. Not here."

*Creak.*

Koenig appearing like a ghost, Luger out. Shaking. "She's *mine.*"

"Shit!"

Hector calm. "Moori, she is all of ours. The nation's."

"Goddamn it, put that fucking thing away." Nobody had ever stuck a gun in Michael's face. The barrel was short and smooth, its mouth itchy darkness.

"*Moori! Please!*" Hector ordered. Moori let his arm drop without ceremony. Points of light gathered around Michael's vision.

"Fuck…"

"Do you dream of Her?" Koenig muttered. Michael felt caged in the closet. His eyes shot to the front door. The colonel carried on, lost in himself: "I do. Even when I'm awake, She talks to me." Koenig's eyes moistened. "It's hard sometimes…"

And he just turned and walked back into the sitting room.

"Somebody picks up another gun, this whole thing's history, understand?"

"It won't happen again, Michael."

"You don't know how I'm hanging my ass out on this."

"I do, Michael. And I appreciate it."

"Just no more guns, okay?" Michael steadied himself. He didn't like Hector seeing him rattled. "What the hell happened to him?"

"Moori was always a man who believed in his nightmares. Leaving him alone here…possibly a mistake." The palms-out Latin shrug: *What's a mother to do?*

"So where do we move her?"

Olivar dead, Koenig checked out, Hector's apartment in the very center of Casa Rosada.

"I have no one left I trust, no place in Argentina that is safe."

"She's gotta sit somewhere for the next week."

"She would be safe on American soil."

Michael not catching the drift at first, then: "The embassy?"

"Yes."

"You're crazy."

"Surely there is a place where—"

"Forget it. A corpse on the fourth floor? What do you suppose I camouflage it as? Norris's coffee table? What the hell do you expect from me?"

Hector lowered his eyes, stroked the dog head of his cane with a hand suddenly old. "A great deal, I'm afraid."

"I'm sorry."

Michael walked out the battered front door, stood on the porch for air. A seagull landed on the stone walk, anxious and depressed at how it could have so misplaced the Atlantic. The garden beside it had run wild, and in the halo of the street lamp you could see flowers.

Cut flowers.

Stacked everywhere along the walk. On the steps. Under Michael's feet. Something chilled in his chest. He hadn't seen them coming in, and that was only an hour ago.

"Unsettling, isn't it?" Hector behind him on the porch now.

"Incredible."

No sound. No scurry of feet. Silence. Hector faced him now.

"You were nothing when you came here, Michael. Frozen out by your own colleagues, ignored by my government, written off by your Washington superiors. Sent as a sheep to wolves to bloody the water. You were smart, Michael, but you were not *that* smart. That unfortunate incident with the Polish ambassador was enough alone to crush you and send you home a failure, your first field rotation a disaster. What would it have been then? Division accounting? Shuffling papers on other people's operational successes? By sharing our information I not only saved your position here, I guaranteed your superiors' forgiveness. You survived, Michael. And Buenos Aires isn't forever. With the files I can give you, you'll be able to name your next assignment. Moscow, London, far away from the Norrises and Millers. The world's yours, Michael. All because of me. So yes, I am asking a great deal of you right now, but not out of friendship, but because I *made* you."

"You crazy one-legged bastard. You don't fucking own me. I did okay here."

"Gulliano? A third-rate postal clerk? Who else? That husband and wife team in naval intelligence? I knew about that, Michael. I *gave* them to you. Oh yes, and Yuri: a Russian who buys you dinner and complains about his wife. Please, Michael, be serious. Think a moment what your career would be without me. Think what would happen if I just disappeared."

"Is that a threat?"

"I would never blackmail you, Michael. I only wish you to see things as they are."

In a red second Michael knew he could punch Hector, knock the crippled spook on his ass. But the feeling dribbled away too fast, leaving a hot numbness.

"Underneath all that detachment about your job is a very ambitious young man, Michael. You want out of Buenos Aires, and I'm the one that can do it. For instance, this week twenty-six military officers, led by General Valle, will be arrested and shot by my office for planning a Peronist coup against the government. Nobody knows these names. Not even President Aramburu. But I do. And I'm prepared to give them to you. Think of the shock waves this will ring through your division. Think of Norris's humiliation that they came to *you*. And that's just the beginning. Help me now, help my country, and I'll provide for you even more intelligence of a quality you have never seen: KGB plans to infiltrate the port unions, shake-ups in the Chilean DINA. I even have the full list of names in Fruende's Nazi ratline smuggling operation, a list you can leverage with Norris and his old colleagues in the FBI legal attaché office if you need to. With this I can take you all the way, Michael Suslov. All the way."

When Michael spoke he didn't recognize his own voice.

"…Okay."

In Koenig's garage was a small Leyland pickup. They put a blanket over Her, and Michael carried the load out. She wasn't heavy— like a box of balsa wood you could hear slip when they tilted it. All the roadblocks were gone now and the drive downtown was easy, Michael at the wheel.

Hector was quiet, his gaze falling out the passenger window, when Michael spoke. "Do you dream about her?"

Hector lifted from his thoughts. The whip of passing lights strobed his face.

"Yes, Michael. I do."

He left Hector with the truck parked around the back of the First Boston, went in front with his key, and opened the loading dock. It shrieked and howled, but the only person inside at this hour would be Wintergreen at his security desk.

There was a rolling cart and they set her on it, backed into the freight elevator, and hit number four. Hector stayed on the loading dock, nodded as the doors closed in his face. Michael's plan was to put her in the same storage closet where they'd put the TSD boxes heading to Milan. It was a risk of course, leaving an extra crate of this size here this far out from Tuesday, but it was all he had right now.

The elevator stopped. Michael opened the doors. The freight let off in a small alcove one turn from the station security desk. Michael peeked around the corner, saw Wintergreen's eyes down in a comic book.

"Get yourself killed sneaking around like that at this hour, Spook. That or get hired as a janitor." Leaving the cart out of sight, Michael came around from the alcove. Wintergreen looked up. "Jeez, you run up here or what?"

Michael looked at his shirt. It was soaked with sweat. "I'm not feeling very good."

"Go to bed. Drink lots of fluids."

"I need to drop something off."

"At five a.m.?"

"Norris coming in tomorrow?"

Wintergreen threw a glance over his shoulder. "Ask him yourself."

"What?"

"He's in his office."

"Here? *Now*?"

"Lofton and Johnny Miller too."

It was more silly than frightening. The odds…

"Well, look who has a nose for parties after all"—Lofton, leaning in the corridor. "Good spy trait that, a nose for parties." Michael considered smiling and backing out, but decided it'd look guilty.

"Just insomnia." Michael consciously loosened his shoulders, thought about Hector waiting in the Leyland. "Little late for a staff meeting, isn't it? Or is this the night you all burn incense to J. Edgar?" He walked up to Lofton, wiping the sweat off his palms onto his trousers.

"Easy, hotshot. I'm the one that half-ass *likes* you, remember?" Next to Lofton he had an angle into Norris's office. Bud was there, so was Johnny Miller, Esther, the embassy FBI legal attaché, and a guy he didn't recognize. They were drinking champagne, some twangy, Okie 78 on a record player.

"So what's going on?"

"Johnny Miller collared his Kraut this morning."

"Schmidt?"

"Eckhardt." A little further up the attorney general's list, but a universe from names like Eichmann or Mengele. "Turns out our lamster SS pal was getting by laundering rackets money for the Gambino mob through his export biz. Busts open a whole Wise Guy–South American money trail. Champagne's direct from Hoover. Hot rumor was Eisenhower himself was gonna call, but we ended up with Nixon."

"Who's the suit?"

"Attorney general rep."

The knot of revelers in the station chief's office didn't notice Michael, and against his will it stung a little. He hated these guys, but being here, on the outside, he couldn't help it…it stung. Lofton, as if sensing it, shrugged. "We would have invited you, Mike, but y'know…nobody thought you'd come."

Michael watched them a beat longer, remembered Hector and what he left outside the freight elevator, and pushed off. "Give Miller my congratulations."

"Mike…" Michael paused. Lofton toyed with his drink. "Take a good look. Guys like me, pre-CIA, we're dying off, retiring. Few more years this place'll be full of bright young Cold Warriors like you. But before you piss on our graves, think about something: Johnny in there just busted a mass murderer and took back some ground from the Mafia stateside. Even a three-year-old can tell you that makes this miserable planet a tiny bit better than it was yesterday. In four years of peeking through Ivan's keyholes, what have you really accomplished?"

Hector's face registered no surprise when Michael returned with the cart, rubbed his eyes, and simply said, "Wrong night." Michael loaded her back into the Leyland and climbed into the cab.

"And if not here, Michael, where?"

Michael cut the engine and coasted into the alley that ran behind his house, stopping in front of a neighbor's garage. He knew the family; they were in Europe for another month. It would be as safe here as anywhere. Hector and he picked the lock, drove the Leyland inside, and pulled the garage door down behind it.

He glanced up at his and Karen's bedroom window down the way. It was dark, and Michael knew he'd never tell his wife the former First Lady of Argentina was locked in their alley. He turned to Hector. "I'll drive you home."

"It's not necessary, Michael. I am very comfortable with the night."

"Then I'll talk to you tomorrow."

"Please get some sleep, my son." Hector lingered, his cane drawing circles in the pebbled surface. "Do you have a gun, Michael?"

In the entire station there was a single .38 locked in a drawer somewhere that hadn't been fired since Bonnie and Clyde.

"No."

Hector handed him a Molina .45, the Argentine version of the US Colt automatic. "Not that I believe you would ever need it, but…well…these are complicated times." The gun was heavy and malevolent, raised grip prickly in his palm. "Are you familiar with it?"

About the time Michael was snatched by a baby CIA during his senior year in college, he was sent a navy draft notice. His spook personnel officer told him he'd have to do his swabby service, but they'd make sure it was in Naval Intelligence, where they could quietly transfer him out after a year. Crew cut and nine to five at Western Pacific Fleet Command, Yokosuka. As a college boy that meant automatic OCS and a pair of lieutenant JG bars. Higher pay, nice white uniform, and officer shore duty once a month: strapping on a .45 and accompanying the enlisted MPs patrolling Yokosuka's red-light district, doing the formal cuffing of drunk-and-disorderly brass the enlisted MPs couldn't touch. It was shitty duty, the biggest danger a hernia from lifting unconscious, vomit-stained captains and commanders, the .45 never coming out of its holster.

Except on ammo day.

At the end of each month, all officers turned in their empty .45 ammo clips for fresh ones at supply. Since target practice was mandatory, it was expected your clips would be empty. But of course nobody ever got around to the shooting range—it was on the other side of town, and the mosquitoes had bloodlust that time of year—so come the thirtieth, down to the beach the officers would go, there to spend the afternoon in a cordite haze firing off clips so the count would match. They'd start with the ocean, move to rocks, then seagulls, crabs, and by sundown, anything that moved.

He'd been hunting crabs with his .45 in the tidal rocks. Crab Killer. Destroyer of crustacean cities. *Blam!* Submit! *Blam!* Tremble before your white-uniformed god! *Blam!* Little side-shuffling bodies obliterated in thundering overkill. By summer the algae-eaters had wised up, gotten cagier, and he had to lie in wait, slinking flat across the rim. He was doing that one thirtieth, frustrated at that day's take of crab pelts, when he spied three magnificent bulls shuffling ten feet below on a table of slick rock. In a single move he rolled, stood, and unloaded—*Blam-Blam-Blam-Blam.* A split second later four ricochets *whoosh-whoosh-whoosh-whooshed* past his ear.

He gave the crabs the rest of the summer off.

"Yeah. I know how to use it."

He didn't go to bed, and Karen found him the next morning in the living room chair, twitching half-asleep, mumbling something about Evita and crabs.

◎   ◎   ◎

He got to the embassy early, threw himself into his commercial attaché cover job, and tried to work the night before out of his skin. Everyone else had apparently decided to give themselves the morning off, and he welcomed the silence. But with it came, at the edge of his thoughts, what Lofton had said about him and Ivan's keyholes.

That afternoon he took the station car downtown and parked behind a strip of green near the Paloma Hotel. A month ago he'd bugged room 710. Every Thursday during siesta a group of cranky military officers gathered there to drink, screw whores, and talk sedition. The station car had a Ferranti mobile radio receiver bolted on the rear passenger-side floor. Michael settled in, slipped on the headphones, and tried to drown out Lofton.

He left early at four. Karen had an obstetrics appointment, and he could use the space to decide what to do with Evita. Wintergreen was just coming on, and they met in the parking lot. "Hey, Jarhead."

"How's the fever?"

"Lots of liquids, right?"

Wintergreen eyed him strange a moment. "Everything okay, boss?"

"Nothing a career change wouldn't cure."

Wintergreen reached over, tucked in the butt of the Molina .45 sticking out of Michael's coat pocket, and walked on toward the embassy. "Don't hurt yourself with that, Spook."

# 13.

He went back to the Leyland, found blankets to help conceal the casket in its bed, sat beside it, and sneezed on dust and unreality. For hours now—was it days?—he'd spent so much time with this box he'd stopped thinking of it as anything but a box. It wasn't, and he decided to remind himself of that.

It only took a few turns with a socket wrench to loosen the bolts, lift away the plywood top, and there She was. So like Her it was nothing like Her. Moments after death, in preparation for two weeks of state viewing, Dr. Ara had replaced the blood first with alcohol, then repeated heated treatments of Formol, thymol, and glycerin pumped through heel and ear. After the viewing, he withdrew the body and spent months bathing it in endless baths of acetate, potassium nitrate, and other secret chemicals he referred to only as his "parafinization method," often sleeping in the same room as his charge, proudly declaring when finished that this was better than mummification, because not a single organ was disturbed. This was Evita *in toto*: flesh, brains, and bone all waxed and sealed for a thousand years. Only the blood was removed, for no matter how well you tried to calm it with preservatives, its life force would not be silenced. She was everything but her blood, because blood makes noise.

Michael fought the urge to touch her luxuriant hair—washed, dyed, and combed for the coming millennia. He thought of a hundred years and tried to make it a thousand, thought about his mother, death…

And the second time he saw Her.

By the time Michael had returned as an adult to Buenos Aires, the Eva Perón Foundation—originally just the plaything of a powerful man's girlfriend—had, under her tireless obsession, exploded into a mammoth organization with assets of 200 million dollars, fourteen thousand employees, and a full staff of priests, all under her name. Funded by shakedowns of corporations and the vast Confederación General del Trabajo union membership, Evita held court in her labor ministry office, the underclass filling the halls with requests for clothes, sugar, a job. Tirelessly, Evita would listen, pull back the sleeve of her fur coat, and grant, always, more than they asked, because she hated charity.

Some wondered how much she granted for herself.

Across the countryside she built hospitals, a thousand schools, dorms for young women. To the wretched she gave cooking pots: two hundred thousand. Shoes: a million. A city: fifteen thousand homes built east of the capital. The poor named it as they named every school, every bridge, every matchstick she produced: Eva Perón. Eva Perón City, Eva Perón Street, Eva Perón Park Bench.

It was fall '51, a few months after her speech on the Avenida 9 de Julio. Michael had been running down Tom Anderson, a United Press stringer that sometimes did sidebar errands for the station. Anderson had left a note saying he'd be all day covering the grand opening of another Eva Perón City. Michael drove down and saw that, as a compliment to her real city, Evita had built one for children: 250 miniature houses with a miniature store, miniature stoplights, a miniature church—an entire miniature universe for a group of orphaned poor, standing there, bewildered, afraid to touch anything. Evita waded among them for the photographers, hugging shoulders, cutting ribbons with oversized scissors.

Michael spotted Anderson standing with the other stringers, scratching his notepad.

"Nice day for an ego fest," Michael said.

"I love this country." The Peronist lackeys hung on her every word. The rest of the foreign press contingent—one Limey, one Italian—were already yawning and drifting away. Anderson, though, couldn't get enough of it. "Look at her, huh?" he bubbled. "The muddy little girl—you know she was a bastard, right?—fucks and sucks her way to the top and tries to make it better for all the dirty little Evitas out there."

"Sort of overkill, isn't it?"

"But that's what makes it great! It's like a guided tour through her screwy past. Look at the kids now. See? Santa Evita trying so hard, and all she's doing is scaring the shit out of them. What theater! You gotta love her, man. You gotta love this whole place."

Michael finished his business with Anderson, as the UP reporter basked in the footlights of Evita's theater of the id. "You oughta stay for the whole show, kid. Better than the Teatro Colón, and it's free."

CGT hacks were shepherding the reporters now on a guided tour of Evitaland. Michael begged off, took a shortcut across the compound toward his car. He was passing the tiny houses, the tiny store, when the tiny church snagged him. Modeled on a traditional, white-plastered Spanish colonial, the arch was festooned with saints as frolicking small children in bas-relief. He couldn't resist and lingered, finally poking his head in the five-foot oak doors.

The light was speckled stained glass. He stooped through the doorway, walked among shrunken pews, and tried to imagine them full of children. Tried to imagine exactly which god they'd be offering their prayers to.

"Are you lost?"

Evita was bending through the doorway. His mind leaped—spook alibi scramble whenever somebody sneaks up on you. "No, I was just going to my car. I saw this, and I guess I was curious. It's very beautiful."

"Yes. My favorite building here. I designed it myself, an exact one-third scale of my hometown church. I wanted to spend a few minutes away from the others, here, before I give it over to the children."

"I'm sorry. I'll leave you, then."

"No. Stay. Honest admiration is always welcome." She was dressed casually—thin maroon blouse and cardigan over tan slacks. Her hair was looser than usual, tucked behind her ears in a way almost schoolgirlish. "You're a *Porteño*?"

"I'm American."

Her face cooled. "You speak without accent."

"Thank you."

"You're a reporter?"

"I'm with the embassy."

From cool to frost. Dean Acheson, the American secretary of state that year, was loathed by the Peróns, and the feeling was mutual. His ambassador to Argentina, Ellsworth Bunker, was the constant target of searing cartoons run in Peronist rags depicting him as a drunk, bootlicking sycophant named Mr. Whiskey and Soda. Michael had some of the funnier cartoons on his desk.

"One of Bunker's boys, then."

"Afraid so, Mrs. Perón."

"I am 'Mrs. Perón' to children and enemies."

"What would you like to me to call you?"

"What do you call Ambassador Bunker?"

"Froggy. But not usually to his face."

She smiled. "I like that."

"You didn't hear it from me, Senora—"

"Evita, please."

"Evita."

"Mr...?"

"Suslov. Michael Suslov."

"Russian."

"Ukrainian."

"I don't like Russians much."

"Neither did my father."

"Your father is in America?"

"Buried there. He died when I was seventeen."

Evita nodded. "I know what it is like to lose a father young. When he was put in the ground, you stood at the coffin?"

"I was the only one."

"You're lucky"—the words struggled a moment—"to have been able to stand there."

The story would not be found in any of Evita's endless autobiographies, but Michael knew it by heart. How her mother had been a third-string mistress to Evita's petty manager father. How, when he died, the real wife refused to allow bastard Evita and her brother at the church service. They could only follow their father's funeral cart on its way to the grave, fifty yards behind the wife's family, choking on their dust, through the roads of their town. In one version of the story, Evita defied her father's legitimate family and rushed the funeral cart, reaching in and snipping a lock of the man's hair.

She seemed to disappear into a private moment, drawing herself back out on steel staves. "Your mother?"

"Dead too."

Evita paused. "Was her death peaceful?"

"I wasn't there."

"You were spared."

"I wasn't invited." It hung there, awkward. "It's complicated."

She watched him carefully, seemed to make some small discovery, and changed the subject. "Why did you go to work in Acheson's State Department, Mr. Suslov?"

"People often ask me that."

"What do you tell them?"

"That you had to be there." She paused and you could see those Latin mental gears searching for the slight, any affront to the almighty *dignidad*. Michael glanced at the door. "Won't they be looking for you?"

"They know better than to bother me."

He smiled. "I'm sure they do." Again the gears. Clack, clack…

"Are you a Peronist, Mr. Suslov?"

"I think every honest man is a Peronist. And every demon."

She grinned ruefully, and that surprised him. "Juan Perón will save this country, you know. His genius is the light in every worker's eye."

"Perhaps. But it is Evita on their lips."

"I am only the General's instrument."

"I was there at the Avenida 9 de Julio." The name, the night, were still burned ice on her. "I saw what you wanted. Half a million did."

Cinnamon eyes appraised him. "Exactly which department of the embassy do you work in?"

"I'm a commercial attaché."

A tug at the edge of her mouth. "Then you must know Hector."

"Everyone knows Hector."

"Especially those of you in the attaché's office."

Michael's turn to smile.

"What do you write home, Mr. Suslov? To Mr. Acheson?"

"As a commercial attaché?"

"Yes, Mr. Suslov, as a commercial attaché."

He should have backed off five minutes ago. What was pushing him? "That Argentina was never great, that possibly it can never be great. But that now, because of you, Argentina believes it is great. And in the end perhaps that's the same thing."

He expected anything and got a small nod. "Few speak to me like this."

"Few are as ill-mannered. I apologize."

"I know plenty of ill-mannered. Embassy Row is full of them. No, you're different. There is something…sad about you. You have a Latin soul, Mr. Suslov."

"I was raised here."

"As I thought."

José Espejo, CGT head and number four in the Perón administration, stuck his head in. "Senora, pardon—"

"Get out."

"But—"

"Shut up and get out!" No dog ever slinked away faster. She turned back to Michael. "I must go. The children…"

"Of course, Senora."

She turned for the tiny door and paused. "I should think, Michael, your life in that embassy, with such a soul, must be a very lonely one."

"I think so must be yours."

"Good afternoon, Mr. Suslov."

"Good afternoon, Senora."

Children's voices could be heard, tiny voices calling her name. "My children await." She smiled with lips famously full and was gone.

Even then cancer was already spreading through her groin, and Michael would always wonder if on that day she suspected all that awaited her come summer would be Ara and his embalmer's syringes of heated glycerin. Along the way there would be small notes left for him in the embassy. Never signed but smelling unmistakably of her. They would be snippets of Latin poetry, always of patriotism and the melancholy thrill of giving one's life. Sometimes there would be a handwritten line beneath the poetry: *For your soul, Michael…*

He never answered these notes—he knew the rules—but they warmed him with maternal affection, touched regions long in ache, and he would reread them often, when alone in the station.

Near Evita's end, Michael came home one night to an envelope tacked to his door, written in a shaking, chemotherapy hand:

*At this moment, I think of the young man with a Latin soul and the mother who never said good-bye. Pray for her, Michael Suslov, pray for me, and protect both our souls.* Included in the envelope was a small lock of blonde hair. Scrawled below it, in handwriting so degraded it was nearly unreadable, a last line: *You Will Never Forget Me.*

Two weeks later her casket, rounded and sleekly black, inched from her bed to the National Congress building through streets heavy with mourners. He was there.

She lay in state for two days, and the faithful waited hours, drenched in freezing rain, for a glimpse. And he was there. Among the farmers and street workers, her army of poor clutching not Bibles but her autobiography. He lied to his wife, called in sick to the station, and stood in the rain ten hours to see the corpse. Ara had done a rushed, temporary job, and it showed. She was still Evita. When the crowds thinned the doctor would take her away, roll up his sleeves, and spend the following year turning her into… his.

The line never stopped moving, but Michael slowed, brushed the rain from his face, and whispered, for her, a prayer.

A glob of sweat rolled off his nose and broke across her lip, running away like rain on polished chrome. *See, look at those lips*, the oligarchy had cried, as if their fullness were in itself proof of her rumored skill at fellatio, a talent reportedly shared with every producer and nickelodeon jockey she met as a young actress. Before the earthquake relief concert and the General she stole from her best friend. Before the sanctifying of that turgid, ruby mouth. Ara's mouth now. Effigy as reality. She was in there somewhere…

Karen came home, baby-to-be and mom given a clean bill, D-day in two weeks. Karen's back hurt, her legs kept cramping, and she knew instantly something was wrong with the house.

"What have you done, Michael?"

"Nothing that won't be over soon."

The hurt ran so deep it was almost lost to the eye. "This is my house too."

"I know. Why do you say that?"

She took in the room with an eerie perception that made Michael squirm. "Is it here?" she asked.

"What?"

"Whatever you've done."

He tried to let the words filter with the confidence of a technicality. "No."

She stopped talking to him.

He fidgeted, tried to come up with something to say. But what was there except what couldn't be said? He bounced off the walls, useless, and finally went to bed an hour after Karen.

He didn't remember sleeping, and waking was a nauseating, fuzzy jolt. He fought for a reason, mine-shaft darkness around him, and was going to let it go when he heard a shadow. Outside, along the foundation wall. His vision flushed hot, and his hand was groping, numb stupid, for Hector's .45 under the bed. It was heavy and giant and his fingers closed over it all wrong. He swung his feet down, smacked a heel on tile, and sat there, ghost frozen.

Karen was asleep, and he measured time by her breaths. He listened till his eyes hurt, finally stood, and shuffled agonizingly to the bedroom window. The backyard stretched out a story below, gardens and olive trees running to the alley. He waited for the backyard to make the first move.

An olive tree shifted.

Something went black in Michael's veins. He bolted through the bedroom, barked his toe on the staircase, barreled without reason through the kitchen to the backdoor. He stood there, gun out, and tried to wait.

Somewhere along the way the sun came up.

His arm was asleep, and he couldn't feel the gun. You could see the backyard now through the kitchen window. Fleshy blue. Silent.

When he opened the back door, his feet sunk in dew. Michael lowered the gun, turned back inside…

And saw the rose tied to the door.

◎   ◎   ◎

"Gotta stop swimming in meat grinders, son."

Michael jerked up. He was in the embassy lunch room—hundred square feet of linoleum, coffee pot, and Coke machine. Lofton leaned on the back of a chair.

"Didn't get much sleep."

"Doesn't look like you got any sleep at all, pally. Trouble at home?"

A jolt of alarm rocked Michael's colon then spread dully through his exhaustion, as nothing registered on Lofton's face. "Got a kid coming. It's hard on Karen. I'm a little nervous I guess."

"It's a roller coaster for sure. Just remember you're not the first. Mommies been doin' this forever just fine." Lofton lingered, and Michael wondered what he was waiting for him to say.

"Yeah. You're right. I guess."

The chair creaked as Lofton rocked it. "Makes a guy think about his future, having a child. What would best serve that future, for you, for Karen, for your baby." It sat weirdly a beat before he released the chair and backed away. "Gotta go back and look busy. Do the same if I were you. Bud's got the green folder out again."

He left, and Michael's mind went back where it'd been all morning.

The rose.

He'd checked twice to make sure it was real, crumpling it before Karen got up. A chance in a million it wasn't what it had to be. One night. One fucking night and it had started. A bunch of old women—and, Jesus Christ, what Wisner would give for ears like that. What Dulles himself would.

The shadow in the yard hadn't looked old.

It was all too much now. He didn't know where to move the box till Tuesday, but it wasn't staying in the garage next door. And he was getting Karen out of there. Today.

Rushing through a budget report so he could duck out early; Karen wary on the phone: "I can barely move, Michael. Why on earth do you want to go somewhere now?" He'd tried to make it sound relaxed, and it came out flushed and edgy. Karen's breath broke and shortened, and he knew she was crying. "Damn you, Michael, I'm your wife. It's my life too. Why won't you talk to me?" He promised he would. He'd tell her everything. But later. Right now, please, she had to pack a case for the weekend. "I've been sick all day, Michael…" A resigned sigh. "Just make it some-place quiet, huh?"

"Promise. I love you."

"Sure."

On the way out Norris hit him with the green folder, a blurry extra hour tracing money transfers through British-owned BA banks. Pumped with Miller's coup, Norris actually smiled. Actually said *please*. Michael fought the need to punch him. A roomful of flatfoots was one thing. A roomful of *smug* flatfoots was one cross too many.

It was dark when Michael got home. He dropped the car at the curb, looked for Karen's bags in the hall—didn't see them—and bounded up the stairs.

She was in bed.

"What are you doing?" He fairly squeaked with it.

One eye opened with difficulty. "Oh. Hi."

"How come you're not packed?"

You could see the shape of her belly under the blanket, a small mountain drifting up and down. "I've been feeling like crap for an hour and half, Michael. If you want to leave that badly, you're going to have to do it alone or carry me over your shoulder."

"You're not just screwing with me, are you?"

"Don't flatter yourself."

He let his shoulders loosen and rubbed his eyes. He was being stupid about this. He sat down beside her. "It's okay. It's not that big a deal. Really. Can I get you something?"

"Some water maybe. Thank you."

She was asleep again when he came back. He set the water on a nightstand, watched her face, easy and soft with a strand of hair over one eye. She was peaceful, and it snuck up on him. The ache of how he could have let so much drift to sea so far.

He'd fix it. He'd ship the Pampa Princess out, and with Hector's promised juice, Karen and Michael Suslov would soon follow. Away from this shit. Away from Buenos Aires.

He made himself something in the kitchen and didn't eat it, settled on coffee, and roamed the living room. Tried to focus but just ended up pacing. Raw and exhausted from last night, he finally turned off most of the lights and sat in his armchair, .45 in his lap, and faced a window that looked out on the neighbor's alley garage. A knee drummed as he waited for shadows.

An eternity passed before he checked his watch. Eleven o'clock. Jesus Christ, it was only eleven o'clock.

He blinked. Looked at his watch again and felt his guts freeze. 4:26 a.m. A five-hour blink…

He sat straight up in the chair, rubbed his eyes, and they were still blurry. He rubbed them again, took in the room.

And knew he wasn't alone.

Something screwy calm in him. Not like last night. Maybe the certainty. Maybe he'd just run out of adrenaline.

It started as just a sense but now it was a creak. From the kitchen. Behind the wings of his easy chair. Hidden, he picked the blunderbuss from his lap. Rammed his thoughts with where to go, which way to leap…

When the lights went out. The fuse box in the kitchen. It had to be the fucking fuse—

Another creak. Hard sole on kitchen tile. He flooded with possibilities, till it all gridlocked and he was jumping out of the chair—blind in his own house—and suddenly his nose sang, his breath exploded, and he was falling backward, the carpet coming up sooner than he expected. His lungs refused to suck, and he realized he'd been hit—body-blocked—and there was shuffling, but you couldn't see…

Something, maybe a leg, and he slammed his fist, breaking a knuckle against bone. The leg shouted—"*Sasiko!*"—a male voice that kicked Michael furiously aside. He rolled, got his gun off the carpet and tried to stand, tried to scream, but nothing came. He rocked to his feet, tumbled after the voice retreating into the kitchen.

He hit the tile and banged into the range. Pain shot through his side. He gasped, spun—

And the room lit up.

A flash, and Michael knew he was being shot at. He wasn't hit—maybe—and threw himself through the opposite doorway, where he locked down and grasped his gun so tight he thought the grip would crumble.

A battery night-light. In the living room. You could see it through both kitchen doorways. He waited. Waited till moving darkness swallowed the pin of light. Then he fired.

He couldn't tell what he'd hit through the pounding whine. The grainy stench of sulfur. Michael wiped his nose, fumbled for a circuit breaker...

And felt his universe cave in.

The round had caught the body midchest and passed through the kitchen wall. The plaster was smeared with blood down to where his target sat against it, swaying punch-drunk. It gurgled and looked up at him and it was Karen.

Black numbness started up his legs. She tried to say something, but he wouldn't have heard. His body, his mind, were swallowed one by one in a cold forever that lowered him gently to the floor, across from his wife, and whispered that it would be all right, all right if he just went to sleep...

# 14.

It was a half hour before anyone came. A neighbor heard the shots but didn't know which house they came from. The first BA police car turned on a street crazy with barking dogs and went door to door, till one cop, running his flashlight through yards, saw the jimmied back door.

The district *capitán* knew they were Yankees and called the embassy. The embassy duty officer called the ambassador, who called Norris, who called Lofton, who wasn't home, so he came up himself.

Norris had to navigate broken furniture to get in. Michael and Karen were still in the kitchen. The cops had taken the gun, but no one had moved either of them. Michael was on the floor, rocking back and forth, keening softly.

Norris kept the cops back, ran interference when the *capitán* tried to question Michael. Insisted firmly that everyone in this room was part of the American embassy and therefore had diplomatic immunity. The US mission would handle it. The officer blustered but backed down, ordering his men, after crime scene photos were taken, to wrap Karen, which Norris gave permission for. They used a pink sheet. As she was lifted, Michael clawed wildly at them, howling as they carried her out, Norris holding him back.

"Get a hold of yourself, Mike."

"*Don't!*" Michael begged. "*Don't give her to Ara!*"

"Ara? Christ, Mike, nobody's giving her to him. She's going to the police hospital."

Lofton came later, and they took turns staying up with him. Lofton was jumpy and had trouble staying still. He'd wander back and forth, wiping his hands on his trousers, mumbling, "Jesus, Mike…"

Norris called in a cleaning lady. She came with dawn and scrubbed Karen's blood from the floor and wall. They pumped up Michael with Seconal and put him to bed. The *capitán* had left a cruiser out front, just to remind them whose beat this was. Norris added a marine guard from the embassy. He washed his face and met Lofton on the landing as they got ready to leave. It was Saturday morning, dead with it.

"Mike going to be okay?" Lofton asked. He looked hammered.

"He'll sleep some. That's enough. I'll leave Casey on the door."

"How far up the chain of command are we going with this?"

Norris shook his head. "I don't want any more of Dulles's SB clowns down here than I have to. Somebody busted in on the kid. Before I end up with the frat-boy hordes crawling all over me, I want to know exactly what this does or doesn't have to do with the station."

"The guy killed his pregnant wife, Bud. Point-fucking-blank. This isn't going away."

◎　◎　◎

That first day Michael slept. He'd jerk awake, feel the flat dullness of the Seconal, and for a moment forget. But the world always came back on ground glass, and he would let himself fade away from it, away into sleep…

◎　◎　◎

The second day Norris came back, gave him more pills, told to sleep more. Told him not to talk to anyone.

That was okay with Michael.

He got up that night on corpse legs, went downstairs to a house destroyed by someone and piled back haphazardly by cops. The son of a bitch had done it while his wife bled to death. While he…while he sat there…

He could see the embassy guard in front, a cruiser's shadow in the alley.

Shadows…

They were plenty in the kitchen. But none of Karen. They had wrapped and scrubbed and taken it all away.

He went back upstairs, curled himself on the chilled bathroom tile, begged for death, and got still more sleep…

Tuesday he rose before dawn and his head was fire. Seconal crowded the edge of his vision and he took more to crowd it further. A guard was still on the door, but the cruiser was gone from the alley. He knew—if he could make himself walk—what he was going to do today.

Barely morning and only Wintergreen on the station front desk. Seeing Michael rattled him. "Go home, Spook. Get some rest, huh?" He talked slowly, as if to a mental patient. "I'm sorry about Karen, man. I liked her…Christ, Spook, what am I suppose to say?"

The TSD photo equipment boxes being sent to Milan substation today had already been brought out into the alcove for the courier.

"Get a coffee," Michael said.

"What?"

"Get a coffee." Just a pair of Seconal eyes, and Wintergreen got up.

"Sure." He disappeared.

Michael brought Evita's box out of the elevator and set it beside the TSD crates. He then went back to his desk and rifled a file cabinet for the station's single .38 pistol. A cable was sitting on his in-box.

**TOP SECRET SELF-RESTRICTED HANDLING EYES ONLY...**
**FROM: PETER NORTH AC/WH/5/**
**TO: FRANK SNIFF BUENOS AIRES STATION**
**SUBJECT: RYBAT BI LETTER**
**MESSAGE:**

**I HEARD. JESUS CHRIST, WONDER BOY, WHAT HAVE YOU DONE?**

Michael sat alone at Wintergreen's desk, station .38 in his lap, and waited till the Hapag-Lloyd couriers arrived, wet from a rainstorm blowing outside.

"Got a pen?" Michael handed him one. The courier ticked off his manifest of transfer orders, including Billy Patterson's fake, compared them to the boxes' attached paperwork, and signed off.

Both the TSD crates and Evita's box were locked inside metal containers and taped shut with US diplomatic seals for their trip on an H&L cargo ship to Europe.

Finished, the courier turned back to Michael, still at the desk with his blown-out eyes, and sighed for the both of them. "Shitty day, huh?"

"You have no idea."

After they left with Evita, Michael wrote two notes. The first he telegrammed to an order of nuns in Milan, Italy. The second he tacked to Norris's door: *I'm burying my wife. I'll be back…when I'm back.*

He hadn't eaten in three days and stopped for a roll on the corner to settle his stomach. It didn't. Barbara DeVries was passing when he came out. "I'm sorry, Mike." He kept walking, was opening his car door, when she leaned in close. "Honestly, I never thought you'd have the guts."

He drove a block, stopped, and vomited in the gutter.

It was in Palermo Park, near the pond, that Hector met him. "A tragedy, Michael."

"Yes. It is, Hector."

Michael took out the .38 and leveled it at the intelligence chief's bad eye. "General Olivar. His throat wasn't cut by a jealous husband, was it?"

"No, Michael."

"Peronists?"

"Almost certainly."

"And Olivar was watching your Senora. Before Moori Koenig."

"Yes. I should have told you. I'm sorry."

"You can't imagine the comfort that apology is to me right now."

Hector shook his head with something that could pass for sadness. "I cared a great deal for Carmelina, Michael. This sickens my heart."

It had all been flat and compartmentalized in his mind that day till the sound of her nickname. The one just for the three of them, and it was molten copper on his soul. His eyes filled with tears and he shoved them aside with his open palm. "You fucking bastard."

Hector's gaze never went to the gun, his voice a calm that made the .38 feel stupid. "We used each other, Michael. And that is the way of the world with us. But I had affection for you, and none less for Carmelina. I never meant for any of this to happen."

You could almost believe it.

And the crazy fucking thing was, who could Michael talk to? Who could he ever share this with? Whose shoulder could he lay just a fraction of this on, just enough to keep his mind from exploding?

Who except Hector?

Under its own power the gun began to shake, lower, and he was jerking with ragged sobs now, as Hector stepped forward and embraced him. "It's all right, Michael. Go ahead, for both of us. The Senora has been a curse for all that have touched her. You needn't worry of her anymore. I'll finish it. I'll throw her into the river if I must."

Michael pulled away from him. "It's taken care of."

A look of uncertainty. "What do you mean?"

"Courier picked her up this morning."

Just a strobe of Hector's mind flying. Considering. "As we had originally planned. I just assumed…after all this…"

"She'll be safe."

A breeze, a faraway cry of winter off the Andes, crept about their feet. "Where, Michael?"

Michael took a long time to answer, then didn't answer at all. He turned and walked toward the car.

"Michael, I must know. I…we…cannot just…" Hector following him now, "*Michael!*"

Michael spun around and shoved the .38 against Hector's face. "She's mine. Do you understand? Mine. If you ask me again, if I ever see you anywhere, ever, I'll kill you. Is that clear?"

"You're upset, Michael. You don't know what you're doing."

Michael lowered the gun and stared at the deputy head of intelligence. "I know, Hector. For the first time in this goddamn country, I know." He slammed Hector then, hard on the side of the mouth. The crippled spook fell to the dirt.

"I think that about finishes it with us."

That next morning Michael Suslov began a thirty-hour trip to Mendocino, California, with another crate: the body of his wife. From Sonoma County Airport, Michael Suslov rode in the hearse, first to the church, then to the family plot in Fort Bragg. At the funeral service Michael Suslov stood and prayed and wept and, having almost nothing to say to Karen's family, said mostly nothing. When her younger brothers hissed they'd kill him if he came through here again, Michael Suslov nodded.

Before leaving Buenos Aires, Michael had visited a document forger he knew operating in an unmarked storefront on the wrong side of Retiro, near the Villa 31 shantytown, who he had make a fake US passport in the name of Gary Phillips.

Now "Gary Phillips," a week after burying his wife, drove to San Francisco and boarded a round-trip flight to Italy.

Gary Phillips looked a lot worse than his picture, looked even more terrible twenty-eight hours later when he landed in Rome. There, Gary Phillips rented a van and drove to the Dun & Bradstreet corporate building on Via dei Valtorta in Milan, where the CIA substation was located. It was a warm day, a happy day, because it was somebody's birthday and the offices were sweet with sponge cake.

The station duty officer that waited on him looked as if he'd been partying most of the afternoon, and Michael thought the CIA substation in Milan must be a nice place to work. The duty officer checked his ID and copy of the transport order and released the box.

The plan had been to retrieve Evita from the substation and hand her over to Hector. Well, not now. Lying in a Seconal haze those nights after Karen's death, he'd considered storage lockers or freezers and finally settled on something more traditional: a grave.

It was a five-mile drive out to the gray industrial gates of Musocco Cemetery. Lining the entrance were the storefronts of gravestone cutters, groundskeepers, and coffin makers. Michael had telegrammed ahead to one, ordering the construction of two caskets: one of galvanized steel that she would actually rest in, and a simple pine coffin that would fit over it.

He arrived now to collect them, had the owner help transfer his "aunt's" body from one container to another, overpaid him, drove to the grounds, and went to the offices of the Catholic order that administered the cemetery. His telegram had explained that he was bringing the remains of his aunt María Maggi, an Italian Carmelite nun who'd died in Argentina and was now returning for burial in Italy. María Maggi was an actual nun from Michael's childhood and was, he assumed, still perfectly healthy.

The local nuns accepted the simple pine coffin of their sister and held a small service that afternoon. She was buried in the quiet, poor section of the cemetery, where the seeds of flowers still jumped the earthen walls and bloomed uncut in forgotten corners.

It was a good place for sleep. Away from Hector and politics, away soon even from Michael. He stood as they filled the grave in, watched pine disappear under Lombard clay. Watched a box holding a general's wife, Ara's masterpiece, and Hector's obsession, become, simply, in that instant…

His.

# OFFICE OF SECURITY
## Investigation report
## October 10, 1956

**CONFIDENTIAL to:**

**Alan Dulles, DCI**
**Frank Wisner, DDP**
**J.C. King, chief WH Div**
**Number of pages in this report, including cover: 37**

**Investigating officers: R. Bonnet, V.R. Howe**

**SUBJECT:** Shooting death of case officer Michael Suslov's wife, Karen Rutledge Suslov, on September 17, 1956.

**REPORT SUMMARY:** Case officer Michael Suslov has reported that during the early hours of September 17, his home was invaded by person or persons unknown. A struggle ensued, during which Karen Suslov was accidentally shot.

Recovered footprints indicates that likely a single individual gained entry to Suslov's home, and fired one M1951 .380 round that struck the west wall. Blood tracked throughout the main floor of the house indicates same male likely conducted a brief search after the shooting.

Karen Suslov was killed by a .45 round fired from a Ballester Molina that struck her in the womb, passing through the fetus and severing the umbilical cord, causing her to bleed to death in approximately ten minutes (see autopsy attachments). The round matches the Molina semi-automatic Michael Suslov  was still holding when BAPD arrived. Suslov has reported that the gun was bought second-hand in Buenos Aires.

No known problems existed between husband and wife and no obvious motive for a murder scenario exists.

Despite continued inquiries, no probable suspect has been identified in this incident. Suggestions have been made of possible Peronist guerilla activity, but this cannot be proved. Likewise, there is no credible evidence at this time of involvement by a hostile intelligence service or elements of the Argentine government, though this possibility will continue to be investigated.

Signed, Robert Bonnet, Office of Security

ATTACHED:    Buenos Aires police report
             Photographs
             Karen Suslov autopsy
             Filed interviews

1957

January 9, 1957

CONFIDENTIAL to:

Frank Wisner, Deputy Director Operations

## 1956 Year End Fitness
## Report for Michael Suslov

Dear Sir,

In writing an evaluation for case officer Michael Suslov, I am somewhat handicapped since only being appointed station chief since Robert Norris' death from a heart attack in November. Case Officer Robert Lofton went to the FBI after Norris' death, and John Miller and Esther Thomas both took immediate retirement in December, all before or directly after my appointment. This has left the unusual situation of an entire changeover in staff, with no one remaining who had personally dealt with Suslov's work performance.

The problem is further complicated by the legacy of inner-station conflict stemming from the FBI/CIA Western Hemisphere consolidation. As the first post-consolidation officer assigned to Buenos Aires, Suslov was routinely harassed by his superiors. As a result, previous fitness reports, in my opinion, must be viewed with skepticism.

However, despite these limitations, and my brief association with Suslov, I feel secure in saying that Michael

Suslov is, as of this writing, a deeply troubled man and a problematic case officer in Clandestine Intelligence.

During daily routine operations, I am confronted by a remote, hostile young man who's job performance is increasingly sloppy and error prone. Embassy officers on the State side recall Suslov as a generally outgoing, positive, and committed personality who changed dramatically after the accidental shooting of his wife.

I am well aware of Suslov's popularity in the DOP for his former quality intelligence gathering on SB activities here and his contacts in both the Peron and successor regimes. But in the last six months, all these sources seemed to have completely dried up. Suslov himself has become unable to take serious direction and often appears in public under the influence of alcohol; a man disliked by the local police, bumbling in his contacts with the East Bloc missions, frozen out of Casa Rosada and not trusted by his coworkers.

Clearly we must take into account Suslov's previous work, but we must also face the reality of a case officer who is a drain on station resources and patience. I think, at the least, serious consideration should be given to removing him from field duty and placing him on administrative rotation, till it can be determined if his decline is permanent.

On a personal note, I enjoyed our dinner last month in Lima and I believe you're exactly right: while this much change at a station can be disruptive, it is also an opportunity to clear the deadwood and get on with the quality work I know Buenos Aires operations is capable of. I look optimistically forward to the challenge.

Fraternally,

George Pompian
Acting Station Chief, Buenos Aires


cc: Alan Dulles, DCI

**February 28, 1957**

**Michael Suslov**
**Buenos Aires Station**

This letter is to notify you that the attached reprimand has been placed in your service folder for conduct unbecoming of an operational officer.

On the evening of February 18, 1957, during an embassy cocktail party welcoming the Mexican ambassador, you arrived an hour and a half late and in a clear state of intoxication. After showing gross inattention to the Ambassador's remarks, you, within clear earshot of several foreign missions, referred to several of your coworkers as CIA case officers. You then spilled a drink on the Mexican Ambassador before abruptly leaving.

Such behavior is a clear violation of both the letter and spirit of operational conduct and a gross abuse of your position as an officer in clandestine intelligence.

This letter will remain in your folder. A copy will be forwarded to the DDP's office for any additional action.

Fraternally,

George Pompian
Station Chief, Buenos Aires

February 22, 1957

**CONFIDENTIAL TO:** Office of Security, CIA

**FROM:** Dr. Allen Silver, Department of Psychology

**Psychological Exam of Michael Suslov**

Please find enclosed my full evaluation. To summarize, subject is an individual under severe psychological trauma, manifesting in anti-social and paranoid behavior.

Though such traits are not completely uncommon in clandestine operations officers, it appears to have advanced to such a degree in subject that it's difficult to imagine how, at this juncture, subject could continue to be considered a functional personality for such work. Recommendation is removal from all field operations and reassignment to Washington staff during aggressive treatment options listed within.

**March 3, 1957**

**Michael Suslov**
**2801 Davis Avenue**
**Alexandria, Virginia**

**Allen Dulles**
**Director, Central Intelligence Agency**
**2430 E Street**
**Washington DC**

Dear Sir,

I am writing this letter to tender my resignation from the Central Intelligence Agency, effective March 15, 1957. This seems to be the best solution for everyone involved, including, perhaps, even myself.

Fraternally,

Michael Suslov

# 1962

MENDOCINO COUNTY JAIL * PRE-BOOKING RECORD * ARRESTING/TRANSPORTING OFFICER COMPLETE

| 'A' NO: 62-1245 | BKG. NO: 62-722 | | C/R NO: 4982742CC | HSNG. LOC: Mendo |
|---|---|---|---|---|

| ARRESTING AGENCY | BOOKING DATE | BOOKING TIME | ARREST DATE | ARREST TIME | OFFENSE DATE AND TIME |
|---|---|---|---|---|---|
| ☒MCSO ☐WPD ☐UPD ☐CHP | 6/13/62 | 3:22 AM | 6/12/62 | 1:06 AM | SAME |
| ☐FBPD ☐T/F ☐OTH: | LOCATION OF ARREST: Dick's Bar, 45080 Main St. | | LOCATION OF CRIME: SAME | | |

| ☒ADULT ☐JUVENILE | ARRESTING OFFICER Burrows | TRANSPORTING OFFICER SAME | BOOKING OFFICER Hazelkirk |
|---|---|---|---|

ARRESTEE'S NAME (LAST, FIRST MIDDLE): Suslov, Michael Alexander    ALIASES (LAST, FIRST MIDDLE): n/a

ARRESTEE'S ADDRESS (NUMBER-STREET): No fixed address    | CITY | STATE | ZIP | TELEPHONE |

| SEX | RACE | AGE | DATE OF BIRTH | PLACE OF BIRTH | HEIGHT | WEIGHT | HAIR | EYES | COMP. | BUILD |
|---|---|---|---|---|---|---|---|---|---|---|
| M | W | 34 | 8/25/27 | Chicago, ILL | 5'9" | 170 | blk | grn | lght | med |

| OCCUPATION None | EMPLOYER OR SCHOOL (ADDRESS - CITY - STATE - TELEPHONE NUMBER) none | SOCIAL SECURITY NO 354-20-6155 |
|---|---|---|

| DRIVER'S LICENSE Y 896769 | STATE CAL | IN CASE OF ILLNESS (PARENT/GUARDIAN/FRIEND/NOK) ADDRESS/CITY/STATE/TELEPHONE none | RELATIONSHIP |
|---|---|---|---|

SCARS/MARKS/TATTO, AND/OR ADDITIONAL IDENTIFICATION CHARACTERISTICS: none    AT PRESENT 44 days / IN COUNTY / IN STATE

| JURISDICTION: | UJC | TMJC | LLJC | RVJC | AJJ ☒ | LXJC | AVJC | D-I | D-II | OTHER: |
|---|---|---|---|---|---|---|---|---|---|---|

| OFFENSE | M-F | WARR. NO. | OFFENSE DEFINITION | BAIL |
|---|---|---|---|---|
| CPC 647(f) | M | 62-883 | Disorderly conduct | $300 |
| CPC 242 | | | Assault/battery | |

| ADDITIONAL INFORMATION/OFFENSES | TOTAL BAIL |
|---|---|

| HOLD PLACED FOR: | PROBATION/PAROLE ☐ YES ☒ NO | PROBATION/PAROLE OFFICER |
|---|---|---|

| VEHICLE DISPOSITION/KEYS: ☐ STORED ☒ IMPOUNDED ☐ LEFT AT SCENE: | LOCATION: | MEDICAL SCREENING COMPLETED, PERSON IS ACCEPTABLE: ☐ YES ☒ NO ☐ NO INJ/ILLNESS |
|---|---|---|

**ARRESTING OFFICER COMMENTS:**

Suspect Michael Suslov, apparent transient (no address, no employment), after becoming severely intoxicated at Dick's Bar, Encountered Mendo. Residents Tom and Harold Rutledge, brothers of Suslov's former wife, Karen, now deceased. After a brief, heated conversation, a struggle ensued with both Rutledge brothers, resulting several cuts and injuries to all participants. Both Rutledge brothers were also arrested. Suslov has three previous priors for vagrancy in Los Angeles, Monterey and Santa Clara counties. Records check indicates his last steady employment was with US State Department till March, 1957.

Suspect was uncooperative and refused medical treatment. Mental incapacity is considered and observation recommended.

Sgt. William Burrows
Badge #123
Mendocino County Sheriff

# ALEJANDRO

**June 1, 1970**

# 15.

Former president Aramburu thought, *This room is not so unlike the room of my youth.* The narrow concrete floor, flaky plaster wall. The tick of heat withdrawing off a corrugated metal roof. The former president was a moody child, or so his father once told him, but he remembered those days fondly, as he remembered few other things in his long, tired life.

He hadn't heard a car pass for several minutes, and that meant he was in an outer barrio. The only light fixture was an oil lamp, which meant he must be in one of the poorer ones too. Probably the north. They always seemed, these people, to come from the north.

He was tied to the chair such that it was difficult to look at anything but the faces sitting directly opposite, of which there were three. Just as well; what glimpses he'd managed of himself revealed only spattered blood…

The Fat One, nervous, whose knuckles were surely wrecked by now—and why didn't he put on gloves?—was on his feet again. He was young—they were all young, these college shits—with the body of a man but the swagger of a cruel child. His face was close, breath ferocious with garlic. "Where is she?"

You'd think he'd have gotten bored of the words by now.

"I don't know."

"Liar!"

Another crack to the numbed, swollen side of his face and he tasted blood, but he was old and bled easily. So predictable, these fiery children. So unskilled. What was one more crack to a destroyed face?

The Fat One stepped back, shook his knuckles in agony, then savagely kicked at the prisoner. A surprised blast of pain shot up former president Aramburu's leg. As the tears cleared from his eyes he thought, *That's the idea, kid.*

The Short One was up now, waving the gun around like a second phallus. He jammed its stubby barrel against one of Aramburu's pulpy hematomas and gushed stupidly, "You think we're kidding? You think I won't do it, old man? You think I won't blow your fucking head off? I've used this, old man. Used it plenty."

And every time a blast of drunken fury from a moving car. *How is it now, college boy? How is it close up, looking into eyes ready and bored?*

"Where is she!"

Sigh. "I don't know." Ironically it was, after a fashion, the truth.

"You were president! You were in charge! You were president!"

President. Yes. Just for a moment a long moment ago. The carnival geek left with Perón's rubble piled to the moon and just a broom to sweep it up with. A couple of strokes with that broom and he was gone, another turn in the endless Casa Rosada revolving door. In that time he had never asked. Never wanted to know.

"No one knew." He hated the way his voice sounded. Sloppy and toothless. "She just disappeared. You don't know what it was like in those days."

"You expect us to believe that? Answer me!"

"I don't care what you believe, *Little Man*." A calculation and it almost worked. The Short One blanched and shook and stuck the quivering barrel in his eye. "You're dead, man! Dead!" But in the end he hesitated, the fury dropped, and he was just another fool too close to his mortality.

Aramburu concentrated and managed his absolutely last smile.

"Carlos. Martin. Get out." It was the Third One, speaking for the first time. The other two lingered, resistant, and the voice steadied with ice beyond its years. "Get out. *Now.*"

So they were alone, he and this calm, young voice that was clearly more than some collegiate firebrand. He rose now, medium height, and paced around Aramburu without hurry. This was no city boy, either. "Senor Presidente…" The voice was slippery gravel. His pace was unhurried and his feet, though clad in loafers, carried the unmistakable weight of a life in country boots. He crouched at Aramburu's eye level. "You know we must have Her. You know what She means to us."

His hair was reddish, his eyes full of the calm emptiness of a boy who was never a boy, living his existence now on the last mile of life. A scar ran from ear to ear on his neck. "And I believe you when you say you cannot tell us."

The young man walked back to the table, picked up the curved blade of a gaucho *facón*, and Aramburu smiled.

Argentina had never developed a myth of the heartland. Like its topsy-turvy place on the globe, this topsy-turvy culture invested all value in urban *Porteño* values. The countryside was a hostile, brutal place; its people, their gaucho cowboy tradition, despised.

Aramburu stared at the ruined young man before him, holding the symbol of his humiliated class, and now understood. It was not the urban spoiled but the pampas, Her pampas, that would rise against his *Porteño* universe to claim Her missing crown. And something untamed in Aramburu sucked deeply on that revelation.

"What is your name, young man?" Aramburu managed through a shattered face.

"Alejandro."

"Did you love Her?"

"Above all others."

"Such a love I have never known."

"I pity thee."

"And I admire thee."

The feeling was not unpleasant, like the stroke of a lover's fingernail, as Alejandro cut the former president's throat ear to ear.

# 16.

A memory:

The air was serrated that first night she came to him. So silent, his father never stirred. So dark, her Indian hair, Indian stillness, waiting over the boy's cot as a vision, willing him to wake, whispering, "Shh, Alejandro, it is your mother. Come with me."

As a boy does in dreams, he released his will to her, finding himself in trousers and country boots, gliding now in the tow of this raven image, away from his father's shack, past the corral where his father broke horses for the estancia, down the gravel path and into the sighing grass of the plain. When they were far from the village and the light on their skins was the frosty rippling of stars, this woman he had never before seen held his hands and knelt down to him, for he was only seven.

"It is a special night, Alejandro, when all the earth speaks."

Certainly it seemed talkative. A warm wind boxed his ears as it surged everywhere in kinetic waves. Grasses hissed in return, cutting snaking eddies around them. A massive ombu tree rose and creaked as deep within its rustling canopy a Chaco owl hooted, and the feeling was electrical dread in the boy's soul.

"Look to the grass, Alejandro. In its patterns you will find your future."

He tried as she said but it was so much, a thousand shimmering ropes roiling in fat, powerful curls to the horizon. At first they seemed as frightening tigers, nipping his ankles; then huge, snoozy beasts chasing one another's tails; finally messengers, conjurings of this woman, speaking in low, urgent tones. The boy could almost feel their fortunes reverberating up his legs— almost—and then they were just indifferent beasts once again, chasing their tails. The woman smiled. "It takes time, my son. There are words to help." She whispered three of them—strange, alien ones.

The owl hooted again, and Alejandro caught just the strobe of a burning eye as his mother whispered into his ear, "Some day, Alejandro, I will tell you of the owl."

Come dawn it was his father above his cot, and there was nothing ghostlike about him as he slammed logs onto the stove and drew water thudding into a kettle.

"Joining us today?" With a smile. The boy snuggled deeper into his blanket, exhausted.

"Come, Alejandro." Sterner now. The boy raised himself up, eyes leaden, as his father poked him playfully in the ribs. "*Mandinga* dance on your eyes?" *Mandinga* was the pampa devil: part Christian, all gaucho, a nighttime seducer whose favorite targets were lonely cross-country travelers and the dreams of children.

The boy smiled, and this pleased his father, who valued the boy's smiles highly. He dressed beside the stove, felt his skin prickle in the heat as he pulled off his bedclothes. The air filled with coffee and chorizo slobbering in a skillet. When his father turned his back, the boy spit on the hot surface of the stove. As he watched the globule hiss to and fro over heated pig iron, Alejandro foggily considered the previous night, thought of telling his father what he had seen, and decided finally with the razor shots of morning that it must have been just a dream, like the spit, noisy but evaporating quickly to nothing.

The day hit its stride as most—the boy's breath puffy white, the horse dung matted with straw, some with its own steamy breath. The workhorses knew him and tolerated the scrape of his shovel as he swept their stalls and picked out their hooves. The boy always brought a handful of spiced, rolled balls of lard. The horses disdained these but for two—his favorites—who lapped them up greedily and nuzzled for more. The boy patted their flanks, blew softly up their noses because they liked it, told them to be fair but firm with the cows and obey their masters.

His father was at the corral. This morning would be spent finishing the breaking in of a new horse for the estancia. His father dressed well for this work: loose *bombacha* trousers with a clean waist sash, pressed cotton shirt, red neckerchief tied at the throat, and rakish gray beret—a touch of the *paisano* blood that flowed through so many gauchos and gaucho tradition. His father was the unchallenged best at this work on the estancia and arguably the whole province, yet the boy could not help smiling at what an awkward, stumpy gait he cut, like a seal on shore, when away from his natural environment, which for his father was always atop a horse.

This one was a male, separated from the others for its spirit. His father had begun the process two weeks earlier, accustoming the prideful male first to a rubber bit and simple halter. While these represented assaults on the horse's freedom, they were largely symbolic. The true challenge to a horse's self-identity, the moment it would or would not accept the dominance of its master, came when a man climbed for the first time upon its back and whispered "*Go.*" Today was that moment.

His father motioned to the boy, and he scampered to the tack room, returning, puffing, with his father's leather saddle. Originally his grandfather's, it was hand sewn by a master in Mendoza and covered with fine, pinpoint stitching and decorative tassels. His grandfather had ordered that he be buried with it, but his grandfather was a son of a bitch and the boy's father—partly for its beauty, partly out of sheer defiance—had kept the saddle for himself.

The horse shifted, agitated by the sight of it.

His father stood beside its head now, soothed it with strokes and murmured patter. As another gaucho laid the saddle onto the horse's back, his father sunk his teeth into the yearling's ear.

Any man can, with enough snaps of a whip, force a horse's submission. And to do so is to be left with a creature compliant but dulled. And in perhaps many places, even most, that is fine.

But not the pampas. Here, on these edgeless tracts of land, where a gaucho can be days from humanity—where the land conspires to confuse, humiliate, and finally consume him—a horse is not a servant but a partner, its intelligence, its spirit, its *will* vital components in keeping rider and mount alive. A true gaucho's steed was ridden because it chose to be. Led because it trusted— even loved—its master.

The boy's father held the horse's ear in his teeth as the second gaucho cinched down the saddle, then released it as the boy tugged tight on the leads, and for just a beat the horse's eyes found his, losing fast their dreamy surprise. Becoming wary.

And his father was on its back.

The boy threw him the reins, and they all gave man and horse distance.

The male was winding up now, trying to make its decision. The boy climbed onto the corral's railing, watched as his father sat rigid and straight. Uncompromising.

The horse lowered its head to the ground, testing if man and leather would slide off. They didn't.

So the horse bucked.

His father carried neither whip nor spurs. There would be no punishment. He would confront this horse with only stamina and certainty.

The horse decided to test his father on both accounts.

It jerked wildly now, staccato blasts of rippling muscle. His father held firm, a force of nature the yearling shook furiously at.

The boy felt pride surge in his gut, then fear for his father as the horse swung to crush him against the corral gate, and the man never flinched, only tugged slowly on the reins till the horse backed away from the fence.

The defiance continued across the corral, but soon the horse tired, the shakes and hops became for show only; then it stopped, panted, and accepted.

His father waited, let the horse feel, in its calm, the power of the man's simple determination. He climbed down and fed it an apple from his pocket, whispered that they were partners now, patted the horse's sweaty flanks once, and walked over to the boy, basking in the heat of his son's affection.

"A fine horse," he nodded, lighting a rolled cigarette. He said that about every horse he tamed. "To break a horse, Alejandro, to shape its spirit, you must tame not with blood but respect. You will find that true, my son, with most things in life."

The next morning was always the boy's favorite: a short overnight trip into the estancia's vast interior to track a cut of the herd and accustom the new horse to its responsibilities. Just his father and he, the boy riding a small criollo he shared with another youth.

After a morning's journeying, they stopped under a solitary ombu for the noon meal: bread, cheese, a thick steak—carried between saddle and horse, where the animal's sweat kept it supple—that his father lovingly grilled over a coal fire. They hadn't spotted the herd yet, but the horse had done well, and his father favored it with extra oats.

"Which direction is the ranch house, son?"

The boy grinned at the challenge and shot a glance at the sun, traced its arc back to the morning horizon, oriented himself two paces west, and pointed. "There."

"And the direction of the cattle?"

The boy studied the trammeled grass and the hoofprints embedded through it. The herd had lingered about the ombu, much like his father and he, then clearly moved south, southwest. The boy pointed.

"A very good guess. But you must remember to be sure of a track's age. Here, feel the edges of each hoofprint. Hard. Baked by the sun for at least four days. And look for the dung heaps. There are none. The birds and beetles have already torn them apart. You are right that the herd was here, and they left in that direction. But they left a week or more ago, and so may not even be the herd we're tracking.

"Time is measured differently out here, Alejandro. Tracks, animals, people. They all fade slower in this place, and so you must be wary of being led astray by ghosts. For nothing disappears here, my son. It dries and bakes and remains. Forever. These tracks are ghosts."

The boy nodded seriously, and his father squeezed his shoulder. "You'll be a *rastreador* yet. You have the look and you have the perception. I think you perceive many things, Alejandro."

Such was his father's world: a practical place full of practical rules and practical heroes. A true *rastreador*, or pampa tracker, was highly prized by his fellow gauchos: a man, in a place devoid of landmarks, who could read the subtleties of earth unchanging and orient himself unfailingly. He could track cattle across twenty thousand square leagues of pampa or find the nearest water by chewing blades of grass. If an estancia produced a single *rastreador* a generation, it was considered fortunate. They were mostly Indians when the gauchos first arrived in this place. But the Indian culture was gone now. Trammeled and dried like the hoofprints and dung heaps.

When the meal was finished, his father brewed *mate*. They drank through perforated metal straws and settled on a blanket for a siesta.

When the father woke, his son wasn't beside him. He rose, walked stiff-legged toward where he saw the boy, nearly a mile off, crouched among blades of tawny grass heaving with breeze. The boy had his back to his father and didn't seem to hear him approach. Clearly he was trying to read the land, and his father smiled proudly, for the boy had located the first stragglers of the herd, far on the horizon. So young, yet so clearly perceptive. A true *rastreador*. He was about to step forward, clasp his son's shoulders, and congratulate him...

When he heard the boy mumbling.

The same three foreign words over and over. And his father recognized the words, saw that his son was not studying the cattle but the sea of grass itself, listening to it, and something caught in the man's chest.

"Alejandro!"

The boy spun around as if caught.

"What are you doing?"

"I...I was looking for the cattle."

"Come here."

The boy rose to his feet, anxious without knowing why.

"What do those words mean, Alejandro?"

"It's for reading"—he felt the withering stare of his father—"the future?"

His father's face erupted, and it frightened the boy. "*Where did you learn this!*" The boy shrunk back with a stammer, and his father felt instantly ashamed. He reached for him, stroked his reddish hair.

"They may seem just words, my son, but they are pagan and not Christian. Do you understand?" The child nodded. "There's a good boy." His father produced a taffy the boy gleefully devoured. They returned to the horses. The boy's tongue relaxed with the joy of the taffy and spoke before he had regained control of it.

"Father, where's my mother?"

His father stiffened, and the boy saw a brief shadow cross his face.

"You know your mother's dead."

They caught up with the main herd that afternoon, flicking tails under a cloud of flies punch-drunk with the day's heat. They drove the cattle a few miles east, his father feeling awkward and the boy guilty without understanding.

At dusk they camped, dropping their gear haphazardly, for all the land was the same here, and ate *puchero* under powerful stars. His father anchored the horses with a cow bone, like ships on an unprotected sea, said a few empty words about constellations, and together they fell into troubled sleep.

It was like the night itself stroking his brow, easing itself into his mind and waking him slowly. When his eyes finally opened and groped for purchase on the eternity all around him, they found not the night but his mother, stroking his brow.

"Alejandro."

He stiffened in terror, his child mind gridlocking on the half-conscious impossibility of it. She reached for his hand, and his only protest was a small whine that must have touched some portion of his father's nightmare, for he stirred and dug his teeth into his lip.

Into the open she took him. Not far, for the open was everywhere here. The woman stopped and the boy waited, head down, fearful.

"What is it, Alejandro?"

"Are you really my mother?"

"Yes, Alejandro. I am."

"Then are you dead?"

The boy was prepared for anything but the shivering, miserable tears that coursed down her face. She sank to her knees, and the cry was hopeless and inhuman, and the boy, against all his expectations, took the woman into his small arms and held her, feeling a hole in him open and fill at the same moment.

"Mommy…"

And she jerked him away at the ends of her arms, so suddenly his head lolled. Her eyes were at once flat fierceness, and the boy crashed back to here, now, and he was scared.

"A boy should not live without his mother," she droned metallically. "A boy cannot live without his mother…"

She released him and was already far away in a place deep inside herself.

When an owl hooted it split the night hideously. The boy's guts spun and he couldn't stand.

"Tell me…about the owl…"

She turned quizzically at the boy, as if noticing him for the first time, and her voice was lifeless.

"The call of the owl means death."

His father found him there before dawn, curled in the dirt, weeping. He gathered the boy up, carried him in his arms on horseback all the way to their shack, whispering over and over into his son's feverish, pallid face, "It was just a dream, Alejandro. Just a dream…"

He stayed in bed the next day, let his father fuss over him with a fearful caution that put wariness at the edges of the boy's thoughts.

By dusk he felt better, restless, and joined his father for a barbecue with the other families and a group of traveling gauchos from another estancia. The laughter, the sharp cackle of the bonfire, felt distant to him, as if experienced through cotton, and he sat apart as men roared with drink, children scrabbled a game of *taba* in clotted earth, and women fussed over a steer slaughtered freely from the estancia, an ancient privilege.

When the iron plates had been cleared and laid in greasy stacks, the community settled themselves on cow skulls around the fire for the *payada*. As with the *rastreador*, each ranch produced a true *payador*, a minstrel, once a generation. That a distant estancia had also produced one, that both were here tonight, sent excitement through the small crowd, for of course there would be a contest.

Each gaucho considered himself a poet, and such qualities were highly prized and severely judged in others, making such a contest a rough, dangerous event. *Payadas* always produced a winner, but if dragged out too long could just as easily end up being decided by knives as words.

The local village champion was Agosto, ancient and red-faced, with a high-parted snow-white mane. He rose now, dressed extravagantly in maroon trousers and satin sash, and unslung his four-string *viguela*. Tradition demanded a gesture of hospitality, and Agosto called out to his opponent a greeting in verse, welcoming him to their fertile land. The visiting combatant, a hatchet-faced stranger, replied with exaggerated politeness, thanking his host.

With the formalities dispensed with, the true contest began. The format was relaxed but generally involved one contestant calling out a question in verse to his opponent, the latter being judged on the speed and wit of his reply. The opening musical query was Agosto's:

*Someone who brags of his valor*
*Yet in danger backs away*
*Is like a paltry poncho*
*Little wool and lots of fringe*

To which the stranger replied immediately:

*No one with the scabbard only*
*Can back down a good gaucho*
*A lasso with such conceit*
*Will not bring down the cattle*

There were hoots of approval from the village. Though Agosto was the local boy, he carried no special favor in such a contest.

The taunts between *payadores* escalated and followed the tradition of hurling sharpened maxims of The Life at one another:

—*One who ignores omens found in bleached bones shows fool's courage.*
—*The wider the wound, the prouder lies the dead man.*
—*He who laughs last, lives.*

The contest continued over an hour with no clear advantage gained.

When at last the crowd grew exhausted of the deadlock, the contest shifted to the next movement. More gnarled logs were laid on the fire, flames jumped and caught careless moths, and the two men each began their ballads. Sung in formal verse, like a Greek epic, they drew on themes close to their audience: the land, the people, their ways.

Agosto followed classic lines and told the well-worn story of the Montoneros, gaucho guerrillas who fought the independence wars against Spain in the last century. It regaled the bravery of great-grandfathers, the character of the men themselves—melancholy, like the ballad itself.

*Nothing in life endures*
*The good and the bad do die*
*Only a sad and lonely grave*
*Will cover us all impartially.*

That never failed to draw tears from his unabashedly senti-
mental audience, and Agosto hung on to it for all it was worth,
stinging his chords, raising his voice from sadness to declaration,
to howl of pride. The acclaim was unanimous when Agosto finished and bowed humbly. Even the earth roared approval, as a
rolling gust caught the trees and hissed accordance.

But the contest wasn't finished and now the stranger, dressed
in layers of black that accented the spectral narrowness of his
frame, rose. From the first distant notes, his audience recognized
his subject as the dark side of The Life—his invocation of the
night, of *mandinga*—and his true subject, the *amborgana*, Indian
witch.

> *With you, your dog, and my horse*
> *We will ride the* pampa
> *There to brew bitter* mate
> *And wait for amborgana*

The *amborgana* was evil, a caster of curses, and came in many
seductive forms. As the ballad described the Indian witch's feral
beauty and dark sexual power, the stranger's voice warbled and
spellbound the crowd. Even the wind seemed to pause and settle
among them, rapt, as the ballad told of how this witch, a shadow
off the pampas, came to the village and there seduced a local gaucho.

The boy looked at his father, suddenly tense. The audience
had become stock still.

> *She bore only a son*
> *But was no mother*
> *Not even human*
> *An enchantress.*

The story burbled luridly in recounting her power over the simple gaucho, her liaisons, spells, and all manner of composting evil. When the good villagers in the poem finally turned against her, as they must, the stranger's voice took on urgency.

*And the village rose and lay naked the witch*
*And drove her into the wine dark night*
*Beyond the edge of the world*
*Forever banished*

*But still, when the southern winds blow*
*Her name carries in the dreams*
*Of gauchos tortured by* mandinga
*Isiola.*
*The witch.*

So fast—a blur—the boy's father shot forward and tackled the *payador* to the ground. A haunting moan escaped the *payador*'s lungs as Alejandro's father pummeled the stranger with fists, and at once the boy understood it all and fled, terrorized, into darkness, crashing into gates, crawling now, feverish, finding only by accident the door of their shack.

There, the boy sank into his cot, let the claw of delirium reach darkly for him…

And felt the breath of his mother.

"Alejandro," she wept.

He didn't move. Couldn't.

"Your name is Isiola…your name is Isiola…"

"Yes, my son."

"You're a witch."

"I am a mother. And I am a ghost." Her face, wet and hot with tears, stung close. "A boy should not live without his mother. And he cannot live with a ghost. Do you understand?"

Her breath was so steady.

"Do you understand?"

"Yes," he choked.

His mother then lifted his chin gently, kissed him once on the lips…

And cut the boy's throat ear to ear.

They caught her a mile from town, stoned her as she uttered a curse of destruction on them all, and buried her where she fell. According to *amborgana* custom, her head was cut off, laid on a termite hill, and she was never spoken of again.

◎    ◎    ◎

He'd lain there two days, wandered the fence between this world and not.

There was no doctor in the village, only an old woman with cotton yarn who stitched his cut throat together with darning needles. Fever descended immediately. The wound swelled, broke a stitch, and oozed muddy pus onto his chest.

He would either die or he would not. But he lived. Lay another fifteen days and rose scarred and unsure if he was nearly dead or the dead nearly living. His limbs had gone cold, and that never changed.

The boy tried to speak, and the sound was tomb gravel. So he spoke little. He didn't ask about his mother, but his father felt the need to say something. The words were vague, self-hating, and the boy absorbed none of it. He had, in his own mind, come to an understanding. His mother had been a ghost, brought the owl as a messenger of his own death and, on leaving, had left him a ghost as well. From the children who had come to gape at the damage, he learned of his mother's final curse laid on the village as revenge.

It was short in realization.

Before the change of seasons, as his mother's head dried and blew away, the cattle began to weaken. Struck as if by plague, they slobbered, bled from ears and anuses, and died in fantastic numbers. Whole herds bloated and putrefied in the sun, legs sticking out cartoonishly. The gauchos tried to keep the cattle moving, as if the curse was something that could be outrun. They tried herbs, faith healers, even priests, and still the cattle stumbled, bled, and died.

When the state biologists finally roared through, exhausted by the enormity of what was sweeping the land, they mumbled only one suggestion, before skidding off to the next devastated estancia: burn them.

And so the cattle were heaped into great medieval bonfires, lighting the edgeless land with a thousand burning hillocks. And the gauchos stood by holding their torches, scarves over their mouths against searing flesh, and as one their eyes fell on the boy and his father. For while the desperate biologists had a word for this, *encephalomyelitis,* the village knew it was the witch's curse. And it was the boy and his father that had brought the witch among them.

On those nights, with an entire nation's identity vaporizing in a million funeral pyres, Alejandro would walk away from the hellish islands of flame into dark grass and there, alone with the wind, would seek his future. The grass spoke to him those horrible nights, but the language was not yet clear. And Alejandro vowed, even as his universe was soaked with gasoline and set alight, that he would listen until the grass revealed itself to him in cadences he could understand.

By month's end, a third of Argentina's cattle had been heaped and burned. By midsummer the estancia was ruined, the village abandoned, the boy and father riding slowly down the path through faces hot with damnation, out of the village, forever. They settled in Córdoba, now just two more of the scores of suddenly rootless, confused gauchos, limping in pitifully on proud horses, begging for work in mills and assembly lines.

His father found a job in the canning factory; the boy scrounged aluminum scraps. They slept outside the town, on a dirty strip that ran south of the river. There were stars here, but his father spoke little of them. The boy, whose voice still carried the rattle of the grave, spoke less and less, till he rarely spoke at all.

Come morning they would stake the horses along the riverbank and cross the bridge to the city. The boy would hunt for his scraps along the slag heaps of the factories, dragging them in burlap sacks to the one-eyed tallyman, who'd exchange them for a small lump of copper coins.

Come lunch he'd be with his father, watching the leathery hands tear themselves on aluminum rims, watching the proud gaucho stance that on the assembly line looked only stumpy and foolish. Come lunch the boy watched his father die a little.

There were rumors of gaucho jobs on far-flung estancias, and the rumors were always false. What few herds escaped the catastrophe were herded jealously in pens to protect them from the rampaging microbe. The cattle no longer roamed free and, as simple as that, the gaucho's life ended.

It had been the hope of returning to the pampa that held his father together, and when that hope crumbled, so did the man.

Gin, then cards, then a cheap particleboard casket after a dispute over gin and cards. They didn't cut his throat, like on the pampas, just shot him twice in the chest, like in the city. The thin casket, still bearing a sawmill's pencil markings, was lowered into a pauper's pit among the slag heaps where Alejandro hunted for scraps. The local priest said some things but never got the name right. Before his service even ended, the small wooden cross tumbled in the wind. The boy righted it, stood there silent, and thought, *Now I am an orphaned ghost.*

The next day they took him to the orphanage.

Listen:

The tiny slap of kerosene on parquet floors. Alejandro's head pounds with the reek of it but he continues pouring through the house, a large house, and the wafts are overpowering.

The mansion belongs to the chairwoman of the Sociedad de Beneficencia, an ancient creature whose precious metal clanks like a Persian queen. The Sociedad benefits orphanages, and this orphan has been sent to the chairwoman's mansion because he refuses to speak.

For a month now he has scrubbed her floors, washed her dishes, all tasks not unusual for the Sociedad's charges, but Alejandro has also stood each night on her carpet and been slapped when he won't speak, and Alejandro never speaks.

Tonight, after her ritual slapping of the boy, the chairwoman leaned down to Alejandro's ear and hissed two words: *Witch child*...And the boy understood that one of them would have to die.

Stirrings above. Alejandro runs for the front door. He can hear the shuffle of slippers on the steps as the great oaken door swings open on fearsome hinges.

"Who is it?" The voice gripped with sleep. "What is this smell?"

The boy draws the match from his coat, strikes, but too hard, and the head snaps off. He fishes for another, drops it, and his reservoir of courage vanishes as the old woman in a dressing gown comes to him in the dark, carrying an unlit candle.

"You there. Who are you?"

And the boy is going to answer when the chairwoman says softly, "Alejandro?"—and strikes her own match to the candle.

The boy remembers the woman's face going bright, then warm nothing as he was blown across the street.

He woke in miniature and thought himself dead. The bed conformed to his nine-year-old body. Through his blurry, damaged vision the walls seemed heaven blue with a short doorway through which tall, indistinct figures in white stooped to enter. He thought they must be angels.

The angels spoke in soft whispers, and there seemed something hidden and bright at their center they were both protective of and deferential to. When they leaned over him, their faces disappeared in streaking ceiling lights and he thought, *I am being judged for what I have done.* With a voice that had but a single burst left, he spoke: "Please don't send me to hell."

The faceless heads in white parted and revealed at their center the tall, slender source of their heat and light. It was wondrous and beautiful and Alejandro thought, *God is a woman with blonde hair.*

God leaned close to his bandaged face and whispered, "You are safe with me, my son, and I will never let you go to hell."

*Shh.*

I'm scared.

*Don't be.*

I can't see.

*You were hurt in a fire, my child. It is temporary and it will pass.*

Can you please hold my hand?

*It is my honor, Alejandro.*

I saw you in heaven.

*You were tired and there were many drugs for your recovery.*
I love you.
*I love you too, my child.*
I looked in the grass for my future, but all I saw was fire.
*Fire is what purifies us.*
Don't ever leave me.
*I am here for all the sons and daughters of my nation, Alejandro, and I will never leave any of you.*

The pain subsided, the blindness lifted, but the memory of Her stood fixed absolute in the boy. An angel's touch, a mother's voice. There were gifts and flowers left for him, for all the children in the ward, each inscribed, *With all my love, Evita.*

Her portrait hung on the walls with a prominence and regularity usually reserved for the Virgin. Each child woke to it, went to bed with it, and like Alejandro, prayed to it. For this was Her hospital, built from CGT funds, constructed, as was Her whim, on a child's scale. There were doctors and nurses, all in the uniform of the Eva Perón Foundation.

The staff spoke daily to the boy, tried to coax friendly words from him, but he needed only the portrait on the wall and nothing else existed for him.

While he waited.

A week turned into two. They asked who he was, how he had come to them. They told him it would be time to leave soon. He didn't acknowledge their words.

Then one day he felt the light without seeing it.

From the door. At the very center of their pointless gaggle, shielded by it.

It was Her.

He hardly reacted, so certain was he Evita would come, morning light kindling blonde hair alive and more than woman.

She gazed down at the scars of old darning stitches on his neck.

"My doctors tell me you do not speak, that you will not leave the hospital."

"I love you."

"And I you, my son. But you are well and should be with other children, where you can play and learn."

"I waited for you."

She touched his forehead. "I am here, Alejandro."

"I don't ever want to leave you again."

She stroked his brow and said quietly, "You have suffered much my child, haven't you?"

He wouldn't cry, and She loved him for that.

"Clerk." Her voice flat and aimed at a colorless suit.

"Yes, Mrs. Perón."

"Where is this boy scheduled to be sent?"

Flipping pages. "Accordia Orphanage, Senora."

"I want him given a family instead. A real mother and father in a real town far from the corruption of this city."

"It is done, Senora."

She crouched down to the boy, took his hand. "You and I are joined in our hearts, my son. Though we will be apart, always will our thoughts be together. Do you believe that?"

"Yes."

"My little *soldado*. When you are older, you will come back and be part of my foundation. You and all the children of our nation will work together to change the world. Can you hold this faith over the coming years?"

"Yes."

"And so it is done."

She released his hand, nodded to the clerk, and was gone.

On the fourth day after Evita died, his stepparents dragged the young Alejandro back into the house. He fought but he was weak and half frozen and his knees bled from nights spent kneeling in the howling open. His stepparents considered destroying the shrine—it unnerved them—but they hesitated, frightened by the boy's devotion, frightened in some measure by the shadow of Her.

That shadow was long and heavy the week after Her death. This had been one of Her towns, the kind of humiliated, wind-blown place that fueled Her climb to greatness. There had been passionate speeches by the mayor, collections taken from people who had nothing to send flowers to a woman dead, all the while the gnawing, numbing feeling filling them that their time, the time of places like this, had suddenly passed. The gait of the town stuttered, conversations failed midsentence, and a ten-year-old boy built a small shrine he prayed to day and night, without food, without care for himself, until his stepparents dragged him, near-dead, into warmth.

He was forbidden to pray to it, but the shrine never came down and with time became a kind of town relic. This tiny pile of stones, a blonde-haired doll, the runny heaps of altar candles. Watched, tended, prayed to secretly at night on bare knees, all by the boy.

The stepparents Evita's foundation had sent him to ran the only gas pump in the village, servicing the infrequent traffic of cargo trucks and slick urbanites weekending at the nearby estancia. The boy did his work, rarely spoke, spent entire days sitting on a stool staring into space, thinking…

Of Her.

And the faraway pressure of something building inside.

Though he lived once again on the pampas, he rode no horse, listened to no *payador* under bright moon. That life, the life of a *rastreador*, was gone. He lived a life away now, an orphan pumping gas and wandering the open tracts outside town in undeveloped thought.

She was slow and didn't go to the parish school. She was young, a child still, liked his reddish hair, and didn't mind the puffy scar that ran ear to ear on his neck. For a month they'd find a clear piece of ground near the river, just sit, say little or nothing. Sometimes he'd try to express a fragment of his relationship to Evita; she'd never understand, would push his shoulder in tease, laugh a dull, retarded honk. He'd stop, sulk, draw stickmen in the dust, put the sudden blossom of emotion into kissing her or touching her flat, pubescent chest.

After Her death he followed closely the march of the Senora's ideas through her husband, Juan Perón. Alejandro's focus now rested on this man, once so unimportant to him, now the nation's vessel of Her word. He read of the rising protests against their political vision, felt dead fury when the oligarchy called Her, in braver and braver tones, just another whore.

"Nobody likes you."

"I know."

"They think you're scary."

"I think they're nothing."

"I don't mind your neck, y'know. I don't mind it…"

A year after Evita's last ride to the CGT, the oligarchy rose and banished Her husband. Her word, Her philosophy, Alejandro's future were in a moment declared nothing, null, finished.

And the throbbing began behind his eye.

The slow girl's father was a brutish drunk, and Alejandro gave him a wide berth, sitting with his daughter at the river, listening to her hum, feeling the throb in his head grow. He turned thirteen, worked in the store, pumped gas for the passing oligarchy and Yankee lackeys. Each night he read again Her autobiography; each day he spent his meager coins on more candles for Her shrine. A boy called Her a name one day and Alejandro broke both his arms. They expelled him from the parish school. His stepfather tried only once to demand an answer to his stepson's behavior but backed down, terrified of the silent eyes. Without school Alejandro spent more hours wandering alone the pampa grass and its snaking eddies, listening for his future.

And one day the future spoke to him.

In words he could at last understand. So he crouched, listened, even as a grass fire on the horizon came closer and closer, even as the smoke and ash stung his face; listened even as the flames rolled over him, and when they had passed he was unburned, and the words of the grass were clear: "You are the immortal protector of Her word, Alejandro. And your meter is fire."

Afterward he brought the slow girl to the shrine and told her he felt his old life dissolving, felt himself blossoming into something beautiful.

"Blossoming into what?" she asked.

"Her word."

And the girl didn't answer, because she didn't understand. But its import warmed her, and she drew him close when he reached out, didn't resist when he pulled her down into dust flickering with the candles of Her shrine.

It couldn't happen, because she was too young, the pain too great, and she was crying, clutching her dress, running away down the road.

He lay there in the dirt, bathed in candle and starlight, and as the girl's footsteps faded, he thought of his mother: headless and corrupted and haunting.

The slow girl was brought to her father, the damage shown, and the father beat his daughter. This brought him no satisfaction and he went to the boy, still lying beneath the shrine, and attacked him savagely, would have killed him, but the boy crawled away to the river. There, heaving shallow breaths, Alejandro washed the hot pain of his body and noticed: the pressure in his head had stopped.

He found the girl's father sitting near his hearth, drinking from a *mate* gourd. The man didn't look up and possibly never recognized Alejandro before the boy killed him with his stepfather's shotgun. He dragged the gun on the floor to the door and was hit by the slow girl—half mad, clawing him savagely, screaming and biting—and he pushed the girl to the ground, reloaded the gun, and shot her too.

The lights were out in his stepparents' home, a *mandinga* wind gritty in his hair. He dropped the gun, hot and spattered. There was nothing left but to leave, and so he did—into darkness, the pampas, into Her.

He had no idea how long he walked.

The sun swelled his lips and blistered his scalp. Rain split his shoes and rent his shirt. He sucked water from muddy holes, cut the throats of dull cattle and ate their tongues. He passed through lightning storms, locust clouds; felt his clothes rot and peel away. Felt himself transformed into something more than dead.

Two months later he entered Buenos Aires the immortal protector of Her word.

**August 15, 1971**

# 17.

They'd refused to come closer than two blocks, Juan and Emilio, his worthless party hacks. The guards at the door had spooked them and they held back, holding a car ready. So be it. Alejandro went on alone, climbing into the building from the opposite roof. The guards were simple militia, not the more effective death squad paramilitaries, with their dark sunglasses and dark-green Ford Falcons. *Was there any sight closer to the rim of hell*, thought Alejandro, *than a pair of Latinos in a dark-green Ford?*

The roof door was brittle with exposed hinges. The room beyond was large, a records-storage area stacked floor to ceiling with files. He moved swiftly through the carefully labeled boxes, mundane catalogs of tyranny. If there was one thing the generals of Argentina had inherited from the Nazis, apart from their war criminals, it was an obsession with documenting in exacting detail the most pedestrian of police horrors. Everything organized and alphabetized and ready for quick burning on flash paper should the merry-go-round suddenly come to a stop.

Choose your secrets well and they will stay buried. But make everything a secret and it's like burying the ocean: it's going to leak.

Alejandro walked past 1971 and 1970, the latest years, sagging with thousands of smiling young men dismembered and disappeared. His own file was there, luscious with broken bones, electrified genitals, transcripts of him howling in the dark for anybody, even his torturers, to keep him company.

The years ticked back, a secret policeman's view of history, wide rows of shelves in the seasons of coups and paranoia, smaller ones in times of distraction and order. They swelled and shrank, each in passing, till he arrived at the particularly thick years of the mid-1950s.

It would not announce itself, this secret. Even the president of the time had not wanted to share in its ugliness. Alejandro remembered the president with fondness: a man, even in death, who understood things as they were. A skill rare enough in this world, rarer still in this city. No, this secret was like the buried ocean: you had to look for the leaks.

Alejandro plied through Casa Rosada memos. The dull work of dull, savage men. Alejandro's efforts, his obsession, was supposedly the charter obsession of all neo-Peronist Montoneros. But theirs had become a commitment thin as a peso coin. With rumors of the government considering negotiations to bring Juan Perón back from exile to stop the country's descent into civil war, many considered the battle essentially won. They were fools. Perón was never the heart of the movement. An old man now, he would easily be manipulated by the ruling junta. This was never about him. It was always about Her. She was the soul of the revolution. If Her body were allowed to be returned under this government's control, even with Perón, it would inevitably become *their* tool. That's why it was absolutely necessary they find Her first and bring her back under Montonero control. Why couldn't these middle-class clowns understand that?

The memo names flitted past, mostly dead now, some in exile, one in retirement, one foreign—an American.

The American.

They'd clearly burned his main file a long time ago, but the ocean is deep and the name dripped constantly on tiny invoices, surveillance chits, patrolmen's musings. The beads of water drew together, began to form a picture…

Footsteps.

Alejandro slunk against the cool metal racks, waited to hear if their cadence was lazy and militia. The pair of footsteps cleared the stairwell and halted several yards away. He had a Walther P88 in his waistband, but to use it now would be to bring down an army.

A radio gagged. "*Suspect is believed in building. Armed and dangerous. Wait for backup...*"

So the army was already coming down.

He pulled the gun from his back and stepped out. The shock of seeing him toppled one backward onto his ass. The second jerked spastically at his gun belt, probably for the first time. Militia. When nothing but Alejandro's stare struck their bodies, the two militiamen—gulping wrecks—backed away and fled.

Sirens outside now on pretty dark-green Fords. These guns would certainly come out of their charcoal blazers more skillfully.

From his own leather coat Alejandro removed two cap-fused tubes of jellied gasoline. The first he laid on the stairwell, played out its fuse and lingered, waiting for dark-green footsteps. Arrogant on new heels, they didn't disappoint. Alejandro let them draw nearer, lit the fuse, and walked calmly back onto the floor as a hot concussion blew down the stairwell and licked out along the ceiling. There were one or two screams, and a great deal of footsteps headed the other way, now distinctly without arrogance.

More footsteps, coming through the roof door now. Alejandro lit the second tube, winged it over the stacks, and there was a blossoming *whump* of thick gasoline droplets pelting the room. The footsteps fanned out, separated, and Alejandro withdrew into darkness.

The fire moved with animal speed, kicking out over 1971 and 1969. Footsteps continued their search but grew cautious, now fearful, now slower still.

And Alejandro waited.

Waited as rising heat stiffened hairs on his arm and stung his eyes. Waited, because he knew he could always wait longer than they.

The fire's voice grew from taunt to bully, and the building offered its first groan of protest. Alejandro couldn't hear the footsteps anymore but knew they were in full, terrified retreat. Still he waited, as his skin cracked and ears blistered, and watched the fire stumble and close around him.

Then he ran. Through its maw and the fire was surprised and made way, tapping just enough to ignite his hair. He bashed through the consuming stacks, took a fistful from the year 1956, felt his melting hair fall in dollops, and went for the roof.

Out across the top where the smoke rolled in iron waves. He could hear shots buzz past as the roof tar began to bubble, and it was hard to get speed as he moved, faster and faster, for the edge, pushing off the granite lintel, falling through air, over the narrow alley, and onto the roof of the building opposite. His hair snuffed out, and his legs rose raggedly, drawing themselves to a ladder, off the building to the street.

His two party hacks were gone.

◎   ◎   ◎

They startled when he entered the safe house. When his party hacks finally recognized the face beneath the destruction, the stupid gaggling began.

"We waited…I swear, man, we waited as long as we could…" The fat one, Juan.

The short one, Emilio, now: "He's right. Shit, the terror cops were everywhere, cutting off the streets. We thought you were dead, man, dead for sure…Goddamn, you need a doctor…We'll get you a doctor…"

Their words bounced off him. Alejandro lowered himself into a chair. Pieces of skin, colored and stiff, dropped in to his lap. *I am a mess*, he thought. *Soon, this is going to hurt.*

In no particular hurry he cut off their jabbering. "Where did you park the car?" He was surprised how a voice could sound so...burnt.

"Don't talk, man, just relax. We'll get a doctor..." He was, just by living, scaring the shit out of them.

"The *car.*"

"On the boulevard. Where we'd be sure to see you. We were there. I swear, we waited as long as we could. We've always backed you up. You know that. That time with the president, with this..."

Parked on the boulevard. Two guys sitting in a car on the busiest street in town, pointed straight at the building. Waiting nervously and not bothering to look like anything but two college terrorists waiting nervously. Anyone who saw them—that is, half of rush hour—would've been blind not to report it.

"I see." His mind was starting to fog. He could let it go of course, but honestly, he was just so tired of their voices.

He shot the fat one in the neck, and the kid registered nothing as he dropped to the floor. The short one blanched, backed up to a chair, and collapsed fearfully into it, an obedient schoolboy once again. He started to moan something, and Alejandro opened a hole in his chest that kicked out plaster in the wall behind.

Academically, he considered that this probably ended his affiliation with the local Montoneros.

◎  ◎  ◎

He spent two nights in Palermo Park, under the abandoned carousel, letting his mind draw together beads of ocean from a fistful of singed 1956–1957 files. He took time. Time for the blisters on his face to calm. Time to absorb the words of the files. The words between words.

Michael Suslov, a mediocre suit at the American embassy during the 1950s—skipped across those words lightly. Alejandro would have passed over him completely but for two facts: this colorless ghost of a man seemed to have a gift for being in the orbit of people like Hector Cabanillas, Pedro Ara, Moori Koenig, etc., all of whom had, in some way, rumored involvement with the theft and concealment of Her.

And Michael Suslov had shot his wife.

The act was so completely without motive, the situation so confused and out of character for the man—this and the fact that it happened almost immediately after Her final disappearance was suggestive, only made more so by a passing reference in a BA police memo that while Michael had sat dazed on the kitchen floor, splashed with his wife's and unborn child's blood, someone had searched his house. Searched it for what?

Maybe this embassy ghost wasn't so colorless after all? Was it possible he had somehow come into possession of Her in the fall of 1956? And if so, would Michael Suslov, fifteen years later, have any knowledge of where She was now? Alejandro had no answers to this, but if the American who shot his wife was still alive somewhere, there, under the old carousel, Alejandro vowed that he and Suslov would have a small conversation about it.

His Montonero friends must have figured him for the north road out of town, for there they waited for him. But his friends were slow, and deep down, he knew, wanted to ask him *why* first.

The leading one he killed simply because he chose to fire first, and that was always the most important thing. The second fled behind a wall as Alejandro faded into shadow. He waited. Felt the anxiety of the other. Waited for the man to fidget, feel the darkness turn enemy, make a mistake.

It came quickly. A break left for the light—a *Porteño* thing to do—when a break right, into darkness—a gaucho thing to do—might have saved him.

The *crack*, echoing off cobblestone, pierced his thigh and he tumbled hard. Alejandro lined up again, then paused, for he recognized the face. Corada, the guerrilla unit's accountant and document forger. Corada's gun had skittered clear, and Alejandro approached leisurely. If the leg shot had frightened the accountant, the sight of Alejandro's face terrified him.

"Oh sweet mother of God…"

Alejandro stood above him. "Corada."

Corada's face crinkled at the voice. "Jesus…Alejandro? I…I didn't mean…it wasn't…" The words stacked up, collided with one another. Alejandro knelt down, drew his *facón* blade and danced it across Corada's neck.

"Do you want to live?"

"…What?"

"Do you want to live?"

"Yeah…yeah…"

Alejandro tapped the blade lightly over the accountant's throat. "I need the address of a certain American. Then I will need a passport, money, and a plane ticket."

The accountant gulped once. "Sure. Sure, Al." He drew his hand to his face and studied the blood. "Christ…you blew half my leg away…" Corada gritted his teeth. "This is for Her, isn't it?"

"It's for the revolution."

"It was always for Her with you, Al." He swallowed. "It was always for Her…"

# HER

# August 22, 1971

# 18.

Sometimes she came in dreams. Young, familiar, forgiving. On bad days she materialized on corrugated waves of desert heat. On those afternoons Michael would stop taking amphetamines.

When he got up for work, the sun hadn't. When he came home it was already a memory behind mountain rims. In between he labored in the mine's darkness, waste water soaking him to the thigh.

Nobody spoke on the bucket ride up. There was a time when this had been a cowboy job—chasing fat, gleaming veins of gold, like drowsy buffalo—a time when you could hold a fortune in one hand. Now you crushed ten million tons of anonymous ore a day, and nothing passed through your hands but your life.

On the surface it was as dark as below, and the transition was a simple one. Nobody got a beer; nobody wanted to talk about it. They just drifted, undead, for home.

He caught a ride the rocky dozen miles to the weak, sodium glow of Beatty. Michael didn't own a car. Didn't see the point of ever leaving this place. He tried to remember the driver's name but couldn't. He didn't know any of their names.

Beatty. The other towns of this desolation zone had folded and died a half century ago when the ore turned against them. But Beatty, the coffin maker, endured, limping through the years an eviscerated truck stop. Then gold was pronounced once more worth the effort to remove it, and again Beatty went into the mountain.

Michael stepped off the pickup at his trailer, shut his eyes against a gritty blast. The wind never stopped. Primeval and bigger than your whole life, Beatty was a speck it didn't even pause over. Flotsam spun about his legs. Nothing rotted here. It was all a time machine: old cars, dead dogs, last year's leaves. They whirled around some, settled, but they didn't disappear. Nothing did, every night faithfully waiting for you on the front step.

There was a small dusty chapel across from the trailer park. Michael had gone there alone once to light a candle for his mother but once there lit one also for Karen, his father, then Maria, Evita...and soon there weren't enough candles. And Michael realized there would never be enough candles, not ever, and didn't return.

He shut the door to his paper trailer, fell on the bed as the swamp cooler banged and drooled down laminated panel walls. The exhaustion cleared a moment, as it always did before he passed out, and that was a dangerous time. The time when his wife came, a woman whose love was someone else's memory but whose death was all his. He needed hate, but she wouldn't oblige. So he brought his own, fermented and self-administered. When finally he dropped into a shallow amphetamine sleep, he was wearing his clothes.

Four hours later he jittered awake, vomited once, and sat on the carpet with his head against the paneling, feeling the vibration of the swamp cooler. It was so ravaged, this night, every night, that it comforted him like a muddy grave.

There would be no question of sleep. He'd sit there, listening to wind buffeting past on its way to Death Valley. Sometimes he'd turn on the a.m. talk shows, hollow voices crackling off the ionosphere from Salt Lake. Sometimes he just sat there and cried.

Come dawn it would be his day off, and the first cold shots of light would freeze him with terror at an entire day available and unplanned. Later it would bring Rosa.

"Mike?"

"Go away."

She'd come in anyway, Rosa. All business as she got him off the floor, stripped down his week-old clothes, and forced him into the bath. He'd curse her, but he'd go, and she'd tell him the news—which brother was in jail, her asshole manager at the bar, the two hippies some highway patrolmen beat the shit out of for being hippies and being in Nevada.

"They were actually *yippies* though, y'know."

Michael swallowed some pills, and Rosa's voice moved to arm's length, where he could handle it. She didn't mind the pills. Alcohol had killed her father, fucked up her brothers, and continually induced her mother to take off her panties in public. That Michael didn't drink much, even if he spent most of his time in a pharmacological haze, put him a notch below sainthood.

Rosa. Gap-toothed with ironed hair dyed a flaxen chrome. Friendly eyes and strong, no-nonsense hands.

"Oh my, what would you do without me, Mike?"

Rosa was certain she alone stood between Michael and oblivion. But Michael needed his pain far too much to ever let that train pull too far out of the station.

"Guess what today is?"

"I don't know." It was the guttural rasp of a drowned man. It'd been…days?…since he'd spoken.

"C'mon, think."

"Sunday."

She blew out a petulant breath. "Oh come on, don't be so *stupid.*"

He could see several fragments of his mind drifting through the bathroom, and he was in no mood to try and collect them for an answer. "I don't know."

"It's your birthday, silly."

He dried himself, but she combed his hair and presented the results proudly in the medicine cabinet mirror. "See? Cute."

He felt absolutely no ownership of the face that stared back.

The shower had roused him to at least a heightened state of stupor as he pulled on clean jeans and a shirt. Rosa was waiting on the bed coyly, hands behind her. "Close your eyes."

He was feeling game and complied. Rosa led him to the bed, laid a package in his hands, and declared, "*Ta da!*" He opened his eyes.

"Well, look at this…" He slipped the ribbon off and pulled away the top. Inside was an antique clarinet. Rosa bit her lip uncertainly.

"I thought you'd want a new one…"

She must have looked forever to find the exact model. The one Michael inherited from his father and lost during one of his three-day disappearing acts in the desert. It was in good condition, just a little tarnished, the velvet box frayed but sturdy.

He lifted it. His father's clarinet had been the absolute last link to his childhood. It was such a thoughtful gift it made him feel mean and unworthy. He turned to Rosa, sitting there now wondering if she'd made some terrible mistake, and kissed her. "It's wonderful. Thank you. It's more than I deserve."

She hugged him back fiercely. "Oh baby, I love it so much when you're happy." Her touch, the feel of her sweater, renewed him. He stood and opened the door, ready to face the day.

It was night.

They had dinner/breakfast at the mom-and-pop steak joint—Rosa's treat—and the food sat foully in his belly, but he felt okay and tried to make it good for Rosa. The evening had a shot, but then they went by her bar for a nightcap, and there was noise and other shithead miners and suddenly she was his girl now and his mood imploded, leaving him hunched in the restroom jamming pills down his throat, seeking the middle distance.

She had a cake waiting for him at the trailer, but he couldn't even count the candles on it, which weren't forty-four anyway.

They ate it, sat there rummaging the wreckage of another night, and fell asleep.

When he woke there was thunder ugly and deep over Tonopah. He disentangled himself from Rosa, pulled on his jeans, and walked out barefoot amongst luminescent gravel. The wind had lost its arrogance and was in full retreat from a thunderhead coming over the mountains, swallowing the sky, black on blacker.

And Michael began to run.

Out of town, across beaten, weedy lots. Through fissured sandstone, into the path of the storm. Thunder throbbed his frame, and it began to rain. He couldn't hear his breath, but when it failed he collapsed to his knees, shot his face up into a sky roiling spun lead above him, and thought, *Oh God, oh God, what have I become…*

**August 29, 1971**

# 19.

Strange time, the ride up. You had to stand still because the bucket swayed easily and there were always too many, shoulder to shoulder. Down at the minehead the weight of the earth crushed and steamed the air. On the way up it relaxed, and the armor of sweat he wore went clammy as he was dumped into a sucking Nevada August.

The crew drifted to their pickups and Suburbans, haphazard in the lot. Michael hated these moments. The ten seconds of forced interaction to hitch a lift back to Beatty. The half-tons and four-wheel drives gunned, and as Michael shuffled among them he noticed the tan rental sedan, puny and awkward. Standing against the door, arms folded, was Hector.

He looked exactly the same, unchanged, and that only deepened the nightmare mirage.

"*Michael.*"

Michael stood there, squinting as the glare scooped out his mind, listened once more to the nightmare speak, then did the only sensible thing with a nightmare: turned his back on it and walked away.

◎　◎　◎

Rosa did his dishes nervously. She knew the troughs of his existence, but this frightened her. Instead of passed out on the bed, he was hunched in the corner, watching the door. The knock startled her. Never in the time she had known Michael had anyone else visited the trailer. He made no move to answer, so Rosa went to the door.

"Don't open it."

His warning chilled her, and she backed away as there was another knock. "Who is it?" she called out.

"Rosa?"

The sound of her name brewed curiosity and she reached for the handle, glancing once at Michael—who offered no further protest—before pulling it open. Standing on the dirt stoop was an old, frail man. He wore a dark-blue suit despite the heat, and rested his weight on a silver dog-headed cane. His face was friendly and alert, his hair slicked flat and white. He smiled.

"You must be Rosa. How beautiful you are."

Despite herself she tucked a piece of hair shyly behind one ear. His voice was soft and smoothly foreign.

"Who are you?"

"Hector Cabanillas," the small man answered brightly. "A friend of Michael's"—the voice changed just a little—"from the old days."

"Michael doesn't have any old friends."

"May I see him?"

"What do you want?"

"Just to talk…visit…" He limped up two stairs to the doorway. Rosa didn't budge. Hector's voice drew close. "I know him, Rosa. I can help."

And Rosa thought, *This is death and devastation standing before me.*

"Let him in." Michael.

Rosa hesitated, then reluctantly stepped aside. Hector squeezed her arm and entered. Michael pulled out a gun.

"I said if I ever saw you again I'd kill you."

Hector registered nothing as he stared at Michael, huddled there on the floor.

"You won't shoot me, Michael."

"You took my life."

"I'm the only one who can give it back to you."

Michael got off the floor, stumbled into the bathroom, and threw up.

She couldn't hear them where they stood together in the vacant lot. Hector spoke in a low mantra, without gesture. Michael hung his head, swayed, listened to the words pouring into his ear. They stood there till pink fell on the mountains and the sky cooled, and Rosa thought, *I'm losing him.*

"The embassy is very impressive now, Michael. Kennedy discovered the south, and everywhere there are great blocks of American diplomatic marble, all full with dedicated, eager young men"—Hector smiled just a little—"who won't talk to us anymore."

He told Michael of how the economy had slid faster and faster through the '60s, how urban guerrillas, Montoneros, calling for the return of Papa Perón, had started the killing, but how the generals had gleefully joined in. How there was a whole apparatus of death squads now, on both sides. How thousands had simply disappeared—thrown from aircraft into the Rio Plata or weighted with lead bars in nameless Andean reservoirs. How the mass killings were isolating Argentina. How most of the world had stopped talking to them...

"Terror, yes, sometimes it is necessary. Useful. But now... terror without reason...without result but more terror...is vile waste. It has become like everything else in Argentina: cyclical, pointless, cruel. A struggle passionately felt and completely misunderstood."

"Why are you here, Hector?"

Hector took off his glasses and wiped them on the end of his tie. "The civil war has taken a disorganized nation and organized it around death. The government and its enemies are in stalemate.

This stalemate is destroying Argentina. Destroying even the notion of it. Something must be done."

Hector slid the glasses back onto the bridge of his nose.

"It is time for Eva Perón to return to politics."

He knew these words would come. Had known for years. Still…"Why now?"

"To wait is to lose everything. Only she can save her nation."

"Why *now*?"

Hector smiled. "Still the smartest CIA officer in Argentina."

"I don't work for the CIA. Or Argentina. Not anymore."

"I know, Michael. And you will do this for neither of these, and certainly not for me. But you will do it. For yourself."

Hector looked up and saw Rosa watching from the trailer. "Are you good to her, Michael?"

"I'm not good to anybody."

Hector nodded and looked away from the worried woman on the porch. "Since that day, for fifteen years, I have never pressed you for the location of the Senora. Perhaps this was self-interest. By telling no one, she has stayed a secret. Perhaps the last secret our country possesses. Certainly it has cost us—a former president, Aramburu, just last year."

"I read about it."

"You knew him, Michael."

"Briefly."

"All presidents in Argentina are brief." Hector turned to the mountains, pink with afterglow. "He came from a place not unlike this, a desperate land full of nothing but men seeking to be consumed by it. Most of them let the place work itself into their bodies, till it found the emptiness within and suffocated them. A few had conviction enough to seek an answer there. Aramburu was such a man. He came from a place, Michael, not unlike this…"

"You want me to tell you where she's buried."

Hector turned slowly from the mountains and faced him.

"No, Michael. I want you to bring her home."

# 20.

The night was in free fall. By the small light of the trailer stoop, Michael and Hector stood where they had for hours.

"How can I go? How can I go like *this*?"

Hector's whisper was fierce. "Hate me, Michael. Hate your whole existence. But understand that your life, all our lives, are great circles. To move beyond this, to find grace, we must pass once more through the beginning. Your circle is broken, Michael. And it is only I, and this deed, that can join it again."

There was silence. There was Michael asking, once again, *why now*?

"Our relationship, Michael, was many things, but it was always private. No written records ever existed of our contacts together.

"But I alone was not the Argentine government. I alone was not even the sum of Argentine intelligence. There were other departments—accounting, security, even the city militia—into whose files your name, during that time, might have wandered.

"Recently an extreme branch of the guerrilla Montoneros attacked and burned a SIDE records center in Puerto Madera. It is unlikely, but possible, that they acquired from there files from the years you were in Argentina. This cell is led by a fanatical revolutionary named Alejandro Morales. He is completely devoted to the return of Eva Perón to Argentina. I know him. He was picked up once in one of our raids. He is a remarkable man. We think he's operating alone now. Hunted even by his own Montonero comrades. He's dangerous and capable, and it is possible he may connect you to the Senora."

"How?"

"Michael, my son, you shot your wife, betrayed your agency, and disappeared with a corpse stuffed in a radio crate. I'm sorry. These are brutal words. It would be unlikely, but absolutely not impossible, for this man to draw together those events and come to a conclusion. If so, you could be in danger."

"You'll forgive me, Hector, if I have difficulty swallowing that you came all this way out of concern for my safety and the unbroken circles of our lives."

Hector's thoughts fell inward for a moment. "I once told you long ago, Michael, how symbols will always be more important to the people of Argentina than ideas. With so much of the nation devouring itself, the Senora—and the time she represents—is the only great symbol we have left.

"The current government has negotiated with General Perón to return him from his exile in Spain as head of a reconciliation government. If he brings with him Evita, peace is assured. But if a Montonero fanatic should hijack her body first, return it under *revolutionary* control, make it *their* symbol…the killing will continue. Forever. Her body, even in death, has become the key to everything.

"The Senora has been safe in your care, Michael. But we cannot know what this man learned from Aramburu and those burned files. What he will surmise. And so we cannot be sure that the Senora is now safe."

"I could just tell you where she is. Send in an armed detachment, claim the body, and bring Her home."

Hector nodded. "That would be the simplest thing. But nothing is ever simple with the Senora. You see, our nation's current fashion of annihilating whole age groups has made it an international pariah. The governments of Italy and France have severed nearly all diplomatic relations with the current administration and would never allow a formal armed detachment of anybody from Buenos Aires to cross their borders."

That left mounting a clandestine intelligence operation to acquire the corpse. But Hector's palpable nervousness, and the fact that he came all this way alone, meant it was likely that he feared his own security bureau was bored full of Montonero holes. And so once again it seemed there was no one the old secret policeman could turn to except an American whose life he had helped destroy.

"Do you have a passport?"

Michael had lost his real one years ago but still had the fake one he'd had made in the name of Gary Phillips. "It's expired."

"Give it to me. I have a contact that can update it overnight. It will be waiting for you at the airport with an airline ticket. I have a nephew at our embassy in Bonn. He can meet you in…"

"Milan."

"Milan, then. He'll help you retrieve the body from…from where you've kept her."

"You want me to turn her over to him?"

"No, Michael. You must, please, transport the Senora alone to her exiled husband General Perón in Spain. Franco has a long connection with Argentina and has promised to open his borders to us without formality. I have personally arranged a quiet crossing location. Once in Spain, Juan Perón and his new wife, Isabel, will be waiting for you in Madrid. But first Evita must reach that border, unannounced and undetected, through Italy and France."

"Will I have any help?"

"I have no one else I trust, Michael. Not with this. My nephew can help you in Milan, but after that, this is a journey you would make alone."

And Michael had always known, at the last ragged edge of his life's broken circle, that was how it would be.

Rosa stood against the laminated paneling, chain-smoking. "You're not coming back, are you?"

He was packing his case. Light. He owned so little. "I'm coming back."

"But not to me."

"I'm coming back."

He buckled the case. He had some things—old spook toys—at a storage locker in Bakersfield he'd pick up on the way. His mind craved chemical distance. He touched her face and she winced because it felt final.

"Rosa...I..."

"Don't," she begged.

And he thought, *Of all the things I chose not to see in her, the most essential was her dignity.*

He lifted his case, opened the door, and was surprised by how rubbery his legs had become.

Hector returned with a car and $5,000. "I'll also need an Argentine ID in the name of Carlos Maggi," Michael said, "and a telegram in his name sent to Musocco Cemetery requesting the exhumation of a nun named María Maggi by her nephew."

Hector nodded, impressed. "A nun. Clever. I'll see it's done at once. I would go myself if I were not such a useless old man." As long as Michael had known Hector, the man had seemed old. "But I'll be there at the Spanish border. I'll wait for you, Michael."

Hector stood outside the trailer as Michael drove away. Rosa followed the car's dust from the porch, her hands folded tight across her middle as if in deep cold.

"You're a monster." There was little rancor in it.

"I love him too, Rosa. You may not understand that, but I do." He turned from the sedan disappearing now on the highway. He was a frail old man on a cane, but Rosa knew he would outlive them all. "But if there are truly monsters in this world, then I suppose I am among them."

Michael took Hector's car over the California line, through the Panamint Mountains, and south on 395, past naval weapon ranges and the skeletons of Japanese internment camps.

He'd promised himself to stay off the pills till Bakersfield, but his mind was growing addled in the heat and he swallowed two with a warm Coke to keep it from seizing completely.

The storage locker in Bakersfield was a serve-yourself series of white catacombs. He'd lost the key and needed the moonlighting ranch kid to saw the lock off. The steel door howled, and the sound brought Michael back to that night on the third floor of the CGT a hundred centuries ago. The kid lingered, and Michael felt his eyes sweep his clammy, bennie-sweat clothes. Michael shrugged it off. "I'm not feeling real good. The weather…"

The kid's expression went dull with an understanding that transcended anything he might have picked up punching doggies, and Michael felt suddenly impatient. "I'm okay now. Thanks for the help."

The kid, in no hurry, gave him the up and down one more time, drawled, "You'll have to pay for the lock," turned on his shit kickers, and ambled away. Michael went inside, braced himself, and yanked the light chain.

On what would turn out to be Michael's last day of operational intelligence in Argentina, his new station chief, Pompian, who had already decided to have his troubled case officer removed and sent to Walter Reed for evaluation, woke up to the realization that Michael had been missing for three days. Wintergreen was given the thankless job of finding him and was getting nowhere till he caught on a PD frequency the local BA cops responding to a drunk American making a scene in La Boca.

Wintergreen ran down the address, and there was Michael, throwing desperate punches at a circle of beat cops on the stoop of an old apartment building. His clothes were ripped, slept in, and soaked with gin. The station marine sweet-talked the angry cops into backing off and came up on Michael easy. Blood drooled down his scalp from police payback. Michael swung a wild fist at Wintergreen and missed miserably.

"Easy, Spook. Just me. What you been up to, man?"

Michael squinted, pushed at the air in front of Wintergreen, hissed "Shit" with annoyance, and sat down hard on the stoop. "I'm just sitting here…Jesus Christ, I grew up in this place and I'm just sitting here…" Michael wiped his eye with the palm of a hand and smeared blood over it. "Fuck it, y'know? I'm from nowhere…I got nothing and I'm from fucking nowhere…" He said something in Ukrainian, let his face sink into his hands.

Wintergreen got on the horn to Pompian, and the ropy son of a bitch was down there in ten flat. He took a single long look at his charge and, without going near him, ordered Wintergreen to load Michael into the car and drive him directly to the airport. They washed him in the bathroom, dressed him in Pompian's blazer to make him presentable, dragged him onto a Pan Am flight with a one-way ticket to Walter Reed, and wiped their hands of it.

Pompian hired a shipping company to box up everything at Michael's house and move it in one day, but a mix-up happened with the new station secretary. Michael's primary residence was in Arlington, Virginia, but he'd recently sent his wife's body home to her hometown of Mendocino, California, and that was where the secretary directed his belongings. There wasn't any commercial storage in Mendocino, so she had it dumped in Bakersfield, figuring, in a Rhode Island way: Well, it's the same state.

By the hard, shadowy light of a single bulb, the room, with its drop cloths and dusty crates, had an attic feel. Fifteen years had passed since he'd looked in on any of this, and it was still about a thousand too soon. The suggestion of tables and chairs under grimy oil covers, the silhouette of another life, gutted him and made it difficult to stand.

After Karen's death—*After I killed her*, Michael reminded himself—during the numb, stupid months he hung on as a husk at the station, he had, during moments of paranoia, begun hiding money, personal articles, even station property in the linings of his furniture. There it stayed during the days of his decline, and there it remained when they crated his life and dumped it here.

He used a box cutter on an edge of a couch, a screwdriver on a cabinet back. From them he removed a Brazilian .25 handgun, a pair of low-light agency binoculars, and a Technical Support Division lock-picking set.

He reached deeper into the insulation of his furniture, and his mental slide presented itself in a midden of stashed fetishes: car keys, fifty-peso notes, routine station memos, his wife's picture, the envelope with a lock of Evita's hair.

The kid came back sometime before dawn. Shined a flashlight in on Michael curled in a drop cloth.

"—Hey."

Michael jerked awake, and there was coma misery in his red-rimmed, mourning eyes.

"You can't sleep here, man."

Michael drifted shuttered streets, found a biker bar, stayed long enough to drown half a ghost and score a box of amphetamines. At first purple light he bought a coffee at Winchell's, spilled half of it on his lap, and left town.

The wingtip caught a cloud, banked, and Los Angeles—stucco white and Central American lazy—filled his window and was pushed aside by an arc of Pacific.

Michael let the seat take him, slipped out the Gary Phillips passport Hector had updated, and looked at the same picture inside from so many years ago. It was a snapshot of Michael at twenty-eight, blown up and cut down to passport dimensions. In it he wore an amused, toothy grin, his black tie askew. Michael recognized the moment: standing against a wall at a garden party thrown by the Indian ambassador. He'd been happy that afternoon, the organization of his life in that instant making a brief, uncomplicated sense. Hector had taken the picture, but it wasn't he who had provoked the amused grin. It had been Karen, a small aside, her arm around his waist. Only you couldn't see her in the frame. Like the day, the moment, that whole stretch of life, she'd been cropped out.

**August 31, 1971**

# 21.

*Goddamn him.*

She'd called in sick to the bar, changed her mind, and now regretted it, swirling damp circles with a beer rag, smiling flatly at miner yahoos. She'd leave, call her sister in Reno, and take the room over the garage. She'd get the hell out of here.

On the way home Rosa steered clear of his place but somehow did a circle and ended up on its porch.

*Goddamn him.*

Softer now, damp.

Another promise to herself out the window as she went inside. Just to tidy up some. For when he came back. When…whatever.

She turned on a single lamp, nosed through the kitchen. There was nothing of him in this place anymore. What little he had, what tiny piece of his aura left behind, was already a century gone. Rosa finished the glasses—nobody's glasses that had come with the place—tried to keep a sigh from worming into a sob…

And realized she wasn't alone.

There was no question of it being Michael. The feeling filled the whole space the way Michael never did, crowding like a hand on her shoulder blade.

"It's okay. You turn around. All right?" The voice was heavily accented. Latin. It had a strange, ruined quality that made it seem to be coming from every corner at once. Rosa set the glass down and turned.

"What do you want?" She faced an empty room.

"We talk, okay? Just talk." It was then she saw him, emerging from shadows near the bathroom. He carried no weapon and his face was a haphazard confusion of burns. His frame had a hard, peaceful core of purpose, freezing Rosa in place.

"Please. What is your name?"

She didn't respond.

"What is your name?"

"Rosa."

"Please sit, Rosa."

She lowered herself on an edge of mattress.

"This is Michael Suslov's home, no?"

She didn't answer, only stared, wide-eyed. The figure sighed and sat down beside her. "I think you understand, Rosa. Understand that I ask questions and you answer them. I think you understand that it is the way it must be. My English is not so good but I think we can understand, yes? You do not know me, but we can be friends, I think." He touched her arm, just a little, let her feel the power ebb through his fingers.

"I know you," she said, not looking at him.

"I do not think so."

"Yes, I know you." She turned to him. "You're Michael's past."

There had been empty pill bags everywhere in the trailer that spoke of a man afraid of his dreams. But that he had chosen this place meant he was also a man with a secret. Such a man would always have a place—a bolt-hole—that in the hollow of a broken night he would flee to with that secret.

He left Rosa in the trailer to her confusion and miseries and walked into the desert. It didn't take long to find the man's tracks. The desperation in each barefoot stagger across the years of his exile here, each always ending at the same protrusion of basalt rock. There, scratched over and over across a thousand nights, were "Garden 41," "Lot 86," and "Milan"…

◎  ◎  ◎

Seven and a half miles out of Beatty, Alejandro pulled into a Richfield for gas. At the same moment he realized the station was closed, they jumped him. Two unmarked Fords screeching in from the back and side. Alejandro hit the accelerator and tried to make the highway. The first shotgun blast ripped out the front tire and fender. Alejandro fishtailed, felt the car hit by another blast from the opposite side, and understood any other theatrics were pointless, as the car spun out into a sandbank.

Figures approached warily across the asphalt, shotguns held low, like cops. They flanked the car, trying to read him. He gave them nothing and they lingered, edging up the fender till two muzzles pushed their way roughly against his head as someone yanked on the door, but it wouldn't open. A voice said: *Shit.*

The opposite door obeyed, and they dragged him across the seat onto hot dirt. It stank of radiator fluid.

"Is he alive?"

"He's alive."

The first voice yanked his head up by the scalp, and even in the fiery halo of a sledgehammer afternoon the face looking down at Alejandro was a wasted mask of years.

"Not that I care if you live. Understand?"

He let go of Alejandro's scalp, but his head stayed up, eyes still locked, even in the glare tearing them apart. The voice snorted and walked away.

"Get him out of here before I get sunstroke."

They put him in the back of their Ford, cuffed, just like home. Even the car was the same—navy-blue instead of dark-green and newer—but the same smell of cigarettes and stakeout coffee. They'd left one of the shooters behind with his peppered rental, and he rode with the other three in silence. They were clearly Americans, though who they represented wasn't pinned either on their clothes or the car door.

The wasted face in the front passenger seat turned and grinned. "Jesus Christ, you're an ugly one."

They took him to the Nye County Sheriff station in Pahrump and parked him in an interrogation room, cuffed to a bar. It was suffocating, but he'd been in places more suffocating still. After an hour the wasted one entered alone, took his coat off, and fell into a chair, .38 visible on his waistband. A cop. From his pocket he unscrewed a small flask and swallowed a bolt. Wiping his mouth he looked at Alejandro across the tiny room. His face was both pallid and flushed at the same time, a universe of veins coursing its translucent surface.

"Go ahead, kid, stare all you want. Believe me, it's a pleasure coming from someone actually less attractive than myself."

Alejandro figured him for a hard sixty-five. This was clearly his show.

"Piece of advice, son. Next time, you, a known terrorist, decide to travel to the United States, don't use a document forger that's on our embassy's snitch payroll."

Corada. So that's why they were waiting for him.

"You want to tell me why you're looking for Michael Suslov?"

Alejandro didn't answer. The cop leaned closer, and Alejandro could smell decades of self-abuse on his breath as he said, quietly, for just the two of them:

"Was it about Her?"

**September 1, 1971**

# 22.

It was clouds as they came in. The stewardess asked him to buckle his seatbelt. He hadn't slept on the way, and the world was a muddy daze. He smiled at the stewardess, but it was awkward. The pilot mumbled something, mumbled it again in Italian. The wing flexed, and the strata below broke away on red-roofed apartment blocks skirting khaki cornfields.

He walked from the plane to the terminal with the other passengers, squinting at the day and feeling his face flush as machine-gun uniforms rolled gazes over his creased sport coat and crumpled chinos. Spook clothes. He folded sunglasses over his eyes, ran a hand through damp hair. Inside he fished for his Gary Phillips passport and was seized with a certainty this could never work. He weighed turning around, getting out…

"Passport, please."

He slid it over along with his second awkward smile in an hour. *Christ, what's wrong with me? Slow down. And take the sunglasses off.*

The passport disappeared behind the counter. "How long will you be in Italia?"

He'd spent the entire landing rehearsing "tourist," his fantasy home address, a sunny, bogus itinerary. It had never occurred to him how long he'd be here. His gears froze on it and he stuttered. The passport kid looked up suspiciously, and Michael forced words out of his mouth.

"Two days."

The kid knotted his eyebrows. "You've come to Italia for only two days?"

*Fuck.* "Uh, two days in Milan. I meant two days here, here in Milan."

"Where do you go after Milano?"

The rehearsal kicked in, and he rattled off Tuscany towns from a Frommer's guide.

"Where will you be staying in Milano?"

He had a hotel name too. A reservation he wouldn't show up for. His voice steadied, heat came back into his veins. He felt human.

"Are you sick, Signore?"

"I don't fly well."

The passport kid studied him some more, sighed, glanced in the direction of a supervisor as if for guidance, then stamped his documents with a fierce wallop.

"This is good for one month."

"Thank you."

"Enjoy your stay."

The smart thing, the spook thing, would have been to pick up his bags right then and walk through customs. Instead he went to the toilet, locked the door, and threw up.

He splashed his face in the sink and thought, *I've lost everything I ever knew of this work.* He swallowed a couple pills to coax a frame of mind, flushed the rest in case it didn't work. He sat on the toilet lid, hung his head between his knees till gravity worked the pharmacology into his brain. Feeling half stable, he retucked his shirt and straightened his fifteen-year-old tie.

*Just walk through like you own the place. The only thing airport stiffs—stiffs anywhere—can smell is dog fear. You took a piss first. So what? They bought a sixteen-year-old passport photo; they'll buy the next thirty seconds.*

A hand banged on the bathroom door. "Mr. Phillips? Are you all right?"

Michael hoisted his bags, unlocked the door, and found the passport kid waiting outside checking his watch. Michael shrugged like the kid was out of his mind and walked resolutely through the green NOTHING TO DECLARE exit.

They stopped and searched everything in his luggage.

The TSD skeleton keys were tucked individually throughout the lining—he'd remembered that much—and the rest was at least vaguely *turistico*. When they'd properly emptied his possessions into a jumble, the customs suits stood back without apology and waited for him to pack and zip them up himself. He did so, forcing with monumental effort to keep it slow and unhurried. Done, he dragged them off the table, avoided giving the day's third awkward smile, and showed them his back for maybe seven steps.

"Mr. Phillips."

The passport kid's voice. Michael stopped, managed an exasperated I'm-late-for-a-train sigh…

And heard a submachine gun cock.

"Please put your hands up, Mr. Phillips."

"What?" Michael fairly squeaked with it. He still hadn't turned, a bag in each hand.

"Your hands, Mr. Phillips. *Pronto.*"

Michael set his luggage down and raised his arms. It was the passport kid who stepped up and pulled the Brazilian .25 from his waistband. He didn't have to bother reaching under Michael's coat to do it. The American tourist on a two-day visit had saved him the trouble by jamming his coattail into his pants along with the gun.

They had him in back now, an interrogation room with a view of yellow fuel trucks. You could feel the throb of jet engines through the walls.

"Why do you bring a gun into Italy on vacation, Mr. Phillips?" It was the supervisor, speaking across a table where the Brazilian pistol lay.

"It wasn't loaded." Not technically. He had two clips for it but they had been in different pockets. The stiffs found both of them. Michael's head throbbed—probably dehydration from the flight. One more addition to his list of blood-chemistry disorders.

"I bought the gun for self-protection."

"Protection from whom?"

"From anyone."

"Are you ill?"

"I'm uncomfortable."

"Are you on medication?"

*Ha.* "NoDoz, maybe."

"Why do you not want to sleep?"

"Bad dreams." *Whole world of truth in that, Mr. Airport Man.*

"What business are you on in Italy?"

"No business. I'm on vacation."

"When was your last vacation?"

"I don't remember."

"1956?"

The supervisor had a telex. Sure. Gary Phillips had been here in '56.

"I've had vacations since then."

"Your last visit to Milan, in 1956, you also stayed only two days."

"Yes."

"Why?"

"To visit a friend."

"Which friend?"

"She's dead."

"When did she die?"

"Then."

"1956?"

"Yes."

"You came for a funeral?"

"Yes. Yes I did."

"What was her name?"

They'd check that. If he made one up and luck wasn't on his side, it would mean a night or two in here at least. Telling the truth would risk...what? Digging her up?

"María Maggi." The truth. Paint it red. The supervisor wrote it down.

"Where is she buried?"

"Musocco." The supervisor wrote that down too and passed it to an assistant who disappeared. Here we go.

"We'll check, of course."

"I'm sure she's still there." That bunched up the supervisor, and for the first time Michael felt on top of the moment. That old, very old feeling.

"What did this María Maggi do for a living?"

"She was a nun."

"Italian?"

"Yes. I knew her as a boy in Argentina."

"And you came all this way for her funeral?"

"She meant a lot to me." And might even be still alive, but that would take time to check.

"Did you bring a gun the last time too?"

"No." Another truth. They felt good. *And the Truth Shall Make You Free*—the CIA's motto, inscribed on the lobby wall. To 99 percent of the people who worked there, its meaning was obvious, even quaint. To the other 1 percent, to the Clandestine Service officers, it held a maxim that was the flip side of *Paint It Red*. Always tell the truth. Even when you lie, make some part of it a truth you know. Only then will a lie take on wings.

"What is your work?"

"I'm a miner."

"Excuse me?"

"I dig holes in rocks."

"Really."

"Really."

He knew they'd run "Gary Phillips" through Washington. That, undoubtedly, would ring some queer bells. But he had time on his side. If they didn't hold him, if he didn't give them another moronic reason, he could still finish this.

"Why did you bring a gun to Italy?"

"I...my wife was shot and killed. In a burglary. Since then I've carried a gun. You can't understand what it's like watching your wife die." A grotesque distortion, but Michael knew, as the supervisor stared into his eyes, that the man saw the real, convulsing pain beneath it. And the lie, all his lies, became real. *And the Truth Shall Make You Free.*

The assistant returned and nodded to the supervisor. There was a María Maggi in Musocco buried in 1956. Michael could feel the wind go out of the supervisor's sails.

"You have a permit for that pistol?"

"In America." And Michael knew they weren't going to hold him.

"We will have to confiscate the gun as a customs violation."

Michael kept his look neutral.

"We have the name of your hotel and will contact you tomorrow or Tuesday. You're free to go."

Michael rose. "Mr. Phillips..." Michael turned to the supervisor. "Be sure to see Siena. It's beautiful this time of year."

"Thank you."

Michael opened the door. As he walked by the passport kid, he heard him hiss under his breath, "Do yourself a favor, Phillips. Stay out of trouble. You're not built for it."

He took the train in from the airport. His eyes stung with their constant, nervous movement, even with the lids closed, which was pointless anyway; he was way beyond sleep. The car clacked through the confusion of a city built by conquerors: Austrian blocks of yellow-washed plaster, Parisian facades of granite and playful lattice, Norman paranoia, Swiss money, and sewers that gurgled of Africa.

The train coughed into the Stazione Centrale, Il Duce's soaring salute to a modern Pax Romana. Michael passed through the terminal of heavy columns and vast marble walls and remembered his first time here, in college, just a year after a war he barely missed, waiting between trains. The great fascist symbols leering from those marble slabs had been hastily covered that summer by acceptable republican flags or simply mangled with haphazard swaths of cement. There were still Allied soldiers everywhere then, eyes cocked no longer on the Italians but the Soviets, mustering over the northern mountains. There'd been poverty and eternal style.

There'd been Gina.

◎　◎　◎

His hotel was a block south of the station. There was a message from Hector, a number in Madrid, and he returned it on a pay phone at the post office.

"Michael." The voice as enthusiastic as always. "Everything went okay?"

"I'm here."

"Excellent. My nephew will meet you at the agreed place at four. He'll have the documents you asked for."

There was a pause on Hector's end. "Michael, Alejandro Morales has disappeared from Argentina on a forged passport. We don't know his destination. It could be anywhere. It could be Milan."

"Thanks for the warning."

"I am here for you at all times, Michael. Good luck."

Michael dropped his bags in his room, lay down on a wafer mattress, locked his arms behind his neck, and looked out the dusty window. He'd clear his brain in a minute, meet Hector's nephew coming down from Bonn in a few hours, and together they'd complete the arrangements at the cemetery for the exhumation of María Maggi.

Beyond the glass was the train station. It hadn't changed much in a quarter century. Fewer bullet holes. The city had seemed bigger then. The whole world had.

Twenty-three years ago he'd finished his summer exchange year at the University of Bordeaux and was drifting magically between the girl left behind in France and the one he'd marry in Chicago.

The train that summer had taken him through the Vichy collaborationist south and a Monaco that was a passing blur of tanned bodies, swimming pools, and the nagging feeling that maybe there had been a war somewhere.

But there had been war, and crossing into Italy, its footprints were on a hundred Lombardy towns. Piles of rubble swept up but not yet removed, cratered fields, and everywhere the sour iron tang of a million obliterated battle machines.

Michael had been on his way to Florence, like all Americans, to taste white-man history older than the Alamo. He'd been restless on the ride and wandered the train, hung his elbows out the side windows, and watched the power lines race up and down, up and down.

She'd spoken first. "Sometimes, people's arms get caught on the mail hooks. They get ripped off so fast the person doesn't even notice at first, yes? If they live, it's important to remember to notify the railway police, so that if they find the arm they can return the wedding ring."

"I'm not married."

"Then you have less to be concerned about."

He pulled his arms in from the window.

She was standing in profile beside him and promptly hung her own elbows out the glass. "I'm not married either."

She was a few inches shorter than he, with the dark blonde of a northerner. Her dress was blue polka dots on white, fitted at the waist and flared to the ankle. It suited her, though not outrageously so. He told her his name in Italian, she glanced him up and down, arms still hanging out the window. "A Yankee wop with a Russian name."

"Raised in Argentina."

"My."

He continued speaking to her in his mother's Italian, and she kept answering in English. "Where are you from?"

She'd only met his eyes once, in her brief appraisal, and had since concentrated on the bushy rush of hillsides and glimpses of coast. "Not far from here. In the mountains. But I live in Marseilles now."

"What's in Marseilles?"

"My boyfriend."

She turned then, and the eye that had been hidden in profile was bruised purple and black. "Tell me about your family," she asked.

"They're dead."

She taught English in France and was on her way home for a visit: mom, dad, a small pharmacy, none of which she seemed to like much. He didn't ask about the black eye. The war had grazed them—an uncle she'd never met killed in Calabria, a little brother's eye lost to a stray B-24 lightening its load over the Alpes-Maritime. Michael felt compelled, stupidly, to apologize for it.

She shrugged. "Life gets you one way or another. At least they never saw it coming."

"And you do?"

"Don't you? You strike me as the kind of guy who sees it coming with both feet."

She took a cigarette out of his pocket, stuck it into her mouth, and walked back down the car.

He found her later in a compartment full of attentive teenage soccer players, slid the door open, and sat down opposite. She didn't seem surprised in the least to see him.

"You're wrong," he said. "Life can't come and get you. It can't, because life is a dumb, blind, thoughtless blunder."

"You believe that?"

"I have to."

She took a long drag on her cigarette and regarded him.

"What's your name?"

"Gina."

There wasn't much left of the train ride, so they talked of simple things: living among the French, the sensation created by the arrival of black American GIs. Then the train was in Milan and there was the pulling down of cases, the flushing onto the platform. They walked silently together past hissing engines, dodged rain puddles from a thousand war-holes in the curved superstructure.

The crowd diluted in the vastness of the station, and they stopped near the ticket windows for local trains.

"Where are you going now?" she asked.

"Florence."

"Of course."

"Is it nice?"

"It's old."

"What's better?" he asked.

"Acereto."

"What's that?"

She pulled another cigarette from his shirt pocket. "My town."

They took the stopping train north, into the hill country. Watched the Renaissance jumble of Milan loosen as towns drew themselves into tight, sober hamlets, felt Caesar's grip weaken with the chill of the barbarian north. As the coal-fired train heaved its way up steeper inclines, the villages compressed tighter and tighter, till the trapped energy squeezed itself out in a profusion of church spires lurching up defiantly against the icy peaks above. Norman cathedrals heaped on Carolingian chapels and themselves topped, like layered Neapolitan, with gussied, Hapsburg clock towers.

Her town was no bigger than others, its church no less layered. They walked from the station, he with his father's suitcase, older than both of them together. He hauled it up steep cobbled lanes, past a small piazza, in its tidiness somehow more German than Italian. It was Sunday, and Sunday people lounged everywhere, having coffee, playing chess. They all stared but Gina made eye contact with none of them.

"Do you know these people?"

"Of course."

They continued down a narrow alley. A young man yelled down from his window, "Gina!"

She stuck her arm in the air but kept moving. Out of the alley, to the far edge of town and a prosperous, two-story home. "This is it."

Gina opened the gate, walked past a battered pet dish. "You have a dog?"

"Had. Killed in the war. Same bomb that got my little brother's eye. Landed right in the pond out behind the house. There's still mud from the explosion up under the eaves. Probably some dried Poitzel too. Poitzel was the dog. I don't know why we still have the dish." She keyed the door and pushed it open. "You'd have to ask my parents."

They walked in, and the house was silent.

"Where are your parents?"

"Oh, they're gone. All week."

They packed a cold dinner, carried it up the wildflower hill behind the house. Sunset flared insects purple and green. The town below glowed coppery and in doing so at last, to Michael, seemed Italian.

They drank hot Chianti, ate hard bread and sliced tomatoes. Gina pulled up fistfuls of fragile mountain flowers. "This used to be a graveyard, long ago. If you look around here, in the grass, you can find bits of marble with Latin on them. Sometimes pieces of iron and teeth. Roman teeth."

"You always picnic in graveyards?"

"All Europe's a graveyard."

She stood with her wine, looking across mountain pastures. "Someday you and I will lie in a place like this, with children picking at the pieces of our tombs."

"I suppose so."

"You don't think about it?"

"Why draw it any faster into your life?"

Gina flopped down beside him. "I'm drunk." She emptied her glass into the earth. "Chianti. Chianti for the dead. Do you miss it, Mr. Centurion?" She broke a piece of bread and let the crumbled fragments fall. "How about some bread?" She lay back on the crumbs, crossed her hands across her chest, and closed her eyes. "It must have been like this, don't you think? Maybe a sword to keep him company..."

He was silent, and she looked at him from a cocked eye. "You disapprove."

"It's morbid."

"Not talking about death won't make it go away. Better to have the courage to look it in the face."

Michael felt his face flush. "*Courage*? Christ, you were in the middle of a war and the only thing you lost was a *dog*."

He regretted it immediately and lowered his voice. "You've got so much. Family, a nice house, a hometown where people know you, things I can't even imagine…Why on earth obsess about death?"

"Because I know life will take all from me, Michael—I just know—and I won't let it have the satisfaction."

"That's no kind of life, Gina."

"What is?"

It stumbled in his throat. "I don't know. I'm trying, but honestly, I don't have the slightest idea."

And Michael, who had never really understood the intentions of women, was surprised when she kissed him.

Just glancing. He held her hand lightly, like a prized lab specimen. And kissed her black eye. She replaced it with her mouth. It tasted of cheese and cigarettes, then didn't, and they were down, fragrant herbs against his cheek. He breathed her in, floated on dark-blonde hair enclosing him.

There were fireflies when he came up for air. Soft, lethargic sparks. He started to get up, his head lightened, and he sat down again. Tiny chunks of Roman tomb stuck to arms and backs. As he rubbed them off himself and her, it came out of him quietly: "Tombs. Nothing but tombs my whole life…"

In her parents' house they built a fire, and the clothes, grass stained with buttons that fastened on opposite sides in America, came off awkwardly. Neither of them had bathed since the train, and there was a tang to their skin. He lifted Gina, curled her close to him, and she was lighter than he expected. Broad, dark nipples on teardrop breasts like small pillows against his chest.

She explored his body, her eyes closed, and found the boy-hood scar on his thigh. "Where did you get this?" she breathed.

He didn't answer, instead brushed his hand across the inside of her thigh. It was moist, warm, and one labia was longer than the other.

"Nobody's perfect," she said.

He kissed it.

In the morning they had brioche and coffee in a sudden and con-fusing silence. It was as if a heavy motorbike, cruising at high speed, had inexplicably begun to tip, and no matter your effort, the momentum was cast.

Words that had seemed so simple the night before now choked midair, embarrassed. He didn't touch her, found it hard to imagine he ever had, and after a few hours of tortured pauses, bewildered, he said he'd better be getting on. She slapped her thighs, said okay, and before he knew it, she was seeing him to the platform, the walk a thousand times longer than the after-noon before. He sputtered some hopeless half sentences about how long she'd be in town, how long he'd be in Europe. He felt tainted and humiliated. She gave him a phone number both of them knew he'd never call.

In the train he took his seat numbly, and shot a glance at Gina out the window, but she'd already given the station, and Michael, her back. The engine lurched, her retreating image slid sideways, and at the last instant, when she was sure he was no longer watch-ing, when he had in fact nearly averted his eyes, she turned to him a face stained with tears, and Michael understood.

Gina fought the chaos of life by giving up to it all that she cared about before it could be taken. Michael had touched her and so was given up.

There was a small note left in a battered novel he didn't find till his return to Chicago. Only a few lines in Italian: *I don't con-sider myself a happy person, but I was happy with you.*

**September 2, 1971**

# 23.

It was knocking that woke him. Insistent. Drawing him up from black lakes. "Signore?" More knocking. "Signore? Is everything okay?" Michael looked at the window. Afternoon slanted through it.

"What?" It surprised him how strangled it sounded. "Of course."

"We were concerned."

"I'm okay. Jesus."

"Will you be staying Monday night?"

"Monday? I don't know. I'll tell you later."

"We need to know now, Signore. Checkout is one p.m. Excuse me."

Michael groaned and struggled off the bed. A cacophony of cathedral bells had begun somewhere and felt like it was going on in the next room.

Michael opened the door. "What's the problem?" He rubbed his face. The nap had left him feeling like shit.

The hotel employee's repertoire was limited to a shrug. "Checkout is one o'clock."

"Why are you bugging me with this now?" The bells were starting a world of a headache. "What the hell *is* that?"

"The church, Signore. They are ringing for Saint Maxima day."

A glimmer of catechism flared in Michael's brainpan. "Isn't that Monday?"

"Of course."

"But it's only Sunday morning. I arrived on Sunday..."

The employee looked at him peculiarly. Michael was growing weary of everyone he met since getting off the plane treating him like a mental patient. "What day is today?"

"Saint Maxima day. Monday."

"That's impossible."

The employee shrugged.

"You mean I slept a day and a half?"

"We were concerned. You never came down for meals."

Hector's nephew. Michael spun around to collect his wits. Get moving. A day and a fucking half.

"Signore. The room."

"Yes, yes. I'll keep it."

The employee nodded and left.

He hit the streets in the clothes he'd slept in, snaked through afternoon traffic to a small café on the Piazza Cincinnato, where he was supposed to meet Hector's nephew. *Yesterday.*

The cappuccino was lukewarm and Michael ignored it, watched instead the sidewalk clutter, bet on the nephew hanging around an extra day. He'd been there an hour, staring at the same dead coffee, when a young man in a black polyester suit and red open-necked shirt appeared before him. "Michael Suslov?"

"How'd you guess?"

"Only an American would drink a cappuccino at two in the afternoon."

The young man sat in the chair opposite, snapped for a waiter, pushed gold-rimmed teardrop aviators back up the bridge of his nose. "They don't have calendars where you come from?"

"I was held up."

"Really? I hadn't noticed during the three fucking hours I sat here yesterday. Slipped right past me." He hunched his shoulders, adjusted his lapels. The guy seemed to be in constant motion. "We can speak Spanish if you want. Or English."

"Italian's fine. It might be the one thing about you that doesn't attract attention."

Hector's nephew did a kind of pimp roll and curled a lip in disgust. "Hey, pal, I don't do this kind of shit, understand? I'm only here as a favor to my uncle. Sooner I'm back on a train to Bonn, the better."

Michael could picture him there. A third-rate embassy clerk haunting fourth-rate discos for country hat-check girls, who probably found him exotic and were five inches taller. Thirty seconds with him convinced Michael there were no dark alleys in this dandy's past—in short, nothing of Hector's essence. Michael understood now why the crippled spook hadn't asked his nephew to take care of this on his own.

"What's your name?"

"Giancarlo."

"You have something for me, Giancarlo?"

Hector's nephew pushed across the table Michael's Argentine ID in the name of Carlos Maggi and a copy of the telegram requesting the exhumation of his aunt. Michael looked up at Giancarlo. "What do you know about this?"

"Nothing. Except that one look at you means it's gonna be low-rent."

The two of them rode the streetcar out to Musocco Cemetery. The day had clouded over but lost none of its heat, beads of toxic sweat tumbling down Michael's temple.

"You okay?" Giancarlo asked.

"I'm fine."

"Well, you look like day-old death."

*How would you know?*

The streetcar squealed to a stop. Musocco was not only the end of the line for its residents, but for the streetcar as well. The remaining passengers drifted away, leaving just the two of them.

"What now?" Giancarlo asked.

Michael explained briefly and elliptically that they were here to complete the exhumation of a certain woman. He'd arranged a hearse for the journey to Spain. Giancarlo would stick around as an extra hand till Michael left Milan, hopefully that same afternoon.

They stepped off onto the broad cul de sac that formed the cemetery entrance. The grand portal to the necropolis was nineteenth century and rose in imposing blocks like an edifice of state. Tall Doric columns supported a sweeping half circle of cement gallery topped by bronze flames. The effect was more of a national frontier than an entrance.

The squat district around this principality had, if anything, declined since his last visit. There was an unnatural silence of abandoned factories and sullen neighborhoods. The autostrada at midday hissed without enthusiasm, and the only voices came from chatty women selling flowers from a dozen booths around the cul de sac.

The cemetery was laid in a complex series of gravel drives, each bending and reforming into districts much like the ancient streets of the city it served: neighborhoods wealthy—expensive marble adorned with life-sized Christs kneeling with tortured gazes to heaven; neighborhoods urban—high-rise vaults looming like condominiums; neighborhoods bourgeois—retouched photographs of the beloved cemented to their crypts like a marble field of high school yearbooks; and neighborhoods poor—simple grass plots with generic markers to keep track of the moneyless dead, whose space would be reserved only seven years before being given over to the next.

An army of workers swarmed this city, sweeping gravel, polishing stone, driving small red buses with smaller old women, conductors announcing lettered quadrants like Disneyland parking lot zones. The cemetery offices were in a faux chapel. Michael left Giancarlo outside among the sighing cypress and went in to find the superintendent's office. He was at his desk, halfway through a coffee and magazine. He bade Michael sit. He wore a Mack the Knife suit and thick horn-rimmed glasses. His handshake was correct, and he smoothed his desk blotter afterward, an action he repeated compulsively.

"Mr. Maggi, a pleasure to meet you."

"You received the telegram regarding my aunt?"

"Coffee?"

"I'm fine, thank you."

The superintendent finished his, set it aside, and smoothed his desk blotter.

"The telegram?" Michael prodded.

"Yes. The telegram…" The sentence died awkwardly.

"Is there some difficulty?"

"You must understand, Mr. Maggi, that we are very sensitive about our record keeping here at Musocco."

"Of course."

"A predecessor of mine has been accused, just this week in this very magazine, of hiding Mussolini's body here under a false name during those confusing days at the end of the war."

Michael felt his chest tighten. "That was decades ago. Surely you're not suggesting my aunt is Mussolini?"

The superintendent looked aghast. "Of course not. I only meant that with this sort of ridiculous accusation hanging over our office just now, someone in my position must be extra vigilant in making sure our records are correct regarding those resting with us."

He smoothed his blotter again.

"Is there some problem with the paperwork?"

"No. Everything was in order. But for one matter."

"What is that?"

"We forwarded your request, as family, for her removal to the Carmelite order. Just a formality. We, however, received an unusual reply."

"Yes?"

"María Maggi died."

Michael let the words sink in. "Well, yes. Naturally she's dead."

"María Maggi died in Argentina *three weeks ago.*"

At that moment Michael understood conclusively both that God existed and that He hated Michael's guts.

"There's obviously been a mistake."

"Of course. I don't doubt that some clerical error has occurred with the Carmelites. It won't be the first time. Still, as I said, we must, particularly at this moment, be absolutely certain of our registration records. Therefore, regrettably, we cannot release any remains till this paperwork issue is resolved."

"Signore, I have a hired hearse waiting at great expense to transport my aunt. Any delay would be a great burden to my family."

"I understand and apologize. But we must verify the paperwork before we can release your aunt."

"How long is this investigation likely to take?"

"Oh, no more than two or three weeks."

"No matter the cost to my family?"

"Again, I apologize."

There was another ten minutes back and forth like this, with Michael trying various tactics, including a thinly veiled offer of a personal donation to the Carmelite order or the superintendent himself, in cash, but the man just kept glancing nervously at the magazine article and shrugging his helpless apologies.

Giancarlo was waiting at the bottom of the stairs smoking a cigarette. "And?"

"Walk with me."

They cut through the cemetery quadrants, Michael's bloodshot eyes eventually finding the numbers he knew by heart: Garden 41, Lot 86.

They marked a simple plot across the path from the daisies of the cemetery's potter's field. Michael stood before the slab, searched for a feeling separate from the general confusion in his body. He glanced up and down the gravel and sighed in disappointment. He'd forgotten how exposed She was. First row. With the openness of potter's field next door, you could see Her grave a dozen yards in three directions.

"A nun," Giancarlo said, reading the marker.

"It'll be harder here. In the more crowded areas you wouldn't be seen as quickly doing it."

"Doing what?"

"Digging her up."

"You are, obviously, insane."

"We'll dig at night. With the airport goons watching me, with Montoneros maybe on the way right now…I don't have two or three weeks to get through this paperwork. We'll do it ourselves tonight and get the casket out a service portal in the wall."

They were sitting outside the cemetery gates now, against the curving gallery of columns. Giancarlo was studying the gelato in his hand intensely, trying to make Michael disappear. The air was so heavy the city seemed to catch its breath.

"We'll need a truck."

Giancarlo finished his gelato and stood. "Get it yourself. I have a train waiting for me."

"Just like that."

"Fuck yes, like that. I do favors for Uncle Frankenstein, understand? But I'm not on his payroll, and this is way, way out of any universe I live in—or anyone but you, I'm getting to think."

Michael climbed slowly to his feet like a man pulled from the wreckage of his own body. The shakes and sweat were getting worse and he wondered a beat if he'd faint. Giancarlo seemed to wonder the same. Michael let him roll with the thought a moment before grabbing the nephew's shoulder pads and slapping him against the column. The kid tensed, and Michael decided, *If I'm going to faint, I'm taking someone with me.*

"Listen." Michael kept his voice close and calm. "You know, I know you're a worthless, pointless piece of shit that only has that third-rate embassy job because you're Hector's last name. And you know, I know that one phone call to said uncle and you're gone, history, back to Buenos Aires, where you're also a pointless piece of shit, only you'll be a pointless piece of shit without diplomatic portfolio, sitting drunk in cheap cafés waiting to be blown up by a terrorist bomb, because, after all, the one thing you'll still have is your uncle's last name."

Giancarlo's eyes narrowed. "Christ, what are you, a spook?"

"Worse."

"You look it."

Michael let him go. "Just buy a truck, get some wino to help dig, and be at the corner service gate at one thirty tonight."

He had his own problems to take care of in the meantime. There was a pharmacy near the hotel on a quiet shopping alley. It was closed now, the block dark, and Michael broke a rear window to get in. He didn't waste time, and he only took the little white ones.

The corner service gate consisted of a locked steel door mounted into the high masonry wall that surrounded the cemetery. Taller than the one dividing east and west in Berlin, it reminded Michael of necropoli favored by the ancients. For them, the dead were unclean and vengeful, their bodies stashed behind secure frontiers.

Christianity supposedly changed that. From howling uncertainty to the gentle metaphysics of a peaceful soul that slept patiently, awaiting not revenge but resurrection. This leached the dead of some of their terror, and the corrupted bodies of family were brought into the churchyards. Villagers visited, picnicked on, walked by their graves to market. For it was only slumber, and the spirit was the soul, and the soul was not a ghost that could wander.

Yet there was something in the northern Italian mind that had never completely accepted this. Their dead, it seemed, still strolled, and taking no chances, these sons of Sibyl continued to hide their deceased behind high walls, just in case the ancients had been right all along.

Giancarlo was at the gate, smoking to look calm, the tight, jerky arm movements accenting his nervousness. Michael, energy in his step, walked quickly across the dirt median. "You got the truck?"

"I got a truck."

"Big enough?"

"For a nun it's big enough."

A three-quarter moon played peek-a-boo behind brewing clouds.

"Did you get someone to help dig?"

"He's got two legs and he's breathing. After that all guarantees end." Giancarlo studied Michael. "What have *you* been doing?"

"Get the truck. Bring it and the guy up to the curb."

A streetlight caught Michael's eyes, and Giancarlo shook his head when he glimpsed the pupils. "I knew it. Uncle Frankenstein sent me a drug addict. A fucking drug addict." He turned to the truck. "Well, at least you'll have something in common with our Igor for the evening."

Michael went to work on the service door with his TSD skeleton keys. The lock was old and burst apart as he picked free chunks of rust. Giancarlo brought the truck to the curb. It wheezed, and a death rattle banged on thirty seconds after Giancarlo shut the ignition.

"It runs," Hector's nephew said sourly.

"And runs and runs, clearly." The whole truck lurched and fell silent. It was a '59 Bedford with a short plank carrying area, corroded but sturdy looking. Tufts of sheep wool were caught in the rear side-slats and drifted like talismans in the breeze.

"Where's the digger?"

Giancarlo looked around him as if noticing for the first time that he wasn't accompanied, sighed, and walked back to the truck. From it, half dragged, appeared the evening's hired help. "Meet Igor."

The man didn't smile, didn't register Michael's presence. He swayed, his hair black and unwashed, bits of dead skin sticking up through greasy clumps. His clothes smelled of low tide. The face was the flat romantic features of a Central European, but the eyes were all Gypsy.

"Igor, this is Mr. Suslov. Your boss for the evening." Igor carried a couple of shovels. Giancarlo looked anxiously up and down the avenue. "Now can we please get off the street?"

They went inside. Threading past dark tombs, scuffling gravel, feeling their hearts jimmy every time the moon broke and shot searchlights around them. A sea of red oil lamps winked tiny patches of hot blood over dead yearbook photos. Thunder rolled without enthusiasm out of town as they crossed the potter's field like thieves, cicadas singing languidly at their feet.

Michael tried Italian on the Gypsy and got in return what might have been Albanian, might have been the man's own secret language. Michael wondered exactly how Giancarlo had negotiated his services.

They hadn't seen anyone moving about, but that didn't mean they weren't there, walking the dead beat. Michael felt exposed, every escaping bolt of moonlight like fire on his cheek. His pulse raced threadily, and he resolved to just get on with it.

They surrounded Her, judged the thin, flecked stone tablet that sat over the grave. Michael crouched, felt for an edge, took the shovel, and pried underneath, using it as a fulcrum. "C'mon. Give me a hand."

The Gypsy seemed to get the idea and knelt beside Michael to lend his effort. Giancarlo lit a cigarette.

"Do you really think a cigarette's a good idea right now?"

"Fuck you."

Giancarlo lit another, stuck it in the Gypsy's mouth, and braced a third shovel underneath the tablet. Together they pushed, and there was a tearing sound as fifteen years' worth of grass roots ripped aside. The marble tablet rose slowly. When it was high enough Michael dropped his shovel and added his shoulder to the Gypsy's, pivoting it up and over with a deep thump onto the grass.

The underside was caked earth swarming with confused pill bugs. They boiled over the grave, considering a sky for the first time.

"Charming," Giancarlo said.

Michael turned to the Gypsy. "Dig." Whether the word was universal, or just that he was following Michael's example, the Gypsy complied.

After a shallow surface of roots, then fine urban grit, the grave gave up soft Lombardy soil. The shovels sank easily and pulled free hillocks of black loam. Giancarlo leaned against the headstone. "You could help us out some, y'know," Michael said. Giancarlo glanced at his own impeccable disco threads.

"Yeah. Right."

It started to rain. Giancarlo hissed something. A sweat had risen on Michael's shoulders and he didn't feel the droplets at first. They began to strike harder, joining across the back of his neck and rolling into his eyes. The droplets plunged into the spongy grave, releasing the sweet remains of previous tenants. The sleepy scent melded with the Gypsy's own personal rot, and the hole came alive in Michael's throat.

Lightning whacked suddenly overhead, close enough to drape them in ozone. Giancarlo reflexively scrunched down closer to the headstone, turning his collar as the sky cracked and dumped. Instantly the grave went to soup, and now they were shoveling as much water as earth. More lightning exploded, strobing faces and turning rain to frozen silver.

Michael's hair plastered to his skull. Giancarlo's blow-dry fell like a soggy hamster. The Gypsy begun humming a dirge but kept digging. The rain was a solid white curtain now, flattening grass, rushing the grave in torrents. Rolling shotgun blasts of thunder bounced off cathedral towers miles away, the succession so fast lightning and sound lost sync with each other. Michael was flash blind, deaf, and couldn't even see the grave anymore...

When his shovel hit it.

The wood was soggy and peeled away like bark. Beneath the humble wood of a nun lay the hardened steel of a First Lady. Beneath the steel, waxed and bottled for eternity, would be the woman herself.

"Oh *shit*..."

Michael barely heard it over the sky's caterwauling, but the fact that Giancarlo had said it reflexively in Spanish spiked his blood. He stuck his head out of the grave and there, across the no-man's-land of potter's field, bobbed two flashlights slowly in their direction.

"Friends of yours?" Giancarlo asked.

"They're guards."

No more than a hundred yards away but the rain made them seem farther.

"Well, you or Igor have an idea?" Giancarlo said.

"Stay low."

"And if they come closer?"

The Gypsy was still humming his dirge in Michael's ear. "I don't know."

"You're not going to do something stupid like shoot them, are you?"

"I don't have a gun."

They were definitely going to pass by. Michael couldn't tell if they were zeroing in on something in particular or following a regular route. He looked at the piles of sludge heaped around the grave. They'd never miss that.

He heard voices. Gruff working-class ones. They weren't laughing but they didn't seem tense either. A flashlight suddenly swung past them, and Michael dropped flat on his back atop the rotten outer casket, softly mildewed as a pillow. The Gypsy fell in line beside him, the rain clattering off their faces and arms. It was warm and he felt mud shifting and reforming around him.

A flashlight beam hit the top of the grave and froze. It was a strange angle, low to the ground, and it held absolutely still, like the untrembling hand of God.

Someone screamed.

A rising, strangled moan, the sound of people clawing up from nightmares. He heard a scuffling, feet darting serpentine through wet gravel.

Michael climbed to his knees. Kept his face out of the light beam and looked over the lip. The flashlight was straight and unmoving because it was lying on the ground. The guards, who had been closing lazily on them, were now dashing wildly in a crazed retreat across potter's field. Through the solid curtain of pounding water, Michael saw a ghoul, dressed in red, baying and loping like a werewolf after them. The guards had dropped everything and bolted in terrorized panic.

When the guards had disappeared, the ghoul paused, straightened, and walked unhurriedly back toward him and the Gypsy, two drowned puppies with their heads above the edge of a grave. The ghoul had lost its lupine gait now, taken on a pelvic swagger, and ten yards from the grave tried to light a cigarette in the rain. The lighter's flare illuminated a horror face of black streaks—cheap hair dye, Michael realized—running in the rain.

Giancarlo gave up on the cigarette and pitched it aside. "You owe me."

From the disintegrated wood casket they lifted the uncorrupted steel inner one. It wasn't heavy, and Giancarlo and Michael hoisted it away as the Gypsy tried to return some dirt to the hole. Not that it would fool anyone. When the storm passed and the guards came sheepishly back, they'd see the disturbance. With any luck, that would be hours from now.

They slipped the steel container onto the truck bed and tied a tarp over it. The Gypsy followed them out, closed the service gate behind him, and they were all standing there, not feeling the rain. Giancarlo gave the Gypsy some bills, and he faded away.

"I'll give you a ride in," Michael said to Giancarlo.

"I'll walk."

"Then this is it. Thanks. For what you did in there."

"Yeah, yeah, fuck you."

Giancarlo tried another soggy cigarette, tossed it with disgust aside, and disappeared too into the wet, dead neighborhood.

Michael drove a few blocks to an inky shell of a nobody factory. He got out, took off his muddy clothes, and stood naked in the storm. He let the rain wash his body, let it roll over him longer than he had to, then put on clean clothes, started the truck, and with the storm thinning and the night plowing its meanest hour, headed for the city line.

# 24.

At Milan airport Alejandro stole a Fiat and drove the ring road toward the city center. Air through the window cooled his face, which even now still generated occasional waves of heat. It had taken almost no effort to match Suslov's scratchings in the desert to a graveyard in Italy. The cop in Nevada turned out to be FBI counterintelligence. They'd been following him since he entered the United States.

The cop made it clear that it was of little interest to them which side in Argentina's war ended up with the Senora, just that they didn't want an American ex-CIA officer caught at the center of it. If Alejandro had information on where she might be and evidence that Suslov might be trying to recover her, they were willing to allow him to continue to Italy and spare everyone a lot of trouble—on one condition: that he allowed the FBI to examine Her to determine the corpse's authenticity before She returned to Argentina.

Alejandro had nodded and never asked why, during this offer, the other cops had been kept outside.

◎　◎　◎

The sky was clear breezes but the cemetery ground was soaked with the night's rain. Steam lifted off roofs as sunlight struck damp shingles.

She'd lain here fifteen years but she was gone now, just broken bits of worm-eaten outer casket sticking up through Lombard clay. The sense of violence and haste blackened his thoughts.

He could still do something about it.

There was a holstered Carabinieri hanging out bored near the spot, leaning on a tombstone, waiting for instructions. He'd eyed Alejandro a few times, but Alejandro was used to the double takes his face provoked lately. Alejandro ignored him, traced trammeled grass and mud back to a service door in the cemetery wall, where a lock hung broken. He swung it open, walked carefully over the weak gravel to the street. Even through the storm's havoc his pampa eyes could detect human tracks, close together, shuffling. Carrying something.

Her.

This was a forgotten street and only one set of tire treads cut through the mud. A truck. Alejandro could tell at a glance the make was unusual. He squatted down, took its measurement with his fingers. Whatever had been loaded into the truck had scraped away some paint off the tailgate, and there were pale flecks of light blue dusting the ground. So a pale-blue truck with unusual tires.

Alejandro walked to a phone booth where he called the number given to him by his new American friend. Into a recording machine he left the paint color and tire dimensions, hung up, then quietly stole a police handy-talkie from a Carabinieri patrol car and slipped away.

On a rise at the bisection of the western autostrada, Alejandro sat atop his stolen Fiat and tuned the police radio. He had traveled west because he knew this was the way Suslov would run. Confuse the jurisdiction, make a fascist border—Spain, the last in Western Europe, and the only one that would have anything to do with him or his bloodstained masters.

Crows scattered on the tracks of plowed earth below. He pictured Suslov out there, making his run. Whatever Michael Suslov may have been in his Buenos Aires heyday, this was now a man at the end of the line, held together by nightmares and the charity of a bar girl. That only confirmed to him how much this was all out of pocket. The choice of a disaster case like Suslov, the utter lack of even the smallest rumor of this operation from the scores of Montonero agents inside Casa Rosada, the end-run around the local Italian stiffs with a messy grave robbing. Hector Cabanillas had clearly hung his neck out on this one.

That evened things considerably. But Alejandro had his own concerns. If his former Peronist comrades caught wind of his movements, they might mount their own operation to track Evita. Time was not on Michael Suslov's side, but neither was it on Alejandro's.

Suslov had enough of a head start to make the border, but Alejandro had begun to grasp—from the files, from Rosa—the rhythms of the man. Trying to keep his mind together, he would pause, grasp at any anchor. No, he hadn't made the border. Not yet.

The Americans had done their part. After receiving Alejandro's phoned tire dimensions, they matched them to a limited production run of Pirelli radials used mostly on Bedford TJ–class trucks in the late '50s, and had the Italians put out an all-points for any truck matching that description. The police radio in his lap spat Carabinieri slang, and Alejandro's gaucho *paisano* was good enough he picked up a car stop on the west autostrada. A light blue, late '50s model Bedford truck. One male. American.

Alejandro pushed off the hood and started the car, and slid it over crushed stone.

Trying to hold his mind together. Sure. Alejandro knew about that. There are secrets to it, Michael Suslov. Secrets.

The arrest had been routine, one of many that 1970 afternoon in Buenos Aires, rifle butts breaking down hundreds of doors. His face was not so different than the others dragged into the streets:

young, hair redder than most perhaps, that crazily stitched scar on his neck.

They were herded into the naval mechanical school and flung into temporary basement cells. It was on these damp, vomit-greased boards that Hector Cabanillas walked, looking past the mediocre faces of the doomed, seeking that one in a thousand…

Finding it in Alejandro.

There was the routine breaking of his body's resistance, and Hector looked in only occasionally on the beatings, the air klaxons every ten minutes to prevent sleep, the mock executions with blank pistols that left blood dribbling from ruptured eardrums.

When they moved from body to mind, Hector sat in more often, never participating, cleaning eyeglasses with the end of his tie. There were interrogations where no real answer was possible, but failure to conjure one brought punishment. There were guards who offered cigarettes then urinated in his face, electrodes fastened to his testicles, teeth drilled slowly in rooms where sunlight never fell.

The usual.

It was a dull, necessary process, the stripping of the externals of a man, and it always ended the same, with a compliant, disoriented human being, without rancor, ready to walk that last tightrope, one side implosion and death, the other acceptance and rebirth.

They'd all long ago coughed away any secrets to Admiral Massera's goons working their bodies, and the young man Alejandro was no different. He wept, shat his pants, but he knew little, was clearly not thought highly of by his Montonero chieftains. Fools. The boy's talent was obvious in his gait, his conviction— even blood soaked—still serene, willingly releasing his body, his minor secrets, but holding tight to that essential that drove him. The Montonero guerrilla hierarchy were snobs who saw only a country bumpkin with a steady trigger finger. No matter. The

Montoneros' loss would be the crippled intelligence officer's gain. For it was not this boy's petty secrets Hector wanted, it was his soul.

"What is your name?"

"You know my name."

"But I want to hear it from you."

It was Hector's first visit to the man's cell. Chilly down here, and he wore a thick overcoat, sitting on a chair provided by the guard, stroking his dog-headed cane.

"Alejandro Morales." His clothes were rags; he stank of a thousand humiliations. Hector was used to it. There was plenty worse here. "What is *your* name?"

"Hector. And you and I have just made our first trade in this place." Alejandro's posture fascinated Hector. The young man could barely stand but insisted on doing so in Hector's presence, leaning his back against the wall on unsteady legs. "Do you have any idea how long you have been here?"

"No."

"Take a guess."

"My whole life."

The beatings of course continued, came each morning with breakfast. Hector came with lunch and never referred to the morning's routine, though he personally prescribed the methods and degree of hurt. He dressed neatly for these lunches and neither smiled nor promised anything, but he was patient and arrived always punctually.

"You are a ward of the state, Alejandro. I am a representative of that state. We form a partnership here, you and I. Each is responsible for his role. This is a road we travel together, both determining the outcome."

"What is it you want from me?"

"I don't know. Perhaps you can help me find it."

"Your thugs already got what I know on the Movement. You might as well shoot me and get it over with."

"They are not my thugs, I may still get around to shooting you, and they never ask the same questions I do."

"Like?"

"Did you love your mother, Alejandro?"

And the young man slid down the wall and sat on the floor.

He had the beatings lightened, just enough to remind Alejandro of their absolute control over his life. Their conversations continued, elliptical, and Hector had a blanket brought to help with the chill.

"I knew Her too, Alejandro."

"What could you have possibly understood about Her?"

"That every nation is given one light, one shining instant, and She was ours. Before Her, after Her, we are just immigrant chaos at the bottom of the world. You think yourself so different from me, Alejandro, but our paths are very similar."

"You despise Her. You and your government. You would destroy Her."

"We despise what has been done in Her name. In the name of what She was. Your Montonero friends—who never met Her, never knew Her—for them She is but a vessel to stuff their college Marx and Mao into. Only you and I knew Her, Alejandro. Only you and I truly understand."

"How do you know I met Her?"

"It is written on your soul."

The boy had resolve, conditioning from a childhood of nightmare shadings, but he had need to talk of Her, to feed that glue of himself, and this was Hector's opening. He decided to move to the next level.

He had Alejandro taken from the basement cell by moonlight and trucked to an abandoned, seventeenth-century Jesuit cemetery, where he was placed in a six-by-ten underground room. It had a single narrow window just above ground that they slid open only after dark, providing glimpses of crooked, bluish ruins. The beatings were stopped, Hector no longer visited, and each midnight a different officer would creep up to the tiny window and tell a ghost story—of pampa *mandingas*, witches—and the horror groans of the young man inside carried spookily over forgotten crypts.

The essence of Hector's work was patience, and the creaking military bureaucracy above him was terminally short of it. Argentina's smudgy war on its domestic enemies was an assembly-line affair, custom jobs not encouraged. The fact that this particular custom job had been IDed as the trigger on at least two high-ranking officer hits—one a colonel—made this government of military officers all the more anxious to get this kid's breathing days over with. There was a limit to Hector's leash, they reminded him. Get on with it.

"You killed military officers."

"If you want to kill a snake, start with the head."

"That's Montonero shit talk. Not that I especially mind killing colonels—I am not terribly fond of most of them myself—but I want to know why *you* do it."

No one had spoken to Alejandro, save the ghost stories, for ten days. When at last it was Hector himself who sat down one midnight beside the cemetery grate, he could hear in the young man's voice the relief, the need for human contact. Most who came this far craved it so deeply they wished even for the beatings again—anything to stop the isolation. But this one in a thousand had proved molded of stronger pampa clay, his sanity holding even as everything else weakened.

Alejandro allowed himself a small smile of vanity now, sitting in darkness, listening to Hector's voice outside the grate.

"Their stupid medals, earned for nothing, peacocks ordering free coffees on sidewalk cafés. They fucking beg for it, man."

"Who are you, Alejandro Morales?"

Silence.

"What is your life's meaning?"

"The revolution."

"That's a stupid Montonero answer. Your life, Alejandro. What drives *your* life?"

"Her."

The next night: "Who am I, Alejandro?"

"A state interrogator."

"Am I like any interrogator you've met?"

"No."

"Then who am I, Alejandro? What drives my life? What do I believe in? *Come*, Alejandro, look in my eyes, look, and tell me what drives my life."

"…Her."

"You and I both. Outcasts from our tribes, committed only to Her word. Alone in woods gone dark for years."

And for the first time he heard the boy sniffle. "Yes…"

"You and I are people apart, Alejandro, and so can make a pact apart. Do you trust me?"

"What a question. Jesus Christ…"

"I come when I say I will. I beat when I say it shall happen. I am a man of my word. Now, within the confines our relationship, do you trust me?"

"Yes."

"Then listen: you will return to your revolutionary cell. You may continue slaughtering colonels, for I care little of colonels. As I shall continue slaughtering Montonero half-wits. But you and I are now joined, Alejandro, and when the moment comes, we will answer to duties larger than these." He paused and let the instant have its twinkling. "I once asked you to tell me what I wanted from you. I ask now again."

"You want me to work for you."

"I want us to work together and change the world."

And the pause was a gust of eternity.

"All right."

Hector never tired of these moments. Honey from the bosom of the earth. He drank of it, sighed, and climbed to his feet.

"Sleep now, my son. Sleep and know the world has changed."

The next night Hector was called to Rosario, and one of the goons tipped off the colonels. They took Alejandro out of his cemetery cell, marched him to a depression filled with rotten leaves, and there shot him. It was cold and they had dates waiting so they halfheartedly buried him where he fell, and went home.

He was unearthed by feral dogs looking for dinner.

They'd spent the effort digging him up and were not to be denied easily. One went for his face, and he locked his arm around it and broke its neck. The others reconsidered, gave him room as he rose—half-mud and blood—and climbed from the hollow. He held out a hand in warning, and the dogs slunk away, watched him move stiffly out of the abandoned cemetery and around an elm that shivered as he passed.

The next morning Hector stood over the small cemetery hollow, saw the blood everywhere on the leaves. What a waste, he thought. What a waste…

**September 3, 1971**

# 25.

Dawn coming fast, purple to blue lances over Michael's shoulder, the air clear and washed, the Bedford's tires singing on damp asphalt.

He was heading west, morning in his rearview, the autostrada empty and flat, for he was still on the Lombardy plain. Milan died stubbornly in the manner of great plain cities, suburbs breaking reluctantly into light industrial tilt-ups that in turn surrendered to open land filled with the seasonal smell of burning fields; their smoke, in no hurry, drifting like pedestrians over the highway.

His cargo shifted, and Michael felt his head lighten with adrenaline. *Hardly started and I'm a wreck.* Two days flat out, maybe a few hours unconscious on an off-ramp in France somewhere, and it would be over. The tarp he'd tied over the back flapped a steady tattoo, but the truck drove firm enough, issuing occasional grumblings. Giancarlo hadn't thought of *filling* the truck when he bought it, and Michael had made a fuel stop at a ghostly all-nighter on the autostrada. The attendant had been incurious, and Michael thanked his god for one in what he hoped would be several dozen small favors. He'd bolted two espressos at the bar to help keep his mind framed, and the pressure of that was making itself known now on his bladder.

A hundred miles out of Milan he crossed the Forty-Fifth Parallel, and the plain turned a pinkish chalk. Caesar had earned his fame on that chalk, and it had tempted every generation since—French, Austrians, Goths, Nazis, papal mercenaries. Still the flowers glowed, the grain flourished, covering over a hundred million boot prints, taking the land, always, back again.

Small hillocks appeared on the smoky plain, standing as gateway sentinels to Asti Province. Beyond them the land began to softly undulate in a motion that a hundred miles further would yield the Alps.

Michael slipped on sunglasses against the building glare. The truck had evened out its hum on the road. He had a headache and his eyes stung, but he was feeling better, more confident...

When the flashing blue light appeared behind him.

A broad, pebbly riverbed fronted the highway, and he could hear the soft rill of shallow water. Alders winked in the breeze, surrounded by plowed fields crinkling with tiny harvest flames.

The Carabinieri four-wheel had just sat there after pulling him over, considering. Michael stayed behind the wheel, fought a thousand possibilities now jockeying for purchase in his mind. Had he been speeding? Didn't Italian autostradas not have real speed limits? Did he have a taillight out? Did they fucking *know*?

The two Carabinieri officers climbed warily out of their vehicle. White shoulder boards and chest strap, high peaked hats, red-striped blue trousers. A radio blurted distorted unintelligibles. They wore old-fashioned military-style holsters, and as Michael watched in the rearview, they unbuckled the flaps on them.

The driver—older, belly folding over his belt—hung back near the front bumper of the four-wheel as his younger partner moved gingerly along the side of the truck to Michael's window.

"Good morning."

He was speaking English. A car shot past and puckered the air, but traffic was light. "May I see your driving papers, please?"

His manner was correct, but he was standing almost completely to the side of the window, as if expecting trouble. Michael took an international driver's permit in the name of Gary Phillips from his wallet and passed it over.

"Can you step out of the truck, please?"

Michael opened the door, and the both of them tensed, so he slowed down, kept his hands in view. "Is there a problem?"

"Wait here, please."

Michael felt his armpits chill as the officer walked back to his partner and compared the driver's license to something on a clipboard. Another clump of minutes standing there as the air rocked with a passing truck. The older officer got on the radio as the partner watched Michael. The radio conversation went on forever, Michael feeling lightheaded and leaning against the door of the Bedford.

The older officer climbed out of the four-wheel, and the two conversed before the younger partner walked back to Michael, carrying a telex in his hand.

"May I see your passport, please?"

"It's in the truck."

"Very well."

Michael slowly unzipped his overnight in plain view and handed the Gary Phillips passport to the officer.

"What are you doing in Italia?"

"I'm a tourist."

"Why this truck?"

"I'm moving some things for a friend."

"What things?"

"A chest with a few belongings."

At that the older officer edged to the back of the truck, and Michael used every ounce of concentration not to watch him peek under the tarp.

"Where are you moving them to?"

"Torino."

"And you came from?"

"America."

"The *truck*."

"Parma."

"Your friend lives in Parma?"

"Nearby."

The driver was tapping the steel box. "Does this open?" he called from the rear.

"No. It's locked. I don't have a key."

"Your friend didn't give you a key?"

"It didn't occur to me to ask."

"May I see the truck's papers, please?"

He had no idea where the truck had been registered, but it sure as hell wasn't Parma. If they were following a lead off the cemetery caper in Milan—a witness?—and the truck's registration read Milan, the water in this pot was going to suddenly heat up several degrees.

Michael opened the glove box and rooted through it, but there was no registration to be found. He stepped back out. "I can't find it."

"Where did you get this truck?"

"I rented it."

"From?"

"A man in Parma."

"He lived there?"

"I have no idea. That's where I met him."

"And he just rented you this on the spot?"

"It's not much of a truck."

Michael knew they'd certainly called in the plates and had the owner's name, that this was a dance to see how long he could keep the balls in the air. Yet they were unsure of something, fishing, and Michael held his narrow ground.

"What was this man's name?"

"I don't remember."

"How were you to return the truck?"

"To a *tabacchi* shop in Parma a friend of his owns."

The two officers exchanged glances; the younger one sighed and looked at the passport once more. "Is this the correct spelling of your name?"

It was then Michael got a glimpse of the telex. It was in Italian and listed a Michael Suslov, below which in bold lettering read, WANTED BY AMERICAN FBI. DETAIN. SUSPECT BELIEVED DRIVING A LATE 1950S MODEL LIGHT BLUE BRITISH-MADE TRUCK, HEADING WEST. NO PLATES KNOWN. FORTY-FOUR YEARS OLD, NO CURRENT PICTURE. HOLD FOR CONSULAR OFFICIALS.

He was in a light-blue British truck heading west, but his documents listed him as a thirty-eight-year-old Gary Phillips, not forty-four-year-old Michael Suslov, and so these officers were stalling, waiting to see if he would solve this himself.

*The FBI?*

Michael couldn't wrap his mind around it. He stood there swimming in his thoughts, barely heard the red Fiat that passed by slower than the others, hardly noticed even as it stopped, shifted into reverse, and whined back at them.

The popping sounds were like bubble wrap. He looked at the older Carabinieri and the officer looked back not at Michael but way beyond, to something infinitely distant, and there were blooming red circles on his chest swelling and joining, and the officer slumped soundlessly against the sidewall of the truck, crumpling to his knees, head bending to the pavement like a supplicant.

The second officer understood faster than Michael, and his service pistol came out of its holster, the barrel snapping and flaring as he shot at the lingering Fiat, punching windshield blossoms and knocking out pale chunks of radiator. The Fiat driver rolled out his door on the protected side of the car. Michael jumped backward into the truck's cab as the bubble wrap sounds started again and there was breaking wood in the truck bed, dully tinkling metal and hornet buzzes over the roof.

The Italian cop was still firing, his gun twice as loud as the other's machine pistol, and Michael flattened on the cab seat and twisted the ignition. The younger cop tumbled through the open door behind him, muttering obscenities. Michael dragged the cop inside right over the top of himself, released the parking brake, and hit the gas pedal with his fist, launching the truck blindly.

Michael couldn't see out the windshield, and the steering wheel drifted on its own whim. He was tangled in the muttering cop, felt wetness spread over his stomach and realized the cop must have been shot, heard first tires squeal then horns blow as the truck rocked across lanes, hit the median, and there was shushing grass, another howl from opposing traffic, and a wallop as the truck bashed across a drainage ditch and spun out in the plowed, burning earth.

Michael pushed the cop against the back of the seat, got up, and the view was violent Dutch angles of a rumpled field wrapped in blue haze. The truck was bouncing furiously toward the riverbed, and Michael yanked the wheel. Chunks of mud and charcoaled husks spun up around the windows, and the Bedford slid sideways, the engine screamed, then a tire caught and it bucked along the edge of the short palisade.

Michael was half sitting on the sprawled cop who kept muttering *Motherfucker*. He whipped a glance back at the autostrada—police four-wheel and Fiat still there—and in the jostling confusion now appeared a single figure running resolutely across the top of the ember-strewn furrows at them.

He stomped the gas and the Bedford fishtailed forward, pitching, and there was no way they'd outrun the guy. Not on this dirt. Michael wrenched the truck away from the riverbed, made for a narrow bricked barn standing in the middle of the field. The truck strained and grinded, and he heard the First Lady of Argentina bounce against the lid of her casket.

The Fiat driver was coming up fast but wasn't shooting. Not yet. His build was strong but his face was a destroyed mask, and Michael thought of childhood dreams as his mouth dried and stung with smoke.

The truck caught a patch of gravel, spat, and he gunned it along the wall of the barn, shuddered around the back, and drove in through a pair of open doors. The inside was high and stacked with hay rolls, light arcing through spaced hollow bricks. Michael forced the Bedford through tumbling bales, stopped, left the truck idling while he closed the barn doors shut and bolted them.

The young Carabinieri officer had stopped muttering and lay now in the truck silently, chest heaving up and down, eyes fixed glassily on the dashboard. He still gripped his service Beretta, and Michael gently pried it from his hand, slid out of the cab, and moved through the maze of haystacks, seeking a vantage.

The truck's idle was laying a pale-blue strata of exhaust that caught beams of morning and bent them. He crouched between bales of hay, aimed at a single open loading door ten feet up the wall, and waited. He'd never held this kind of automatic before. The last time he'd pulled a trigger had been on his wife, and the gun shook now in his hand with its promise of disorder.

Straw stuck to his pants, wet with Carabinieri blood. He'd left the engine on, afraid it might not start again, but its drone kept him from hearing any movement outside. There was the barn door, locked, and the loading window leading to a china sky.

Something stirred and he spun on it, furious, and it was feral kittens nesting in the hay. The abrupt move strained a muscle in his eye and the pain radiated back into his head. He rubbed it with the cold butt of the cop's Beretta, turned again to the loading window—just as the Fiat driver swung in firing.

Their weapons erupted follow-the-leader, and if Michael never saw where his rounds hit, the other's announced themselves by slicing straw and rattling planks before dying in the clay floor. Michael's leg suddenly numbed and he realized one of the rounds must have died there too. The Fiat driver dropped from the window, and Michael followed the motion with two shots, but the gun bucked and he was so *fucking* bad at this.

The driver was moving the moment he hit the clay, and Michael backed up on all fours in a panic. He couldn't make out his own blood from the cop's on his trousers, and it wasn't till his foot collapsed under the weight that he realized the shot had gone clean through his ankle. Hopping, he retreated through the stacks, fell, heard two single pistol cracks, and figured the driver finally out of submachine-gun rounds.

There was a tractor in a corner, and Michael crawled behind one of its tires. His own gun was empty and he knew it would only be a moment before the driver flanked and killed him.

"Michael Suslov."

Michael's blood seized with unreality at hearing his name.

"Michael Suslov," he called out again. "You're shot, no? You have nowhere to go, no?"

Michael's arm was getting soaked with oil from the tractor's bleeding crankcase. A bullet had found its way there, and Michael had a desperate thought.

"Who the fuck are you?" he called back at the driver.

"We only want the truck."

"We?"

And he could hear the son of a bitch smile. "I."

Michael unfolded his pocketknife, jammed it into the spare plastic gas can on the tractor, felt cool evaporation roll over his arm and spill onto the clay.

The driver spoke Spanish now, and it was an ancient sound from his throat. "You work for murderers, Michael Suslov. Why go to the wall for them? You're outnumbered, hunted by police in a foreign land. We just want the Senora. We will care for Her, I promise."

"You don't know the first thing about me."

"And certainly you're wrong."

He didn't think the voice was moving, but it was hard to tell. The floor had a slight tilt, and the gas was slithering away from him, soaking up hay.

"What can possibly be worth all this to you, Michael Suslov? What is it that you could need so badly?"

"How about the name of the town I'm dying in?"

"Torrazza."

Michael had a lighter in one hand and was sliding on his ass away from the tractor. *If I've gotta die, at least all of Torrazza's going to hear it.* He was only seven or eight feet from the tractor when the Fiat driver appeared over the top of the bale. So the voice had been moving after all. Michael struck the lighter, and the fuel on his hand ignited in a festival of racing blue flames. The driver fired once, and Michael struck his arm out across the cool floor, touched a fuel-soaked clump of hay...

And the place blew up.

Tongues of hay-fed flame ratcheted violently to the terra-cotta roof as he ground out the fire on his hand. Michael couldn't see the driver and hobbled on one leg to the truck as a shot he never heard spun away a side mirror. The cop was where he left him, and Michael climbed over the officer, shrieked the transmission into reverse, and looked up. The Fiat driver was standing atop one of the blazing haystacks like a nether angel, holding in one hand his pistol and in the other its empty clip. He cried out, and the voice rose above the burning tirade below as a note played on shattered glass.

"*I am Alejandro, Michael Suslov! I serve Her and you will never keep Her! I am Alejandro!*"

Michael slammed the accelerator, and the Bedford flattened the barn door off its hinges, snaked backward over smoldering dirt, and he braked, turned, and churned out over the field for the road. The Fiat, the Carabinieri four-wheel, and the older officer were where they'd been left, unmolested, and the barn was already slow-motion destruction on a smoky plowed sea.

He made the frontage road, thudding bluntly as mud kicked itself free in breaking clumps over the tarmac.

"Should have given him the fucking truck," the cop said, one eye open, curled like a child on the seat beside him.

The road chinked southwest, shadowing the pebbly river. Michael had no idea what he was doing, but he was going to do it as far as possible from the autostrada. Getting onto a country lane, he ran down faded asphalt, pushing the barn, Alejandro, the whole mess over a burning horizon. He pulled the truck into the shelter of tangled brush and looked at his ankle. The bleeding had slowed but his entire shoe sklished with fluids. It didn't hurt much, but that was only a matter of time.

Michael listened to the raspy breath of the pallid cop beside him. His shot leg barely bent now when he got out and held on to the truck's side panel, walking it back to the bed, where he rooted inside for the cleanest rag he could find and fixed it around his ankle. *That* hurt.

There was a long scrape along Evita's casket. Scorch marks dotted the Bedford here and there, tufts of hay standing spikily from taillights and wheel wells. Michael tied back the corner of tarp loosened by the older Carabinieri officer lying now face-up on the autostrada.

He'd have to get the wounded cop to a hospital and hide Evita along the road somewhere during the inevitable insinuations that would follow. Doing this would give Alejandro and whatever friends he had time to regroup—Michael might even get summarily deported—but there really wasn't any other choice. The Carabinieri bleeding in the cab was the only witness that the Bedford license number his partner called in wasn't the car that started the shooting. Finishing this would be hard enough with a bullet through his ankle. Getting there on the run as a cop killer—forget it.

And the thought came to him again that he could walk away from this. Through the trees, over the field, a train, a plane, back. Back to nightmares and nothingness and broken circles of life wobbling hopelessly anew each dawn. He could go back. And back, certainly, would be waiting for him.

He finished cinching the tarp, took a handful of rags for the cop's wounds and hopped back along the truck, his shoe hissing wet prints on the concrete. He tossed the rags into the cab and eased himself in to check on the curled Carabinieri officer.

He was dead.

Mindless miles. Unnamed country bends. Instinctually following the sun southwest, drifting now into regions steeped and flecked with vineyards.

He'd laid the cop among the bramble at roadside, taken the last pistol clips from his white belt, placed a rag over his vacant features—because he'd known him, if just a moment. His ankle had swollen and begun to bark with a low thudding he knew would only build. He cut away his shoe and the skin was tight as a water balloon, blood oozing through the bandage, and there was so much of it—his and the cop's—over the cab, smeared on the dash, lolling in puddles on the floorboards.

He drove without destination or purpose. He was a cop killer in a blood-soaked truck carrying a dead First Lady with a bullet in his leg, and the border—any border—would soon be as closed to him as the moon. Still he went on, chasing the day through tiny villages of old men sitting beneath *tabacchi* verandas, sipping brandy, all of them indistinguishable, all of them watching Michael's truck labor and vibrate noisily over stone lanes.

His blur deepened—blood loss, exhaustion, caffeine jacks, amphetamine withdrawals—and the villages, the space between villages in these rising hills, melded. He lost whole miles, jerked back by the cobblestone drum of another main street. He had nowhere to go and kept going, following the imagined arc of the sun, drawing himself toward dark peaks in a silhouette distance.

From the Monferrato headlands the way opened in a long, narrow valley to Cuneo. The truck wandered the road, skirted shoulders that became abysses then shoulders again. He had trouble remembering where he was, what he was doing. The throb in his ankle shook all the way up his thigh, and all he knew how to do was keep on.

He began closing his eyes in shifts, snatching thimblefuls of peace, and the howls of cross traffic always brought him back and he repeated his name, Her name, and not the name of this place, for he didn't know where he was, only that he was tailing the day, ambivalent now at noon, and he guessed roads—always small ones, always steeper—leaving the narrow valley onto plateaus where the air cooled and bushy foothills emerged from the haze. They rose and fell in rhythms apart from the road, until falling away completely before the Alps, appearing now as an impenetrable granite wall unknowable miles ahead.

He closed his eyes again and everything packed and grinding in his mind loosened, floated, and he held on to the feeling—a moment, more—and when he opened them the world was a white flare. He teared, wiped his eyes with a hand smelling of gasoline, burned hair, rough with tiny blisters. He'd lost the road, was on a smaller one that quickly went gruff, and led his truck out over a spur of mountain and into the insecure town fastened to its spine.

A thousand sparrows exploded through the glare in furious chevrons. There were hot smells of manure and damp, rotting grass, then there was the town and he was quickly lost in its old, meandering streets, passing the same fountain, the same butcher, the same curious child over and over, and it was like a dream as he tried to find his way out looking through cotton, feeling through cotton, thinking through cotton, driving in circles, a merry-go-round with stripped gears, and he gave up trying to slow the slur of movement out his window and let it all stop instantly of its own volition and the world was suddenly quiet and dark and he let it be.

A minute or year he sat, happy in darkness, reluctantly pulling his face off the steering wheel. The impact had only been the low brick of a planter but it lit up the radio, and he was drowning in Austrian *oompah,* pawing at the dash till it snapped off and the afternoon was ghost quiet, blood-savvy gnats humming softly on marionette strings out his window.

He'd come to a stop in the small piazza of a small town full of silence and poverty in equal measure. Three cows lingered in the square enjoying views over the steep ridge. Across the short, sloping campo of rough cement was a humble Romanesque church cheesed up with Doric columns and a baroque portico only painted on, this being a poverty town even then.

Michael breathed through his mouth—deep, fat gulps to slow the sour bile fighting up his throat. The cab smelled of blood iron and burned hay, and he had to get out, out of the glare, out of here. Stiff and swollen, he moved deliberately from the truck. There were coffee-colored leaves blown over the square and they stuck when he dragged his shot ankle. He shuffled like this a dozen steps before sitting down hard and silly like a rodeo clown.

He was dimly aware of the horror he presented: singed clothes, rigor-mortis leg, blood worn like pudding head to toe. He resolved to make the shade of the Romanesque church and rose, swaying drunk in cool shock. The three cows followed his agonizing movements, rechewing their lunch, and one took a step forward and bellowed warningly.

At the speed of a frustration dream he crossed the patched concrete and lent his weight in a stumble against the carved church door, opening it. As Michael's eyes adjusted, the church inside rose in gaudy blue wash and more fake baroque paintings of high-fluted columns and windows that didn't exist looking out on imagined fields of romantic splendor. The altar was sculptured like a general's tomb. No candles burned atop it and the pews were empty. Pigeons roosted somewhere in the tower.

It was a church originally raised in times of chaos and fear, thick walled with windows high and small, built to both serve God and protect the village as a keep. In the centuries that followed it had been tricked up with vanity into a painted harlot of its former simplicity. There were echoes of it, tombs of forgotten cardinals beneath Michael's weakening gait, each etched with a crude skull and crossbones wearing a churchman's miter, reminding a later era that despite all the blue wash, the marble statues to merchant barons, we were all just bones under the floor, and God knew it.

He caught his foot on a kneeling bar, fell hard to the stone, and his cheek rested cold on the cardinal's grave and he didn't— couldn't—rise, and the blood from his foot ran in small eddies through the chiseled words *Ciordana Prap Pro Sacerdotibus*. He crawled forward, dragging his forehead on the stone, leaving a snail's trail to the sacristy door, where the floor turned to terracotta, where he pulled a phone down with a crash from the table and dialed the only number he knew in Italy.

"*Pronto?*"

"Gina."

"Michael?"

"Help me."

# 26.

On Christmas morning Michael walked on Lake Michigan. The coldest afternoon in a generation, and the horizonless gray table seized suddenly at the shore, stiffened, and went white silent a mile out.

Children came down to its edge to taunt its lifelessness, to slap hockey pucks among the frozen sailboat moorings, to stare out at the wonder of it. For freezes happened on Erie, on Huron, but never on deep Michigan. To see it conquered like this brought the entire city to its shore.

Where Michael began to walk.

Past the hockey games and breakwater, where the freeze beneath him was the conviction of granite. Out beyond the hand-off voices of children, first into stillness, then into the battle-ground of ice and water, lake and winter, its howls rumbling in his bones. Further out the water clenched at different levels, creating pressure ridges that exploded as craggy mountain ranges. Michael scaled them, slid down their backs. He didn't understand exactly what drew him out here, so far alone, only that he was nine, bursting with it, and he had to see it, speak with it, climb its whitened heights.

And he saw wonders for himself alone, and his lake did speak to him and the sound was history breaking.

He struggled up the tallest mountain of ice, not half a day old, stood on its forming pinnacle, thrust out his arms, and declared, "I am nine years old and I am master of all I see."

The ice boomed in reply, endless, but there was another sound now, a new one of low cracking. Michael squinted at the shimmering expanse, past seagulls stomping the dead lake angrily...

And saw the freighter.

An iron smudge near shore, lumbering for Gary, cutting the lake in a dirty slice.

Cutting off Michael.

He watched it, geared so low it vibrated windows on Randolph Street, tried to believe, to work out a way it wasn't dividing him from the city, murdering him. And Michael slid down the zippered ice-mountain and began to run. On the way out his steps had been sure, confident. Now, in a mad desperate lunge to beat the freighter to shore, he slipped, stumbled, and tore his hands on razor shards of frozen lake.

And the harder he fought the ice, the more it conspired against him as he went down and down again. It was only when he surrendered, accepted that the freighter would cut him off forever, that the ice began to deliver up purchase. The moment he tried to dominate it, the lake's frozen back turned on Michael and drove him down until he once again submitted, accepted, and the lake would once again lift him, push him, slow the freighter...

It was like that, here on the sacristy floor. When he fought the fog, it closed over and smothered him. When he let go, gave it run, the fog thinned and he could move a little in one pointless direction or another.

The phone receiver howled off the hook, jumbled up somewhere near him. At some point he twisted up in its cord and snapped it off.

He had no idea how long he'd been there, tried to measure time in the growing puddles of his blood. The tile floor ate without prejudice the heat from any part of his body that rested against it, and he had begun to shiver and chatter and it felt absurd...

"Hold still."

"Gina?"

"I'll get help."

"Gina…"

The face seemed bigger than he remembered. Darker. Its voice nervous and unsure, and it was the priest of this trampy church, not Gina, hovering above him.

"Please. Stay still."

"Gina."

"You are very sick."

Fluorescence. Stiff cotton coats hard on his cheek. Dreamy voices, none of them Gina.

Till one is.

And across the years, the blood loss, the lactate stabilizers pumped into him, it's the same. And nothing, nothing about him is the same, and he can hear it when she speaks his name.

"Michael."

"I'm sick."

"You're a mess."

"Do they have guns?"

"You are in a clinic."

"Do they have guns?"

"No, Michael."

"Take me away."

"They are going to move you, Michael. To a bigger hospital. This is only a small town."

"You have to take me."

"You're hurt, Michael."

He reached up blindly, crushed something in weak fingers, and drew it close. Dark-blonde hair. "If I stay here I die…If I stay here I die…"

Repeated till his strength failed and his sight clouded milky lead. "If I stay here I die…"

◎    ◎    ◎

In the end they just walked out.

She gave him her shoulder so he could limp. Put him in the backseat so he could lie down, drove slowly because the curves hurt, to her town, where she eased him to bed, half-conscious, and shot him up with painkillers, because she had these things.

He begged her, over and over in his delirium, to go back and get the truck. She asked him why, and he only repeated that she had to get the truck…She had to get the truck…

Feeling that he was stable enough for her to leave, Gina drove to the poverty town, and the truck was where Michael had crashed it, soaked with blood the local police assumed was from the accident. No one from the hospital had apparently told them their patient had a bullet hole in his swollen ankle, and so the truck remained unmolested outside the church.

There was no one in the piazza, and Gina simply drove the truck away. She parked it in her garage and sat up with Michael as he slept, dreamless.

The next day he woke, looked at her, said he was sorry. Gina nodded. Told him not to move too much. It was the same house from so long ago. The same room, and the room had changed little. She was quieter than he had remembered. Measured, as she carefully tested his shot ankle. She wore her hair to the shoulder, pushed behind her ears, and her eyes were still deep brown but steadier than memory. She was Gina and she wasn't, and he could only imagine what she thought of the wreckage stirring now in her childhood bed.

She told him, with her help, to get up. As he swung his legs slowly over the edge he asked, "Are your parents still out of town?"

"Careful," she said, but he bumped his foot on the plank floor anyway and the pain was white thunder clear up to his jaw.

She eased him across the hall into another room that, to his surprise, had been converted into a small medical treatment space. Gina lowered him onto a raised, stainless steel examination table, asked him to lie down, and it was cold and too small for him.

"Curl up," she suggested.

"It's too small."

"It's made for dogs." He didn't understand. "I'm a veterinarian, Michael. Curl up."

He obeyed, and she began taking off the bandage. Michael watched his foot, purple and swollen, oozing juices clear, juices yellow, juices red.

"They left the wound open. That's normal. They were probably concerned about contamination from the bullet. The blood flow helped wash away foreign fragments. I'll sew it closed now."

"Have you done this before?"

"People shoot dogs too."

She took out a length of sterilized thread.

"Did the doctors call the police?"

"If not they certainly have now."

"That means I'm wanted, Gina. By the police. By…everybody."

"I know." She pumped the wound with lidocaine, and the first tugs of the suture were a dull, tearing sensation. "You said it in your sleep."

"What else did I say?"

"Lots of things. Were any of them true?"

"Were they awful?"

"Worse."

"Then they were true."

She put him in her childhood bed, lit a small coal fire in the grate, and opened the windows to the mountain breeze. He hunkered in the blankets, and she told him to sleep.

"Did you talk to me? When I was asleep?"

"Yes, Michael."

"About yourself?"

"Yes."

"Was it awful?"

"No. But it wasn't the truth, either."

It's dark and Michael wakes to a shutter creaking. He gets up and limps to the phone in her living room. The codeine's worn off and with each downhill pump of his heart the foot backstops a thud of agony. He lifts the phone from its cradle, keeps his foot above his heart on the back of a chair, because that seems to help, and dials a Madrid number. The line hisses, and the ring on the other end is sleepy, but not the voice answering, for it never sleeps.

"Michael."

"Hector."

"Where are you?"

"I'm alive."

"What happened?"

"I just wanted to talk to a friend. Are you still my friend, Hector?"

"Of course."

"Why does the US government have a warrant out for me, Hector? Why does every Carabinieri here?"

"I can find out, Michael. Has there been any sign of the Montoneros?"

"Oh, one or two."

"Is She safe?"

"She's with me." Hiss crept over the line, far off, like wind on the moon. "I'm alone in this, aren't I?"

"Was it ever any other way, my son?"

"I'm going to do this. But not how we planned. No highways. No safe houses. My way." You could hear a breeze, probing the house. "It's cold here."

"Are there stars?"

"They are not my friend."

"I'm your friend, Michael. And I'll be waiting for you."

He hung up, limped back along the wall toward his bed. Stopped first at the examination room and rifled the drawers till he found the amphetamines. Stuffed them under his mattress, because the trip would be long, because he was hurt…just because.

**September 5, 1971**

# 27.

He read the telex again, looking stupidly for a nuance he might have missed, but it was a telex and the message was clear: *no*.

*No* to floating the loss. *No* to delaying the payment of the futures. *No* to extending the line. *No, no, no.* The registered letter beside it was longer, flowery in a way only New York legalese can manage, direct even in its evasiveness: it was gone.

All of it.

Oh, there'd be fire-sale recoveries, pennies on the dollar, globs of meat pulled from the feeding frenzy that had followed, but it was only tailings, for the stake in main had resolutely gone down with the ship.

Otto Spoerri spread the telex and registered letters out like roadkill and reached for his glass, but it was empty, so his hand drew a bottle from the desk and filled it. It was a nice desk, one of the finest here, because he was family.

He sucked a bolt, traced its burning journey. The nice desk faced the nice wall of Brazilian rosewood covered in nice portraits of un-nice men, all of whom were his ancestors. He disliked their gaze on the best of days and this was not the best of days.

The office was nice but not the nicest, because another man now sat there, a man to whom he, and these paintings, were not related. A man who knew utterly the inventory of each item in Otto's office but two: the letters before him and the Luger Otto had stuck into his own mouth this morning but hadn't fired, dried saliva still on the barrel.

The Luger he kept at his side, but the letters and telex he tore into strips and burned in an ashtray.

His father lay dead a decade now, but the family crime was now run by a man not family but more son than he.

The secretary stuck her head in, concerned at the thick haze of burned paper. "Herr Spoerri?"

"Get out."

She did. He drank.

The same gene pool that humiliated him also gave him a vague portfolio, if not trust, at the bank for life. For that, for a chance to honorably claim his birthright from a dead man he loathed, Otto Spoerri had taken a chance. The kind of chance his father, or grandfather, would have taken.

And lost.

It had been a sure thing, an absolute money-maker for the bank, and he couldn't even remember how now.

Otto had taken, against every Swiss banking law known, deposit funds to do it. Millions. And they wouldn't miss it at first, but there would be an audit soon enough and then the man in the nicest office to whom he was not related would disgrace Otto—perhaps imprison him—and so, though the bank carried his name, the Luger seemed to speak it louder. He had already tasted it once, its tang still in his mouth, when the other piece of paper had arrived.

It was not flowery nor a telex nor much but a phone number. He had burned it, but not before calling, and after a brief conversation had set the Luger aside. For now…

He swayed on the way out of his office, and the secretary avoided his gaze. Fuck her.

The bank was quiet so near lunch, and the reps were trying to look busy, pretending not to notice him pass, adjusting their ties, straightening creases. He despised them.

The drinks tapped louder than expected; he wanted to sit down but not in front of these clowns and so went into the safety deposit vault, took a bench under the eyes of guards that wore the suspicious gaze of their real boss in the nicest office. He sat there ignoring them, letting the tapping pass.

And, looking up, realized he'd forgotten just how big hers was.

Even here, among a thousand oversized safety deposit boxes stuffed with a century's trespasses and unburied skeletons, hers was a standout. Two enormous separate boxes, cut and joined as one mammoth unit.

Over the years he had never told anyone of that night, when, as a young man, he made the midnight arrangements for the acquired fortunes of Eva Perón. No one at the bank knew the unnamed owner would never return for it personally, and nineteen years after her death, clearly no one who knew her would either. He'd toyed with the idea of raiding the box, saving himself with it, but he didn't control the guards or seals or laws, and so the fortune would sit and rot until the Swiss government—which had, after all, not grown fat on chocolate and cuckoo clocks—finally claimed the absentee funds for itself.

The city had shirked the warmth of only a week ago and embraced its true nature: gray. Otto turned up his collar, stepped from the bank onto the walking street. Lampposts were already ticking on and in the glow he could see the faces, streaked with freezing drizzle, thinking, *Jesus Christ, it's only September.*

The conversation on the other end of that phone number had been short and unconvincing. But he was a man with the alloy taste of a Luger still in his mouth and required less convincing than usual.

The Limmat was high, rain swollen, and dark as asphalt. They had suggested meeting nearby at the McDonald's, a three-story monstrosity on Banhofstrasse. He disliked immediately the din inside, the music, the burble of school kids wearing fluorescent backpacks.

He found them on the third floor, against the large window overlooking the colorless street, looking so obviously American, even here. The seat was cold plastic, bolted to the table, and he couldn't remember the last time he'd sat on plastic—maybe never.

"Herr Spoerri," the old one said. He was drinking coffee from a Styrofoam cup, and it must have been a rare moment, for the alcohol devastation on his face was absolute. A younger man sat beside him, forty maybe, severely parted dark hair and steady, powerful hands. He stirred a hot chocolate.

The older one saw Otto's annoyance at the surroundings and smiled. "Nobody watches McDonald's, Herr Spoerri." His nose looked like melted plastic. The younger one pushed forward a coffee and a cheeseburger. Otto let it pass.

"So I'm here."

"Yes."

They seemed in no hurry, and he wondered if that was technique, wondered if they could sense the cognac's havoc in his veins.

"You're a man with problems, Herr Spoerri. Big problems."

Against his will, Otto found himself tearing off a corner of burger. "Who are you?"

"People who know of your difficulties."

"Which people?"

"Just people."

"You're misinformed."

The two concentrated on their dissected breakfasts, and he wondered if they'd heard him. Then the young one lifted a stack of papers from his coat pocket and dropped them unceremoniously into Otto's lap. "SEC records on a commodities collapse five days ago." His voice was more clenched than the older one's. Impatient. They both wore haircuts unfashionably short. Government short.

"Your name is on it, hidden but not very well hidden, honestly. The money's all gone, zip, and it couldn't have been yours—not that amount—so yeah, I, we, think you have a problem."

Otto crossed his legs, toyed with his cashmere sock. "The bank invested in some commodities. We lost but we're a large institution, as you must know, and my name is on the building. There's no problem."

And they just stared at him, as though he were a sad, arrogant child.

Down below were families window-shopping—simple people with simple, uncomplicated lives.

"Is this blackmail?"

The older one smiled. "We're here to make your life less complicated, Otto, not more."

The three of them joined the simple people on the street, storm clouds hurrying night, the city washing through a spectrum of slate grays. They arched their collars, threw puffy breaths over their shoulders. It was September.

The older one with the melting face was running through the bank's safety deposit policies with Otto. "And if I want access to a box?"

"If you are on the authorization list, you present your secret account number and the box is removed in the presence of the bank manager and a security detail, who must both code the locks."

"Impressive."

"These are special boxes not often accessed and our clients appreciate the trouble taken to protect them."

It was the young one who spoke now, his eyes window-shopping an appliance store. "What if I just had a key?"

"A key?"

"Just a key."

"We don't do that."

And now the older one joined his friend, gazing at displays of Krups coffeemakers, as if Otto had suddenly vaporized.

"…Not normally."

Both Americans looked up from the shop window and smiled. They walked on. "So if a certain box turned out not to have an authorization list," the older one mused, crouching to cluck the chin of a small child abandoned in his pram, "and just a key, the matter would be more simple?"

"You'd just walk in and open it. If you had the key."

"Even if the box's owner were, say, dead? Dead for years?"

"In the case of abandoned safety deposit boxes, the Swiss banking commission would freeze access and begin a search for claimants."

"How would the bank or Swiss government determine the box was 'abandoned'?"

"If the person is famous or notorious, then through news reports of their death. In other cases, it's usually when the annual box fee stops being paid." Both of them walked along silently, encouraging Otto to connect the dots. "Then the key is no longer enough. The account is frozen."

The two Americans nodded proudly at Otto. "Particularly, I would imagine, in the case of famous, even notorious, clients," the older one prodded.

"The law was mostly created for such clients. To allow governments or individuals to make claims against deposits illegally acquired."

"But I'm guessing, Herr Spoerri, that it's possible a bank manager might, just once, when he was very young—at the time the account was established, you understand—not actually enter a famous person's real identity on the forms."

"Especially, say, a young bank manager with his name on the building," the younger one offered.

"That same bank manager, I would think, knowing the box of a certain famous person is anonymous—anonymous even to other executives of the bank itself—could have, quietly over the years, to avoid having the box declared abandoned, continued to pay the box fee himself. And, if provided with the key, could thus quickly access the account with a minimum of fuss or attention."

They stopped there on the curb, the drizzle turned fairy light, and Otto Spoerri felt a tingling in his legs.

"Do you have the key?"

# 28.

Closing his eyes, he would empty his mind with a memory of the pampas. A bowl of freezing stars, and he would rise into them, focus on each glowing fragment, let it help him sift the Carabinieri radio traffic coming over the head-phones.

Alejandro knew there were other interested ears somewhere, and though a lot happens in northern Italy in a day, it wasn't hard to recognize Suslov's footprint. A shot American, Gary Phillips, brought to a local clinic by a priest's phone call. The priest's town is mentioned, and Alejandro is instantly in motion, racing for the mountains.

Where once there had been indifference thick enough for an unnamed woman to simply drive both Suslov and the truck away, now a small army of Carabinieri crawled over the town, excited with the possible connection between a small-town accident and their fellow officer face-up on an autostrada.

Alejandro slipped past them and entered the church through the rear, following the puddled blood back to the sacristy. There, in the small anteroom, Michael had made his real mess. Chairs tipped over, an end table standing with one leg broken. Blood, in huge looping pools, dried on the floor. There were outlines in the blood, including a clean square of floor, four inches a side. Alejandro glanced at the telephone now sitting on the righted table. There was dried blood on its bottom metal plate. A plate four inches a side.

Low on blood, Michael Suslov must have pulled down the phone to make a call. To whom?

Alejandro stepped out to a pay phone and spoke to the operator, borrowing the name and badge number of a Carabinieri officer he'd seen inside. His accent was lousy but so was the connection and the operator did as asked, connecting him to her supervisor who read off the last number called on that line. It was, of course, the local hospital. The priest had picked the phone off the floor, called the hospital, righted the table, and set the phone upon it.

Alejandro doubted the priest would have called anyone before the hospital, so the second-to-last call would be Michael's. It would take them longer to get an actual address, but the exchange was in a hill town not far from the church. Judging by his blood loss, Michael was there now. Alejandro was sure of it.

"—Getting a brainstorm, butch?"

Alejandro hung up the pay phone. It was the old American and his younger attachment, both in suits, both leaning against the wall beside him like they owned it.

"You asked me to find him."

"We asked you to find *her*."

"I'll find Her, you asking or not."

"Certainly. Our cooperation is testimony to our confidence of that. But we also have an…understanding, right?"

The American looked across the campo and shook his head. "Son of a bitch sure bleeds a lot." A thought seemed to pass through the American, far and worn, and his voice changed slightly. "He's not a bad kid, really. But he's smart…"

"He's committed."

"Well, I suppose you know all about that."

A Carabinieri marshal approached, and the younger American pushed off to deal with him. The older American smiled. "Little cross-jurisdiction discussion. Michael Suslov is wanted by the FBI. Now he's wanted by the Italians. We're here, in the spirit of international cooperation, to help in any way we can."

The American stepped up close, and his breath was a riot of metabolic meltdown. "I know you'll find him, Al. You've got the look. I just want her first. Understand?"

"To authenticate Her."

"Yes, Al, to authenticate her."

Alejandro held his gaze till the American turned and walked for the church.

◉  ◉  ◉

Gina bought him new clothes and oversize slippers. She told him of a friend who did car repairs in a shed behind his house, and at sundown packed her vet bag in the truck, and together they drove the Bedford over. Michael gave the man a handful of lira, and if Gina's friend ever wondered why the damage looked like bullet holes, he didn't ask.

Michael considered moving Evita's locked casket but decided it was as safe here as anywhere. He could limp now, painfully, and Gina lent him her shoulder as they walked from her car to a small café.

"Does it hurt?"

"Constantly."

"You're at your limit on painkillers. I'm figuring you two and a half times the weight of a German shepherd."

"Comforting."

"It'll get better. When the swelling goes down."

A waiter brought coffees.

"Where will you go?"

"It's probably better if you didn't know."

"And in the trunk?"

"A woman's casket."

"Evita's? You mentioned it in your sleep."

"I should sleep less."

Outside two men stepped up to a pay phone on the sidewalk. They were Italian—big, with short haircuts and dark, ribbed sweaters.

"I'll give you some pills tonight. Barbiturates. The sleep is dreamless," Gina said.

"Doggie downers?"

"No. They're human. I have a bottle left."

"From?"

"When I tried to kill myself."

Michael spooned his coffee thoughtfully. "What happened to us, Gina?"

The dark sweaters finished their call as a sedan collected them and sped off. Big guys. Short haircuts.

"Know them?"

"No."

Something stirred in Michael. "Let's go back."

Two blocks from her house the road was cut off by a pair of local police cars. Gina and Michael held back at the corner. "Are they there for you?" she asked.

"For both of us. They must have...they must have found me." Michael craned his neck back down the dark road leading to town. "We have to get the truck."

It was still in the shed, Gina's friend still sanding Bondo by a hissing propane lantern. She spoke to him quietly, and he left with only a nod to Michael. "Where will you go?" she asked.

"Away." He held open the driver's-side door.

"They'll catch you. Out on the road. They must be everywhere now."

"They won't be interested in you. Just say I was an old friend."

"You are an old friend."

He got in and closed the door.

"There's a way," she said. "A small dirt trail that leads up over the border. It isn't on any map. I could show you. Any other way and they'll be watching."

He sat there. Watched the blonde in her hair catch the propane lamp. "Okay."

They drove without headlights, feeling the ruts by starlight. The Bedford's engine whinnied at the strain, and Michael thought it impossible that someone didn't hear them, but no lights showed on the dirt road behind.

"That's my house. Down there."

Michael stopped the truck, and taking the low-light binoculars from his overnight bag, stepped to the edge of the embankment. Her house was visible 250 yards below, bathed in rotating police beacons.

Staying in shadow, he edged up behind a pine and lifted the binoculars. There were half a dozen cars in her drive, most unmarked, some Carabinieri four-wheels. Black sweaters wandered the grounds, shadows crossed upper-bedroom windows, shoulder-strapped uniforms leaned on car fenders.

There were a pair of suits, standing apart, watching the others, toeing gravel in a way somehow not European, their faces in shadow. One's hair was thin and gray, the other thickly black. The gray-haired one turned directly to Michael as if sensing his stare, and a slap of red police light struck his face. It was worn, beaten. It was fifteen years older.

It was Ed Lofton.

The other turned to reach something in his back pocket, and Michael knew the face too: Wintergreen, the embassy marine.

They tossed the house, and he was all over it. Bloody bandages, clothes, poppers of codeine. The old American, Ed Lofton, wondered who the woman was. A long-time resident of the town, she didn't figure as Hector backup. Still, why did she take him in?

The Carabinieri were pounding doors in town, but Lofton knew Michael was gone. Wintergreen lit a cigarette. "Day late and a dollar short."

Lofton grunted, strolled away from the whipping lights that were giving him a headache. He leaned on his unmarked at the end of the drive, tugged on a bolt from his flask…

…And was slammed into the driver's-side window. His cheek bounced off the glass, and he spun around and faced Alejandro, who had his hand on his throat.

"You idiot. What are you doing here?"

Lofton ran a tongue round his cheek for any damage. "We followed you. Cute stunt with the phone number. Should have thought of that."

"You ruined everything. I had him. I had *Her.*"

"Look, all's fun, butch, but why don't you take your hand off my throat?"

Alejandro held him at arm's length. "This is my operation. My mission. Don't get in my way."

"Or?" Wintergreen now, .38 pressed against Alejandro's temple. "*Or?*"

Alejandro turned and looked directly at the ex-marine, without a flinch. "Or I'll kill you both."

"I do like his spirit," Lofton wheezed, still hanging by his neck.

"Let the man down." Wintergreen cocked his gun. "C'mon, Al, I was stare-out champion two years running on my schoolyard. Save it for someone who cares."

Alejandro stared at Wintergreen a moment longer, then let the FBI agent go. Lofton coughed and rubbed his neck. Wintergreen lowered his gun.

"Point taken, Senor Morales," Lofton gasped. "Wintergreen. Be a sport and find my flask." Wintergreen fished it out of the gravel.

"There's a good lad." Lofton drank. "Did you know, Al, that Master Wintergreen here is Spanish Basque? Who knows? Maybe thousands of years ago your ancestors were fucking the same sheep."

Alejandro looked at them each silently, then turned and faded into the dark.

"We need her before she gets to Spain, Al," Lofton called to his back. "Before she gets to Spain..."

"We're gonna have to kill that son of a bitch," hissed Wintergreen.

Lofton massaged his Adam's apple. "He'll find Suslov first."

"Then?"

Lofton turned back to the car. "Then we'll worry about then."

The moon was bright as a blast furnace as the Bedford rocked over short grass and flat slate. They stopped, feeling naked and exposed, the silence enveloping.

They were off the tiny road, following sheep trails, and you could hear them, small tinks on shale rises. The wind carried a gentle chill.

"Across these grasses is an unmarked dirt road. Two kilometers farther...France."

Michael got out, leaned against the truck.

"How's your foot?"

He shrugged. It hurt, but the hurt was becoming familiar and dependable.

"Stay on the road another eight or nine kilometers and you'll reach a junction in Isola."

"Thank you. For everything."

"Wait a week. If your foot doesn't fall off, thank me then."

He nodded, touched her once on the shoulder, and turned for the truck. He was reaching for the handle when his foot caught an edge of broken slate and he fell violently on his side.

Gina rushed to him. "Michael..."

He couldn't even speak through pain-clenched teeth. She lifted his shoulders and cradled his head. "You can't drive. Not the way you're hurt."

"I just need to get in the truck."

"You've reopened the wound. You'll never be able to shift like this."

"I have…I just have to…"

"Go home, Michael. Go back to your life. What could possibly be worth this?"

"You wouldn't understand."

"I might."

Clouds crept up from France and tore themselves on granite sores.

"I know hell is only half-full. But maybe, just maybe, if I finish one thing, keep one promise to one woman in my life, even a dead one…hell will forget my name…"

"Do you really believe a person can fool hell?"

"I have to."

Gina looked out over the ridge and its few scattered German pillboxes, long abandoned and stained with lichen.

"I can drive you further. Get you into France…or Spain."

He turned, and her face was pale as a candle. "Gina. I have nothing left but this. Do you understand? Nothing. It doesn't matter what happens to me. But it matters to me what happens to you."

Gina stood and reached for the driver's door.

"Maybe that's reason enough."

Somewhere they crossed into France.

The road fell off grassy flats, switchbacked down, and pierced a tiny hamlet shuttered tight against mountain ghosts. There were no street lamps or cars, and it passed and was gone.

"What about your family?" He had his head against the seat, window open though the air was cold, because the truck stank of blood and fire and two days of confusion.

"I gave them up."

"Husband?"

"Him too. Did you marry?"

"Once. Why did you try to kill yourself?"

"I'd given everything else up. It just seemed…natural. Turns out I wasn't very good at it. Where's your wife?"

"Dead. A thousand years now."

She was driving well, shifting better than he, and the Bedford appreciated it.

"Everyone you know dies, Michael."

A half hour later they reached the edge of Isola, a cluster of bluish street lamps set among tiled roofs. Dogs howled, a single car made the corner and passed indifferently with amber headlights. French headlights. They turned at the small town-center, crossed a bouldered river into the woods on the other side, shut down the Bedford, and the sound was fast-moving water over smashed rock.

"It'll be morning soon. We probably shouldn't drive by day."

"Will the gendarmes be looking for you?"

"Only takes one angry Italian police call. They must know I'm going west. They know everything else about me."

She did what she could for his ankle and redressed the bandage.

"Those people at my house. You knew them."

"Two of them."

"Are they friends?"

"I worked with them once"—he looked through the trees, across the river and into Isola—"and I don't think they're friends anymore."

Michael opened the door. "We better not risk a hotel. You can sleep in the cab. I'll lie in back." But he was on amphetamines, and she could hear him as she rested her head on the seat, walking circles in the gravel…

She found him at noon, curled asleep among leaves. She left him there and crossed the bridge into town, where they accepted her lira, selling her brioche, ham, and coffee.

When she returned Michael was up, sitting in the open passenger door reading a Michelin map. He waved off the food but took the coffee, and Gina could see it burn its way down his throat.

"There's another dirt track." The map was spread over his knees. "I think it could get us out of the mountains."

"I don't know it."

"We'll have to take the main road to Saint-Étienne to pick it up."

"All right."

Gina turned to the stretched tarp over the truck's bed. "Is she really in there?"

"Yes."

"She's been dead a long time."

"She hasn't begun being dead."

After nightfall they drove the road to Saint-Étienne, picking up the gravel track that wound through crumbling ghost towns going to ruin in the mountain wind. The Alps released them at Barcelonnette and they passed attractive villages. Nobody looked at them. Nobody turned on a flashing blue light. They skirted a man-made lake with shores of concrete dust.

"I smell gasoline."

Michael did too. The engine was hesitating. "I think something's wrong with the truck."

"Can you fix it?"

"Not if it needs anything more than a quart of oil."

The ground lost its mountain gray and sprouted irrigated fields of apples, peaches, cows. One-blink towns crowded neck to neck on the road.

Outside of Sisteron, at the joining of two valleys, the Bedford went into steep motorized senility, forgetting how to shift, how to combust gasoline, forgetting which way was left and which right. "It's dying," Gina said.

He decided on the next repair stop and parked at a small garage, till dawn brought the owner, older and thickset in dirty blue coveralls and crushed beret. He listened patiently to Michael describing the truck's death rattles, then told him this wasn't a repair garage but part of the local farm, which he worked for. The next service garage was ten or fifteen kilometers.

"English?" he asked.

"Irish," Michael lied.

"Ah. Then we both hate the English." With that bond he insisted on looking under the hood. Gina took up a position beside him as assistant, and he liked the attention. Michael felt his mind drifting and sat on a stone curb. The sun burned here but the air held its cold. The old mechanic was grumbling localisms about the engine's condition when he pulled out of its gullet the crushed remains of a bullet.

"You know. Kids," Gina said.

A few minutes more and he came up with additional lead remains and clumps of burned hay.

"Were you in the Resistance?" he called out jovially to Michael.

"Wasn't everyone?"

The mechanic laughed. It was an old and—at the time Michael was in college here—touchy joke about how this most accommodating of countries to its conquerors produced, during the war, a resistance movement a thousand times larger in memory than it ever was in real life. It was shameful history and so now didn't exist. Everyone, you know, had been part of the Resistance.

The mechanic stuck his head back under the hood. Gina walked over to Michael just in time to see him slip two white pills into his mouth. He shrugged. "Helps keep me awake."

"How long have you been awake?"

"Fifteen years."

The mechanic looked up from the engine and drew a finger across his throat. "It's finished."

Michael sighed. "Can it be fixed?"

"It's old. It wants to die."

"But I don't want it to die."

"Such is life."

Michael concentrated on his wounded foot. "Do you have another?"

"Another opinion?"

"Another truck."

"To buy? Right now?"

"This moment."

"I admire your style." He smiled to Gina. "Is he this way with his women too?"

"In all things but his past."

"I've seen the past," the mechanic nodded. "It's not as good as they say."

"I agree," Michael said, and he knew this was a piece of it. Old men like the mechanic, in tattered sweaters and philosophy, had once been everywhere. But they were disappearing from the villages, expendable weight in the race for a future somehow more Teutonic than French. Such men had courage and memories, and the courage of memory was a sometimes dangerous thing in France.

"I have a truck."

At least that's what he called it, one of those horrendous Renault clatter traps with corrugated metal floors, three speeds, and a rubber-band engine. "Does it run?" Michael asked.

"It has never failed me."

"When was the last time you drove it?"

"1968." The bed was big enough. Barely. "I'll give you a good price."

At that moment an army truck rumbled past, full of weapon-ready conscripts, and Michael was standing there, right in plain view, and they didn't stop. He watched the soldiers fade, waited for his heart to steady, then turned to the mechanic. "I need it today."

They agreed on a price, US dollars from the money Hector had given him, and the old mechanic spent fifteen minutes oiling, fussing, and wiping down the dust inside with a rag. He helped load the box, and Michael tried to hide his lame foot, for surely it marked him. But then the casket, which the man never inquired after, probably marked them more than anything. They settled the tarp, settled the paperwork, on which Michael lied from one end to the other, and Gina and he got inside.

"The battery is good but low. It will be fine after an hour or so." With that he gave them a push, Gina let the clutch pop, and the engine started gasping in neck-crunching bursts. "Choke! Choke!" the mechanic cried out. She yanked on it and the engine revved uncontrollably. "Less choke! Less choke!" He was running alongside them now, coaching her. "There, you have it!" He stopped, let the Renault rattle away and called out to them, "Enjoy your vacation!"

First stop on said vacation was another license plate off a field junker. The afternoon had turned warm and swooned with lavender and thyme. Vineyards appeared at Mollans, and Michael had an idea. They bought bread and meats at a market in Entrechaux, pilfered some wooden crates, and under the cover of a vineyard hedge, filled them with stolen grapes so ripe you could see the liquid slosh inside. The crates they stacked in the rear of the Renault, hiding Evita's box.

"So now you're a farmer," Gina said.

"A real farmer wouldn't have bought this truck."

"How's your foot?"

"Killing me."

Out of Entrechaux, in daylight, they traveled down the volcanic side of Mont Ventoux, where the land became the south: brushy hills, cypress trees, people hanging out on doorsteps. The drive was slow, for there were lumbering harvesters everywhere. A provincial cop went past and didn't brake and U-turn. There was nothing to do but accept the favor and keep on.

Michael closed his eyes and listened to the vibrations of the truck. When he opened them they were among castles ruined by time and villages by war.

"Where are we?"

"Near Avignon."

It was getting dark. After a few kilometers he told her to take the next road. She did, and it fumbled along past once-grand estates. The farther they went, the creepier the road became, until Michael told her to stop.

They were in front of a mansion probably considered gentle in its time. Set back behind a wide garden run riot, its tall, latticed windows were mostly broken. "Pull into the drive."

"Here?"

"We can stay."

"Michael, it's barely dark. I can keep driving. We're nearly halfway to Spain."

"No. We'll stay here."

They got out of the truck, Michael limping ahead, leading her up the front steps. The inside was empty but not as ruined as she expected. There was a smell of feral cats. "This way."

He seemed to know where he was going and Gina followed, up marble steps into a grand suite lit purple with twilight. He stood in its center, pointed to a square of oak floor darker than the rest. "The bed would have been here." He pointed to another, smaller square. "The chair, maybe, there."

"Why are we here, Michael?"

He stared at imaginary furniture and told her of how, when Evita arrived in Paris as part of her 1947 European tour, she requested an audience with the pope. While it was arranged, she was brought here to wait. Her personal assistants left for Rome to prepare, and she was left with a small French staff of strangers. What no one realized was that until then, in her entire life, Evita had never spent a night alone.

There had always been brothers and sisters in her bed. Or men. And finally Perón. Even in Paris one of her maids slept with her. But when the sun went down in this room, she was alone. Later, the French staff reported that Eva Perón, First Lady of Argentina and one of the most powerful women in the world, had pushed a chair against the door and wept all night in terror.

He looked out at fading light through broken windows. Sparrows had begun their nightly insect hunt. "There are a thousand stories of her being arrogant, cunning, vengeful. This is the only story I know of her being scared." He turned to Gina, and only half his face was lit in afterglow. "I'm sorry I brought you here. You're right. We should have kept driving."

She hadn't noticed how red his eyes had become, the jitteriness in his hands. She reached out and took one. "Why don't we bring her in so she isn't lonely?"

They placed the box near where the bed would have been and lit the fireplace, cobwebs alighting and drifting through the room like Gaelic fairies. Gina pulled down the musty drapes into a heap, and they sat among them with the bread, meat, and grapes.

"Does she seem truly real to you, Michael? Something more than just a box?"

"Do you want to see her?"

Her voice faltered. "It never occurred to me."

"It's okay." He stood and limped to the box. He worked at the bolts, but a few were determinedly frozen. He hit them with the base of a wine bottle and the screech was like grave robbing.

"Michael…"

But the lid was open. And against her will, Gina walked toward it. Michael's shadow kept the contents in darkness, but as Gina came slowly alongside he stepped away and the firelight bathed her. "Oh my God…"

"Dr. Ara, the man who embalmed her, spent a year and a hundred thousand dollars doing it. Each night he slept in the room with her, so she wouldn't be alone."

After nineteen years moisture had stained the casket's silk lining and the tip of her nose had broken off. "Month after month, he submerged her in baths of acetate and potassium nitrate. Month after month he injected into her formol, thymol, and pure alcohol in secret combinations only he knew. Month after month he coated her in thin layers of liquid plastic."

Gina turned away. "How could they do that to someone?"

Michael studied Evita's face a moment, then shut the lid. "She belongs to the people."

"How could the *people* have done that?"

"They did it from the beginning. From the first day they saw her. They lifted her and changed her and made her theirs. They never cared who she really was. They don't now. Men have fought and died for her, and who she really was doesn't matter at all. In fact it's probably better for them that she's dead. Now the only sound she can make is what they put in her mouth."

"Is there anything left of her?"

"Everything. That was Ara's genius. Everything but the blood."

Gina went back and sat among the drapes. "She's nothing but a flag to them."

"Yes."

"And to you?"

"A flag of a different kind."

"What kind, Michael?"

He stepped carefully back to their makeshift bed and lowered himself. "A promise."

"A flag for a promise?"

"A flag for one promise kept."

Gina stared into the flames. "You knew her."

"A part of her."

"I think we die twice. The first time is physical. The second is when the memory of us dies. When the people who loved us for who we were are gone. That's when we're truly dead." She turned to him. "Everyone who knew her as a person is dying. One day you could be the last."

"And when I die?"

"Then she'll be truly nothing but a stuffed flag."

# 29.

It was dark but the air still gusted a hot madness that cracked Hector's nose membranes. For the second time he wiped blood from them, standing there in Juan Perón's library at the villa at 6 Calle de Navalmanzano. Outside, Madrid was rising and looking for dinner. It was a thick book in Hector's hands, *History of South American Horses*, horses being one of the general's obsessions, and the only one that seemed to raise him anymore.

"My first cavalry horse. A criollo. There's a picture in there of it. God, I loved that horse. A wonderful book, no?"

Hector looked in the direction of the voice and found an oil painting of the General. Commissioned at the height of his vitality and popularity, he was an imposing man, ramrod straight in brown uniform and presidential sash.

The man sitting beneath the portrait wore a stained Hawaiian shirt, faded slacks, and no shoes. His voice was weak, and gray tufts of hair bushed from his nose. "Yes," Hector said to General Juan Perón, "it's a lovely book."

"You never rode, Hector?"

"I was weak as a child."

"Ha! Weak like a snake!"

Hector closed the book and returned it to the shelf.

"They say I cannot ride anymore," Perón said. "What good am I? Seventy-eight and now I drink tea for whiskey, eat soup for beef, sleep with a bar dancer for…" Still, after all these years, he couldn't bring himself to utter her name.

"Good enough to be president again."

"Bah. A nation of imbeciles. They eat themselves until there is only a mouth left, and now the mouth wants me, a man who has not set foot in that cursed land for sixteen years."

"The junta has agreed to elections. The Peronists—your Peronists—will win. You will return as their true leader, bringing peace to your home."

"Spain is my home now. I expected to die here. I may still."

"You will return with *Her*."

Perón's eyes reflexively rose to the attic they were enlarging for her arrival. The man was a ruin. A shell. He rose late, was in bed by nine, spent his days wandering an unfashionable villa given him by Franco, his old friend who had not bothered to visit in the years Perón had been here. "Yes," Perón said quietly, gazing through the ceiling into the attic, "the mouth must ultimately have its fill. Even of the dead."

Isabel, the third wife, entered. "Darling, Lopez Rega says you must unfasten your trousers. For your digestion." Perón complied, right in front of them, and Hector knew Perón was finished. Anything he might have been once had drained away years ago in this mausoleum. A turn or two in the revolving door and he'd be gone—replaced, Hector knew, by his ratlike ambitious wife, Isabel. Isabel and Lopez Rega, of course.

Perón sat there like furniture stuffing, his pants unfastened and lying in peeled flanks. You could glimpse underwear, urine-stained. Their leader. This was not stability before Hector but merely a pause before deeper chaos. Still, one nightmare at a time...

Later that night, Isabel—bar dancer, future First Lady—roamed the darkened villa with a candelabra, singing incantations of power. An entourage of maids and cousins followed her in a train, and Hector watched them from the upstairs gallery, a sinister glowworm, the light rising and falling through the house.

When he looked up, Lopez Rega, Isabel's spiritual advisor, stood beside him. He was a short, brutish man with the hot eyes of a demon. He preferred to stroll the house in silk pajamas and stank of lavender toilet water. It was Lopez Rega who now screened all the General's letters, decided whom he saw and whom he didn't, prescribed the General's diet, read his bowel movements; the one who led endless séances to call spirits to Perón's side. Claiming to be in daily contact with the archangel Gabriel, he drew up complicated horoscopes only he could interpret. It was Isabel who first brought him into the house, but it was Rega—all Rega—who stayed.

"Dr. Ara is coming," Rega said. Even normal sentences had a way of sounding perverse and obscene in his mouth.

"The embalmer," Hector answered.

"He's much more than that." Lopez Rega's eyes fell to the glowworm, snaking its way through the dining room. "Isabel shall usher in a new age for our nation. I have seen it in the stars, read it in the leaves, seen it in my own dreams."

"And the General?"

"All this through the greatness of General Perón, of course."

Of course.

"She will need not only support but tools to help this dream come to pass." Rega's lips quivered when he spoke in a manner that made Hector avert his eyes.

"Tools?"

"Money."

"She will be First Lady of a great nation."

"A nation broke. Defeated…"

Lopez Rega thought a moment. "You liked Evita."

"I like everyone I work for, Lopez."

"You admired her."

"Yes."

"Even though she stole."

"Even though everything."

Down below, Isabel's childlike songs echoed strangely, and Hector thought of graveyard interrogations.

"Don't you ever still wonder, Hector, after all these years, where she put it?"

**September 7, 1971**

# 30.

He isn't taking the highways. We have men watching all the westbounds. They stop any trucks that fit your profile."

The Surete Nationale officer stood at a map of the area. He was speaking French, and it was Wintergreen who translated for Lofton, sitting there in a chair, staring at a map of highways and the clouds of lesser roads between highways.

"He's taking the country roads." Lofton's words went up and back along the language chain.

"It would take him days that way to reach Spain."

"He has days."

"All the local provincial police have been notified."

"Have they set up roadblocks?"

"We cannot stop all of France."

Lofton stared glumly at the map, then smiled brightly at the French police official. "Thank you, Captain. I appreciate your help. I know you and your men are doing everything possible." The captain nodded. "Master Wintergreen, why don't you and I take a stroll in the delightful southern French sunshine."

They did. Lofton stopped a dozen yards from the police station and sighed. "Am I correct in detecting a certain lack of urgency on the part of our frog comrades?"

"An American guilty of American crimes, dead Italians or no, I'm sure a part of our police captain would just as soon see Suslov make Spain. It'd be out of their hair."

"Do you think he'll make it?"

"Suslov?...No."

"How's our bloodhound?"

"Off sniffing his own trails."

"Has he checked in?"

"Of course not. He's switched to a motorbike, but there's a transmitter in the radio we gave him. He's still on a leash."

"Homing transmitters. Haven't done one of those since…"

"Buenos Aires." Lofton looked at his feet and was somewhere else a moment. "They're smaller now," Wintergreen added, "the transmitters."

When Lofton looked up, his bloodshot eyes were somewhere else. "Do you ever have second thoughts? About all of this?"

"Not really."

"Me neither, son." Lofton turned and started back for the police station. "Though I was rather hoping you would."

You could smell the ash in the fireplace and know they had been here the night before. You could see the imprint of two bodies left behind in the wadded drapes, and that meant Michael had brought the woman with him into France. Alejandro had understood Michael would have to stop at this place, one of *Her* places. And of course he would have brought a woman—he seemed always to keep women near—to prevent his mind from completely melting down.

Rosa was such a woman. Michael hadn't brought her, because she clearly knew him too well, and he had reinvented himself with old clothes for this last mile of life.

It was easy to smell the ash in the fireplace, to interpret the drapes on the floor, and it was no harder to see the small white envelope peeking out from a crevice beneath the window. It was sealed, and when he tore it open he recognized Hector's handwriting. *My thoughts are with you, my son. Consider the other. Consider the unity of both your missions...*

And Alejandro wondered if he had written it to Michael or him.

# 31.

The drive was slow, choked with harvest and grapevines so vital they leapt the road, went native, and strangled trees. The sun stung, mountains elbowed them south toward the Mediterranean. The day grew hot by the hour, and Michael slumped in the sawtooth shoals of an amphetamine crash.

"Michael?" She was driving and he had trouble remembering where he was. "Are you okay?"

"Sure." He looked down at the floorboards. "I think my foot is beginning to stink."

"It's just the bandage. We'll change it later." He leaned back and thought, *I've been shot. I was actually shot. I'm driving the French countryside and I have a bullet hole in my ankle.*

"Where are we?" he asked.

"Between Pont du Gard and Nîmes."

"We're getting nowhere in these hills."

"These hills have only one direction out going west, Michael."

"Meaning?"

"If I were the police, I'd be watching that road."

Michael looked at the map. "What are you thinking?"

"Stay on this road till the last moment, then slip into Nîmes. They won't expect that."

"Because it's insane. Us, Her, in the middle of a city?"

"Only for a moment. Just south of Nîmes, four separate roads branch back into the hills *after* the western exit. Four roads they would have to watch, Michael, instead of one."

"We'll be sitting ducks."

"We've been sitting ducks since we started."

◎  ◎  ◎

He drove as fast as the stolen motorbike would let him, air howling around his sunglasses. He stuck to the coastal highway and blew in a rage through flat, insular towns grouped around funnel-shaped water towers. At a roadside mall he bought a two-franc bottle of wine he poured in the dirt. At another he bought an alarm clock and wire. At a gas station he filled first his panting bike, then the wine bottle, adding powdered Jell-O and corking it.

Alejandro no longer noticed if people blanched at his face. He had been following Michael too long, spent too many days just reacting to him. The time had come to anticipate, to reach into the lost man's mind and cut him off. The bottle of gasoline, stinking of Jell-O, clinked in the saddlebag, and Alejandro thought, *It's a medieval plan, like this land, and yet all Argentine…*

◎  ◎  ◎

The one road west curled two turns below them. European bugs hummed European songs in the grass. Wintergreen handed Lofton a Coke.

It was sticky outside the tree shade. French cops sat on the trunks of their cars, smoking. Some kicked around a soccer ball.

"You should get out of the sun."

"I find its rays today…medicinal."

"You look like you're going to have a stroke."

"And will, I'm sure. But not before we finish this." There hadn't been a car in twenty minutes. Lofton sighed. "Think you could suggest that our Gallic colleagues be ten percent less obvious? You can see the roadblock from bloody Normandy."

Wintergreen nodded and turned. Lofton held him with a touch on the sleeve. "Speaking of international cooperation, our boy Alejandro still sniffing his own tail?"

"Moving like a bat out of hell along the coast toward Béziers."

"Young man has the conviction of a crusade. Any idea what he's doing there?"

"Transmitter says where, not why."

"Amuse me with a guess, son."

"Alejandro thinks he has a bead on Suslov."

"An empathy."

"One doomed fuck to another. Maybe he figures him for the coast."

"Suicidal, isn't that?"

"Mrs. Perón went the same route, on her trip here in '47."

Lofton paused, thoughtful. "Think Suslov's really that screwed up?"

"No. But I think he's that doomed."

Lofton tapped a fingernail against his tooth, a habit that had driven Wintergreen crazy since BA.

"Get the car."

"Where are we going?"

"You."

"Where am *I* going?"

"Béziers."

"And then?"

"Don't lose Al, Mr. Wintergreen. Just don't lose Al…"

◎　◎　◎

He felt as if a large sign was painted across the side of the truck: HERE! EVA PERÓN IN HERE! He sensed the stares of every face and had the time to concentrate on them because they were stuck flat dead in traffic.

"Are you all right?" she asked.

"I need caffeine."

"You need a week's sleep."

"Till then I need caffeine."

Nîmes was hard, a faded city laced with the danger of the coast. They kept to its scarred fringes: hypes sleeping under palm trees; Africans selling out of suitcases; easy, loose-stepped women in shorts; and young men appraising every-thing.

They turned right on Rue du Gard and just like that there was a beat cop on the corner. Michael felt the top of his head float slowly away as the officer looked directly at him. Michael stared back, was afraid to break the connection too hastily, and every detail of the officer's blue pillbox hat, his epaulet, his gun strap and buckle were burned into his brain. He would never forget that face, would sooner forget Karen's. They were locked together forever.

The cop turned away. It was only after a moment that Michael realized he hadn't been breathing. He wasn't sure if he wanted to start now.

"It's okay, Michael," Gina said.

"I need some caffeine."

◎  ◎  ◎

Farther from the road than he had in mind, but better because this canyon was just tight enough to form a natural chimney and loose enough to keep feeding it air.

Alejandro picked his way through dry brush to the bottom. There he stuck a length of wire into the bottle of gelatin gasoline, capped it with wax, and ran the other end to an alarm clock. Alejandro needed a time, an exact time, and he set the hands at 8:25 p.m.: the moment She died.

He hiked back up, stood on the ridge, and thought, *I don't sweat anymore. My pores have been cauterized shut.*

Below, bunched up close, were four roads heading west.

◎   ◎   ◎

Hector had his contacts in the French police, ears bought over time the way everything is ultimately for sale in France. Road-blocks were being thrown up across the western routes of the country. There was a circulation picture of their quarry, and it was such an old photo Hector wondered if Michael had photographed any part of his life over the last fifteen years.

The Italians wanted Michael to avenge a dead cop. But the French wanted Michael because the FBI wanted Michael.

The FBI. It was a piece Hector had trouble fitting. He didn't force it, rather let it glide over the puzzle, seeking its own place. The FBI knew Michael, but was it really Michael they wanted? They'd turned loose a damaged Argentine boy to hunt their quarry down, a boy they couldn't possibly come close to under-standing, but was it all for Michael?

Or Her?

That night Dr. Ara joined them for dinner at Perón's Madrid villa. Long since retired from diplomatic service, his body imploding on itself, he still carried that elfin face and Castil-ian superiority Hector let wash over him like dull wind. Evita's embalmer spoke of his travels, of lazy sunsets on Greek islands, of chance cadavers in Africa and Bombay on which he practiced his art of preservation. He spoke of many things and many places, but never of Her. Yet she was at the table just the same as if she were his date, and no one could help think, each time the doctor opened his mouth, of his promiscuity with her fluids and tissue, with her essence, and of the room he supervised being readied in the attic for her return.

Hector watched Perón. While Isabel clattered her dinnerware in a child's attempt to reclaim attention she felt being sucked from her, Perón grew silent. He had difficulty looking at Ara directly, as if the months the embalmer had spent alone with his wife's body were a kind of adultery never confronted.

Hector excused himself to bed early enough to avoid the night's offerings of witchcraft. He slept well as usual but awoke late with a call to the toilet down the hall. It was at the stairs that he saw Lopez Rega on the landing below, speaking quietly to Dr. Ara. They could have been talking of almost anything sacred or vulgar, but they weren't.

They were talking about Evita's stomach.

# 32.

At 8:24, the western hills filled with sunset.
At 8:25 they filled with the tingle of an alarm clock and, a moment later, the liquid *pop* of glass.

It wasn't long before people smelled it, but this was the season of harvest burns and no one was sure. And when they were, when the orange glow set the ridges against the sky like a second setting sun, it was too late.

They were not long out of Nîmes on a road headed west when the traffic suddenly came to a stop. Gina got out, walked the line of impatient French drivers, and saw a fireman holding traffic. When she got back in, you could see tufts of ash on the seat. "They're stopping traffic. There's a fire."

"I don't trust our luck twice in Nîmes."

"The whole ridge is burning."

"We can't stay here. We've got to find another road. Some-place to wait this out."

Gina watched the growing radiance in the sky. "Do you ever think about God, Michael?"

"No. But I've always had the feeling he spends a lot of time thinking about me."

Gina slipped the truck into gear, pulled out of traffic in a U-turn, and started back down the road.

◎  ◎  ◎

Trapped drivers sat like lemmings on the four western roads, in four barricaded lines, each growing longer with the futile hope that the fire wasn't that bad.

Alejandro dropped his motorcycle and walked the rows, just another irate driver, and his no-face dipped in and out of shadow from the burning glow. He stopped at any vehicle big enough to carry a coffin, sometimes scaring small children, always looking for Suslov, knowing, in his heart, that the man had more in him than to wait and die at a roadblock.

The police would be shutting down the exits from Béziers or Montpellier, so either they were bottled up in town, in which case the gendarmes would eventually trip over them, or they were up here, between roadblocks, alone with him. Alejandro felt he knew Michael now. And he knew they were close. Each advancing barrier of fire he set shrunk the remaining distance between Alejandro and Michael. Alejandro and Her.

*You would return Her for the use of a government that despised Her. I want only to return Evita to those that love Her. Love Her, Michael Suslov.*

*Like you, I'm starting to think.*

◎  ◎  ◎

Lofton watched the fire from the edge of Béziers. Ridge after ridge consumed silently miles away. The air was still here but you could tell it was devilish at the center of that.

"Your boy does subtle work." Wintergreen on the radio. He was out there tracking Alejandro south of the fire. "Though I suppose if you're going to create an international incident, you might as well make it a good one."

"Where is he?"

"Al? Doing circles up here somewhere. I think. Fire's playing fuck-all with his tracker. What do you want me to do in this mess?"

Lofton swallowed from his flask. The taste had gone metallic. He keyed the radio. "Wait."

To get off the barricaded road they took the first gravel path they came on, and it went to dirt immediately, dying altogether in a rumpled field. They backtracked to the road and sought out another path. It was getting hard to see, the smoke thickening and no longer smelling of harvest but of sage and dirt and things wild. The power must have gone down in the few villages, for there were no lights anywhere to orient with.

Gina chose another path, and it finished even sooner on a locked cattle gate. Michael got out and shook it, but the gate held firm. "We're going to end up in town," Gina said.

"We can't."

"Maybe with all the confusion of the fire—"

"He lit this."

It began to snow. Millions of dandelions bursting in the heat, their soft white bodies filling the air, like a blizzard. It was getting hard just to see from the truck to the gate. Gina caught a dandelion in her fingers and looked with apprehension at the swirling dark around them. "Would he really do all of this?"

Michael was going to say something pointless when a bloom of heat stung his back and he turned from her instead, faced the current of fleeing dandelions, and watched smoke boil away to reveal a wall of flame marching across the hill toward them. "We have to get out of here."

They backed down the path, traveled again the main road till it suddenly disappeared in a fiery maw ahead.

"Oh God…" Gina said. He didn't have to tell her to stop, turn around, run. Neither of them were sure which way to go, but the fire left few choices, reducing even those by the second. Smoke descended on them heavy as soup, and the world went a dull, glowing black.

Gina took a trail—maybe it was a trail—and the Renault shimmied and spun on soft earth as they climbed. Nothing was visible in the headlights but the few feet of dirt directly in front of them. Michael had no idea how far they traveled—it was impossible to judge either time or speed—only that the trail flattened out on a knoll of some kind.

"Stop the truck." She did. Michael opened the door and it was getting hard to even breathe out here.

"Where's the fire?" Gina asked.

Michael looked out on what passed for a foggy horizon and saw only murderous red. "Everywhere."

"Where do we go?"

Fire had already closed over the trail they'd driven up on. Everything was only unfocused scarlet, hot and dark, on every side. "Christ, I don't know."

As his eyes clouded at the lashing smoke, a silhouette emerged from the darkness coming resolutely at them. It held a pistol at the end of an arm outstretched and moved without pause till the pistol was in Michael's face, and it was Alejandro.

"You. Come. Now."

Alejandro half tugged, half threw Michael into the cab. Gina moved on her own, compliant, and Michael wished she'd run. Alejandro jammed inside beside Michael and they were three upfront, the young Argentine practically in Michael's lap. He kept the gun aimed both across Michael's nose and at Gina beyond. "Drive."

"Where?"

"Straight. Right a little."

There was only fire everywhere she looked. "Are you sure?"

"This is my fire."

Gina steadied herself and edged the Renault forward. Alejandro's face nearly touched Michael's, his free hand a vise on Michael's arm. The face smelled like rotten cotton and looked like boiled hamburger. "You killed those cops," he said to the mask.

"I haven't begun killing."

Gina stepped harder on the gas toward what seemed to Michael only a sheet of flame. The whirl of heat jumped all over them but was thinner here than elsewhere—a facade—and Michael thought, as they popped through the other side, *This boy knows his fire.*

They rummaged a path, squeezing carpets of embers as Alejandro ordered Gina when to turn in the gray-black sameness. Michael found it hard to believe the man had any real sense of where they were. How could he?

"I am curious," the boy with the destroyed face said, his gun occasionally bumping Michael's cheek, and the memory was instantly Moori Koenig and a Recoleta closet full of Evita. "Why you do this? I think not for money or patriotism."

"To finish this."

"That is important to you?"

"I don't know. I've never finished anything before."

Alejandro gazed at the unstable blackness around them. "You knew Her?"

"I met Her. I'm not sure anyone knew Her."

Alejandro seemed jealous of the familiarity. "Tell me about Her."

"She was strong and frightened. Pure and dirty. She suffered badly but died well…"

"She was the light of my life."

"She was the end of mine."

Alejandro seemed to think a moment. It was difficult to tell under the mask. "It seems strange we should be on different sides."

"You serve chaos."

"You serve murderers."

"But mostly I serve myself."

"I serve only Her."

"Keep telling yourself that, Al…"

Like an errant herd of buffalo, a churning arm of the fire slid over the road behind them and gave chase. "We must go faster," Alejandro ordered Gina. She drove harder, tires banging furiously the ruts, and the fire stayed on their tail in pursuit.

There was nowhere to go but straight ahead, the fire leapfrogging at unbelievable speed. Gina pushed the Renault to its maximum, the little truck's rubber-band engine screaming in pain. But the way had turned to steep switchbacks, and like all fires this one liked switchbacks.

Out of the gusting ash ahead emerged the faint shapes of concrete blocks. Spaced one after another along the road, open on one side with rounded, oriental tops, they seemed like guard shacks to a raja. "Where are we?" Michael said.

One of the concrete shacks slid past Gina's window. Its insides, blackened by smoke, held a sculptural tableau of Christ being crucified by the Romans. "They're stations of the cross…"

The road ended.

Right at the base of a broad set of stone stairs. It was difficult to see the top, the only things visible being three massive, oversized crucifixes.

The fire, perhaps smelling blood, doubled its efforts and was now a lazy wave of death sloshing up at them. "Drive up the stairs," Alejandro ordered.

"You're crazy," Gina said.

"Do it!"

"It's impossible!"

Alejandro leaned across Michael and leered the gun at her. "You want to die? To burn? Here? Now?"

Gina exploded. "Stop shouting at me! Stop threatening me! I don't care, do you understand? I don't care!"

And to Michael's surprise Alejandro spoke softly to her. "Please. Gina. Drive up the stairs. I'll coach you."

The truck held its traction better than Michael expected, as the insides jostled madly on each step. Unburnable stone gave them a small jump on the flames, now washing up at the stairs' base, fumbling and yowling like pack dogs.

At the top they reached a flagstone square and climbed out where the three oversize crucifixes loomed in smoky silence: Jesus flanked by Dismas and Gestas.

There's an inherent gothic horror to crucifixes everywhere, but these...the arms bound instead of nailed—the way the Romans really did it—the stains on Christ's loincloth, his face not beatific, not accepting, but caught as if in midspasm, lips parted, the human in him dying hard and lonely. It was horrible.

"What is this place?" Gina asked.

Ruins, mostly. Collapsed stone blocks choked by brush lit by the fusillade of embers carried on fire wind. There was nowhere to go. Nowhere to protect the truck. Michael felt the lake of flame below watching, waiting for the signal when it would simply move in and consume them.

Alejandro had left them for a stretch of wall. There were two *pops* from his pistol, the sound of chains pulling, and Alejandro was back, gun out, for this was not a discussion.

"Get Her out of the truck."

Gina shouldered her vet bag. Michael did what he could on his ruined foot, but it was Alejandro and Gina in the end who took most of the casket's weight.

The chained doorway Alejandro had shot the lock off of led into a musty basement that smelled of rat feces. Michael's last glimpse behind him, as they descended the steps carrying Evita's casket, was of fire washing around the crucifixes and licking the ruins' grounds.

The roof was fractured stone and the firestorm above cast unearthly shafts of red over faded religious mosaics and smashed crypts. They set the casket down, got their breath, and Gina gazed at the mosaics. "*Tot co que's Dieu...*" she read. "It's Occitan."

"Occitan?"

"The ancient language of the Cathar heretics. The King burned the last of their priests in the fourteenth century. This must have been one of their monasteries..."

Alejandro's gaze was on the ceiling, as it breathed threateningly. His eyes fell to the plundered tombs around them, most smashed and covered in graffiti, but one with a stone lid was still in decent shape. "Put Her in there."

"The casket'll never fit."

"Then take Her out of it."

Michael stared at him a beat then complied and pried open the lid. The woman was as they'd left her. Unchanging. A biological sculpture lit freakishly by the probing flames above.

Alejandro looked stupefied, and Michael realized this must be the first time the Argentine had actually looked upon the face of his obsession as an adult. His eyes couldn't stop moving over her. "Get Her inside..."

Gina's face shuddered with reluctance, but together they lifted the former First Lady, Michael awkward on his foot, and when he slipped Alejandro pressed the gun's muzzle to his ear. "You put the goddamn bullet in my ankle, so why don't you give me a break, huh?"

"Just be careful."

"I knew her too, okay?"

They set her easily into the marble tomb as the roof began to groan. "Now what?" Michael asked.

The firestorm howling up the sides of the ruins was developing the low rumble of an approaching tornado. "It's going to kill us," Gina whispered.

Alejandro looked at them both then waved his gun. "Get in the tomb."

"With Her?"

"This place is all rock. The fire will pass over quickly. There's only brush above to burn."

"You're insane."

"Get inside. Now."

They stepped into the dank interior. Built to be roomy for one, it was instantly tight for four. Michael went first, scrunching himself to one mossy side away from Evita. Gina lay beside him, her back to his face, and he held her from behind to make their profile smaller. Alejandro then pushed the stone lid nearly closed over them, climbed in on the opposite side of the body, and tugged the lid closed.

"I'm scared," Gina whispered.

Michael held her tighter to him. "You and I and tombs, huh?"

She gave a small laugh, his face full of her smell.

As the burning tornado above lashed and sought their hiding place, Alejandro said in a strange voice, "What did the Cathars believe?"

"They rejected all earthly matter," Gina answered, "and believed Satan as powerful as God. And as eternal. Earth to them was the soul's chain and the only real power rested in the dead..."

The tornado hit.

The air around them lifted and attempted escape as sudden stabs of red forced themselves through cracks in the crypt, and Michael saw Alejandro holding Evita against him, his voice tiny and broken: "*I saw you. I saw you in heaven...*"

The fire screamed and instantly began pounding their hiding place like a furious child…then just as abruptly grew bored and moved on.

Michael could feel the radiant heat left in the marble cooking his back. "We have to get out."

There was no answer from Alejandro, just a child's snuffling. Then in one movement he rolled on his back, raised his powerful legs and forced the crypt's lid aside.

They rose cautiously from the tomb, careful of the Senora, and the room around them, including Evita's coffin, was completely fried. The fire may have only glanced this place, but it glanced it completely.

Alejandro no longer bothered with his gun and lent his full support in lifting Evita's body, carrying her up blackened steps into a world fire had consumed and abandoned. The Renault had been cooked into nothingness, small flames licking its carcass. One of the massive crucifixes—Gastas—blazed like a Klan burning. They stood between it and the destroyed Renault, like some punished and sacked funeral procession.

"How are we going to get out of here?" Michael croaked as he gazed across the charred land around them. They set Evita on a flat rock, like Abraham's sacrifice of his son. Tiny hands still grasped the rosary to her breast. Gina rifled her vet bag for burn ointments.

"Hey. Spook."

Michael looked up. It was Wintergreen coming up from the smoldering courtyard, looking like he'd had his own close call with the night's events, his pistol loose in a sooty hand. "What a fucking disaster," he breathed, hard from the effort. "Nice work, Al. We'll only spend the next decade trying to smooth this over." Wintergreen shifted his position, gun still easy in their direction, and for the first time saw Evita resting on the flat rock beside them. "Christ, is that her?"

"It's Her," Michael answered dully. He could see now, at the far end of the courtyard, a surprisingly undamaged French four-wheel that must be the ex-marine's.

"She's smaller than I expected," Wintergreen said.

"Where are the others?" Alejandro asked.

"They're nearby, don't worry. We've had loads of fun looking for you in all this. Borrow your radio? Don't know where the hell mine's got to."

Alejandro handed his over, and Wintergreen muttered something into it, receiving a muddled squawk in return. Finished, he looked back at Evita. "Y'know, I saw her once too. On a street corner. All mink and attitude. Look at her now..." He stared a moment longer. "I never got you and her, Mike. The ice princess and the schoolboy spook with 'lost' stamped on his forehead."

"I don't remember any of this stamped on yours."

"Just didn't look hard enough."

"What did I miss, Wintergreen? What did I miss in all this?"

Wintergreen sighed. "You bought their bullshit, Mike. Evita the divine. Evita the wondrous. Just a whore who got lucky, that's all. A girl on the make with cheap dyed hair and a hundred million she looted from her beloved *descamisados* and stuffed in a Swiss bank. Evita may be a saint in the *arrabales*, but she was smart enough to figure she might have to buy her way into heaven."

Michael could feel Alejandro stiffen with rage beside him. Wintergreen must have too, for his smile became forced and his gun gripped a little tighter. "Nothing personal, Al."

"What is she to you, Wintergreen?" Michael asked. "You don't care about Argentina. There's no reward for carrying her over the border into Spain."

"—They want her money." Gina.

Wintergreen swung his gun around at her. "What's in the bag?"

"Medical kit."

"Put it down."

Gina squatted gently and set it in the dirt.

"Is that it, Wintergreen?" Michael asked. "Is it her money?"

Wintergreen considered, then a smile broke out over his features. "Acres of it, Spook. Stuffed in a drawer."

"What drawer?"

"Think about it."

Michael did, and the answer was cloudy and unsatisfying. "But there'd be rules, access codes, signatures…"

"Not when you're the First Lady, son. Not when you're *Santa* Evita. *Santa* Evita just gets a key."

"Where's the key?"

Wintergreen just smiled, his eyes darting to Alejandro. "Why don't you ask Dr. Ara?"

"What does he mean?" Gina asked.

"I told you about Ara," Michael said. "He embalmed her. The Ara method. Everything intact inside but the blood."

The ex-marine seemed pleased. "Remember that café bomb in '55? Right in broad daylight at the one place you could get a decent hamburger? Only killed that drunk, Tomi-something? He was delivering X-rays for Dr. Ara. X-rays of a certain dead woman. X-rays blown all over the sidewalk, just waiting for someone to pick up."

"You think she took her own key with her."

"Don't just think, Spook."

Michael turned to Alejandro. "What did they tell you? That they needed her body first? Just for a little while?"

"I don't care about Her money," Alejandro answered. "It is Her person that will save the revolution."

"But what did you think they were going to do, Alejandro? Search her pockets? Pat down her hair? The woman *took it with her.*"

It was hard to read a man without a face. But it wasn't hard to read Wintergreen at all. "Why don't we keep this friendly, Spook, huh?" He waved his gun at Michael. "Take her to my truck."

"What are you going to do?" Alejandro asked.

"We're going to borrow her, Al. Just long enough to authenticate her fingerprints. We're on your side."

"Where are you taking Her?"

"I don't know, okay? You'll get her back. Like we said."

"It's not her fingerprints they're after," Michael said. "They're going to find a table. And then they're going to find a butcher. And when they're finished, they'll find some plastic bags to give her back to you in—"

"Stop talking shit," Wintergreen snapped.

"Look at her, Alejandro. Think about what they're going to do to her. She took the key *with her*."

"I don't care about Her money!" Alejandro shouted.

"But they do, Alejandro. They care a lot. And they're going to carve her to pieces for it."

Wintergreen swung his gun squarely into Michael's face. "You're under arrest, Suslov. Murder and about a thousand other charges. Now why don't you start behaving yourself and help us move the lady before she catches cold."

Michael didn't react, and Wintergreen jammed the muzzle into his cheek, hissing, "I know how to use this, Suslov. *I* won't miss and kill my wife."

Michael's eyes went flat. He stared at Wintergreen coldly and something in the ex-marine paused. He seemed about to say more but stopped. Maybe because of what he saw in Michael's eyes; maybe because it occurred to him that he should never have taken the gun off Alejandro.

Wintergreen spun, and Alejandro had an elbow ready that he slammed into the ex-marine's eye. Wintergreen howled as Alejandro shoved his other arm into Wintergreen's side, hard enough he pushed Wintergreen against the Renault, far enough away to get his .38 up and, with one eye, blow a hole in Alejandro's stomach. The Argentine dropped to his knees as Wintergreen whipped the gun at Michael—then jerked it suddenly, a jet of flame erupting in a wild arc. His arm hit the Renault for support, and when he turned Michael could see a hypodermic sticking out of his lower back.

Wintergreen tried to bring the gun up again as his arm jerked madly. Michael rushed him and Wintergreen collapsed, the gun tumbling to the dirt with the FBI agent swaying stupidly now on all fours. Gina stood behind him, her vet bag open.

Michael looked at her amazed. "What was that?"

"Robaxin. Canine muscle relaxant."

Wintergreen couldn't get his face off the ground, and a thick drool rolled from his lips. Evita lay above it all, serene on the flat rock.

"…Please don't take Her from me."

It was Alejandro, still kneeling on the ground, voice wet and shallow.

"What do we do?" Gina asked.

Wintergreen was still drooling on all fours. Michael went to Alejandro, leaned down to him and said, "You're dying."

"Yes."

"If I promise you that you'll never leave her side, will you behave?"

"Yes."

Michael pulled Alejandro to his feet. "We're bringing *him*?" Gina asked, still finding ways Michael could astonish her.

"He's the only one that knows how to get us out of here."

Michael handed off Alejandro to Gina, accidentally stepping on Wintergreen's hand as he did, and the ex-marine gurgled a curse: "*Sasiko!*"

Something old in Michael died.

He stood there, frozen, above his old embassy guard. "What did you say?"

Wintergreen was all drooling incoherence, trying to crawl away, and Michael put his foot in his back. "I know that word…"

Images rushed Michael—that night in his Buenos Aires house, the figure shooting at him, the curse it hissed when Michael struck its leg. "*Sasiko*…"

Michael bent down to Wintergreen's ear. "You son of a bitch. You all knew. You all *knew*." Michael pulled the FBI agent's face from the earth. "Were you going to kill us both? Make it look like a robbery? *Sasiko*—it's fucking Basque, isn't it? That was you. Why? *Why*?"

"We…we…" Wintergreen's mouth was as unhinged as a shark's. "We knew you were trying to ship her out through the station…some BAPD joe saw the truck in your alley that night… you weren't supposed to be home…you *said* you were leaving that weekend. Nobody was supposed to be home. Your wife, that's on *you*, asshole."

Michael drove the rancher's son's face into the dirt. Wintergreen struggled feebly, but Michael only pressed harder, digging a crater with the man's face, pressing till Wintergreen's body slacked. Michael stood. Gina had helped a stumbling Alejandro into Wintergreen's dark blue four-wheel and returned, the two of them staring a beat at Wintergreen's body before wordlessly loading Evita onto the backseat.

Michael climbed in beside Alejandro. Gina was behind the wheel, and after starting the engine she eased them along the gravel path leading down the opposite side of the ruins.

"I'm having trouble understanding," Alejandro said through clenched, bloody teeth, "exactly who your friends are."

"Don't bother," Gina said.

# 33.

They came out of the night hills briefly, south of Narbonne, and quickly passed small settlements that reminded Michael of eastern Montana or western Argentina. Ash danced in the cab. Alejandro stared at the silk-shrouded body of Evita in the back as they drove, and for an instant, beneath the destruction, Michael saw the eleven-year-old farm boy.

Wintergreen's four-wheel had maps jammed between the dashboard and windshield that showed the local dirt paths and, more importantly, the locations of French police roadblocks. Even half-dead, Alejandro had an uncanny sense of direction, and they skirted roadblock after roadblock on the feeder roads west.

Thirty kilometers later dawn snuck up, and the Mediterranean appeared in the distance like dull chrome in moonlight. They crossed stale mudflats where a forever wind crippled trees and carried the stench of low tide and sewage. The swamps here had been drained in '63, but the decay went on remorselessly, and the pseudo-Italianate apartment blocks laid over them sagged, corpse-like, and would never look, or smell, finished.

"We'd better stop. It's almost day..." Gina said. Michael nodded. It was the end of the tourist season, and he told Gina to cruise the outskirts of Perpignan and look for a vacant holiday cottage.

They patrolled grassy, smelly hillsides in Wintergreen's truck, three damaged heads rubbernecking low-rent, wind-blown streets, and every place looked vacant, looked never used, and it was a matter of picking one. Michael broke the lock on a garage and they parked the four-wheel inside.

Gina took Alejandro into the cottage, laid him down, and did what she could with her vet bag. Michael tried to sleep and for his trouble got amphetamine-warped half dreams of blood and Argentina, waking from them exhausted, his clothes soaked and clinging, Alejandro groaning incoherently on the couch.

Michael stepped outside, and it was nearly sunset. He popped an amphetamine, felt the sweat on his body chill, and looked out across the breezy mudflats, the disorganized farms climbing the hillside, the toffee-colored bay. The Pyrénées sat in hazy distance, old with rounded, gentle tops, pushing the coast farther to sea, and that was the Spanish border that he, Gina, and Alejandro—if he lived—would try for tonight.

Gina offered him an espresso she'd rounded up inside. Michael sipped it like a child, and they both watched the day sink behind mountains as dark clouds raced the sun, their torn undersides bleeding pink. "Have you eaten?" she asked.

"No."

"You should."

"In Spain."

Inside, Alejandro shouted out in dreamy agony, and it should have fried Michael's nerves, but he had nothing left to fry and so just stared at the sunset. "I gave him some morphine," she said, "some antibiotics. He's bleeding inside."

"He's bleeding everywhere."

"It's the inside that'll kill him."

"I think I'm losing it. I keep seeing things, in the dark."

"I'm here."

He looked at her bag. "Do you have anything for pets losing their minds?"

"We just put them to sleep."

Michael held her hand. "I think that was your first joke."

"How did I do?"

"Terrible."

She pressed herself against him, and he let his face rest in her hand. Over the Pyrénées a last defiant shot of sunset had caught the clouds, and the horizon exploded one last time. There were insects in the grass, and Alejandro's screams on the couch.

"I think it will be a good thing when this is over," Gina said.

# 34.

Hector napped till four o'clock. He rose, bathed, put on the old suit coat and a new tie he bought the day before near the Prado. The villa on Calle de Naval-manzano hummed with heat and the snores of siesta. Even the flies drowsed. Though rest never failed him, Hector did not like sleep as a rule and found naps especially bad for the soul. But the General would nap—would nap until Hector returned his dead wife and would only wake then if Lopez Rega said it was okay.

He could see through the window a sedan pull up to the villa's gates. One of Franco's drivers. Michael had chosen his own route, his own schedule, but from what Hector could glean from his French contacts, from what he knew of the boy himself, Hector felt sure Michael would make the journey into Spain tonight. Hector would let Franco's driver take him across the dry plains to the border crossing he had arranged a thousand million years ago in Beatty, Nevada, and wait.

It had been hot that day too in Beatty, with tiny grains of sand aloft as time tried to bury them all early. Hector felt a grain of sand strike his cheek through the sedan's passenger window. He held it between fingers and crushed its sandstone core. Time would have to wait one more night.

◎　◎　◎

There were no crickets, and the silence as they left after sundown was total but for gusts of salty wind. The cottage, lifeless once

more, receded on the unlit street as they chanced the small road
that webbed southward into the foothills.

Alejandro was still breathing. He sat between Gina and
Michael, the dog morphine forcing his eyes open to cartoon size.
He held a soaked compress to his belly and he didn't moan, though
his teeth chattered occasionally. He spoke to Michael in Spanish,
dreamy, drugged. "She is the light, the mother of the revolution."

"She'll be safe."

"We didn't trust the government. We didn't even trust Perón.
Not in bringing Her home."

"Perón will bring Her home. We'll see to it."

Alejandro's eyes were frozen open, unblinking. "I may still
have to kill you."

"I understand."

Gina tried to pretend she wasn't listening and heard the
sound of a helicopter.

"Turn off the lights," Alejandro said. She did. They slowed
and crept in darkness, the treeless, wind-battered land around
them emerging as moonscape.

Michael held a penlight in his mouth and a map in his lap.
"Take the next right. Toward Col de Banyuls."

"Will someone be waiting?" Gina asked.

"Only if we're unlucky."

○ ○ ○

The wind that never stopped shook the low brush just over the
Spanish border. Generations spent on the exposed flank of the
Pyrénées bred them thick and low to the ground. They hissed first
this way, then that, and Hector thought himself kin to them: bred
thick, low to the ground, flexible to shifting winds.

The customs post was small, little more than a shack and
striped barrier bar. A single dirt road ran off in both windy

directions, and not much disturbed the three Guardia Civil officers' evenings of pulp magazines and TV. Hector's driver carried with him a letter from Franco himself to the effect that one
Michael Suslov and cargo were not to be disturbed or detained
in any way, whatever hysterics the officers heard over their
radios from the French or Italians. Or Americans.

One letter, three guards, a quiet little adjustment of routine
quickly forgotten by everyone involved.

The road went gravel and they drove slower, in deference to the
steepening terrain, in deference to French police officers Michael
imagined around each bend. There was little moon but you could
see, far off, the faint winking of white caps on the Mediterranean.
The truck growled through its gears.

No one seemed to be on the road anywhere, and Michael
wasn't sure if he should be thanking God for the favor. Ahead,
the ridgeline appeared faintly, and that meant Spain. The
French had their border checkpoint down the mountain,
nearer town, and by sidestepping it on a dirt track, all that
remained between them and the border would be the Spanish
post.

Hector waited in the sedan with Franco's driver. It would be dawn
in less than two hours, and he hoped Michael would be out of
France before then. He longed for an espresso, Italian-style, and
was surprised when the local guards hadn't at least offered him
some Spanish instant coffee. No matter. Hector smiled to the
driver, let himself out, and trudged against the wind, with his
cane, toward the guards' duty shack.

Amber light spilled from the doorway; the soft purr of Spanish military frequencies carried on the wind. Hector stepped into the shack. There was a warm kettle, half-drunk plastic coffee cups…

And no guards.

Hector stepped back into the wind. It took a moment for his eyes to adjust. When the land around him came back, he saw his car and driver were missing. In their place, standing in the clearing, were Lopez Rega, two young malevolent men Hector didn't recognize, and Ed Lofton. "Good morning, Hector. Or nearly morning. You look good."

"You look exactly the same."

Lofton smiled. Hector turned to Lopez Rega. "This your idea, Lopez?"

"I work only for the interests of the General."

"Ah. And is he aware of this particular interest?"

"Your Michael Suslov is a wanted criminal, endangering the vessel of our nation's beloved Evita. We want what you want, Hector: her safe return with the General to Argentina."

Hector's eyes went back to Lofton. "I suppose this has nothing to do with the money?"

"It always had to do with the money, Hector," Lofton said. "Just ask Evita's brother, Juan."

Hector drifted back over the decades to that night with him, Perón, and Juan Duarte's official suicide. He sighed. So many suicides. Pity, really.

Lofton again: "You'll get her back, Hector. Clean as a whistle. Argentina will be saved. There's enough of the Senora for everyone."

Hector turned to Lopez Rega. "I never thought the money would matter to you, Lopez."

"The General cannot last long after his return. You've seen him. A year? Two? Then it will be Isabel's turn. She will need the money, Hector, to help the poor. To secure her reputation…"

"To become Evita."

"There will be only one Evita. But the beloved Senora will be in Her crypt, and Isabel will live, will carry on the Senora's work, and I will be right beside her, guiding her…"

"You've forgotten one thing, Lopez."

"What is that?"

"You can only become a hero in our country after you're dead."

Lopez Rega smiled. "Dear Hector. Perón's favorite. And Edelmiro's before that. And Ramirez's before he. And how many before Ramirez? I've done your horoscope, Hector Cabanillas, read your signs, and I think you can become Isabel's favorite too."

They could hear the truck engine. Lofton craned his neck down the dirt path for a glimpse of headlights. One of Lopez Rega's men raised the striped barrier bar, and the other rested a machine pistol against his leg.

"Well, don't be rude," Lofton said to Hector. "Go and welcome them."

Around a bend the post came up suddenly, and Gina braked to a stop at the concrete marker dividing France from Spain. The barrier bar was open and a single figure stood in the road. Dark and backlit by the guard shack, it leaned on a dog-headed cane.

Michael got out as Hector stepped up and grabbed his arm. "Michael. Michael. You made it. You're injured."

"Just mortally."

"We'll get you a doctor immediately." Hector set off to the cab. Leaned in and saw Alejandro ashen faced on the seat. "Alejandro. My son."

"Hector…"

"I knew you and Michael would find each other. Are you hurt badly?"

"He's dying," Gina said.

"No one need die, my lady. Not now." He touched Alejandro's face, icy and wet.

"Don't let them take Her…" the young man wheezed.

Hector glanced at the passenger in the backseat and shook his head in amazement. "Remarkable." He swept back Alejandro's hair. "We are an understanding apart. You and I. Do not worry about the Senora's safety. She is with us, both of us, now." Alejandro nodded. Hector backed out and turned to Michael beside him. "Please. Michael. Climb back inside." Hector spoke brightly, enthusiastically.

"Why?"

"Let's get you out of France, no? Just a few meters, and we can make it official."

Michael did as he was told. As he went to close the door, Hector grasped it with surprising strength, and now the secret policeman's voice was quiet and stern. "Michael Suslov, within the confines of our relationship, would you say you trust me?"

"Within the confines of our relationship."

"When I say, please drive as hard as you can, as fast as you can, and don't stop. Not for anything." Hector looked at Gina, behind the wheel. The engine idled beneath them. Gina nodded.

Hector withdrew from the cab and his voice was bright again. "Ah! I think I see it!" Hector drew his eyes low, to the rear tire, and walked back as if looking for something. When he had reached the four-wheel drive's rear he opened the hatch and said evenly, "*Now*."

With whatever strength remained in his ageless frame, Hector jumped into the four-wheel as it jerked into reverse and spun itself backward into France.

Gunfire erupted from the darkness and clattered against the truck like hail as the windshield exploded into snowing glass. Gina kept the pedal jammed in reverse, unable to see, and the truck careened over brush and rocks. Lofton, Lopez Rega, and his two thugs, they were all in the open now, guns spitting short flames.

Alejandro drew his blood-caked machine pistol from the floor, laid it on the dash, and fired through the destroyed windshield, hot shells ejecting against Michael's arm, till the magazine clicked. Michael had no idea if he hit anything. But the truck did—a rock—and stopped neck-wrenching dead.

Hector, flung against the rear seat, half draped over Evita, said with surprising calm to Gina, "I meant drive into *Spain*."

Gina hit the accelerator and the four-wheel flew in rocky confusion off-road over bramble and roots. Michael had no idea what direction they were heading, the world outside blurry, windblown insanity.

The land dropped quickly away, a cleft rose on Gina's side, blocking the customs station with an earthen berm, and that probably saved them. The steering wheel leapt from Gina's hands with every bone-jarring bounce, knocking the truck to a different point on the compass. They serpentined madly across open ground like that, Gina never letting up the pedal, and when Michael made eye contact with her he wanted to shout *slow down*! or *speed up*! or *look out*! and only managed "*Un-fucking-believable!*" And Gina laughed a gulping, panicked laugh, and it was the first time Michael had ever seen her laugh—a beautiful laugh—and he knew he loved her, if only for the five or ten seconds they had left to live.

"The road!" They crashed right across it, would have missed it entirely if not for Hector's shout. Gina fishtailed right, bounded along in a cloud of dirt, and at about the same moment the right fender tumbled away, Michael saw a surveyor marker stuck in the roadside and the language was Spanish. "Keep going...keep going..." Michael closed his eyes, and it was sandpaper. He opened them again as a fat blood bubble rose from Alejandro's mouth and broke over his chin. "Sorry."

"It's okay," Michael said.

There was only one way out of these mountains: down. They jerked along the path, horseshoe after horseshoe. Everyone knew without speaking that the others had a vehicle, were probably just behind them, and that this was now a race to…where? The Guardia Civil weren't a problem; one call from Hector to Franco would bring help from the next station. But if the Guardia station was too small, Lofton and Lopez Rega might be tempted to just shoot their way through to Michael. They needed a bigger town with a bigger Guardia squad. They needed luck. They needed to keep going…

But there were no towns in this part of the world—not real ones—only the road, and dawn was working it in soft purples as they tumbled from the Pyrénées into the dry plains of the Aragon Reconquista.

The land flattened, stars retreated, and the engine sprayed mists of oil through the smashed windshield.

"This thing's finished," Michael said.

"What do we do?" Gina asked.

The mountains had quit, but the wind had only gained enthusiasm for the treeless, dusty plain. It rocked the truck broadside so hard Michael thought it would topple. "Keep going…"

The horizon was now a pale line, and they could see clouds of orange brown clawing into the air everywhere. A dust storm. Gusts of it struck their clothes and muddied itself with engine oil.

Michael scanned the horizon and it gave up dark, silhouetted towers. "There's a town. It looks big…"

"Yes, Michael," Hector said from the rear. "I see it."

Gina took a smaller dirt road toward the spires. Drifting mountains of dust played peek-a-boo with the image, and she traveled the road on faith.

They kept their scratched eyes on the three or four yards of dirt in front of them until they were stopped before an earthen wall. Gina drove along it till she found a break. They passed through it onto what could have been cobblestones...and the truck shut down. She turned the key a few times, but Wintergreen's four-wheel was finished.

Michael, Gina, and Hector climbed from the truck and were stung by dusty gulps of air. The wind lived here, was born here, and spun with the arrogance of someone who knew it.

"We've got to find a Guardia Civil station," Hector shouted. Michael nodded. The sun was up, up for real, and lighted only swirling sand. The wind found strange eddies within the city's walls, and the dust bunched into four-story traveling storms. One drew other strays to it and shot along the inside wall, giving Michael a brief glimpse of the town. It was old, its cathedrals and apartment blocks the color of the earth, rising from it, like a mirage, hastily thrown together and left a thousand years.

"Where is everyone?" Gina shouted.

It was dawn but the streets weren't dawn quiet. They weren't even dust-storm quiet.

The clouds of earth pulsated once more, an apartment block came into view, and it was a normal apartment block but for one wall completely sheared away. Orderly rooms and toilets stared at Michael like the removable wall of a dollhouse. He looked to the cathedral's spire. It had seemed indistinct, fuzzy, and he had blamed the dust, but now, with the weak strikes of morning, he saw its fuzziness came from having been so smacked by artillery that it had lost the edges of its shape, like sandblasted glass.

"What is this place?" Gina asked.

Hector smiled his secret smile, the one irony owned, and turned to her. "*Los Martirizados*, Gina."

"What do you mean?" Michael asked.

"The martyred ones. Civil War relics. Cities destroyed and abandoned forever. Aragon is littered with them."

"So no one's here?"

"Not for forty years."

Michael hobbled back to the gap in the city's walls. About a mile off a car was approaching. It could be any car, but Michael knew it could only be one.

"They're coming," he said.

Alejandro had his machine pistol, which he kept with its one remaining magazine. He wouldn't leave the Senora, so they helped him behind a rubble pile nearby. Hector had a small derringer four-shot, nickel-plated and scrolled from another century; Michael and Gina had nothing. Michael turned to her. "Alejandro's finished. I'm crippled. Hector's a thousand years old."

"And?"

"You could run."

She stared at him a long time. "Where?"

And Michael knew there wasn't anywhere. Not for any of them. Blowing sand crept up his back and he thought, *Don't bury me yet.*

Lofton and Lopez Rega upfront, two of Lopez's thugs in back. They came through the gap in the wall, navigated the clouds of lashing earth, saw Wintergreen's four-wheel at a corner as Lofton parked the Opel. They all got out, armed, and stood in the blowing dirt.

"They could be anywhere," Lopez Rega said, an edge in his voice.

"Tell your men to fan out. Slow," Lofton answered.

Lopez snapped at his two thugs, and the four of them began moving with caution through the orange wind.

Michael and Gina saw the car, saw briefly through the flying dust the four climb out. Michael took Gina's hand and limped to a half-destroyed apartment block nearby. The lower apartments had been stripped, and Michael searched them in frustration. "What are you looking for?" Gina asked.

"Anything."

It was useless. A staircase led up. It was strewn with tumbled masonry, and the whole wall breathed with wind. "Maybe the apartments upstairs."

Outside, twenty yards from the truck, one of Lopez Rega's men moved along a wall. Abruptly he shredded like a red doll from machine-pistol fire.

The others dropped for cover. "Well, I recognize the gun," Lofton said, lying on the ground beside Lopez Rega. "Is that you, Al?" he called out. There wasn't any answer.

Lopez Rega couldn't take his eyes off the blood-drenched wall that a moment ago framed one of his boys. "You said they were finished. That this was the end."

"It is the end, Lopez. Right here."

"They could kill us!"

Lofton stared at him. "No matter what happens, Lopez old boy, it's a pleasure to know that the future of Argentine government is in such brave hands." Lofton unscrewed his flask, shuddered a bolt, and motioned to Lopez's remaining thug to flank Alejandro on the left. Lofton slipped the flask back into the breast pocket of his seersucker jacket, checked his gun, and rose creakily to his knees. "That boy out there, the one with no face, he's your country's best, Lopez. He could have saved your nation." Lofton began moving right, flanking the opposite side. "Now let's kill him so we can get out of here."

Gina went first, hands and knees up the collapsed stairs, panting, reaching now past the debris and helping Michael over. His foot caught a brick and he twitched a full minute in agony as Gina held him. His senses coming back, shaking, he stood and together they eased up the remaining steps, grasping a wall that shifted each time they touched it.

On the next floor half the roof was missing, but the rooms were less looted: rotten mattresses, ceiling fans, a crumbling chair. Michael went into what was left of the kitchen, ripped open drawer after drawer, and came up with one rusty butter knife.

"Michael..."

He turned. Gina was standing in a fragment of living room and staring down at something hidden by tumbled ceiling. He limped over.

Partly buried by debris, blown in half by whatever brought the ceiling down, were the mostly skeletal remains of a Spanish Nationalist soldier. He was clad in a '30s dark khaki uniform, and his face showed no peace in death. He had died up here, and his fellows had clearly written MIA on his form, and Missing in Action he remained, staring at a crumbling chair—ugly even when new—bird shit running down his cheek into a clenched mouth. He held in one hand a rusted German-made Karabiner grenade launcher.

There was a clatter of fire outside from Alejandro's machine pistol. The second battle for this town had begun.

Lofton was gone into the maze of collapsed stone immediately, leaving Lopez Rega alone, clutching his gun, looking feverishly around him. He heard two pistol reports and the return burst of machine-gun fire. He heard Lofton's voice calling out "Al?" Blowing sand cut him like glass, and he cursed it, cursed Lofton and this godforsaken place.

Lopez Rega moved in the direction of where he thought the Opel would be. He got lost immediately, his only orientation in the orange sameness Lofton's voice pitching around him: "Al, I don't know what Wintergreen told you, but we're with you, man. We're with Her and Argentina..."

The buildings all looked the same, their destruction relentlessly anonymous, and Lopez Rega began to run, away from this town, away from Lofton's voice…

And into another one.

"Lopez…"

Lopez Rega spun and shot from his pistol and saw only a frail shape fall behind a tumbled Moorish statue.

Michael and Gina pried the grenade launcher from the dead man's hands and dragged it to the blown-out apartment wall. "Will it work?" Gina asked.

"Of course not."

He blew clean as best he could the trigger mechanism, pulled what he thought was the safety, and stuck the bulbous head through a sheared part of the wall. "Keep the rusty knife," he said.

Lopez Rega's thug kept tossing off shots in Alejandro's direction, and Lofton muttered at the stupid bastard. He was just shooting dust. They had to get closer. Lofton's voice flew in every direction in this wind, but the shots didn't. Each one announced his position, and if Alejandro had many bullets left, he wasn't wasting them on that fool. Alejandro was the key. Mike, the girl, Hector: they were a carnival show. He had to get the kid. Could have used him in this. Where the fuck was Wintergreen?

There was just enough room around the edges of the grenade launcher for Michael to look over it and see…dust. A world of swirling orange. He knew the truck was down there somewhere, Alejandro, Lofton…His foot throbbed hard enough he felt it in his spine. He couldn't just fire. Not without a shot. The whole building wheezed, and when he rested one hand on the wall, four bricks fell away to the street. He never heard them hit.

Lopez Rega, his gun shaking in front of him, walked slowly toward the fallen Moorish statue. It was of some feudal lord, hands on his shield, one eye squinting down at Isabel's confidant. Lopez kept bobbing up and down, trying to see over it, but the statue was a big one to a big lord and he couldn't glimpse the other side.

Pressed against it, Lopez Rega drew his face up its pitted, marble flanks and there were...drops of blood. Emboldened, he jerked his arm and head over the top, and all he saw was the face of a dog, silver, racing at him, puncturing his eye, and he fell back—gun jerking pointless, spasmodic shots into the sky—screaming in agony as Hector appeared over the top of the Moor's mustache, his dog-headed cane bloody, his derringer aimed flat at Lopez Rega's face. "Hector!" Lopez squeaked.

"Stick with horoscopes, Lopez."

"Don't shoot me!"

Hector came around the Moor's head, a bloody bullet graze on one cheek, and stood above him. Lopez Rega babbled, one hand over his ruined eye, gun somewhere in the dirt. "You can't kill me! I'm part of the government! You work for me! You can't kill me!"

"You're right, Lopez. I can't kill you..."

Lopez Rega calmed some, put his other hand over the first on his eye, and moaned, "My eye...Look what you did to my eye..."

"I can't kill you...but I can still *shoot* you."

Lopez Rega stuck his hands out to protect his face, but it was his knee Hector blew into a ragged pulp. Most of Lopez Rega's screams went into the dirt, and it hardly mattered if he heard Hector walk away. "Casting spells for Isabel, Lopez, you don't need to *walk*."

Lofton listened to the pair of shots—two guns—and the direction was impossible in this caterwauling. They must have confused Alejandro as well, for the young Argentine responded this time when Lopez Rega's thug teased a shot over his head.

A dull burp of half a dozen shells, and it wasn't the reflection of bullets on masonry that caught Lofton's ear but what was almost imperceptible just beneath it.

The click of an empty ammo magazine.

Michael waited on the ancient Karabiner grenade launcher. He had no shot but could hear the patter of gunfire below. He couldn't decide which was worse: never getting a shot, or actually having to use it.

Then the dust lifted.

Bunched up into a whirlwind, it dragged away like a curtain the barrier between Michael and the street below. There was the truck, high and right. He couldn't see Lofton or Lopez Rega, but there was the other thug, coming up slowly on a dead-looking Alejandro, curled behind some debris. Alejandro had let his machine pistol tumble away from his grip and it lay two or three feet from his unmoving body.

The thug was in no hurry, measuring his steps, and Michael knew he had one shot, if that, and where was Lofton? Then he saw him. Arcing from the opposite side of Alejandro, coming now nearer the thug, now himself right below Michael's building. And the dust cloud had grown weary of its journey and was returning now, bearing down on them, and Michael knew it was now or never. Even if he hit Alejandro. Or the truck. Or nothing. The dust cloud smacked against the building, sand clogged his eyes, and Michael squeezed them shut and pulled the trigger.

Silence.

Then a hiss. A trail of smoke at the grenade's base and Michael waited a million years till he couldn't take it anymore and pulled the launcher back from the wall opening, tried to get a sense of where the hissing smoke was coming from…

When the grenade launched.

Straight up into the roof, and a thousand roosting birds died instantly in a concussive blast that flattened Gina and threw Michael into the wall.

Which gave.

A brick cascade that annihilated the remaining thug in a rolling catastrophe that might or might not have swept Lofton and Alejandro into it.

Michael went out with the first brick but caught a handhold, which went too, and he was scrambling the wrong way up an escalator of collapsing building till there wasn't any more escalator and down he went. And if he could have felt it, eighteen feet down into a brick pile would have hurt. But he was numb and the world turned slowly in a dusty, dreamy way, and maybe that was Gina's voice, screaming his name from somewhere over him. Heaven maybe. She'd be in heaven. He? He'd be, well, lower, just like this, listening to her voice above, waiting on the devil, and here he was in chalky orange seersucker.

The devil carries an FBI .38 and drinks too much.

"I can't figure out if that was on purpose or not, you crazy fuck…"

There's too much wind in hell. It's hard to hear anyone.

Lofton had his .38 pointed at Michael's face now, the barrel taking up way too much of his vision. "Long road, Mike, huh? Should have just stayed out of it…" Michael nodded. There was wisdom in that. Lofton straightened his gun at Michael, and that meant bullet time. "Sorry about your wife…" Michael nodded again. He'd forgiven Lofton. Forgiven everyone. He just wanted to float away.

Lofton squeezed the trigger. The gun jammed and Lofton smiled. "Son of a bitch. Just a second, Mike…" *Sure. Take your time.* Lofton flipped open the chamber and tried to clear the sand clogging it. "You and Wintergreen. The two of you were always my favorites at the station. The other stiffs. Never got on with them, really. Too bad you turned out to be such a company cock-sucker."

*Was I ever a company man?* Michael thought. *Oh yes. A long time ago. Something to do with Argentina. My mother and sister were there. And Evita. They're all dead now. Everybody's dead. Now I am too. Please don't be mad at me. I tried and please don't be mad at me.*

"Still with us, Mike?" Michael blinked. "Just checking." Lofton finished cleaning the gun, flipped it closed, and there was a noise in the rubble behind him. Over the wind and settling concrete, Lofton turned and was hit broadside by a rushing, screaming Alejandro. The impact drove them both off the top of the rubble into a wind-piled dust dune.

Michael watched Lofton struggle to get out of the dune, which was sucking him down like quicksand. He could see Alejandro, tangled around his legs, holding on, sinking with him. Lofton fought feverishly against Alejandro's hold, striking the Argentine's hands, dragging himself forward, working his gun around, firing over and over—*pop, pop*—point blank—*pop, pop, click*—and still Alejandro's grip held, the boy almost completely below the sand now, Lofton clawing desperately up its sides but only clawing a grave that was closing around him.

At a certain point Lofton stopped struggling, turned back from the dune's lip, and stared into the boy's face. He was dead. Cold flat dead, but his arms held on like steel. And Lofton smiled improbably, patted the dead boy's head, and together they sunk beneath the surface of the dune.

You see the strangest things in hell.

# 35.

**M**ichael."

That face. Lingering again between this world and another. She really has to stop doing that. Purgatory's maître d' is beside her, pleasant concern etched on a face recently also etched by a bullet.

"Are you all right?" Gina asked.

"What a strange question."

"It's a doctor's question, Michael," Hector answered.

The doctor had her own etchings, tiny cuts over her face. He had liked that face. He liked it now. "Maybe. I can't hear very well."

"None of us do after that grenade," Hector might have said.

"Can you feel your toes?" Gina asked.

"Yes."

"Your nose is cold."

"I'm not a golden retriever."

Gina smiled and turned to Hector. "He'll live."

"Excellent." Hector kneeled down beside Gina. "I'm proud of you, Michael. Of what you've done. You and Gina. She's a remarkable woman. If I were a younger man…"

"You'll outlive us both." He blinked hard, fought a spasm of pain.

"There's another town a few kilometers down the road," Gina said. "A real town. I walked down and phoned a Guardia station."

"They'll be here shortly, Michael," Hector said. "Medical care for you, a truck for the Senora."

"Lofton? Alejandro?"

"Dead. Everyone's dead, Michael. Everyone but Lopez Rega, and he wishes he was."

"What about their bodies?"

"This is a place of war, Michael. What better place for them to be buried?"

"Dig them up. Lofton and Alejandro."

"Why?"

"We're taking them with us."

By afternoon's end the Guardia medics had helped Michael off the rubble and splinted his broken arm. They were leading him to an ambulance, but he insisted he and Gina ride with the Senora in the army truck. They agreed, making Michael as comfortable as possible on the benches.

Lofton and Alejandro's bodies, bleached orange like Etruscan statues, were dug from the dune, wrapped in tarps, and laid beside Evita on the truck bed, which they had delicately covered with canvas. Hector sat in back with them, all three sporting bandages and salve, Gina wanting to sleep against Michael but it hurting too much for both of them.

There was only the few-hundred-mile ride to Madrid left. Hector smiled his reassuring smile as they bounced along the road, but he was not at ease. It was only a small thing, but Hector had noticed, sometime in the last hour, that his derringer was missing.

Michael smiled back.

Across the dry wastes of Aragon and over mountains Michael stopped counting, the small military convoy continued, past sunset, becoming a string of grated headlights on slow, two-lane highways. The back of the truck vibrated, a note musical and awful.

"How much longer?" Gina asked.

"A few hours. No more," Hector said. "Then everyone can get to a proper hospital." Hector smiled at Michael, who was thumbing through Lofton's wallet. Michael looked back at Hector and closed his eyes.

It was on the high-altitude plains outside Madrid that Michael asked Hector to stop the convoy.

"Why?"

"Let's take Her in alone, Hector. Just us. No army. No guards. Lofton, Alejandro, you, me, and Gina. One happy family."

"The driver?"

"Keep him."

There was nothing threatening about Michael's stance or the way he stared. Just one hand, the one not splinted, resting in his pocket. Hector smiled. "Of course, Michael. I appreciate the symmetry. We started this journey together, let us finish it that way."

Michael didn't nod, didn't smile. Hector leaned out the back of the truck and spoke to the Spanish escorts. Thanks much. Appreciate the effort.

The troops gathered in their other vehicles, pulled back onto the ring highway, and with just the driver, Evita and her closest friends moved slowly into Madrid.

Fashionable only slightly, crowded with villas threatening to go to seed, the Puerto de Hierro neighborhood was well lit but silent, the truck's engine vibrating windows up and down the street as the driver stopped at the gates on Calle de Navalmanzano.

"So we have finally arrived," Hector said. "I always had the faith that you would make it, Michael. I always knew we would stand together here one day."

"Dr. Ara is waiting in there, isn't he?"

"Almost certainly."

Two military police officers stood guard at the villa's gates. "Tell them to send for the good doctor, Hector."

"Of course. But why don't you and I give the news to General Perón together, Michael?"

"Just tell them to get Ara."

Hector leaned out and spoke with forced casualness to the guard nearest. The guard disappeared inside, and Hector found himself again facing Michael across three dead people.

"You are a continuous source of surprises, Michael Suslov."

"There's nothing surprising about me at all, Hector. You should have learned that by now."

"Is the Senora in danger?"

"Not unless you're stupid." Michael's hand was still in his pocket. "Within the confines of our relationship, Hector, would you say you trust me?"

Hector paused a long time, then the smile that irony owned crept over his face. "Within the confines of our relationship, Michael Suslov, yes."

The guard returned from the villa with a scowling Dr. Ara. The former Spanish cultural attaché to Argentina looked with disdain on the dusty and bloodied pair inside. "Where's Lopez Rega?"

"He'll be along," Hector said, "one way or another."

Dr. Ara's eyes fell on the smallest of the three canvas wraps, and his voice changed completely. "Is that Her?"

"Come with us, Dr. Ara," Michael said. "Come with Evita."

Ara looked at Hector suspiciously. "It's quite all right, Doctor," the secret policeman said.

"We want only a brief moment of your time," Michael added, "for this final part of her journey."

The doctor scrutinized Michael's features as best he could in the dark. "Do I know you?"

Michael pulled Hector's derringer from his pocket. "Just get in the fucking truck."

Ara glanced over his shoulder for the guard—he was gone—and merely shrugged, accepting Gina's hand and climbing aboard beside them. "Tell the driver to go," Michael said.

"Where?" Hector asked.

Michael stared at Ara's bald, elfin features.

"His house."

It was a suite of generous apartments, three floors up, and they sat in the rear of the truck outside it. "We'll take them in with us."

"All these bodies?" Hector asked.

"No. Just Evita." Michael gestured to one of the shrouds. "And Lofton."

You could see Hector trying to make the pieces work. "Dr. Ara's apartment is on the third floor, no?"

"Yes," Ara confirmed.

"The Senora is no stranger," Michael said, "to back stairs with you and me, Hector, in the middle of the night."

"That was a long time ago."

"And I'm sure that in the meantime the doormen here at Dr. Ara's building have grown accustomed to all manner of strange boxes being delivered to his apartment. They probably even help."

Ara stared at the canvas wrap between them. "Is it truly Her? After all this time?"

"Yes."

Ara let his hand touch the rough material. "Have your driver take us around back," Ara instructed. The command was relayed, and the military truck grinded itself to a service door. Ara turned to climb out. "I'll be right back."

"Not so fast."

Ara stopped and shook his head, every motion an ooze of breeding. "Please, young man, I'm not a child, hmm?"

Ara climbed off the truck. "Go with him," Michael said to Gina. She paused. "Please." Gina touched his shoulder and stepped out behind the Spanish dwarf.

"I must confess I'm intrigued." But Michael ignored Hector and focused what was left of his mind on Gina, now returning through the service door with Ara and two doormen.

"The doormen will take them up," Ara said. "Do what you want with the other one. Just have respect for the neighbors."

Michael came off the elevator with Gina and walked to the only door on the floor. It was open, and Hector and Ara were standing in the living room with the bodies of Evita and Lofton on carts between them. Michael entered and collapsed onto a couch. The derringer stuck out from his pants' pocket, a cut on his neck had begun bleeding again, and his entire nervous system felt like melted copper traveling his spine.

"Where are the toys, Ara?" Michael asked. "Not the farmer's head you keep in a hatbox for parties. The real stuff. The play-room, Dr. Ara. Where do you play?"

Michael coughed violently, bending over, and that ripped open another cut, soaking his back. "What's wrong with him?" Ara asked. The doctor looked over Hector and Gina, their dusty clothes, the broken scabs on their faces, and shrugged. "Never mind."

"The room, Ara. Where's the room?"

"Nobody enters that room. Not alive."

"Your choice."

Ara chuckled to himself. "For the Senora then, yes?"

"Open the room."

Ara took from his coat a string of keys, pulled back a faux bookcase, and unlocked the steel door behind. He gestured to the others. "Please."

The door led to what was once, years ago, an adjoining suite of apartments. The long entryway had been left paneled in pre-war woods. Along each wall, mounted like Roman busts, were embalmed heads. African heads, Asian heads, Indians, Gypsies… some clothed in native headdresses, most of their eyes closed but some open, sparkling clear irises and imprisoned souls.

You couldn't help but linger, and Gina, who thought she had no tears left in her life, wept silently as she passed these trapped horrors, filed here in Ara's personal purgatory.

"Excellent collection," Hector said, nodding.

"Thank you."

The corridor of heads guarded a larger room, maybe the old parlor, also richly paneled. Here were entire bodies, stretched out in glass cases like a rare library. Some wore magnificent costumes, others the simple worn coats of cobblers and street vendors. There were children, smiling, and Michael willed his eyes from them.

A large, snarling black bear stood on its hind legs in one corner. "I wasn't aware you did animals, Dr. Ara," Hector mused.

"An early dalliance. I never took to them, though. No soul. Or a soul that flees too quickly. With people you have more time. To *capture* them."

It figured that it would be here, among his stable of horrors, that Dr. Ara would at last warm to his guests.

Hector noticed, among the cases, Soviet founder Vladimir Lenin. "One of your celebrity copies?"

"I was asked to consult during his embalming in '24."

"I remember."

"January in Moscow. No heat. Unbearable. But I had ample time for a thorough study of the man."

"The work is exceptional."

"Yes. An excellent piece."

"What was your basic model? Your materials?"

"Well, Hector, who says this one is the copy?"

"Remarkable…" Hector muttered.

"Insane," Gina said. She had Michael's arm, helping him along, as Ara opened the final door that led to his laboratory. It was all white tile, deep autopsy sinks, and steel worktables.

On one bright metal table rested a three-month-old infant. Smiling, eyes open, arms out, cooing to its mother, and Ara's guests froze in numbed desolation. Gina turned away and placed a hand over her eyes. "We're all mad…this entire trip… madness."

Ara covered the child with a sheet and lifted it away. "Just something I was working on."

They brought Evita in, placed her atop the table, and cut away the canvas covering. She seemed less strange here, with her creator fussing over her dress, her hands. It's extraordinary, Michael thought, what you can get used to.

"Her skin is fine, only a few small cracks. Her hair needs cleaning, of course. Some small damage to the nose. There's ash in here."

"It was a long trip."

"I'll begin work immediately."

"Not just yet."

Ara straightened up, his enthusiasm replaced by imperial bearing. "Yes?"

"Take the key out."

Ara just stared at him. "Come, Doctor," Michael said, "don't play dumb. You've always known it was there, right? It was your X-rays blown over that Recoleta café."

"The safety deposit key," Hector said, nodding to himself. "Of course."

"You didn't know?"

"The key?" Hector said. "No. We suspected, even cared once. But now? Now is just politics, Michael."

"Was Evita's brother, Juan, murdered for politics or money, Hector?" Ara asked.

"As I said, once we cared."

"Why didn't you keep the key?" Michael asked of Ara. "You had her. She was yours for months. Why wait nineteen years for Lopez Rega to bring it up?"

Ara stepped away from the body and faced Michael directly. "Assuming the money mattered to me, young man, I was the only one who knew. Why hurry? Bank rules would never allow the money to be touched for years. Possessing the key would only cause me danger. Especially after the X-rays were stolen by your friends. It was perfectly safe with the Senora...till she disappeared..."

"The key still with her," Hector finished, "and only Michael knowing where she was..."

"Get the key," Michael said.

"You'd defile her? Now? After all this time?" Ara challenged.

"Don't butcher her like Lofton would have. Use your skill, Doctor. Your knowledge of the woman. Make it clean. Make it respectful. But get on with it."

Ara turned from Michael and opened a surgical tray. From it he removed a scalpel. Gina looked at Michael, horrified. "The money? Was it about the money for you too, Michael?"

Hector, who was also watching Michael and perhaps gleaning his thoughts, answered her for him. "No, my lady, I don't think so."

"What, then?"

"A close of the cycle. Yes, Michael?"

Michael didn't answer, was watching silently what they all watched now: Dr. Ara drawing the scalpel across Evita's burial gown. The stiff muslin parted, and Ara made another incision, through layers of impregnated plastic and chemical injections, reached into the dry but intact viscera with a pair of forceps, and removed one specially made, multialloyed key. He wiped it with a towel and handed it to Michael. "Satisfied?"

"Nearly."

"What now?"

"Bring in Lofton."

Gina rolled in Lofton's wrapped corpse and together they laid it roughly onto a second examination table. "Open the shroud."

Ara drew his scalpel along the material, and Lofton emerged from within not looking much different: old, wasted, eyes half-mast, orange dust everywhere. "Some journey," Ara said.

"It's not over yet."

"What do you want with him?"

Michael stood beside Ara and looked down at Lofton's face. "Ed Lofton drank too much. Since the day I met him. Didn't eat well, either. It always left him skinny and emaciated looking. His body seemed to me in those days almost…feminine.

"I was thinking of Lenin out there, of the fake celebrity heads you used to seduce women in Buenos Aires. After Evita died, we were doing surveillance on a house one night, and I saw you show off Evita's head. Only it couldn't be *Hers*; Hector had the entire article. You'd made a copy. Surgery on some poor dead peasant woman. Just a game, right?"

"My art was never a game, young man."

"Fair enough. Where is the head now?"

"That was years ago."

"Where is it?"

Ara measured Michael. "Here."

"Get it."

"And then?"

"Make Lofton Evita."

"You're insane."

"Still…"

"He's five inches taller than Her."

"Cut his feet off."

"He's a man."

"Is someone going to look up Her dress? Now? He's a skinny man. Put her head on him and people will see what they need to."

"Why, Michael?" Hector.

"A promise."

"And Argentina?"

"Argentina wants an empty vessel to jam their superstitions and dreams into. I wouldn't deny them that." Michael pointed Hector's gun at Ara. "Now cut Lofton's goddamn head off."

Michael waited with Gina in the living room. The one without the displayed heads. He closed his eyes, and the room spun with viciousness. He reached out to Gina, she held his hand, but he was running low—too low—and when he passed out, Gina took the gun, kept it in her lap, and with the Guardia's medical kit, dabbed and redressed his wounds.

Michael screamed when he woke and the nightmare lingered too long before his eyes. When it finally cleared, he felt Gina beside him and saw Hector waiting on the sofa opposite. "He's finished."

Michael fought to remember what he was talking about. It took everything just to lean forward. "Bring me Ara."

The doctor was along presently, wearing his physician's smock. "Success?" Michael asked him.

"It's a sixty-five-year-old man with the head of Evita. A monstrosity."

"*Success?*"

"It is not my best work. It is not even good work. I spent nearly a year on Evita, do you understand? A year!" Ara took off his smock and threw it over a chair. "But in a limited way, it could work. In a *very* limited way."

"Sit down, Doctor." Ara sighed and took a seat beside Hector. Michael closed his eyes, closed them a long time, and Hector wondered if he was coming back. He did. "Dr. Ara, I remember you told Hector once, in a dark alley a long time ago, to remember that though Evita was a symbol to so many, she was also a woman. Do you remember?"

"Yes."

"You cared for her."

"I still do."

"I could shoot you now, Dr. Ara, and release every soul trapped in this horror den. But I believe you when you say you cared for Evita. I care for Evita too, Dr. Ara, and I believe her service to her country should end here.

"I intend to deliver to General Perón that monstrosity in the other room, which they may parade through the streets, run up a flagpole, or rip in half looking for a key. But they will not disturb her peace. You can help in this by authenticating the body we deliver, or you can destroy it and me the moment we walk in. I am asking you, in the name of her, to help."

Ara was silent a long moment. Something small and alien crossed his features. Something…human. It rested strange on his elfin mouth. "In return you guarantee her peace?"

"And several million dollars."

It was midmorning when the military truck arrived at the gates of Perón's villa in exile. Michael wasn't sure what he expected, an honor guard maybe, but it was the Spanish cleaning staff that emerged and carried Evita inside—now protected in a makeshift casket from Ara's office. They set the casket atop Perón's dining-room table.

Michael, Gina, Hector, and Ara were shown into the parlor, where General Perón and Isabel awaited them. Both had dressed for the occasion, and if they noticed the condition of the others, didn't say. Perón sat on the sofa, Isabel standing at his side. "She's here?" he asked.

"Yes," Hector said.

Perón turned to Dr. Ara. "You've examined her?"

"The body of Eva Perón is in excellent condition."

"I have prepared a place for her. Upstairs. Until our return. This a great day for my wife and me. For all of Argentina."

"Yes, General," Ara purred.

"This is Michael Suslov, General," Hector said. "He and his friend Gina brought the Senora to us."

"You're a remarkable man, Mr. Suslov."

"Just one with nothing else left."

"Well, that describes all of us, doesn't it?"

"Where is Lopez Rega?" Hector asked.

"The hospital," Isabel said.

"There was trouble at the border."

"So I understand," she added without emotion. Isabel turned to Gina. "You helped bring our beloved Senora to us?"

"Yes."

"You are always welcome in my home." Isabel rested her hand on Perón's shoulder. "Shall we go see her?"

They filed from the parlor into the dining room. "Michael," Hector said, "will you do the honors, please?" Michael unbolted the coffin lid. He looked once at Hector, longer at Ara, then opened it.

During the final weeks of Evita's cancer death, Perón had never visited her. His first wife had also died of cancer, and the strain of another had been too much. He had waited, in the hall, silently each night as she slipped away. Even when Ara had begun his long preservation process, he had come no closer than the embalming door. And when she was paraded through the streets, when she was put on public display, he had stayed at home.

Now that wife lay on his dining table, and it was the new one, Isabel, who approached first. She studied the face, the rosary-clenched hands. "I never met her…"

"Isabel," Perón said, his voice cracking, "this is Evita." Isabel reached out and touched Evita's hair. "I'll comb it. Every day." She looked up and offered the general her hand. "Come, Juan." Perón was still in the doorway, his view blocked by the coffin lid. He walked now anciently toward Isabel, came up beside the casket, and took her hand. Husband and wife smiled to one another, then, with great reluctance, for the first time, Perón turned to the image of Evita.

"She shall be with us always, Juan," Isabel chanted. "She will be our inspiration, our hope and future…our power…"

And as Perón fell deeper and deeper into the image, as he reached out and touched the surgically altered head of some nameless peasant, as he caressed the stiff body of FBI officer Ed Lofton, his eyes filled with tears of melancholy love, and he turned away.

# 36.

They stood outside the villa in singeing heat and were not missed. "And now, Michael?" Hector wore his suit coat, the ubiquitous dark-blue one, and as usual was impervious to temperature.

"We're wanted, Gina and I. We'll need new passports. Argentine if you like."

"Done."

"You'll need one too, Hector."

"Oh? Where are we going?"

"Switzerland."

A week later Michael, Gina, and Hector stood on the cobblestones outside Kredit Spoerri Bank, new clothes, bodies banged up but clean. "I'm supposing," Hector said, "that you have a reason for coming to this particular bank."

Michael pulled from his pocket Lofton's wallet. Choked with sand, among his FBI ID, driver's license, and passport was a Kredit Spoerri business card for one Otto Spoerri.

"Herr Spoerri?" His secretary on the speaker box. Otto was pacing his office, glaring at his ancestors.

"I asked not to be disturbed."

"You have three visitors."

"What visitors?"

"They say they represent friends."

Otto sighed. What was the use of a secretary? "What are they wearing?"

"I'm sorry?"

"Their clothes. Open your eyes. What are they wearing?"

If her voice had showed any sign of hurt, even annoyance, it would have improved his day. But she merely sighed back. "A woman in a print dress, two men: one in sweater and slacks, the other in a dark-blue suit."

Not likely the uniform of the Swiss banking police or American SEC. "Is one old and wasted looking?"

"Why don't I just send them away?"

"Is one old and wasted looking, please?"

"One's old. They're all wasted looking."

Otto stared at his ancestors. God he hated them. Was it those crazy Americans? The government ones?

Was it the key?

The last portrait on the right was of his father. Death did nothing to reduce his proximity. Otto met the hateful gaze sneer for sneer and turned to the speaker box. "Send them in."

He took a seat at his powerful desk that signified nothing. He closed the drawer with the Luger and did his best to rub the liquor from his breath. The hated secretary opened his door, ushered in the three, and excused herself. His visitors stood together on the carpet. "Can I help you?"

"May we sit?" Dark hair, arm in a sling, a limp.

"You may tell me what your business is."

The dark-haired one stepped forward and laid on his desk an open passport. It was filthy and contained the photo of the older, wasted man that had first visited him. His name, apparently, was Edward Lofton. "A passport that isn't yours in terrible condition. What is the point?"

"Know him?"

"Who's asking?"

"Friends of his."

"You don't look like friends."

"Most of his friends don't."

"Were you all in a car accident?"

"Several."

"You are in the director's office of one of the most trusted banks in Zurich. Again, what is your business?"

"We'd like to sit down."

Otto reached for his secretary's speaker box and pressed the call button. "Yes, Mr. Spoerri?"

"Please come in."

The door to Otto's office opened at the same moment Michael tossed onto the desk the safety deposit key.

"Yes, sir?" the secretary asked, entering. Otto was suddenly frozen a long moment.

"Please bring my guests some tea." The secretary disappeared. Otto turned to Michael. "Why don't you and your friends sit down?"

They did, their bodies creaking with damage like a World War II VFW meeting. Otto picked up the key and turned it in his hand. It was freakishly shaped, with strange reflections catching rare alloys. "It's Her key, isn't it?" Michael said.

Otto continued to turn the key in his hand, and you could see the brush of memory on his face. "Who?"

Michael shrugged and reached for it. Otto reflexively jerked back his hand. Michael reached further and held tight Otto's clenched fist. "Lofton had something else. A letter from the SEC. Something about missing deposits. A *lot* of deposits."

Michael took the key from Otto's grip and sat back. "So why don't you loosen your tie, take a hit from the bottle in the drawer you keep glancing at, and start talking to us."

Otto had the three of them stay in his office till nearly closing.

"Will this be a problem?" Gina asked.

"Less when you're president of the bank."

At closing time Otto led them down to the vault. They signed in with their phony names, completed formalities, and two bank officials witnessed the placing of the bank's partner key by Otto in one lock, then Michael's key into the corresponding one. It slid in like it was made yesterday and turned with a smooth *click*. Three bank guards were needed to remove the massive box. They carried it into a private viewing room, leaving the four of them.

Michael opened the top. There were four smaller boxes inside. Michael handed one each to himself, Gina, Hector, and Otto. "Should we open them?" Gina asked. Michael nodded. There was a clinking of metal. Then there was silence.

"I don't understand…" Otto's voice trailed off.

"Is this right?" Gina said.

In Gina's box was a small wooden horse. A child's toy. In Otto's an envelope of common earth. Hector lifted from his the torn pleat of a black funeral dress. In Michael's was a lock of a gray hair.

"This can't be," Otto gulped. "Why? Why this? What does it mean?"

"It's her life," Hector said, "that most private part of her she kept to herself."

"Her childhood," Michael joined in, "a toy, dirt from her town. A lock of her dead father's hair."

Hector nodded. "A bastard clinging to some tiny piece of her family history."

"Her most valuable possession."

Otto had gone fish-belly white. "But the money…"

"Here," Gina said. They peered in. Stacked beneath the small boxes of her life were gold bars and diamonds. "My God…" Gina breathed. "Is it a lot?"

"Millions," Michael said.

Hector glanced at the fortune, but his interest seemed more on the fragment of black funeral wear in his hand. "So we have her riches. All the money she set aside during the years of feeding the poor. You brought us here, Michael. What are we to do with it?"

There was a sudden rattle of steel outside, startling them. "The bank is closing," Otto said. "Even the bank president will be forced to leave this area shortly. We must decide now."

Michael's eyes never left Gina as he spoke. "Mr. Spoerri here may take what he requires to cover his bank debt; Dr. Ara will receive some for his continued cooperation; Gina and I will need a little to fade away. The rest will return with Hector to the people of Argentina." Michael turned to Hector. "That's it."

"I'll get cases to transfer it," Otto said, and he was out in a rush, headed upstairs, and Hector nodded quietly to Michael. "This money will do much good."

"This money will keep you alive."

Hector smiled. "So you are becoming a student of Argentina after all." His expression became more somber. "What will you do now?"

Michael placed a modest number of gold bars into one of the smaller boxes. "Keep a promise."

"To the Senora?"

"The Senora and myself." Michael shut the box. He collected Evita's childhood belongings into another and handed it to Gina. "We're leaving now, Hector. Gina, me, and Evita. Don't follow us, don't call us. Know only that whatever peace is left to me I'll divide equally between the three of us."

Hector nodded. "So you're taking her."

"I made two promises, Hector. That I would watch over her soul and that I'd never take Alejandro from her. Whatever I might have been, whatever I might become, here, today, I am a man who keeps his promises."

Hector nodded thoughtfully. "Well, I suppose she spent one lifetime in your care. Why not another?"

"It may be more than one lifetime, Hector."

"In Argentina, Michael, the dead always have one more life-time."

Hector took Gina's hand. "You're the best possible thing that could have happened to Michael."

"And you're the worst, Hector."

"I shall miss you, Gina. You are a rare creature."

Michael hoisted his box, and together Gina and he started for the door. "You always understood, didn't you, Michael?" Hector said. "About the box."

Michael paused. "She built that box for the money because that was Her way. But she had the key made to protect Her child-hood. And she swallowed it to save Her soul."

"Go with God, Michael."

"And you, Hector."


Michael and Gina had a rented van. They loaded the gold into the back, next to Evita, climbed behind the wheel, and sat there as Switzerland went by.

"Is it just the three of us now again?" Gina said.

Michael was silent a moment. "It will be a responsibility for the rest of your life. In return you get no name, no future, nothing except me."

She hugged him then, held his wounded body close—close enough to feel his blood pound—and Gina thought: blood makes noise. If you're lucky in this life, blood makes noise...

# EPILOGUE

**June 21, 1973**

On the shortest day of the Argentine calendar, the body Dr. Pedro Ara authenticated as Eva Perón was returned to her country. Her husband, Juan Perón, had been already dead a year and never did gaze again on his wife's remains after that day in Madrid. His third wife, Isabel, now in control of the government, with a limping Lopez Rega, welcomed the casket to a private residence in Olivos, there to be cleaned and prepared for the nation. But Isabel's turn in the revolving door of military coups came shortly after, and it wasn't till October 22, 1976, that the authenticated remains of Eva Perón made their final journey along streets lined with half a million well-wishers to the Duarte family crypt in Recoleta Cemetery.

On that same day, 150 miles away in the small, dusty pampa town where Evita was born, two strangers laid flowers on a pair of graves in the church cemetery. No one was sure whom the graves belonged to. They had been told only that they were distant Duarte relatives from Europe, mother and son, who had asked to be buried here.

The two strangers held hands a moment beside the plots. They said something quietly to themselves that no one heard, then turned and walked to their car. When they were gone the children ran to the graves, snatched the flowers, and the little girls among them adorned their hair with them and ran home, singing as they went songs of Baby Jesus, Mother Mary, and Santa Evita.

# Author's Note

Of all the strange things presented in this novel, perhaps the strangest of all is how much of it actually happened. Though this is a work of fiction, it may surprise the reader to know the degree to which the story adheres to known facts.

The imperious Dr. Pedro Ara was a real person, who was known indeed for carrying with him to parties a hatbox containing the perfectly preserved head of a Spanish peasant. A consultant in the embalming of Lenin, he spent the better part of a year preserving Evita—forming, some thought, a bizzare, paternal relationship with her corpse. He's also known to have created a "spare" head of the Senora for his own, if unclear, use. If you read Spanish, a description of his embalming "method" can be found in the somewhat creepy and obsessive memoir, *El caso de Eva Perón*.

The early 1950s—when the real-life Colonel J. C. King ran the Western Hemisphere Division as a personal fife—were, as described, a time of internal tension within the CIA in Latin America. Michael's embassy experiences are based on actual stories related by retired intelligence officers from that period.

The restlessness of Evita's remains after her removal from the CGT in 1955 was also largely as depicted, from the flowers that always followed where she went, to being sheltered by the very real and odd Moori Koenig, who, when ordered to find a hiding place for Evita, instead became infatuated with her corpse, keeping it in his home while slowly losing his mind.

The tragedy of an embassy employee who, after inheriting the body from Koenig, accidentally shot his pregnant wife during a home invasion, is also based on true events.

In life Evita's remains did end up hidden as described under a nun's name in a Milan cemetery, and Montonero terrorists did in fact murder an ex-president seeking her location. The fear of that information possibly being revealed by both the president's murder and an attack on a records center spurred the abrupt and secret operation to move her to Spain.

Everyone's favorite demon uncle, Argentine military intelligence officer Hector Cabanillas, was a historical person, as was Perón's third wife, Isabel, and her bizarre astrology-casting Rasputin, Lopez Rega—all of whom existed, doing more or less here what they did in life, including casting nightly spells and presenting Evita's body during dinner at Perón's residence in Spain.

And finally, of course, there is the mysterious and wonderful character of Evita herself. The dusty pampa bastard who climbed her way to the top of a society determined to throw her away, who gave dignity to so many while stealing from them at the same time; a fearsome dervish who stormed for justice yet made a still-unexplained trip at the height of her fame to a certain Swiss bank. A woman who was, as in this tale, a whore to some, a saint to others, and, at least to one person, a promise finally kept.

—Gregory Widen

# Acknowledgments

Ah, so many. To Richard Green, who first turned me on to the story of Evita's body's restless journey; to Rima Greer, who believed in the novel longer than even the author; and to Bernadette Baker-Baughman and Victoria Sanders for their support and creative advice and, most important, for finding a way to sell a novel like this. To my sister Kathleen, who helped with much of the early research. To Alan Turkus, Alison Dasho, and the rest of the editorial staff at Thomas & Mercer for their enthusiasm and careful editing to help make the lamer parts of this book less so. Any that remain are my doing alone. Thanks are also due to the numberless friends who took time out of their much more interesting lives to read this manuscript and offer suggestions, an incomplete list that would have to include Michael, Viggo, Adara, Don, Gerard, Brett, and a certain CIA station chief friend living not so quietly abroad.

# About the Author

Photograph by A. S.

A native of Laguna Beach, California, Gregory Widen is a former firefighter, NPR station host, and mountain-rescue team member. While a film student at UCLA, he penned the script for what would become the movie *Highlander*, starring Sean Connery. Among his other screenplays are *Backdraft* and *The Prophecy*, and his television writing includes scripts for *Tales from the Crypt* and *Rescue 77*. A committed traveler, his explorations have taken him to war-torn Somalia, Uzbekistan, Namibia, the summit of Mount Kilimanjaro, the arctic island of Svalbard, Indonesia, and Argentina. He lives in Los Angeles, where he is at work on a film for Universal Pictures.